Blood Sweep

Books by Steven F. Havill

The Posadas County Mysteries
Heartshot
Bitter Recoil
Twice Buried
Before She Dies
Privileged to Kill
Prolonged Exposure
Out of Season
Dead Weight
Bag Limit
Red, Green, or Murder
Scavengers
A Discount for Death
Convenient Disposal
Statute of Limitations
Final Payment
The Fourth Time Is Murder
Double Prey
One Perfect Shot
NightZone
Blood Sweep

The Dr. Thomas Parks Novels
Race for the Dying
Comes a Time for Burning

Other Novels
The Killer
The Worst Enemy
LeadFire
TimberBlood

Blood Sweep

A Posadas County Mystery

Steven F. Havill

Poisoned Pen Press

Copyright © 2015 by Steven F. Havill

First Edition 20145

10 9 8 7 6 5 4 3 2 1

Library of Congress Catalog Card Number: 2014954926

ISBN: 9781464203879   Hardcover
      9781464203893   Trade Paperback

Poisoned Pen Press
6962 E. First Ave., Ste. 103
Scottsdale, AZ 85251
www.poisonedpenpress.com
info@poisonedpenpress.com

Printed in the United States of America

for Kathleen

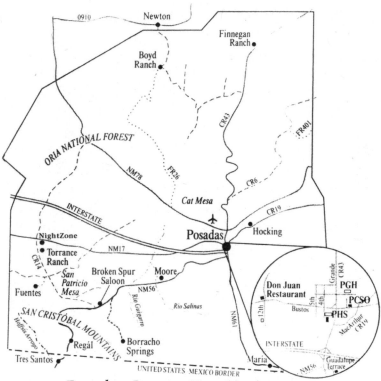

Posadas County, New Mexico

Chapter One

The antelope posed motionless, nostrils flared, enormous eyes taking in the sweep of prairie, trophy horns heavy and black. Robert Torrez's right index finger remained relaxed, resting on the side of the trigger guard. The mature buck dominated a small hummock where he could watch his five ladies and the collection of bandy-legged fawns. The little ones had survived their first month—two sets of twins, three singles, and off to the left, a weary-looking doe with week-old late summer triplets.

The range finder built in to the expensive scope calculated the distance at 480 yards. A minute shift of the rifle moved the field of view yards to the right, where two more does grazed fitfully. Their concern was a second, younger buck who drifted ever nearer to them. Now beginning his second year, the young buck was new to the game, but smart enough to be apprehensive about the dominant male. The herd master ignored him.

Torrez let the crosshairs drift across the juvenile buck's flank. Summer rains had been generous, the under-grazed gamma, fescues, and wheatgrass abundant. While the mature trophy buck's sides showed the slight caving of age, this youngster was powerful and sleek, ready to begin the quest for a harem of his own. His horns were still runty, but a trophy didn't interest Torrez. Dust kicked behind the buck as two tawny streaks shot past, the fawns enjoying their muscles and footing, accelerating and dodging with bursts of speed that flashed their white rumps.

Ignoring them, Torrez watched the young buck, his inspection as complete as a county fair livestock judge patting down a prize 4-H lamb—he saw well-padded ribs, a satisfying bulge of haunch muscle, even some weight building on the withers up through the neck. A minute adjustment of his hands and the scope's image drifted back. The older buck now picked his way down a slight rise toward the does. Aging as he might be, the animal was still heavy enough, untouched by mange or scarring, still managing a healthy, productive herd. He'd be active for another year or two, maybe longer.

Torrez shifted his position, seeking relief from a pebble that dug into his hip. He blinked, glad that this day had dawned with a rare overcast, a pewter blanket in no hurry to either shed moisture or burn off. No wind stirred the prairie grass or ruffled the antelopes' butt ruffs. The distance between shooter and game was so great that a hot, sunny day—the norm for southern New Mexico in August—would have made the shot an impossible guess with heat waves distorting the scope's image. But the overcast permitted a clear, crisp view.

Having kept a close watch on this herd for weeks, Torrez was in no hurry to take his shot. He knew that the veteran buck favored the sweep of pasture close to County Road 14, close to one of the windmill-filled livestock tanks around which the grass stayed lush as the tank sweated and leaked. And Sheriff Robert Torrez had taken the time to prepare for the hunt far more thoroughly than he usually did—in his wallet was a folded letter from the landowner, rancher and developer Miles Waddell, granting him permission to hunt on this private, thoroughly posted property, a favor that might not be possible after the huge, three hundred million-dollar astronomy theme park being built by Waddell was complete and flooded with tourists.

For several weeks, Torrez had kept track of this herd. He'd had to pause more than once out on the county road as they shot across in front of him, often to disappear behind the steep prairie swell to the east. This morning, he'd hiked over the swell, saw the herd, and slipped down to this little mound of cover and support for his rifle.

There was nothing about this hunt to make Torrez's heart hammer with anticipation, no excitement of the chase. Rather, what he planned was a simple culling of the herd, a carefully managed stocking of the freezer. Torrez took one more visual tour of this herd, and then settled back on the youngster. The cross-hairs rested on a spot between eye and ear, and Torrez's breathing slowed and then stopped as his right index finger moved into the trigger guard. Ten seconds, twenty, a full half minute, and finally he allowed his finger to actually touch the trigger.

A heartbeat later, the .264 Magnum bellowed, the recoil punching the hunter's shoulder hard. So instantly did the skull shot drop the antelope that by the time Torrez had recovered from the recoil and once more acquired a clear scope view, the animal was down, one leg kicking spasmodically. By then the rifle's sharp report had reached the herd. Unsure at first, they milled about and then charged off, the old buck circling toward the left to pick up the straggling fawns.

Even as Torrez's hand relaxed away from the trigger guard, his scope exploded, sending aluminum, glass, and plastic shards in all directions. A heavy piece was flung backward, clearing the bill of his cap and whacking him over the left eye. Another fragment stung the middle of his left forearm, still another raked his left shoulder. When the crack of the gunshot reached him, it seemed to float in from a dozen directions, rolling across the prairie, finally bumping up against a nearby mesa, to echo and re-echo.

With an instinctive lunge, he spun away and scrambled back-ward, to dive under a thick, runty spray of creosote bush, unmindful that the bush might include unwanted company. There wasn't enough bush to hide his six foot, four inch body, even though he tried to curl his two hundred forty pounds into a tight ball. He clawed out his handgun at the same time—a useless long-range prairie weapon, but one step better than his folding knife.

For a moment he lay perfectly still, letting his breathing and pulse even out, waiting for a second shot or the thud of boots charging toward his location across the rough ground. His wrist-watch told him that it was shortly after noon. Twisting slightly, he studied the watch until the exact time was engraved in his memory: 12:12 p.m. Torrez turned his head, scanning the prairie through the tangle of branches.

The ocean swells of prairie prevented most straight-line shots and the runty bush would blur the outline of his body, but the shooter had the advantage. Storm run-off had carved the arroyos and washes in a wild crisscross pattern. The terrain rose between him and the county road to the west, a long berm of shattered limestone that hid from view the gravel road and all the con-struction activity on Waddell's Mesa. Farther to the south, the berm subsided, and Torrez could see the pale line that was the county road winding southward.

He took a moment to dig his ear plugs out and flick away the rivulet of blood that threatened to run into his left eye. Ten yards away, the rifle lay where he had dropped it, partially cushioned by his folded vest. The expensive scope was a shattered tangle, the rear portion jerked to the left, the forward half blasted free of its mount. That fragment lay on the ground five feet away… also to the left.

Torrez edged around the creosote bush, giving himself a view to the south. Empty prairie rolled down to the vast arroyo that scarred the prairie south of what Torrez still thought of as Herb Torrance's ranch. Now that land belonged to Miles Waddell as well.

Upgrade shots were always a challenge. The single shot had missed Robert Torrez's head by ten inches, and the terrain might explain why. But there were dozens of places where the naturally folded prairie could conceal the shooter.

He raised his head and breathed in hard. Far away now, the antelope herd had slowed as they drifted up the west side of a prairie swell, the big buck out ahead of them, alert and nervous. *They* were all looking off toward the south, and Torrez risked enough movement to holster the pistol, then find his compact binoculars. The leather lanyard was still looped around his neck.

Trusting the antelopes' interest in what lay to the south, he backed away from the cover and moved due west, following the rise of the rough, rock-strewn berm. He bent low and slowed every few feet to drop to his knees while he scanned the prairie. Several of the antelope had spotted him. They stood stock-still, regarding him from the safety of eight hundred or more yards. Their gaze shifted from him to whatever in the distance had attracted their attention and then back again.

A soft, distant thud froze Torrez in his tracks. Far less intense than a gunshot, the sound still carried, and this time he could both identify and place it—a car door slamming off to the west, down at the county road. He ducked down and sprinted up the berm, legs pistoning like a Marine charging a challenge hill. He reached the crest of the prairie swell and dropped prone. To the west, County Road 14 snaked north-south. His truck was parked in the shade of a juniper clump on the shoulder of that well-traveled dirt road, a long, hot trudge away. And there was company. A second vehicle, less than two car-lengths south of his own, now accelerated on the county road. The white Ford pickup drove at a conservative pace, and despite the overcast, the lack of rain encouraged the billow of rich dust.

He hadn't seen the pickup truck actually pull out from a stop…perhaps it had just idled by, innocent as can be, the driver wondering if the owner of the parked, decrepit Chevy needed assistance. But Torrez was absolutely certain he had heard a door slam. Even as he watched, he dug the cell phone out of his pocket. Twenty-five miles to the east, Sheriff's Dispatcher Ernie Wheeler picked up on the first ring.

"Posadas County Sheriff's Office. Wheeler."

With his typical lack of greeting, self-identification, or small talk, Sheriff Robert Torrez asked, "What's Guzman's twenty?"

"She's just headed out to Gastner's for a bit, sir. Then she's got a string of meetings this afternoon."

Torrez paused. The white Ford's dust trail was about to disappear around the west end of Waddell Mesa. He turned in place, surveying three hundred sixty degrees of prairie. He could easily interrupt his undersheriff's activities, but the dispatcher prompted him.

"Pasquale is free. And Sutherland should be out of court in a few minutes."

"Okay. Look, have Pasquale head south on 56 and then north on 14. If he sees a late model white Ford pickup, extended cab, have him find an excuse to stop it for a chat and run a twenty-eight. No holds at this point. Just tell him to be careful. Tell him twice so he hears you. It's a newer model. No camper, no tool boxes. I don't have a plate yet." He didn't need to request that Deputy Thomas Pasquale not let the moss grow. Foot to the floor was Pasquale's favorite mode.

"Affirmative. This is in regard to..."

"I'm not sure yet. Somebody took a rifle shot at me out here just east of the cattle guard where I was huntin'. Might be the Ford, might not. So give Pasquale a head's up."

"You're all right, sir?"

"Yep." He didn't offer any further explanation to the dispatcher, refusing to dwell on the image that he had been less than twelve inches removed from joining the downed antelope. He switched off the phone and slid it back into his pocket.

He walked north, staying just below the spine of the ridge. A hundred yards from where his shattered rifle lay, he found a large rock bench and dropped down with his back against it to continue his scan of the prairie with the binoculars. If the cruise-by pickup was indeed the shooter's ride, it would be long gone by the time Torrez trekked back to his own vehicle. He knew better than to attempt some teenager's wild sprint down the rocky slope, dodging rocks and cacti. By the time he had returned to his truck, if he could make the dash without breaking an ankle, leg, or neck, the Ford might be anywhere, blended in with a myriad other ranch trucks. Besides, Torrez had work to do. He had no intention of leaving the antelope carcass to rot. If the Ford turned east on the state highway, maybe Pasquale would get lucky.

He turned and looked carefully at his own truck, and swore under his breath. The sun-faded, bent hood, dappled in a dozen places with dings, dents, and scars, was sprung open. He cradled the binoculars against his knees to steady the image. Finally, face set hard with anger, he rose and returned to his jacket and rifle.

The sheriff had never used the phone's camera feature, but he grumbled his way through a series of snapshots of the rifle and busted scope *in situ,* acutely aware of how much he'd like to have department photographer Linda Real—or Undersheriff Estelle Reyes-Guzman—at the site to do the job properly. Then he collected as many scope parts as he could and bundled them into his vest, leaving the rest hanging off the rifle. As an afterthought, he jerked off the dangling fragment of eyepiece and left it on the rock as a marker.

Satisfied that he was now alone on this particular reach of prairie, Torrez trudged out to the dead buck. As he had planned, the single high-velocity rifle slug had fragmented the animal's skull. The sheriff took no particular satisfaction from the careful, calculated shot. The animal was down, mercifully or not, and the job now was the first step toward cuts in the freezer. After knotting his hunting tag around the split remains of one horn, he set about field dressing the small carcass with swift efficiency. Even as he finished, a raven wheeled past, a low fly-by that stayed a respectful distance away.

"Just a minute," Torrez said aloud. "You'll get yours." Himself no connoisseur of dining on entrails or organs, no matter how disguised as fancy cuisine, he spread out the guts several yards away. In a couple of days, there wouldn't be a trace remaining. All the while, he kept up a routine scan of the prairie horizon. He didn't *feel* watched, except perhaps by the raven.

From a back pocket he withdrew a square of thin folded plastic, shook it out, and covered the carcass. Except for the obvious—that the high-powered rifle bullet had smashed in from his right, from the south as he lay watching the herd—he had no answers to any of a host of questions.

Chapter Two

The row of Post-it notes cascaded down the side of the under-sheriff's computer screen. Usually more apt to embrace modern gadgets for posting his messages, Dispatcher Ernie Wheeler this time had chosen the old-fashioned approach. He had routed nothing to Estelle Reyes-Guzman's little electronic secretary that rested mute in her pocket during the morning-long session of District Court. Her cell phone was set on vibrate, but had remained quiet. No bailiff had appeared at the courtroom door to beckon her for a message.

Now, with the session adjourned, she settled in behind her desk in the Sheriff's Department office in the Posadas County Public Safety Building. She ignored both her computer's voluminous crop of e-mails and the voice-mail on the phone.

Instead, intrigued, she scanned the rainbow of demanding little 3x3 paper notes that featured the time written boldly on the upper right corner, with the name and number of each caller printed neatly below that. Of course, Ernie had posted them on the slick screen in order, newest at the bottom. Estelle plucked off the last message, penned by dispatch at 11:31 that morning, less than half an hour ago.

D. M. again for you. Estelle frowned. And who might D.M. be? Ever discreet, the dispatcher also hadn't included an *re:* to illuminate things. She moved up the line, picking out the four D.M. notes until she reached the earliest, having by then surmised that the caller was Dennis Mears—he'd called for the first time at 9:30 that morning, just after Estelle had left for court. And then again. And again. And again at 11:31.

The president of Posadas State Bank and twin brother of Sheriff's Department Lieutenant Tom Mears, Dennis was a model of decorum, and it must have embarrassed him to be so persistent. But he hadn't tried her cell phone, which ran the risk of interrupting her in the middle of something important—in this instance district court testimony during a domestic violence docket.

Equally curious about the other messages, Estelle plucked off the note from Camille Stratton. Brassy Camille, former sheriff Bill Gastner's oldest daughter and denizen of Flint, Michigan, surely had both her father's contacts and Estelle's cell, but she hadn't gone that route either. Like Dennis Mears, Camille had left no message when she had called at 10:26 that morning.

The remaining note, posted from Estelle's youngest son, Carlos, had come in at 10:46. "*Mr. Mears is trying to find you,*" her son had reported.

The undersheriff looked up at the wall clock. Now a minute or two after twelve, odds were good that the banker had left for lunch, either at Rotary, which met on Wednesdays at the Don Juan, or with one of his colleagues. Estelle dialed the bank anyway.

"Good afternoon, Posadas State Bank. How may I direct your call?" Rosie Ulibarri sounded cheerful.

"Rosie, this is Estelle. I see that Dennis has been trying to reach me all morning. Did I catch him?"

"Well, yes, you did," Rosie said with enthusiasm. "Hang on, please. Oh, and how are those kids of yours?"

"Hale and hearty, thank you." Rosie Ulibarri had no children of her own, but made up for it by nesting any child within reach.

"Everyone is still talking about that wonderful concert last winter. When do we get an encore?"

Estelle laughed. "I'm not in the loop," she said. "But soon, we hope."

"Has he been home for the summer now?"

"The conservatory is year-round, so no. If we're lucky, we'll see him on Labor Day weekend. Maybe."

"They do make them work, don't they? And he is how old now?"

"Francisco is fourteen in October. Carlos just turned ten last Sunday."

"My goodness." She sucked in a quick breath. "Listen to me. Estelle, forgive an old maid's rambling on. Here's Dennis."

"Thank you, Rosie."

Circuits clicked, and Dennis Mears' quiet voice came on the line.

"Estelle, I don't mean to pester," he said without preamble, "but you know how time slips away. Is there a possibility that you could swing by the bank this afternoon sometime? Or if it's easier, I can drop by the S.O."

"How about two at your place?" Estelle offered.

"Could we make it one?"

She glanced at the clock. The banker's lunch hour had already been shaved of four minutes. "One is fine, Dennis. This is concerning what?"

Mears hesitated. "I'd appreciate it if we could discuss it in person, may we?"

"You bet. Your office at one o'clock." She hung up, more than a little puzzled. If the bank president wouldn't discuss the topic over the phone, his absolute discretion was being put to the test. If it were an issue with her husband's clinic, which now included a dental suite as well as general family surgery and a full-scale pharmacy, Mears would not have called Estelle. The Guzmans' personal accounts were impeccable, well-padded, and under the care of a CPA. Mears wouldn't have bothered her about a goofed check.

That left the Sheriff's Department as the most likely target of concern, and there were any number of ways that some of the deputies, hard-pressed to make ends meet, or not mindful of their credit card balances, could misstep with the bank. Still, Estelle couldn't image Dennis Mears calling *her*. She wasn't in charge of Sheriff's Department employee banking unless one of them had tried to rob the place.

She sighed and reached out to paste Camille Stratton's note on her desk calendar. What Bill Gastner's daughter wanted was anyone's guess, but long-distance from Michigan didn't necessarily add urgency. Camille called often, keeping close tabs on her aging and stubborn father—and at the same time, nurturing the ties with the Guzmans and their two boys, for whom Bill Gastner was an active godfather—their *padrino.*

Even as Estelle withdrew her hand from the calendar, her desk phone rang, the dispatch circuit blinking.

"Estelle, Camille Stratton is on line two. Did you want to talk with her?"

"Sure. And I'm meeting with Dennis Mears at the bank at one. I need to keep things clear. I don't know what's up with him." She glanced at her calendar. "And I have another meeting at three. Don't let me forget."

"Who could forget Leona Spears?" Wheeler said dryly.

Sure enough—the great waft of the county manager's perfume would mark the undersheriff's office for the rest of the day. The grand lady—grand in many ways—would fill the doorway, her habitual, voluminous muumuu patterned as usual with gigantic sunflowers. Estelle was sure that Sheriff Bob Torrez, painfully taciturn and monosyllabic at the best of times, was embarrassed by Leona Spears. He ducked meetings with her whenever he could. But the department budget was the undersheriff's turf anyway, and Estelle—who *could* talk easily with the stubborn sheriff—knew Bobby Torrez's wants and wishes list. And she found it easy to enjoy the ebullient county manager's company.

She pushed the button for line two.

"Camille? What a nice surprise!"

"Well, good afternoon to *you, hermana.*" Camille Stratton's Midwest twang grated on the Spanish. "Say, did you happen to talk with Dad this morning?"

"I haven't. Court's been taking a lot of time this week. We're going to try for dinner tomorrow evening." She glanced at her calendar to make sure that Friday was still clear.

"Court," Camille said with disgust. "I was *so* relieved when that silly manslaughter lawsuit against Dad got tossed. I mean, there were absolutely no grounds, but you know how those things can drag on and on and on until every last lawyer has sucked up every last shekel."

"Worrisome," Estelle allowed. "And we're all glad it's over."

"Well, if you shoot somebody, I guess you can expect that to happen, but Dad certainly didn't have any choice, did he? The asinine judge should have just chucked the whole thing on day one."

"Everyone gets to have his say, silly or no," Estelle said.

"I suppose. Anyway, done is done. Did you happen to talk with him yesterday?"

Estelle's mind went blank. Had she? Court proceedings had taken all day on Tuesday, and then her mother had been a worry—detached, far from her usual acerbic self, obviously preoccupied about something—but at age ninety-nine, who knew what? Estelle talked with former sheriff Bill Gastner so routinely that for a moment she had to think hard. "The last time I talked with *Padrino* was Sunday night at dinner, Camille. Carlos made green chile lasagna."

Camille laughed. "God, those kids of yours. We need to clone them. And, oh," she said suddenly, "we had some friends over the other day and watched the CD of the Posadas Concert with Francisco and that other youngster. His classmate."

"Mateo Atencio," Estelle prompted. "The flutist."

"About the tenth time for us, I think. Just breathtaking. And I think my youngest—she's home now from Berkeley—is in love with your son. Or maybe it was Mateo who made her swoon. Or both. Hell, I don't know. Anyway, once again it was quite a treat. Mark did some Internet skimming and found that the boys are giving a concert in *Chicago* in late September. Did you know about that one? At the Garden Auditorium downtown?"

"September fourteenth." Estelle had noticed the concert promo in one of the Leister Academy's flyers. "Quite a venue." She hadn't taken time to read the details, but had been struck by the name of the place, and the small color photo included that showed an indoor glass dome with Lake Michigan in the background.

"We were thinking of going...it's not all that far. *Anyway,*" she said, "if you see Dad today, would you have him call me? I've tried about six times yesterday and today. I think his answering machine is off or something."

"That's not surprising. But, yes, I'll swing by there this afternoon if I can't make contact before."

"I'd appreciate it. I know I'm a worrywart, but with Dad, there's no telling. I wish we could find the old badger some live-in romance or something."

Estelle laughed. "He's been spending a lot of time out at our new astronomy theme park. That's his current romance. Right now, they're in the middle of building the tramway up the side of the mesa. That's neat to watch, but I think *Padrino* is more interested in the site archaeology."

"Well, no wonder, then. I'm glad he's busy." Camille laughed ruefully. "A cranky, busted-up seventy-six-year-old heart and stroke patient climbing around on cliff-side boulders and such, swatting at rattlesnakes? *That's* not much of a worry. Especially since he refuses to carry his cell phone at least half the time. And I bought him one of those medical alerts he's supposed to hang around his neck. Does he do that? Noooooooo."

"He does what he does, whether we know where he is or not. And loves every moment of it. He's incorrigible."

"Ain't that the truth. When you see him, have him call me, all right?"

"I'll do my best."

"How's your hunky husband doing? You know, Mark and I want to visit down there sooner rather than later. Mark is fascinated by the international clinic concept that Francis has going. Especially since you guys have let the dentist in."

"Camille, I wish you and Mark would treat us with a visit. Francis is talking about adding a *veterinarian* to the mix, if you can believe that." Estelle knew that, with his own wealthy patient load, oral surgeon Mark Stratton would find the small, rural Posadas clinic a culture shock, with its large percentage of patients from south of the border.

"Ye Gods, dogs and cats. Just what he needs. But look, is there any chance of you guys coming for the Chicago concert? We could have a nice reunion over here. It's been too long. And you know our guest room situation. We could quarter an army."

"We have been talking about it."

"Well, talk some more, and then do it. These moments are fleeting. I mean, fourteen years old and in concert at *the Garden*? Who woulda thunk? Next thing you know, this handsome little kid musician is going to be celebrating his fortieth birthday for God's sakes, and where will *we* be? You could bring Dad up with you. September is easy traveling. He'd love it."

"I'll talk to him about that." Bill Gastner had visited Flint on more than one occasion, and *loving it* had never been a description he'd used.

"And you'll check on him today for me? He thinks I try to smother him from a distance, but my gosh, Estelle."

"He's a tough case," Estelle laughed. "We'll be in touch, though. Thanks for calling, Camille."

"And do think about September. Really do."

"I really will."

She hung up and took a long, deep breath. Camille's agenda was indeed to smother her aging father with long-distance care. Bill Gastner didn't accept smothering well. On the infrequent occasions when Camille visited Posadas, Estelle had learned to stay well out of the epicenter. Still, because she had promised to do so, the undersheriff dialed Gastner's home phone. No answering machine came to life even after a dozen rings, and no life in the cell phone.

She had fifty minutes before her appointment with Dennis Mears—she could be at Gastner's spreading adobe fortress in three. On her way out of the Public Safety Building, she stopped at dispatch. "By some remote chance, does three hundred have his radio turned on?"

Wheeler frowned and turned just enough to touch the transmit pedal with his foot. "Three zero zero, PCS. Ten twenty?"

The radio remained silent. "Who knows?" Wheeler shrugged. "Half the time he forgets." Long retired, Bill Gastner still carried a Sheriff's Department radio in his SUV. Never a meddler, never looking to be underfoot, he still continued to be a valuable information resource for the department, a walking Posadas County gazetteer.

"Okay. I'm going to take just a minute and swing past his place. Camille is fretful. Then the bank, then Leona in my office." She took a deep breath. "Is there anything else on the horizon?"

"It's been a long, boring day," Wheeler replied.

"Did the sheriff happen to mention that he would attend the meeting with Leona later today?"

"I saw him for a minute or two when my shift started, then he went out. Lemme see." Estelle could picture Ernie twisting to look at the staff *in-out* whiteboard. "Doesn't say. When he comes in, I'll remind him about it."

"Good. Because the county manager might have some questions for him."

Chapter Three

Bill Gastner's spreading adobe hunkered under clusters of scruffy trees and one or two towering cottonwoods trying to compete with a pair of giant elms, a place Estelle referred to as a "Badger Den."

The undersheriff pulled into the graveled driveway, the crunch of tires loud on the stones. Nosing the county car up to the garage, she switched off the engine and out of habit sat for a moment, windows down, feeling the summer heat waft in with a bouquet from the thick hedge of creosote bush by the front door. Thirty percent humidity hardly qualified as muggy, but the overcast was a welcome relief from the usual five or six percent.

"Hey!"

Estelle froze. The single word had been so faint that had she merely rustled her clothing, she wouldn't have heard it. As it was, she had no sense of the direction from which the exclamation had come. She waited another few seconds and then got out of the car, closing the door without clicking the latch.

"I'm in…the garage." This time, she recognized Bill Gastner's voice, heard the strain of vocalizing only two words at a time.

"*Padrino?*" She tried the lift handle, but the door was held secure by the electric opener's mechanism.

"Go through the house," he said. "The…" and he hesitated. "Front door is open." His voice was a faint rasp, and then just a little stronger as he muttered, "God damn it."

"I'll be right there." Even as she turned toward the front door, she pulled the cell phone from her jacket pocket. The pleasantly musty air from the old house greeted her as she touched the speed dial.

"Ernie, I need an ambulance at Gastner's. I don't know what the deal is, but get 'em rolling. I'll be back to you in a minute."

"Roger that," Wheeler responded, "We got…" but the phone was already back in Estelle's pocket. The undersheriff turned right off the foyer, through a small bedroom that now stored the old man's collection of "perfectly good" cardboard boxes, to the hallway and the door to the garage. The door was ajar, and she reached in and snapped on the overhead lights. One of the bulbs worked, enough to cast deep shadows around the shiny red Dodge Durango SUV.

"Hey." Gastner's voice was small and rusty.

Between the SUV and the collection of boxed and unboxed junk that had bred over the years, and the rows of shelved paint cans whose contents had crusted, there was at best eighteen inches of clearance to sidle along the vehicle on the driver's side, the space in deep shadow. In that shadow lay an even darker shadow, securely wedged, head toward the rear wheel.

"Open the goddamn overhead door," Gastner whispered. "The remote is on the visor. Damn button by the door doesn't work."

Estelle had already started to slide past the truck's projecting mirror. She was five foot seven and slender. Gastner was an inch shy of six feet, rotund and beginning to stoop a little with age. How did he manage? One of her boots touched something.

"Don't be walking on me." He tried a half-hearted chuckle. By awkwardly straddling the fallen man's legs and sliding along the side of the truck, she was able to reach inside the cab to the visor and push the garage door remote. With a rumble, the door started up. The surge of fresh air stirred the other body odors of a man too long down.

The blast of daylight was harsh, and in the distance Estelle could hear a siren.

"Help is on the way," she said, bending low to rest a light hand on his shoulder. "Are we going to be able to help you up?"

Gastner lifted his left hand just clear of the floor in protest. His face was inches from the back wheel, legs awkwardly crumpled toward the front of the truck.

"I think I broke my goddamn hip," he growled weakly. "Hell, I *know* I broke it. So here I am."

She reached over and took his left hand. His fingers were cool, and he returned her touch with a gentle squeeze.

"Concrete floor is damn hard." He tried to shift his head. Estelle slipped out of her khaki jacket, wadded it into a small pillow, and lifted his head just enough to be able to slide it under.

"What brought you by?" His voice was a raspy whisper.

"Camille called a little bit ago," Estelle replied. "She'd tried to reach you, but here you were."

"Here I was." He suppressed a cough. "Here I was. I heard the damn phone. She doesn't give up, you know."

The ambulance turned off Grande onto Escondido, charged past the trailer park, and swung into Guadalupe, backing into the driveway beside Estelle's county car. Matty Finnegan was first out, crash kit in hand.

"Oh, good," Gastner murmured. "My favorite."

Always bubbly cheerful, Matty set down her gear and wormed her way along the truck to Gastner's head.

"What did you *do?*" she said. "This is no place for a nap."

"I tripped over my own goddamn feet," Gastner managed. "I couldn't catch myself. I think I broke my right hip."

As he spoke, Matty surveyed the tight spot.

"How's the pain?"

"Morphine would be nice."

"How long have you been here?" She grimaced at the aroma.

He cleared his throat. "Since yesterday afternoon. I think you better just tip me into a hole and bury me. Of all the goddamn times for the bowels to work…"

Matty murmured in deep sympathy, and half-turned toward her partner, Doyle Maestas. "IV, board, the whole thing. And we gotta get this out of here." She rapped a knuckle against the slab side of the SUV.

"The keys are in it," Gastner said. "But I think my right foot…is under the front tire."

"Oh, now don't worry about that. We'll just back out right over it."

"Thanks, sweetheart."

Matty stood up and turned to Estelle. "Hop in there and back this boat straight out. I'll make sure we don't squish any vital parts. We need room to work."

Estelle hustled to her own vehicle, started it, and spun it out of the way.

Returning to the garage, she slipped through on the passenger side and maneuvered over the center console to the driver's seat. Only months old, Gastner's SUV still offered the showroom smell, making for an interesting potpourri. It started instantly with a heavy-engined rumble.

"Okay, now I have to move this foot just a little bit," she heard Matty Finnegan say. "Slowly now, just an inch or two. Let me do all the work." Gastner sucked in a sharp breath and muttered an oath. "Okay, Sheriff. Straight back, nice and smooth."

Foot hard on the brake, Estelle pulled the gear selector into reverse. The truck twitched.

"Slooooowly," Matty said. "We don't have any extra room down here."

Estelle eased off some brake pressure and the SUV glided back on the smooth concrete.

"Let's get that elbow tucked in just an inch or two," Matty said. In another moment, the Dodge was clear, wheels on the gravel of the driveway. Making sure she had left room for the EMTs and their gurney, Estelle switched off the SUV.

Back in the garage, she could see that Gastner was lying on his right side, crammed against several boxes, the remains of a power mower, and his collection of empty paint cans. Moving him out on the floor so that he could lie flat was going to be agonizing.

"We want an IV right now," Matty said. "What time yesterday did you fall?"

Gastner closed his eyes. "Since just after four."

"p.m.?"

"Of course p.m."

"'Cause you're *never* up and about after dark, right?" Matty quipped. She bent down and looked him in the eye, a hand lightly on his forehead. "So you've been sacked out here for something like eighteen hours, huh?"

"Yep."

He kept his eyes closed as she went through the string of vital checks. "We're going to give you a sedative to take off the edge," Matty said, "and no, it's not morphine. But it's pretty good stuff anyway. But then we'll get you hydrated up." As she prepped the IV, she studied Gastner's face. "Are you still on the heart meds?"

"Uh huh."

"Don't be so grumpy. That's a yes?"

"Yes." He took a long, slow breath, as if marshalling his energy. "The three bottles are in by the bathroom sink. Estelle knows where they are. And, no. I'm not too good at remembering to take 'em."

Matty cranked her head around so she could look up at Estelle. "Would you? They'll want them at the hospital."

"You bet." And sure enough, the bottles of blood thinner, anticholesterol, and statin meds were lined up in the bathroom, along with half a dozen others. Beside those was an unmarked and unfilled plastic seven-day meds organizer. She swept the entire collection into a large zip bag.

As she returned to the garage, Estelle heard Matty chide, "You know, I always expected to find you diving headfirst off some boulder, a thousand miles out in the boonies."

"Me too," Gastner whispered. "Good way to go."

"But that's the way these hips happen," Matty added cheerfully. "My mom broke hers when she turned to pick up a dish towel. Tripped over her own feet." She held the IV bag out to Estelle. "You hold that while we work him onto the back-board?"

"There's nothing wrong with my back," Gastner groused.

She knelt beside him and touched his cheek. "This isn't going to be any fun, but we gotta do it, okay?"

"Have at it." His speech was already slurred a little from the sedative.

With Estelle holding the IV with one hand and preventing an avalanche of garage junk with the other, Matty at his legs and Doyle Maestas at his shoulders, they worked Gastner away from his bed in the boxes. By the time he lay flat on the back-board, a sheen of sweat soaked his forehead. He kept his eyes tightly closed. Matty checked his vitals again, and then glanced up to see a Sheriff's Department unit slide to a stop on Guadalupe.

"Oh, look at this," she said. "We've got the cavalry. You're such a lucky guy." Deputy Brent Sutherland got out of the car and walked quickly to the garage.

"Hip," Matty said succinctly to him. "And you couldn't have timed it better."

She glanced at the deputy. "You're the guy with all the muscles, so you take the head end. Doyle at the other, and fly-weight me hovering." She looked at Estelle. "And you're set with the IV. Let's do it."

"How about lunch first?" Gastner whispered.

"You'll get lunch, all right," the EMT said. "A nice bag of potions at the hospital. And maybe if you *really* behave yourself, some morphine-diluted applesauce."

"You're a cruel woman," the old man whispered.

Despite Gastner's two hundred twenty pounds, the trio managed the lift as if they were using hydraulic assist, and then with a web of straps to hold the boarded patient secure to the gurney, wheeled him out to the ambulance. Matty took the IV from Estelle and affixed it to its stainless tree. "You're going to follow us in?"

"You bet. I'll secure the place and be right behind you."

She stepped back and watched as they buttoned up the ambulance.

"Anything you want me to do?" Deputy Sutherland said. Estelle turned to him and shook her head.

"Thanks, Brent. Any surprises in court?"

"No problemo. The sheriff has something going on out at Waddell's, though. Pasquale is headed out that way."

If only it was *no problemo* here, Estelle thought, unable to imagine how long those eighteen hours must have seemed for *Padrino,* trapped on that chilly concrete floor. She snugged the SUV back inside, then methodically closed up Bill Gastner's house and garage. She dropped his key ring in the center console of her car, and sat back. She slumped as the urgency released. She needed to call Camille, but she would do that from the hospital, when she knew the full scope of the patient's condition.

Instead, she called Posadas State Bank. Dennis Mears had stepped out, Rosie told her, but she knew that the bank president was planning on meeting with Estelle in just a few minutes. "And if it's really, really important, I'm sure that Mr. Mears can find *you,* " Rosie said.

"I'll be at the hospital, if you would ask him to stop by there," Estelle said.

Rosie sucked in a breath. "Oh, dear. I hope nothing…"

"Me too," Estelle said, and let it go at that.

Chapter Four

The field-dressed antelope carcass weighed no more than sixty pounds. Torrez carried it over his left shoulder, the damaged rifle in his right hand, and by the time he reached his truck, the sun had burned through the overcast, with the temperature hovering in the low nineties. The large cooler in the back, protected by an old, musty tarpaulin, had been untouched. With deft dismembering and wrapping, he managed to stow the entire carcass. He rearranged the bags of ice to cover the game, and made sure the lid was firmly latched before jerking the tarp back in place. He took a deep breath, regarding the truck.

"Shit," he said aloud. The hood sure enough *was* open. Instead of rounding to the front of the truck, he backed up, retracing his steps until he was twenty paces away. The gravelly dirt on the side of the road bore a number of vague prints, but with some imagination, they told the story. They'd be laughed out of court as evidence, Torrez knew. He guessed that someone had pulled in around his truck, parking ahead of it. The single set of boot prints, deep in the heel and smooth-soled, headed directly to the driver's door. One of them was clear enough that a casting might be possible.

The driver's door hadn't been locked, so it would have been easy to open it and pull the little hood latch handle—it was one of the few accoutrements of the truck that still worked as it should. The tracks then retraced the route to the front of the truck. From five yards away, Torrez could see that the man had stood in front of the old truck, perhaps fumbled for the release, and jerked the hood open, fighting against the bent metal and the dry hinges. To what end?

Careful to avoid scuffing existing tracks, Torrez slipped his fingers under the edges of the hood and lifted. The hinges squawked. For a few seconds, he saw nothing amiss. "Huh." He bent his head to one side. Sure enough, the high tension wire from distributor to coil, both tucked at the rear of the engine under the air cleaner housing, was missing. "Ain't that clever," he said. It was a simple, surefire technique. He dug out his phone.

"Posadas County Sheriff's Department, Wheeler."

Torrez's handheld police radio was in the glove box, but he was loath to blab over the air.

"Pasquale made contact yet?"

"That's affirmative, Sheriff. Sutherland is headed that way, too, now. It's a white Ford, 2013 model, Arizona license November…"

"I don't need that. Look, I ain't got wheels. Someone needed my coil wire more'n me." He turned and gazed down the road at an approaching contractor's rig—headache rack, side rail tool boxes, mini-crane swung tight in the back. "I need Guzman and her camera out here asap. That's one thing."

"Ah, sir…"

"And then have somebody swing by the Dick's Auto Parts and pick me up a coil wire for a '68 Chevy half ton, 350 box engine and bring it the hell out here. We got a good set of tracks out here, so before Pasquale lets that truck go, we need to take a look at its tire prints."

"Sir, the undersheriff is going to be tied up for a while. It looks like Bill Gastner managed somehow to fall in his garage. Broken hip, for one thing. I don't know just what the deal there is going to be. They're transporting now."

Bob Torrez pushed his cap back and frowned. "Okay. Look, get both Taber and Linda on the road, then. I'm going to need photos, and *I* sure as hell ain't going to do it with this Mickey

Mouse phone camera. And tell Pasquale to handle that end. How many in the truck?"

"One, sir. Arizona registration on the truck, a Dominic Olveda, current Arizona license, negative twenty-eight."

"New-issue license?"

"Yes, sir."

"Have Pasquale hold him until I get there."

"You want him arrested?"

"Not yet. Just make sure Tom holds him until I get there."

"Hope he's not just a tourist."

"Then we'll all apologize."

Torrez switched off, then immediately hit the speed dial to reach his undersheriff.

"What's up with Bill?" he said without salutation as soon as the call connected. There was a pause as Estelle Reyes-Guzman took time to make the mental switch.

"Hip," she replied. "Somehow he got his feet tangled and fell in his garage. He got stuck on the floor beside his truck… he was there since yesterday afternoon, Bobby. Like eighteen hours or more."

"Well, that ain't good."

"No. He's lucky it was August and not January."

"You got everything you need?"

"I think so. This is going to be one of those wait and see things. I'm sure they'll transport, but I don't know yet whether Cruces or Albuquerque. Can you take my meeting with Leona this afternoon at three?" She asked the question more than half in jest, already knowing the sheriff's answer.

"County manager will just have to wait," he said with surprisingly even temper. "Look, I'm going to be occupied out here for a little bit. Taber will handle the meeting if you're not free by then." He caught himself. "Scratch that. She'll be busy out here. Wake up Mears. He can do it."

"We'll see," Estelle replied. "What do you have going?"

"I had a good shot at a buck, and then someone took a long-range rifle shot at me just after I fired. Missed me, but wrecked my rifle scope. And then I find out that he stole the coil wire off my truck to give himself a little extra time. Pasquale might have him stopped down on 56 right now. Sutherland's on his way down, too, and I got Taber and Linda comin' out here. Lots of tracks, maybe prints. We'll see. We're going to need pictures."

"Is this likely somebody you had talked to before?"

"Don't know. I didn't see him parked down on the road, or hear him before the shot. Just one round. I was kinda startled and fell backward, so maybe he thinks he got me."

"*Kinda* startled," Estelle repeated dryly. "I would think so. Okay. Let me know. I can break from here if I have to, but this doesn't look good for *Padrino*. You're sure *you're* all right?"

"Yep. Catch you later."

Phone pocketed, he walked over to the juniper and found a spot in the shade. The contractor, driving slowly with his windows open, drifted his rig to a stop beside Torrez's truck, then pulled past it when he saw Torrez.

"Need some help, Sheriff?" Carl Bendix peered back at the pickup's partially raised hood. "Miles told me you might be out here huntin' today. Any luck?"

Torrez shrugged. "Runty buck is all. I'm just waitin' on some folks now. How's your project comin'?"

Bendix, rotund with a shaved head under his blue cap, shifted in the seat uncomfortably as Torrez finally rose and approached. "You know," he said, "We're going to be out on this goddamn mesa project for *years.*"

"That's a good thing, ain't it?"

The contractor shrugged in resignation. "Damn hot place to work, if you ask me. Could fry an egg on them rocks when the sun comes out." He nodded at Torrez's truck. "What's the trouble?"

"Coil cable."

"Give you mine, but it's a Ford. Then *I* could sit in the shade all day." Bendix laughed.

Torrez slapped the truck's window sill in dismissal. "That's okay. I got one comin'. You take it easy."

"You betcha."

Taking a wide circle around his truck as the contractor pulled away, Torrez opened the passenger side door. The door hinges groaned, and not for the first time, Torrez reflected that it would be convenient if the door locks actually *worked*. Nothing in the glove box had been disturbed. The twelve-gauge shotgun in the rear window rack was still latched in place. The full gas can in back was bungeed tightly in front of the fender well. The rest was junk, not worth the taking.

"Just to give yourself a little time," the sheriff muttered.

Chapter Five

"He's comfortable, and will have surgery first thing in the morning, Camille. Up in Albuquerque as soon as we can arrange a transport." Estelle's delivery of the news prompted a loud sigh. Gastner's eldest daughter had married an oral surgeon, and would understand that euphemistic word "comfortable" perfectly well when she saw for herself the X-ray and the illuminated jumble of bone fragments. Unless *Padrino* was slumbering under anesthesia, he wasn't comfortable.

"He just fell *in the garage?*"

"That's how it appears," Estelle said. "The most dangerous thing is that he spent eighteen hours there, on the concrete floor, wedged between a pile of old boxes and the truck. He couldn't move himself, so there he was."

"Why are they waiting until morning for the surgery, then?"

"To make sure he's stabilized before anesthesia, I suppose. And he has a little cough. I think they want to make sure he isn't working on pneumonia or something like that. And his heart issues, you know."

"Oh, my. A really bad break, then? Although I guess *all* broken hips are bad, huh."

"Yes. That's why the choice of UNMH. My husband's favorite orthopedic surgeon is there."

"What's that, six hours by ambulance?"

"They'll fly him up. Maybe an hour."

"Well, at least *that's* good news." Camille fell silent for a moment. "He wasn't wearing his alert call-button, was he?"

"Of course not."

"And the cell phone…"

"Was in the kitchen. And he couldn't reach the sheriff's radio in his truck. He was stuck."

"What are we going to do with this old guy, Estelle?" Her tone had softened, her vexation draining away.

"Just the best we can."

"I want to come out for a little while, at least. He's going to need somebody underfoot."

"He'll enjoy seeing you," Estelle was not sure if that was the truth. She knew that Gastner was sometimes as much irritated by his eldest daughter as charmed. "Whatever time you can spare would be good."

"Well, there's a whole bunch of things we're going to have to decide, I suppose. Rehab, things like that. The recovery time for a new hip isn't just a day or two, after all. Not for somebody his age. He'll need help even with a walker for a long time."

"We'll just see," Estelle said. "He's sedated now, but he's been lucid. He'll have time to think about all this. Time to make up his mind."

"You have power of attorney?"

"Yes, I do. He made sure it was active when he had his kidney stone last year. He said he wanted to leave the POA in place. Just in case."

"That's a relief then. Are you going to Albuquerque with him?"

"I *think* I'll be able to, if things stay quiet here. I could fly up with him and figure out the ride home when the time comes."

Estelle turned as a couple of chatting nurses walked past the waiting room, and to her surprise saw Dennis Mears sitting across the room in one of the yellow plastic chairs, forearms on his knees, hands clasped together, steady blue eyes regarding her with a mixture of patience and sympathy.

"I'll talk to Mark and see what he says," Camille said. "And when I get there, I'll sit down with your hubby and see what *he* says."

"Sure." *And don't forget to talk to your father to see what he wants,* Estelle almost amended, but she kept the thought to herself.

"I'll let you know when I'm on my way," Camille said. "Don't worry about picking me up. I'll just rent something at the airport. I should be able to fly out tomorrow, so maybe you and I can meet up there. Then we could ride down to Posadas together. I'd enjoy that."

Dennis Mears rose as Estelle approached and extended his hand. He held the position while Estelle finished her call, then shook her hand warmly.

"How's he doing?"

"He needs a new hip," Estelle said. "We'll be leaving for Albuquerque here in a few minutes. Last we heard, the air ambulance was in Gallup, so we have a little time."

"Hip…that's a bad deal." Mears turned and nodded down the hallway. "The atrium is half in shade. Shall we use that—if you have a couple of minutes?"

The warmth of the sun-warmed concrete was welcome after the sterile, refrigerated air of the hospital's interior. Estelle sat at the small concrete table in the shaded corner, and the banker sat on the bench across from her as if he were astride a horse. Despite his hours behind a desk, Dennis was fit and trim, looking like a polished version of his brother, Lieutenant Tom Mears. Maybe he even awoke each morning with his blond hair perfectly coiffed, with not a whisker in sight.

He frowned and examined the pebbled texture of the table for a moment, running a manicured fingertip along the edge. "Estelle," he said finally, "I'm a little bit concerned about your mother." When she didn't respond, Mears added, "As if you didn't have enough on your plate at the moment." He smiled gently. "This is really a difficult position for me professionally, so I'm going to ask you to forgive the indiscretion."

"Of course."

"Your mother has requested a significant withdrawal." Mears stopped, and Estelle felt the first surge of uneasiness. He grimaced as if uttering the news was actually painful. "This is none of my business, of course, but I'm assuming that you have some sort of understanding with your mother? I mean, she's how old now?"

"Just turned ninety-nine. And yes. I have power of attorney for her as well."

"As well?" Mears looked puzzled at first, then the light dawned. His sparse, nearly white eyebrows rose. "Oh…for Bill, you mean. Of course. Now, in your mother's case…and she's a remarkable lady. She's still sharp as can be, isn't she?"

"She's been fortunate."

The banker shifted on the concrete bench. "Your mother's account has not been particularly active."

"I wouldn't expect it to be." Estelle smiled. "If she buys anything at all, she must store it under her bed. I never see it."

"Needs are few at her age, I suppose."

"We try to make it so. You mentioned a withdrawal. How much is she asking for?" When it came to figures, Mears didn't back and fill. He rested his hand flat on the table.

"Eight thousand dollars even."

"*Ay,*" Estelle startled.

"Now," Mears hastened to add, "my problem is that, first of all, the transaction is none of my business. I mean, it's her money, in her account. And just because she's elderly doesn't change the rules."

"I understand that. But she must have a good reason. When did all of this come about, Dennis? She called you?"

"That's exactly what she did, late last week. Friday, in fact. She wouldn't talk with either of the tellers who were working, or with my VP. She could have, of course."

"What time did this happen?"

"She called me shortly after ten-thirty Friday morning."

"And she just wanted the money deposited in her checking account? An even eight thousand?"

"This is the part that worries me, Estelle. She asked for a cashier's check, and as you well know, those are on demand, negotiable by anyone."

Estelle found it difficult to imagine her mother doing any of this. The details of a vacation trip in 1947 to Monterey might be crystal clear in Teresa Reyes's mind, but remembering the topic of a sentence just started was a challenge.

"She just called you and asked for a cashier's check?" Dennis Mears nodded. "Did she say who was going to pick it up for her?"

"She asked that we bring it over to her. Now, we normally wouldn't do that sort of thing, but in some instances we will. Your mother has been a good customer for twenty years or so. And we understand that she doesn't get around like she used to. She said that you would be doing this, but that you were busy with court."

"And I wonder what *I* was supposed to do with a bank draft for eight thousand dollars."

Mears held his hands palm up in surrender. "Will you talk with her? I'd worry a whole lot less if you would."

"Of course. Maybe she's giving a donation to someone, but why not just write a normal check?"

"We can always hope that's the case, Sheriff. I tend to be cautious, though. There are a number of scams going around, and some of them specifically target the elderly. When someone who is beyond the normal consumer's loop suddenly wants a large sum of money, my ears perk up a little. If she was buying a new car, the sum would most likely be a whole bunch of numbers. Eighteen thousand, six hundred and twelve dollars and thirty-eight cents. You know what I mean. And I have to tell you." He patted the table top gently. "I got a scamming letter last month myself. An e-mail from someone I met years ago, saying he was stuck in the Philippines after his wallet was stolen. He needed twenty-two hundred dollars to get out of there. The police were dragging their feet, things like that."

"Only twenty-two hundred, though?"

"Interesting number, I think. The sort of thing where someone *might* be willing to just dash off a check, or an electronic transfer. I didn't respond in any fashion, and just deleted the e-mail after making a copy for my collection. So when your mother called me…"

"You haven't cut the check for her yet?"

"No. I confess to dragging my feet. I had just the one call from her, and she said she'd get back to me this week to arrange the transfer. I'll certainly cut the check today if you give me the word. And that's what makes me uncomfortable. Your mother is perfectly cogent. If she wants the money, she'll get it. That's the rule of the game. But…I didn't think waiting a day or two would hurt. If it inconveniences her in any way, I apologize."

"No, no. Let me talk with *Mamá* and get back to you, Dennis. I'm sure there's a simple explanation." Estelle extended her hand. "Thanks for taking the time to give me a head's up. I appreciate it, Dennis. You did the right thing."

As they rose, the banker's face brightened. "Any chance of another local concert soon?"

"September in Chicago is the next one I've heard about."

"No CD releases?"

"You know, Francisco isn't in any hurry to do that. I'm not sure why. He told me that he walked into one of those huge chain book-and-record super-stores in Joplin, saw the racks and racks of CDs by hundreds of artists, and said it all made him want to run the other way."

"He's fortunate that he understands the concept of exclusivity at such a young age."

"We'll see where it all goes. Right now, he's still excited about live concerts. That's what he loves to do. And he loves all the related academic work, believe it or not."

Mears nodded and pointed at the doorway to the atrium. Estelle turned and saw the nurse waiting.

"Sheriff Guzman," the young man said, "Mr. Gastner wishes to talk with you for a minute when you get the chance."

"I'm on my way." Estelle shook hands with Dennis Mears once more. "And thank you, Dennis. I'll be in touch. And yes… please hold the check until you hear from me."

"Give Bill my best wishes, please."

The thirty-year Sheriff's Department veteran, former New Mexico livestock inspector, inveterate historian and repository of a gazetteer's worth of information about the Southwest in general and Posadas County in particular, lay plumbed, padded, and monitored in one of the two intensive care beds. His eyes were closed and as Estelle Reyes-Guzman hesitated at the door, he opened first one and then the other. He reached for his glasses and settled them in place. Owl-eyed, he regarded Estelle with something akin to amusement.

The undersheriff stood beside the bed for just a moment, then reached out a hand and patted his left knee, letting her fingers trace the outline of his kneecap.

"So," she said.

"I'd walk out of here if I could." Gastner's voice was raspy.

"We've done that before, haven't we? Are they managing the pain all right for you?"

"Oh, sure," he said dismissively. "Some really good stuff. And maybe I need it. Your hubby showed me the X-rays. I'm in a hell of a lot of pieces." He eyed Estelle critically. "You're lookin' good."

"Well, up until your taking a dive, it's been kind of a downtime. Lots of sessions with Leona on the budget, everybody behaving themselves...I think I've finally caught up on some sleep." She smiled at him as he raised his right arm in slow motion and settled it on top of his head, fingers idly scratching his closely cropped hair. "You'll be okay, *Padrino*. They were kind of worried about some congestion."

"Nah. A little too long camped out on the garage floor is all. But I did a thorough job on the hip. Anything worth doing, you know. They've really got me cornered this time."

"You were just standing beside your truck when you lost your balance?"

"Well, essentially. I turned a little bit for something, I don't remember what, and the next thing I know, I'm examining the concrete floor. I'd like to be able to say, 'you should see the other guys,' but I can't claim heroism for this one."

Estelle glanced at her watch. "The plane should be here in less than an hour, *Padrino*. Then you'll get a new bionic hip, and you'll be running sprints in no time."

He huffed a feeble chuckle. "Sure enough." He lifted his left hand, the right still in place on his head, and examined the tips of his fingers. "You know, a few dozen times over the years, I've watched other folks play out this same scene. I know what the goddamn score is." His face brightened. "But see, I know some things they don't. The secret road to healthy bone growth and repair lies in green chile. We'll find out how good my credit is with Fernando Aragon." He lifted his head a little, looking hopeful at his own mention of Aragon, owner of Gastner's favorite restaurant, the Don Juan de Oñate. "I don't suppose you happened to bring a snack with you."

"I've failed you," Estelle said with deep, mock sympathy. "I was going to propose that when you break out of here that you buy yourself one of those luxury RVs and park it right in the Don Juan's parking lot. That way, your restaurant therapy would be just a shout away."

His eyes narrowed in speculation. "That's a profoundly good idea, sweetheart."

"Dennis Mears sends you his best, by the way."

"He's worried I'll fall behind on some payment now? We gotta keep *him* happy, except I don't owe him a goddamn cent. He's the one who will finance the RV that you're suggesting, though."

She laughed. "I want to see that."

A knuckle rapped on the door and Melinda Gabriel bustled in. As wide as she was tall, the ICU nurse advanced to the head of the bed so that her face was a foot from Gastner's. "We're gonna get you ready to fly, lover," she said. "Fun times, huh?"

She reached out and tapped the IV feed. "You're doin' okay?"

"As long as I don't move."

"Boy, oh boy, roger that. Well, Doc wants you snoozing through the whole trip, so we'll get started with the goodies."

Gastner turned his head and nodded at Estelle. "We'll see you when I get back from drug rehab," he said.

"So *you* think," Melinda scoffed. "She's flyin' with us the whole way, just to make sure you don't try something foolish like hatching some weirdo escape plan." She patted his left arm affectionately. "I've heard about you."

That brought a deep frown from the patient, who glared at Estelle. "You're not going to waste all that time…."

"A little R and R," the undersheriff said. "Anyway, I want to chat with Camille when she gets in, and this will work out just fine."

"Camille?"

"That would be your oldest daughter, sir."

"I know who the hell she is. You called *her?* Jesus. "

"The other way around. She called me, *Padrino.* That's why I happened to show up at your place when I did." She watched as Melinda introduced a new medication to the drip line. "We've hatched a grand conspiracy, you see."

"Oh, for God's sakes," Gastner whispered. "Now I'm really finished." He looked up at Melinda. "My daughter is a professional Jewish mother."

Melinda squeezed his shoulder. "Maybe that's what you need just now." She grinned at Estelle. "You have your over-nighties and all that?"

"I'm on my way to do just that. How much time do I have?"

"The plane left Gallup a few minutes ago, taking a youngster back to Chinle. So what, two hours?" Gastner muttered something, and reached out a hand to point toward the door. The burly, bearded Dr. Francis Guzman had entered as silently as a cat, and after picking up the bedside chart, surveyed the various monitor screens.

"Things are lookin' good." Guzman moved to Estelle and hooking an arm through hers. In his hug, she look tiny and frail. His left hand settled on Gastner's wrist as if checking to see if the overhead monitor was correct.

"You should have told my daughter to stay in Michigan," Gastner rasped. "She's going to set my convalescence back a month."

"I don't have the nerve to tell Camille *anything,*" Dr. Guzman said. "You can try when you see her."

Gastner relented a little. "Oh, she's not that bad, really. But just fix me up here, Doc. I have a whole can of screws and bolts in my garage you can use. Christ, we don't need to tie up a god-damn med-evac airplane for a busted hip."

"Normally, that's exactly what I'd do," Dr. Guzman said. "Raid the hardware store and get on with it. But some folks luck out and get the full VIP treatment." As he said that, he turned and urged his wife toward the door. "I'll be back in a minute," he said to Gastner, and ushered his wife out into the hall, clos-ing the door to Gastner's room behind them. "Camille's flying in as soon as…?"

"Tonight, probably. Or tomorrow morning. She'll rent a car in Albuquerque, so maybe she and I can drive back down here together the day after tomorrow. We'll just have to wait and see."

Enveloped in her husband's bear hug, she lingered for a moment, letting his strength bolster her own optimism. Nothing was ever simple. *Padrino* had pulled on a brave face, but with his health on the edge, he faced a dangerous surgery—and then a long recuperation and a troublesome road of physical therapy. All of those complications would present the challenge of a complete lifestyle change, from ambulatory and independent to dependence on home health care. She thumped her forehead against her husband's chest and then drew back a little.

"I need to talk with Bobby before I go. He's got something going on with a couple of the deputies out at Waddell's. And I need to talk with *Mamá*, too," she said. "Dennis Mears came to see me."

Francis stood with his hands featherlight on her shoulders. "What, she tried to rob the bank?"

She laughed. "I wish it were that simple. He's concerned about her request for an eight thousand-dollar withdrawal—all in a negotiable cashier's check. And asap, of course."

The physician frowned. "New solar-powered hearing aids, maybe? An electric wheelchair with jewel-studded mud flaps? Is she making a down payment on a new golden flute for Francisco?"

Estelle took a fistful of his neatly trimmed beard and twisted. "I don't think so."

"She hasn't mentioned any of this to you?"

"No."

"Well, talk to her sooner rather than later, then," Francis said. "I'm not surprised that Mears came to you if there's a problem, but I'm *very* surprised that Teresa didn't talk to you about it first. I didn't think that you two guys had any secrets from each other."

"*Yo tambien,*" Estelle murmured. "We'll see."

Chapter Six

Turning his phone so that the two officers could see the tiny screen, Torrez gave Linda Real-Pasquale and Sergeant Jackie Taber a digital tour of the shooting scene. The phone images were disappointingly flat and featureless.

"You go to the top of this ridge." He nodded eastward. "And where I was shootin' from about a hundred yards from there, downhill to the east. I left a broken piece of the scope on a rock to mark it. The antelope were another four hundred yards out." The close-up he had taken of his shattered rifle and jacket was spectacularly blurry. He saw Linda's right eyebrow drift upward. "It's a damn phone," he said.

"Maybe one day you can move up to a pinhole camera, Sheriff," Linda said, sober-faced. He gave the pudgy young woman a withering glance. Half his size, she was never intimidated by his glowering, his abrupt manner of speech, his ignorance of tact.

"We'll find where you field-dressed the carcass," Taber said.

"Yes!" Linda chimed in with mock enthusiasm. "A pile of guts!"

"That's it. Then just back up due west four hundred yards or so, and you'll have the spot where I was shootin' from. I want *pictures*," and he looked hard at Linda, "that show something." He swept an arm in a large circle. "And then I want to know where the shot came from. Got to be to the south. I'd guess maybe as far as five hundred yards out. And then here," and he turned to face the old truck. "Tire tracks, boot prints, see if you can lift a print off the hood release. Maybe off the hood near the latch."

"Some measurements will be easy," Taber added. "The way he pulled in there in front of your truck, that's a tight turning radius."

He held out his hand. "I need to take your unit," he said to Linda. "If I ain't back right away, you can ride with Sarge."

"You got it. Let me get my camera bag."

As she half skipped, half jogged off, little bursts of dust rising from her boot falls, the sheriff regarded Sergeant Taber. "Gonna be hard," he said. "But from up there, you can get a good lay of the land. Maybe you'll see something." Torrez was not alone in believing that Jackie Taber saw patterns in the land that no one else did. Her thick sketch pad and art pencils always rode in the patrol unit for those quiet moments when sitting with windows open and listening to the prairie talk was more productive than racing back and forth on the highways.

She hitched her utility belt up on her generous waist, frowning toward the hill to the south. While the pudgy Linda Real looked as if she needed some concentrated time in a fitness center, Jackie Taber carried her heft with power and grace. "The shooter skirted from here around to the south somehow, that's what you're saying?"

"Yep."

"And you never saw or heard a thing until your rifle scope exploded and then that was followed by the distant gun shot?"

"Suppose so." That thought irked Torrez, who enjoyed quiet pride in his own hunting skills, his ability to outwait an animal until conditions were just right for the shot. That someone had been able to do that same thing to *him,* taking advantage of the same long-range shots that average hunters would neither consider nor accomplish, made him uneasy.

"And nothing after the shot?" Taber persisted. "No metallic noises of the rifle bolt being racked, or no boots crunching on gravel?"

"Nope."

"But you're thinking that he missed with that one shot, or just wanted to scare you?"

"*Maybe* he did."

"Or not. May I see the rifle?"

Torrez opened the truck door and slid the case out. Opening it wide, he spread out the scope pieces. Taber leaned forward, but touched nothing. "Right on the windage adjustment knob, it looks like."

"Just a little below it. Whole thing burst up and out."

She reached up and touched Torrez's left eyebrow. "Nice little souvenir."

He flinched back, not from any pain, but from the discomfort of the close contact. "Couple of places. Nothin' serious."

Taber held her index fingers about a foot apart. "That far to the left, and *your* brain pan would have been frying in the sun along with the antelope's."

The sheriff looked irritated and zipped up the rifle case. "You need anything else before I go on down and see what Pasquale's into?"

"I think we're set, sir. We'll see what we can find."

"If somebody shows up with a coil cable, just put it on the driver's seat."

"I have it, sir. The invoice is stuck in the box."

He nodded "Thanks. I shouldn't be long."

As he settled into Linda's Expedition, the SUV now a decade and well over a hundred thousand miles old, he smelled the light fragrance of perfume. The girls talked, obviously. The perfume was the same fragrance favored by Gayle, his wife. And that thought brought him up short. He'd come within a few inches of leaving her a widow and his month-old son, Gabriel, fatherless.

Fifteen miles down County Road 14, he paused for the intersection and then turned east on State 56. The engine pulled strong, but at eighty miles an hour the approximate alignment and worn tires set up a shimmy that he could feel both through the steering wheel and his seat. He backed off, settling for seventy.

"304, 308 ETA eight minutes."

"Ten-four, 308." Pasquale sounded bored.

There was no point in pestering Pasquale for information—in a few miles he'd know for himself.

Not far southwest of the ghost town of Moore, the Rio Salinas crossed the highway, and just to the west of the sign announcing the grand name for that dry wash, Deputy Pasquale had stopped the Ford pickup. His SUV was parked well off the roadway, front wheels cocked toward the pavement. Sutherland's vintage Crown Vic completed the bookends.

Torrez passed the three vehicles. The tailgate of the pickup was down, and a chubby man with well-oiled hair sat comfortably on it, feet swinging like a kid on a playground swing. The palms of his hands rested flat on the tailgate. His posture said he was merely waiting for a friend, not in the least defensive that the minions of the law were congregating around him. The sheriff swung onto the shoulder and parked.

Torrez was certain that the pickup, shiny new with just a blush of red dust, was the one he had watched through binoculars. Deputy Pasquale stood on the shoulder side of the truck where he could keep the man in view. Brent Sutherland was intent on inspecting the front of the 150, and moved around it as Torrez approached. The man craned his neck as the officers congregated, but none of the activity appeared to make him apprehensive. Pasquale intercepted the sheriff.

"Sheriff, this is Mr. Olveda," he said quietly. "No wants or warrants, nothing inside the vehicle except personal luggage. He tells me that he drove down here from the airport, and is on his way back to town."

"Huh," Torrez murmured. The airport was seven miles out of town on State Road 76, and then from there, several miles west to the intersection of County Road 14. What followed, south to the sheriff's hunt area, was about fifteen miles of dusty road, crowded with lumbering trucks and contractor traffic of all shapes and sizes.

Olveda offered the beginnings of a smile, and then glanced at his large watch and shrugged. When Torrez was within reach, the man bent forward and extended a hand. Torrez ignored it, but his attention was attracted to the gold watch, multi-dialed and probably expensive, nestled in the thatch of wrist hair. A linen short-sleeved shirt with just enough wrinkles to be fashionable, off-white chinos with a black leather belt, and pricey leather running shoes—and the shoes certainly did *not* have raised heels and smooth soles. He was not dressed for hunting.

"I hope you are having a pleasant day," he said. "But I know how these things can be." His accent was careful with the English, as if he rehearsed each line before uttering it.

"What things are that?" Torrez's voice was flat and disinterested. Olveda tipped his head and looked at the sheriff curiously, taking in the size, the heft, the stance…even the lack of fashion statement in the sheriff's hunting attire—worn, blood-spattered jeans; a work shirt in even worse condition; baseball cap with the brim crumpled.

"You are looking for something, no? Officer Pasquale stopped me when I was driving but fifty in a sixty zone. What do they say…*rubbernecking* at the countryside." He mentioned the deputy's name as if they had been acquaintances for years. He raised both hands in surrender. "Seat belt secure, all lights working. I wondered, of course, what he was seeking." Olveda's accent was modest, certainly not border Mexican. He looked at the watch again. "And now detained for close to an hour." Again the shrug, as if the hour didn't really matter. "So I assume that not all is as it seems."

Torrez stepped to the truck and leaned an elbow on the side. Olveda could not have failed to notice that he was now flanked, the big, roughly dressed man on his right, the younger deputy in snappy uniform just behind his left shoulder, the second burly deputy filling in the middle.

"Were you on County 14 earlier, sir?"

"I was." The answer surprised Torrez, who had expected to hear the standard, "*Where's that?*" Olveda shrugged. "It seemed a natural way to go, you know. Earlier this morning, I was at the airport on business, meeting with the county manager. And then I had some questions for the developer who is funding this enormous project of which I've heard so much…this astronomy park? Really quite remarkable, really it is. I drove down then, but was told that the developer was not on site at the moment." He smiled pleasantly. "Then I proceeded south to this highway, planning to return to Posadas for a late lunch." He shrugged. "And that's it. That is what I did." His expression clearly added, *I'm telling you all of this because I'm a nice guy…and I know people.*

Torrez was silent, and Olveda shrugged again. "I do not know why the officer stopped me." He glanced over at Pasquale with good-natured patience. "Of course he has his reasons, and will tell me in due time. And then I was informed that we must wait for you, Sheriff. So here we are. Here *you* are."

"Mr. Olveda, when you drove down 14, did you see an older model Chevrolet pickup pulled off the road? Maybe a mile short of the project?"

Olveda pooched out his lower lip and frowned. "I did. It was parked with the hood partially up. I wondered if assistance was needed. But there was no driver in sight, so…"

"The hood was *up?*"

"Well, unlatched, so to speak. As if it had been opened, and then not closed completely."

An observant man. "You didn't stop?"

"No. I slowed, but then continued on when I saw no one. I'm not sure what I could have done anyway, except possibly offer a ride. But, as I say…" Torrez's eyes assessed the clean, neat business man with the immaculate, manicured hands. He didn't look like the sort who stopped to render roadside assistance to strangers.

The sheriff dropped his arm off the truck, glanced back down the highway, and then stepped out so he could see the pickup's tires. The highway tread on the Michelins was clearly no match for the heavier lug impressions left near his own truck.

"What time was that?"

"I did not check the time, Sheriff."

"From there, where?"

Olveda frowned at Torrez's shorthand grammar. "I drove to the project site, and spent some time there, inquiring about the whereabouts of the owner. I wanted to drive to the top, but it did not seem appropriate at that moment."

"Mr. Olveda, what other vehicles did you see in that area?"

The man smiled. "That project that is underway…a most busy place. I suppose that from the time I left the state highway—the airport road, that is—to the time I passed the site gate, I was passed by a dozen vehicles of one description or another. And several overtook me." He shook his head. "They do not waste any time raising a dust. Such enthusiasm!" He chuckled and shook his head.

"Where are you headed now?"

"Well, I'm just exploring. Now tomorrow, I will be talking with your county commission with a proposal for the airport. That's why I was up there a bit ago."

"Huh." Torrez nodded. The mesa-top astronomy project had garnered nationwide attention, and with the construction phase now in full swing on several fronts, the population of Posadas County had taken an exponential leap. "What's an Arizona interest in the Posadas Airport?" It was the sort of question that Olveda certainly had no need to answer, but he seemed bothered not in the least.

"Well, Sheriff, we'll see," Olveda said. "It's a very long runway for such an underpopulated area. Much potential. I have several ideas that could be mutually beneficial to both my associates and the county."

"Such as?"

Olveda looked askance at Torrez. "It's best that we're not premature," he said simply.

"I need to see your license and registration," Torrez said abruptly, as if the man's answer had annoyed him. Before Olveda had a chance to reply, Deputy Tom Pasquale released the documents from his clipboard and extended them to the sheriff. The Tucson address matched what he had been told, the insurance was up to date, and the registration listed the truck as a 2013 Ford, color white. He handed the paperwork to Olveda. "Thanks for your cooperation," he said. "You're free to go."

"If I can be of any further assistance," Olveda said, "I'm staying at the Posadas Inn for a day or two." He turned and slammed the tailgate closed. "It's been pleasant meeting you gentlemen." With a deferential nod, he got in the truck, started it, and turned onto the highway.

"What do you think, Sheriff?" Pasquale asked.

Torrez's dark face remained expressionless. "I think I'd be pissed at being detained for an hour for no good reason."

"He was way cool. Do you think he's up to something?"

Torrez shrugged. "Don't know. I'll be interested to hear what he has to say to the commissioners."

"Are you going to the meeting?"

"Well," Torrez said, "that ain't so rare, is it?"

"Yes." Pasquale's snappy response almost earned a smile from Torrez.

Chapter Seven

With her afghan enveloping her like a colorful tent, Teresa Reyes sat in her rocker, aluminum walker within easy reach. Her right elbow rested on the arm of the chair, and she cushioned her chin in her hand. Once a sturdy, bustling woman capable of managing a one-room schoolhouse filled with twenty-five noisy, obstreperous children, she was now a tiny sparrow of a person. Her gaze didn't shift from her thoughts far away as Estelle entered the house.

"*Mamá*, are you doing okay?"

"Oh, sure." The elderly woman ever so slowly pulling her gaze back from her personal horizon.

"I'm going to be flying with *Padrino* to Albuquerque here in a few minutes." Soft footsteps in the hallway announced their housekeeper and Teresa's caregiver, Addy Sedillos, and Estelle's comment was as much to her as to Teresa. "He managed to break his hip somehow."

"Should I go over?" Addy asked immediately.

"He won't be home for a while, I'm afraid. He has to have surgery—Francis says a hip replacement. Maybe a plate besides. We don't know what he'll need." She had crossed to her mother, and bent down to give the tiny woman a gentle hug. "We just don't know yet."

"*Aye.*" Teresa shook her head. "The hip…that's a bad thing." Her voice was little more than a whisper, raspy as a dried leaf.

"Yes it is, *Mamá*. But *Padrino* has a stout constitution. He'll be all right. Anyway," and she stood up and stretched, "the air ambulance will fly us up. And guess what?" She bent down again so that she was face-to-face with her mother. "Camille's coming out. She'll fly in tonight. I'll be able to meet her at the airport."

Teresa brightened. Despite what Bill Gastner might imply, his daughter Camille Stratton was indeed welcome company. She would pamper and chat with Teresa Reyes, drawing the elderly woman out, savoring Teresa's stories of her childhood in northern Mexico, of life in Tres Santos, just a few miles south of the border.

Estelle quickly packed what she needed in one compact gym bag, and then returned to the living room. She sat down on the fireplace hearth next to her mother's rocker. "Will you tell me about the cashier's check, *Mamá*?"

The elderly woman looked blank for a moment, and then one expressive eyebrow lifted a bit. "Sometimes you find out things faster than you should," she said. "I didn't want you to worry. You have enough on your mind."

"Tell me, *Mamá*. Is this about something with Francisco?" Her husband's offhand remark about a new flute had seemed logical to her, since the boy's passion had grown to include the wind instrument as well as the piano that he'd been playing since the age of five. But eight thousand dollars would pay for just a note or two from the sort of flute Francisco would favor.

With the fourteen-year-old boy hundreds of miles away from home, living at Leister Conservatory in Missouri with his world heavy with theory, practice, and performance, it wasn't hard to imagine his agile mind coming up with some scheme—a new instrument of some kind, or perhaps he had changed his mind and was planning a personally produced CD of his music. But he would never try to cajole finances out of his grandmother, whom he revered.

"Do you recall…Francisco's friend? Remember…" Teresa squinted at the window as if her memory lay outside…"Do you remember the boy who played in the concert…was it last winter?" Her speech was halting as she both tried to recall what she wanted to say from one sentence to the next, but also struggled to cope with English—not a language for which she had much affection.

"Of course I do." Mateo Atencio, the fifteen-year-old youngster from a tiny village in south-central Texas and also a senior performance major at Leister Conservatory on a full-ride scholarship, had stunned the audience with his virtuosic flute performance, playing both solo and accompanied by Francisco Guzman on the piano.

"I hear that he got in trouble somehow," Teresa said slowly. "In Mexico. Maybe it was Mazatlán."

"*Ay.* Did my *hijo* call you?" Estelle knelt beside the chair, both of her hands covering her mother's. *And why would he do that?* Estelle knew that both her sons treasured talking with their grandmother, who was now never left alone. The boys knew that. Had Francisco had such important news, he would have asked to speak with his brother, Carlos—who would receive and deliver messages with perfect accuracy. Failing that, he would have spoken with *Nana*, Addy Sedillos. If not her, then whichever dispatcher was on duty at the Sheriff's Department. Or their father at the clinic. Or, or, or…

The Spanish word opened the floodgate, and when Teresa replied, it was in the elegant, old-fashioned borderlands Mexican dialect with which she'd spent the first eighty-five years of her life in Tres Santos.

"*Su amigo, el Capitán…*" and she stopped as if recalling that difficult name had exhausted her circuits.

"*Tomás,* you mean?" Now a colonel in the Mexican *judiciales,* Tomás Naranjo had been a valuable resource for the Posadas County Sheriff's Department when matters had spilled one way or another across the border. "He called here?"

"I told him that he could reach you at the office, but he seemed in such a hurry, that man."

Estelle frowned. Naranjo being in a hurry was a difficult concept to accept. It was unlikely enough that he would have called Estelle's home during the day—and even if he had, he would have been the epitome of genteel manners. He would have taken time to court Teresa over the phone, asking about each family member in turn. Eventually, he would have gotten around to the problem at hand. And what help would Teresa be? Naranjo would certainly have called Estelle at the Sheriff's Office had something urgent arisen. That he might have called her home, choosing to speak with Teresa, was incomprehensible, and stirred Estelle's suspicions.

"Did he explain what he wanted? What was going on with the boy? Why would they be in Mexico?"

Teresa looked distant again, and for a long moment didn't answer. Estelle had long since learned to simply wait, not pushing her mother with impatient prompting.

"I don't know," Teresa said finally.

"But the eight thousand dollars? Did Naranjo himself request that?"

This time Teresa nodded thoughtfully. "That was last week, *mihija*. That is the bail that is necessary. And I know that the two boys have concerts coming up." A fleeting smile touched her lips. "They always do, those two. Maybe that's what it is."

"Bail." Her stomach felt as if it were full of lead. "Tomás asked you for the money? It was him, *personally,* who made that request of you?" How completely unlikely, Estelle thought. The colonel would never do such a thing.

Teresa nodded. "I believe that is what your friend said."

"*Por dios,* whatever for?"

"The captain explained it to me, but he talked faster than I could listen. But you've always trusted him, no?"

"Of course." Trusted *him.* "So he asked for the bail money, and you then agreed to send the cashier's check?" Tomás Naranjo was a colonel, his most recent promotion not something that Teresa would remember. But he would not have tried to cajole money out of Mateo's friends or relatives. Unthinkable. No, it would have been much simpler to order the boy's release and—if Mateo had actually been in Mexico in the first place, had been caught with one hand in the Mexican cookie jar—send him packing back across the border. Anything serious enough to warrant custody, like an unlikely weapons charge, assault, auto theft, or a rough night at a cantina, wouldn't be assuaged with a mere eight thousand dollars. Had such an improbable thing occurred, her son Francisco would have called immediately. At least she hoped he would.

But a *cashier's check?* That took a moment to digest, and then Teresa nodded slowly. "Maybe I shouldn't have," she whispered. "But the bank is so slow now, you know. I thought that this was something I could do. Without bother to you. He said I would have the money back promptly."

"No harm done," Estelle said. "Mr. Mears has not cut the check yet." *And won't.* "I think I know what happened," she added, and rose to give her mother a hug. She didn't bother explaining the continual flow of telephone predators…and the phone scams trying to lever emergency money were common. "Let me check with Francisco." She frowned hard. True enough, trying to force that kind of money from Atencio's parents—his mother a *nana* like Addy and father a day laborer—would be a fruitless pursuit. But a ninety-nine-year-old woman might be an easy mark.

As she dialed, she walked out into the dining room. Addy Sedillos was busy with four huge baked potatoes at the sink-side cutting board in the kitchen, and she glanced up as Estelle leaned against the counter, waiting on the phone connection. After four rings, Francisco's cell went to messages. "Long chance," Estelle muttered. "Francisco, this is *Mamá.* Give me a call as soon as you can, please? Love you."

She disconnected and then scrolled down through the catalog of numbers. Selecting Mateo Attencio's cell, she tried that, and left another message. "Ay," she said with impatience. "Wouldn't you know." She selected the landline to the Leister resident hall's dean.

"Dr. Baylor's office. How may I direct your call?" The secretary's voice was brisk, almost dismissive.

"This is Undersheriff Estelle Reyes-Guzman in Posadas, New Mexico. I need to speak with either Francisco Guzman or Mateo Attencio, please. It's urgent."

The woman's voice warmed instantly. "Do you have a number I might use to return your call? It'll only be a moment. I'll leave a short message at the Sheriff's Department, if that will suffice."

"That will be fine." Estelle rattled off the number and disconnected. "Nothing can ever be simple," she said to Addy.

"They're responsible for a lot of talent," the young woman offered. "Lots of adoring fans out there."

"I suppose. I haven't gotten used to that yet." She watched the seconds tick by on her watch, and sure enough, two and a half minutes later, the phone chirped.

"Guzman."

"Estelle," Ernie Wheeler said, "Leister Academy just called us to patch a message through to you. I gather you were expecting them to call."

"That's great. What's up?"

"Dean Baylor's secretary, Lucy Delfino, called to tell you that both Francisco and Mateo are in Mazatlán, Mexico. They left yesterday with two members of the faculty, and will return Sunday. End message."

Estelle stood silently, phone pressed hard to her ear, hoping that Ernie would add something else. The young man didn't, but said, "That's it." When Estelle didn't respond, the dispatcher gently nudged her. "You still there?"

There was no point in asking Ernie to repeat the message, or to suddenly recall a vital detail that he had overlooked.

"Thanks, Ernie."

"You're welcome. By the way, the med-evac is fifty-five minutes out."

"Thanks." Estelle disconnected and immediately redialed Leister. Her fingers flashed on the tiny keys, but her mind was deep in Mexico. Mazatlán…the fabled city with snow-white beaches, impressive and colorful historical district, and nestled in an area with one of the worst reputations for cartel violence in Mexico.

"Dean Baylor's office. How may I direct your call?"

Estelle kept any pleasant deference out of her tone. "Ms. Delfino, this is Undersheriff Guzman again. Dispatch informs me that the two boys and two faculty members flew to Mazatlán for several days. They'll be back Sunday. Is that correct?"

"That's correct, ma'am."

"May I speak with Dean Baylor, please."

There was just the faintest hesitation before Lucy Delfino said, "Ma'am, Dean Baylor accompanied the boys on the trip this time. He and Dr. Lucian Belloit."

"This time?"

"Well, I mean *this* trip. We take part in a fund-raising concert in Mazatlán every year. The Angela Peralta Conservatory is one of our sister schools. Just a beautiful, beautiful place."

"Have you heard from them today?"

"In fact, Dr. Baylor calls here twice a day, Sheriff. Angela Peralta's concert of greeting was last night, and a great success, he said. The two boys play tonight, and then on Saturday night, we have the combined concert as a finale."

"Sounds wonderful. I wish I had known about it."

"Ah, that's our fault, and I apologize. If you look at the schedule on the back page of the July newsletter, you'll see the concert series with Angela Peralta listed, but we neglected the follow-up contacts with parents—all the details. I'm not sure what happened, but it won't happen again, rest assured. Your son didn't inform you either, then?"

"No, he didn't." *A fourteen-year-old isn't in charge of travel arrangements and details,* Estelle almost added, but Leister clearly *knew* that. And parents were in charge of finding these things out, no matter what. That was the baseline.

"Is there a number I might use now to contact Dean Baylor directly?"

"You mean *right* now? In Mexico?"

"Yes."

The secretary hesitated. "Would it be adequate if I have Dr. Baylor call you at this number? Or Francisco, if he's handy?"

Or even if he isn't, Estelle thought. "If he will do so in the next ten minutes. I'm about to catch a flight, and I can't guarantee how good the reception will be once we're airborne. If you can't reach them, I'll need his contact number so that I might try later."

"I understand. Either he or I will be right back to you, ma'am."

"Thank you." Estelle disconnected and let out a long breath. She could hear her pulse pounding in her ears. "The boys are in Mexico," she said to Addy. "A three-day concert series in Mazatlán."

Chapter Eight

While she waited, Estelle first rummaged through the file of Leister material that they kept in the carousel in the living room. Sure enough, the July schedule of events listed a gig in Mazatlán at the Teatro Angela Peralta. Performers were listed as Guzman, Atencio, and *guest artists.*

"It pays to read the fine print," Estelle muttered, furious with herself. She used the landline to call Colonel Naranjo's office in Chihuahua, her cell phone ready and waiting in the other hand. The colonel would rather have been covered in fine dust, with his kidneys jolted out of place by the rough country roads, than spend time inside behind a polished desk, puffing a cigar. On top of that, Mazatlán in Sinaloa was far from his home state of Chihuahua, no more in his jurisdiction than a San Diego cop trying to work in Albuquerque. But Estelle knew that he would have contacts. Naranjo was as much a walking gazetteer of northern Mexico as Bill Gastner was of Posadas County.

She took a deep breath while circuits clicked. The officer who answered sounded about twelve years old, his Spanish rapid and melodious.

"Colonel Naranjo, please," Estelle replied to his greeting, and identified herself. The Mexican officer hesitated, and Estelle could hear papers shuffling.

"Hmm," he said as if coming to an important conclusion. "*Agente,* may he return your call, please? The colonel is, ah…

somewhat indisposed." He said the word *indispuesto* as if the situation possibly amused him—or as if the correct words would present discretionary complications.

Estelle glanced over her shoulder at the kitchen clock. "Will he be able to do that in the next few minutes?"

Again the hesitation. "I would think so, but I cannot be sure. Would you care to leave a message for the colonel?"

"Just that I called, and that I need to speak with him."

"It is of some urgency, then?"

This time it was Estelle who hesitated. "Yes, it is." She gave the officer both her landline and cell phone numbers and disconnected. "*Ay,*" she whispered, and glanced across at Addy. "Am I being a suffocating mother?" Estelle smiled ruefully. "But Mazatlán?"

"A beautiful place," Addy offered without much enthusiasm.

"Yes, it is, parts of it." Hefting her modest overnight bag, she gave Addy a quick hug. "Thanks for staying tonight," she said. "I'll call from Albuquerque. If Francisco should call here…"

Addy nodded quickly. "I'll forward the message."

"Thank you." In the living room, Teresa Reyes sat quietly, nestled in her afghan.

"What do we do now?" she whispered.

"Well, *Mamá*, we wait. I have my net out. I'm sure that if something really is wrong, the conservatory would have called before this. Or the director will call. Or Francisco. They gave a concert last night, and the dean said during his phone call to the school this morning that all went well. He's going to call me as soon as he gets the chance."

A half dozen thoughts tangled in Estelle's mind, and for a long moment she sat beside her mother, brows furrowed.

"This worries you?" Teresa asked. Her withered right hand touched the back of Estelle's, and her bottomless black eyes roamed her daughter's face.

"The whole thing. We could start with the two boys being down there in the first place. Mexico has changed so. I'm not sure Leister appreciates that." She didn't mention the fundamental improbability of Naranjo's calling Teresa Reyes to ask for bail or bribery money…or anything else for that matter. And yet, Teresa had been suckered in.

"I know that people fall prey to these scams all the time," Estelle said gently. "It's easy, because we're concerned for the safety of loved ones." Teresa frowned at that, looking as if she'd bitten into something sour.

"I should know these things perfectly well."

"Yes." Estelle patted her hand. "But there's always this nagging doubt, *Mamá*. What if the boy is *really* in trouble. What if? What if? It's hard just to dismiss it."

"It is impossible."

"Perhaps it is all a silly mistake. I have a call in to Tomás, so we'll know soon enough." She paused, but her curiosity held the upper hand. "You said the colonel was in a hurry when he called. Did he ask about the rest of the family?"

Teresa shook her head slowly. "Most of the time, I could not understand him."

"Did he specifically ask for me?"

"It surprised me that he didn't," Teresa said.

"*Yo tambien.*" Estelle looked at her watch again. Was Naranjo's supposed rushed phone call somehow related to his now being 'indisposed'? "We'll find out soon enough. I'll call you from Albuquerque."

"Addy will be here?"

"Yes, she's staying until I return from the city."

Teresa nodded and closed her eyes. "She or Carlos can answer the telephone, then. It's impossible, that thing."

That thing buzzed again just as Estelle turned the ignition key in her unmarked car.

"Yo," Sheriff Robert Torrez said by way of greeting—the single syllable unusual, since he was in the habit of simply starting the conversation without greeting of any sort. 'What's the deal with Bill? Do we know yet?"

"A badly broken hip. We don't know what complications, if any. I'm on my way to the airport to ride up with him to UNMH."

"How come you're goin'?"

Ah, Mr. Sympathy. "Camille won't fly in from Michigan until this evening. I can catch a ride home with her. But he needs someone with him right now."

"Huh." The line fell silent, and Estelle edged the gear lever into Drive. "I'll be back as soon as I can. Any luck on the hunt?" She was about to pull out of the parking lot when she saw the emergency lights, and she waited for the ambulance to pass.

"Yup," Torrez said again. "Tell Bill we got us enough antelope rack to make green chile stew for a year." The sheriff's sympathy was dished out in tiny bites, Estelle reflected.

"That will cheer him up."

"Yup," Torrez said. "You ever meet a guy named Dominic Olveda? Says he's from Tucson?"

"No. Should I know him? His name is on the county meeting agenda. That's all I know about him."

"Just wondered. He's talkin' to the county commissioners tomorrow about some airport deal. Thought maybe you'd heard."

"I haven't."

"You're not going to go to that meetin', then."

"I really can't," Estelle said. "*Padrino* is in a bad way."

"Maybe I'll go and see what he's about."

"That would be good, Bobby."

"We'll see." He disconnected as abruptly as he had begun. For the eight-minute drive out to Posadas Municipal Airport, Estelle found herself clutching the phone, willing it to ring, willing it to carry her son's quiet voice with the news that all was well, that the concerts were drawing huge crowds, and that the phone call to Teresa Reyes had been nothing but an empty scam by some opportunistic jerk who had been able to put all the numbers together.

Even though *she* hadn't paid as close attention as she might have, the concert would have been well publicized within the private circles of that world, and it would not have been difficult to pick up tidbits of information. Still…

The lights of the ambulance outdistanced her, and by the time she pulled through the chain-link gate that accessed the airport's office and apron, the EMTs were already lifting the gurney out of the vehicle. And by then she had reached no conclusions. How could the scammer know the Guzman's family connections with Naranjo? How would they know enough to use his name? How would they know that Teresa would be the most vulnerable target?

The med-evac aircraft, a jet-prop Beech King Air, was parked just off the fuel island donut, one of the crew conferring with Jim Bergin, the airport manager.

Estelle parked beside Bergin's pickup truck near the office and took a moment to organize her thoughts and her mobile office before turning once again to the cell phone. Gayle Torrez was now working dispatch, and picked up immediately, and just as quickly informed Estelle that she had heard nothing.

"We'll be in that air here in a few minutes, and it's about an hour to Albuquerque. I'll be in touch."

"Is Bill hanging in there okay?" Gayle asked.

"I'll try talking with him in a minute," Estelle replied. "I would expect that he's so heavily sedated that he's off in la-la land for the duration."

La-la land or not, Bill Gastner raised his head and regarded Estelle as she ducked into the crowded Beechcraft. He was strapped into narrow confines on the right side of the aircraft, the rig looking more like a high-tech torture device than a bed. A rack of tubed gadgets hung from the wall and ceiling above him, almost obscuring the most forward of the five windows. If the patient had been able to stretch out a hand, he could reach across the narrow aisle to touch either one of the two passenger seats. "What the hell are you doing?" His voice was little more than a slurred whisper.

"Making sure you behave yourself, *Padrino.*"

"What a goddamned waste of taxpayers' money." He turned his head so he could see past one of the EMTs who was fussing with his IV tubes. "Did you hear from my daughter?"

"We'll be meeting her in Albuquerque," Estelle answered, and nodded as one of the aircraft crew pointed to a small jump seat toward the rear cabin bulkhead. The undersheriff reached out and patted her friend's arm. "I'll get out of their way. You ride easy."

"I don't have a choice," Gastner whispered.

"It's better than taking the ride in the back of a buckboard," Estelle said.

"I'll have to think about that."

Tucked into the small seat aft of both the door and the medical section, she had a fine view of the interior, but not much outside. By leaning forward, she could see out through the tiny aft cabin windows, out over the aircraft's right wing. She watched as the pilot continued his conversation with Jim Bergin. The airport manager was pointing off into the distance while the pilot stood with his hands on his hips, nodding. In a moment, the two men separated, the pilot trudging toward the plane, Bergin jogging toward his pickup truck.

The pilot boarded and paused when he saw Estelle. "Well, it's good to see you again," he said. She remembered the Hollywood face, and the name tag reminded her that she'd flown with Ben Woods on at least one other occasion. Woods shook the undersheriff's hand cordially, then made his way forward. He slipped past the EMTs, took a moment to exchange pleasantries with the groggy Bill Gastner, and then slipped into the cockpit to join his co-pilot.

Even before he'd settled into his seat, the right hand prop began to windmill, accompanied by the shriek of the turbine. Woods didn't call for the left engine until the aircraft had been buttoned up, the EMTs making one final check of their patient, and then strapping themselves into the two seats. Connie Tingley, who facing forward with her back to Estelle, rode with her right hand across the aisle, resting on her patient's shoulder. The second EMT, Brad Salazar, occupied himself with a sheaf of paperwork, then unbuckled, rose, and adjusted the screen brightness of one of the monitors over Gastner's head. He settled again, and the copilot, a young woman with fair hair streamlined back into a ponytail, leaned out of her seat to survey the aft cabin.

"We'll be rolling as soon as the traffic is off the runway," she said. "All secure?"

"All secure."

"Flight time is one hour, sixteen minutes," she added, and Estelle heard the port engine whine into life, and within seconds they were drifting forward, turning tightly to the east to catch the taxiway.

Connie twisted around to smile sympathetically at Estelle. "Not much room for you, but once we're airborne, maybe you'd like to sit up here for a little bit?" She glanced at Gastner, who lay with his eyes closed, strapped and wrapped. Estelle could see by the determined set of his jaw that he was neither asleep nor relaxed.

"I'm fine," the undersheriff said. The aircraft taxied smoothly for a moment, then braked, swinging wide. For a moment they parked with the nose facing southwest as the crew finished the check list. With props cycled and everything else in the green, Estelle looked forward as Captain Woods made a final adjustment of his headset.

"Posadas Unicom, one eight eight November Mike will be departing on two-eight. Departure to the northwest."

She couldn't hear what Bergin said, but Woods nodded and laughed at something. Bergin had returned from his sweep of the runway, and apparently they were good to go. "Have a good day."

Even as the airport manager radioed back acknowledgement and barometric information, the pilot was feeding power to the turboprops, and the aircraft tracked out to the runway, pausing just a moment on the white line. Woods turned once more to survey the cabin, and Connie Tingley shot him a thumbs-up.

Accelerating hard, the King Air flashed past the first intersection from the taxiway, and Estelle caught a glimpse of Jim Bergin leaning against the tailgate of his truck. Another hundred yards took them past the gravel pit on the south side of the runway, and Estelle turned her head away from the right side windows. She saw a flash of brown out of the corner of her eye, an indefinably quick wink of color, and then a loud bang and jolt shook the aircraft.

For a moment, the Beech tracked straight, and Woods pulled off the power. Still charging along at eighty miles an hour, the plane shook hard, and Estelle waited for the pull of brakes. She knew that nearly four thousand feet of runway remained, and Woods was in no hurry to slam the aircraft to a stop. By the time they had slowed to what Estelle guessed was forty or fifty miles an hour, the left engine windmilled to a stop, and they coasted all the way to the final donut that connected runway to taxiway.

Woods made the turn when the aircraft was inching along at walking speed, and as the plane swung onto the taxiway, the copilot nodded. "Very nice," Estelle heard the young woman co-pilot say.

"Talk about out of nowhere," Woods muttered. He touched his boom-mike. "Posadas Unicom, one eight eight November Mike is clear the active."

Pulled along by one engine, the King Air swung onto the broad apron in front of the office. The right engine sighed to a stop.

Woods pried himself out of the narrow cockpit confines. He held up both hands in apology as he saw Estelle out of her seat and bending down near the foot of Gastner's gurney. "I'm glad one of you had your rabbit's foot engaged," he said with a rueful grin. Gastner opened one eye, raised an eyebrow at Estelle, and promptly dozed off. The pilot looked at the two EMTs, busy with the equipment.

"We encountered an antelope or two," Woods said. "I don't know what our delay will be, but I'll see what I can do to make other arrangements. I think our chopper is in Farmington. We'll just have to see."

Through the window, Estelle saw the airport manager jogging toward them, and then sunshine blasted into the cabin as Connie Tingley wrenched the door open and lowered the steps.

Seeing that Gastner was zoned out on his drip with the two EMTs hovering nearby, Estelle clambered down from the plane.

Woods and Bergin were standing near the left propeller. The Beechcraft's characteristically long turbo-prop engine nacelles put the propellers well forward of the cockpit, within easy view of the flight crew. Six feet or so behind the props, the landing gear and gear doors were tucked under the shadow of the wing.

Bergin knelt, his bronzed and lined face scrunched in grimace. "Antelope burger." He looked at the undersheriff as she joined him. Sure enough, a large mess of bloody remains, some of the fur still tawny with a trace of white, complete with a portion of skull attached, was jammed against the landing gear strut above the wheel. A portion of the retractable landing gear door was bent back against the strut.

"Sure glad I took that drive to clear the runway," Bergin growled. "Miserable little bastards. Had to be hidin' behind the brush, just waitin' to commit suicide."

"There were two," Woods said. He knelt and stroked the fuselage belly, and then looked at his fingers. "A little spray this way. It's the prop I'm worried about, though." He backed out carefully from under the wing, and watched as Bergin ran his hand down the leading edge of each blade, hand-turning the big three-bladed propeller gently. Shaking his head, he wiped his hand on his trousers.

"So how did he do that?" Bergin said. "That takes some skill. Get hit by the prop and go straight back into the gear."

"Only some of him went straight back," Woods offered. "I think he turned at the last minute. Not enough." Woods saw Estelle's camera. "I need to do that, too," he said. "For our flight office."

"He did hit the prop, though," Bergin said. "Prop overhaul at the minimum, with a run-out on the shaft. That's if you're lucky."

"We've already been lucky," Woods said.

Chapter Nine

The ambulance, lights flickering in a garish kaleidoscope, lumbered westbound to the airport turnoff just seconds ahead of Bob Torrez. The sheriff hadn't heard a radio call for an ambulance at the airport, and he could see the med-evac King Air parked on the apron, a group of people standing nearby. His first thought was that some medical emergency had prompted Bill Gastner's sudden off-loading, with the old man headed back to the hospital for emergency treatment. Whatever it was, it had drawn Dr. Francis Guzman, along with a full ambulance crew.

He frowned as he drew closer, since while the medical crew's attention appeared focused on what was going on *inside* the aircraft, the flight crew members, along with airport manager Jim Bergin, were concentrated around the left engine and landing gear.

Parking well out of the way, he stepped out of the truck in time to hear Dr. Guzman call to the crew from the top boarding step as he nimbly deplaned, "No chance of a departure with this aircraft, then?"

"None," the four-striper replied. Torrez recognized Ben Woods, who turned to Estelle and added, "If the med-evac chopper is clear to come down here, he's three hours north. And then with the return flight adding time to that? Hell, you might as well drive up. Straight shot up I-25."

Estelle Reyes-Guzman caught Torrez's eye and then looked heavenward.

Matty Finnegan, the EMT who had been in on the initial rescue at Gastner's garage, looked expectantly at Dr. Guzman as he approached. "Let's change the game plan, then," the physician said into his phone. "If you're willing to do that, that's wonderful." He grinned broadly at something the other person said. "I owe you big-time, Barry."

He took a deep breath to collect his thoughts, beckoning Estelle. "Game plan calls for Las Cruces," the physician said. "Las Cruces is just a little more than an hour. By the time we get there, they'll be ready for us."

"I hear that." Finnegan's face lit up. "Let's rock and roll."

Guzman nodded and strode back to the airplane, taking a second to reach across to squeeze Torrez's arm in greeting. "Round and round we go," he said, and didn't wait for a reply, ducking up the narrow stairs into the King Air.

The undersheriff held up both hands in surrender, shaking her head as she joined the sheriff.

"So what now? Ambulance to Cruces?" Torrez asked. Estelle nodded, and Torrez added, "Let me talk at him." The cramped aircraft was awkward for such a large man, and once inside, Torrez had to turn sideways. He moved up close to Dr. Guzman, who was himself no petite figure. The physician was kneeling near Gastner's head, eyeing the monitors above him.

"You hanging in there?" Guzman asked, and Gastner's eyes fluttered.

"How long is this day?" the older man murmured.

"Just relax and in a few minutes we'll have you out of this crate and into the Cadillac. Is there any pain?"

"Aches."

"It's going to do that," the physician said. "Look, we had an argument with a couple of antelope, and they changed our plans. We'll be vacationing over in Cruces."

Gastner opened his eyes and regarded Guzman with clear skepticism, and then his gaze drifted over to Bob Torrez.

"I thought you had killed off all those critters," he said weakly.

"I'm tryin'."

"Look, Dr. Cushman will meet us either later this evening or tomorrow morning, just before the surgery," Guzman assured him. "He's the best." The physician grinned. "We're playing some musical chairs here. Cushman *was* in Albuquerque, but the cards fell just right for him. He's on his way downstate right now. And his jet is a whole lot faster than our ambulance."

"What a goddamn waste," Gastner muttered. "Just screw me together, give me some aspirin, and let it go at that."

Guzman laughed and moved aside. "I don't want to disappoint Cushman. He looks for any excuse to fly that fancy jet he has. He can make the trip, and then write it off his taxes."

Matty Finnegan had ducked halfway through the door, glowering at Torrez. "You big lugs are going to have to vacate," she said sternly. She dug a fist into Torrez's ribs. "God, the high sheriff himself, the undersheriff too?" She reached down and waggled Gastner's toes as Guzman and Torrez made their way out of the cramped confines. "How do you rate all this attention?"

"It's all who you know," Gastner whispered.

Torrez approached Estelle as she watched the careful transfer from airplane to ambulance.

"He's not talkin' for a while," Torrez observed.

"No. Way too much juice sloshing around in his system. What did you need to know?"

"Just…" Torrez let the thought go with a shrug. "So what now for you?"

"I'll take my car down," she said. "I'll be right behind the ambulance."

"You're worryin' too much," he said gruffly.

Estelle punched the sheriff in the middle of his chest, none too lightly. "I'll remind you of that next time you're down with a rifle bullet through the butt," she said. When that episode happened a decade before, it had been Bobby Torrez being littered out of a landfill pit and med-evaced to Albuquerque.

He grimaced at the reminder, and saw the dark worry circles around Estelle's eyes. "He's tough," he said. "Give me a call later on when things are settled down there. I got some things goin' on right now and I ain't going to break away." He turned at the sound of an approaching car. "Oh, shit. Here she is."

A boxy, compact Ford Transit with government plates and the county logo on the doors swept into the parking lot and parked beside Estelle's sedan. Leona Spears, the county manager, made notations on her dash-mounted computer before getting out, then donned her purple hard hat—a perpetual on-site trademark for the theatrical woman. Rather than her sunflower patterned muumuu cascading from throat to ankle, Leona was a fashion statement for utility workers everywhere. Sharply pressed tan chino trousers and shirt showed not a drop of perspiration dampness. Her name over the right breast pocket, and her title, *Posadas County Manager,* over the other, left no room for doubt.

"She precedith herself," Gastner had once remarked about Leona's bosomy figure.

She stood for a moment, surveying the scene. When she was sure she wasn't going to walk into the middle of something, she gave the aircraft a wide berth and made her way toward the officers. She favored Torrez with a bright smile.

"Don't tell me," she said with an expressive wave of the hand. "Aircraft problems?" She reached out and rested a hand affectionately on Estelle's shoulder.

"We had some antelope damage to the aircraft," the undersheriff replied. "We'll be heading over to Cruces here in a minute or two with the ambulance."

"My word. That would have been easier in the first place." Leona managed to say it so that it didn't sound like a criticism.

"It would have," Estelle replied. "But the surgeon Francis wanted was in Albuquerque." She smiled at Leona. "And by plane, it would have been an easier trip for Bill. Now he's headed over to Cruces by ambulance. So there we are."

"How is he?"

"Bill? He'll be all right. Heavily sedated, so the world's just a blur. His hip is a jumble of pieces, unfortunately."

"But now you have to settle for a second choice in doctors?"

"No. Cushman is flying to Las Cruces. He'll be there before we are."

Leona's eyebrows shot up. "My word. *Somebody* owes *somebody* a favor or two, don't they now?" Leona didn't fish for a response, but sighed and surveyed the airport. A former highway engineer for the state highway department, she had found a beloved niche with the county when she retired. A woman easy to underestimate at first meeting, those working with Leona found out soon enough that her insightful mind included a broad streak of the artistic, mixed with a clear understanding of what was practical. The little van was a case in point. It accommodated her rack of maps, her computers, her CAD printer, her transit, and a host of other gadgetry and paperwork that she referred to collectively as her "necessities of life outside the office."

"Well, when you are able, I hope you'll pass my best wishes along to our patient for a speedy and complete recovery."

"He'll appreciate that."

"When he's back home, we'll have to be sure to visit. Keeping the spirits up is so important at a time like this."

Sheriff Torrez muttered something, looking impatient. Estelle added, "I'm sorry that I have to stand you up this afternoon."

"Oh, bosh. Don't give it a second's thought. Just budget *stuff,* if you know what I mean. I had to come out to ask Jimbo a couple of questions." She nodded across the fuel apron toward the airport manager. "We need to move a little faster constructing the airport perimeter fencing so this doesn't happen again. Mercy." She touched Estelle on the shoulder again. "And one little tidbit that perked my ears. Homeland Security wants to give us a 1.2 million-dollar grant to change Mr. Waddell's narrow-gauge railroad to standard gauge. Just that one little change." The powdered crinkles around her eyes deepened slightly, perhaps because Torrez's interest was immediate. "Actually, it was just a message of exploration on their part. I mean, they *offered.* I didn't seek them out. Apparently they don't fully understand that Mr. Waddell's mesa project—and such a lovely name for it, too—is a matter of private enterprise. They get their standard gauge approach, then it will be something else. I took the liberty of telling them that we had no interest in their grant, and no authority over Mr. Waddell's private property, and that if they wanted to deal with our gentleman rancher directly, then that's what they should do."

"I can't imagine that Mr. Waddell's *NightZone* project either wants or needs a standard gauge railroad," Estelle said. "The narrow gauge route is giving him problems enough." Miles Waddell had made dozens of changes in his proposed railroad route out to the mesa-top observatory from the village of Posadas, the thirty-seven-mile line now in the final planning stages.

"I do see their point," Leona added. "I mean, *narrow* gauge is totally useless to anyone other than Mr. Waddell. HSA tends to think always about improving infrastructure. If they think of his mesa as some kind of potential installation," and she said the word as if it had an astringent aftertaste, "then rail access is certainly something to consider. And if you don't think *that* will raise some hackles…"

Matty Finnegan had approached, and now stood deferentially to one side, waiting for the county manager to wind down.

"We're ready, Sheriff," she said. Torrez knew who she meant, since no one bothered with the cumbersome title *undersheriff,* and rarely was anyone confused. He didn't acknowledge Matty's presence.

Estelle reached out and touched Leona's arm. "Excuse me, please."

Her husband glanced up as she approached. "I think I'll just ride back here with Bill and the folks," the physician said. He patted his own chest, a motion that was not lost on Estelle. "You're taking your car, right?"

"I'll be right behind you."

As the ambulance doors closed, shutting off any chance to finish conversations, Estelle Reyes-Guzman realized that during all the comings and goings, in all the hustle, she had never explained to her husband about the second enormous worry in her life…their son in Mazatlán. She had mentioned the eight thousand dollars and they had joked about what Francisco might be planning to do with it, but she hadn't discussed the conversation that she'd then had with her mother and the potential for disaster in Mexico.

As they pulled away from the airport, taking the seven-mile loop back into town and then down to the interstate, Estelle tapped into the sound system of the county car, activating the little telephone icon on the steering wheel spoke. In a moment, Dispatcher Ernie Wheeler was on the line, his voice boosted by the car's sound system.

"No word from anyone," he reported. "Did you happen to speak with the sheriff?"

"I just left him at the airport."

"Oh…good. Then you guys had a chance to talk."

"Actually not much. Someone took a shot at him and broke his beloved rifle. We don't know who or why. That's what I know."

"Well, that's about what they know, too. Linda has a ton of pictures, and Sergeant Taber found the spot where the shot came from. I just talked with the sheriff, and he's coming back to the office to sort through all the stuff. And Gayle was going to insist that he see the doc about his eye."

The line fell silent, and then Wheeler, sounding less sure of himself, said, "He told you, no?"

"Told me *what*, Ernie?"

"A piece of the broken scope nicked him over the eye. Might need some stitches."

I saw no nick over his eye, Estelle thought. Torrez was Torrez, the rock. Her concerns hadn't been directed at him, even when they spoke face to face. As usual, he wore his baseball cap pulled low over the bridge of his nose, military fashion.

"Look, when he comes into the office, tell him that I'm going to call. I'll get the full story from him then." She switched off with a burst of irritation aimed at herself for not noticing, at Sheriff Robert Torrez for being such a taciturn, uncommunicative oaf, and finally at her immediate concern, the dimwit drivers on the interstate.

Ahead, the boxy shape of the ambulance paced them down the highway, smoothly moving in and out past the endless cavalcade of traffic. Most of the time, drivers darted out of the way as the dazzle of red lights caught up with them. Others were loath to give up the passing lane. Just outside of Deming, unbidden and unexpected, they were joined by a New Mexico State Police unit. As the black sedan roared past, Estelle recognized Lieutenant Mark Adams, who raised a hand in salute. He pulled several car lengths ahead of the ambulance and aggressively ran interference.

"*Padrino* still has clout," she mused aloud. Or maybe it was simply because it was an election year. Adams was running for sheriff against Bob Torrez. The State Police lieutenant was confident in his dreams.

Chapter Ten

The quiet that hung over the airport was heavy. The big Beech-craft had been pushed into the main hanger out of the sun, to wait for someone with the proper state-sanctified credentials to arrive and work on it. Jim Bergin, the airport manager and a crack A & E mechanic himself—but with no contract to supply services to the state—was amused but unruffled.

The flight crew and two EMTs were effectively stranded in Posadas until one of the other aircraft, or ground crew, came to fetch them—in hours or days, who knew.

"So, Mr. Sheriff." Bergin relaxed behind his sales counter in a vinyl chair repaired with duct tape in a dozen places. He waved toward the coffeepot. "Relax. You know, if it wasn't for some possible damage to the prop, they could just fly on to Albuquerque with the gear locked down. No big deal. But you ding the prop, and that's got to be checked. That's not something I can do here, even if the state gave me the okay."

Torrez bent and rested his elbows on the glass counter. He ignored Bergin's assessment of the plane's damage. "You know a guy named Olveda?"

Bergin lit a cigarette. He frowned and spun the lighter between his fingers as the cloud of smoke drifted up around his raisin-like complexion. "You talking about Cal Olveda, over at Posadas Electric?"

"No. Little guy. His license says he's from Tucson. Kinda slick. Pudgy."

Bergin grinned. "*Dominic* Olveda."

"That would be him."

"Well, I know what I read in the papers."

"Yeah, well…"

"Be good for you, once in a while. Reading, I mean." He leaned forward and pointed a finger-gun at Torrez's face. The red gash over the sheriff's eye was going to color nicely. "Gayle take after you again?"

Torrez ignored Bergin's jibe and curiosity. "He's makin' some sort of presentation at the county commission meeting tomorrow."

"That's what the paper said." Bergin sucked on his cigarette and directed a thick blue stream of smoke at his lap. "He's another one of those dreamers, Bobby. Thinks that if he builds it, whole flocks of dumb-butt tourists will show up. Manna from heaven."

"Build *what*?"

"Well, he's got a flashlight factory, for one thing. I mean, ain't *that* just what we all need—more goddamned Taiwanese flashlights. And what is…" Bergin's face, already lined like an aged piece of leather, screwed up against the smoke. "The other thing? Oh, shit, yes. He's got a small factory that builds solar panels that wants to relocate here. And some other shit. All of this down at the west end of the runway in a little industrial park."

"Huh. That's it?"

Bergin pointed his cigarette at Torrez. "And a hotel. Can't forget that. For those vast hordes of folks who don't want to stay out on Waddell's mesa or here in town with the Patels. And a car rental. And a parking area for aircraft. And, and, and. You got to have some place to dump all that drug money." He chuckled at his joke, chuffing out little bursts of smoke.

Torrez turned and looked out the window, past the tumble-weeds and bunch grass where the black asphalt of the new runway vanished across the prairie. "Huh," he said again.

"Fly in, taxi right up to the hotel portico. Maybe I can make a few bucks with valet parking." He hacked a dry cough, his wiry little body almost bouncing off the chair with each spasm. "You don't sound impressed," he managed after a moment.

"Well, I don't need no flashlight, and I guess if he can stay in business with two tourists a month, maybe the hotel idea might work."

Bergin laughed. "Where'd you run into Olveda?"

"Out on 14."

"What'd he want with the law? Or was he just chasin' down old Waddell? Them two are birds of a feather, if you ask me. Always dreamin'."

Torrez shook his head. "Don't know."

The airport manager stubbed out his cigarette and then locked his hands behind his head, leaning far back in his chair. "Old Bill is the one person who'd be most amused at what went on this morning. And ain't that a kick…all he's been through over the years. Take a tumble in his own garage, and then mow down my pet herd with the air ambulance." Torrez nodded. "Damn lucky, is all I can say. I didn't get a chance to talk with him except to wish him well. That's a long drive when you're all busted up." He exhaled a long sigh. "And I never did see those damn critters…and I took a drive down the runway, *looking*. Christ almighty, they can be hard to see."

"He's so doped up now he don't know what's happening." Torrez pushed himself upright. "I gotta get to work."

"You break away to hunt yet?"

"Yeah, I did."

"Luck?"

"Good little buck for the freezer. That's what I got to do, is get him over to Sandoval's." He nodded toward the hanger where the med-evac crew still conferred. "If those guys need anything while they're stuck here, Leona is around to help."

Bergin grinned. "She already offered, Bobby. At least I think I'm gonna get that boundary fence now."

Torrez slipped into the truck, its interior well-baked from the sun. As he started to turn toward the gate, Deputy Sutherland pulled his unit into the airport apron and stopped window to window with the sheriff.

"I'm headin' to the office now," Torrez said.

"They have a bunch of stuff for you to look at, sir."

"I got to swing by Sandoval's for a minute, then I'll be along."

"Yes, sir. Get a good one?"

"Good enough. I coulda just waited and got me some free antelope hamburger here." He twisted in his seat and looked back at the hanger. "If these guys need anything, fix 'em up."

"You bet. If the Game and Fish wants to tag what's left of the carcass, do you want it?"

"Nope." He flashed a rare grin.

Fifteen minutes later, Torrez pulled into the Sheriff's Office parking lot. Both Sergeant Taber and Linda Real Pasquale waited in the small conference room and he was surprised at the spread of articles on the table. His rifle was now tagged, and haloed around it were a dozen or more bits and pieces of the scope—those that he had recovered, plus an extra handful. He picked up the threaded cover that originally had protected the windage adjustment. Half of its perimeter was dented and torn, the impact blowing it right off the threaded mount.

Jackie Taber reached across and touched part of the undamaged edge with the tip of her pencil. "That's a good match for what cut you on the head bone," she said.

"What else we got?"

"Okay. This is where you gutted the antelope," and she pulled a large glossy print from the assortment. "It's four hundred sixty-four yards from where you fired the shot. Now," and she handed the photo to Torrez and selected a topographical map. "This," and she touched an X penciled lightly on the map, "is your spot." Dragging the pencil eraser southward, she stopped at another location where the topo lines seemed to merge. With her other hand, she slid yet another photo across the table. "We found just enough tracks to place the shooter here. The little cut in the arroyo bed allowed him good cover for the shot." She drew a line northward to the X.

"And I don't get it," Linda said. "Did this bozo *follow* you out there? Did he see your truck and just *assume* that's where you hiked? I mean, how did he know? Did somebody know you were out there?"

"I told Waddell one time," Torrez answered. "He musta told Carl Bendix, the head honcho." He stopped, but Linda followed the thought.

"Who knows who *he* told."

Taber tapped the photo. "But from here, he could shoot and then jog back to his car or truck, without being seen by you."

Linda slid another photo toward Torrez. "These are the best we could do with the prints. They're not much." With a good imagination, Torrez could make out the boot prints, including the smooth heel.

"No prints on the truck, sir. The tire tracks are clear. Goodyear Wranglers, and the size that fit any number of vehicles."

Torrez let out a loud breath. "Nothin'."

"Not much, that's true. We know that he took a shot of more than three hundred fifty yards, and only missed by eight inches."

"He wanted to miss," Torrez said.

"How do you know that?"

"If he was out for a kill shot, he would have checked afterward to make sure. And takin' the coil cable just made sure I couldn't follow."

"Why would he want to do that, though? A warning shot of some kind?" Sergeant Taber arranged the photos into a neat pile and smiled. "Politics, maybe. Somebody wants you to stay out of the race this November. Trying to scare you off."

"Nobody shoots a high-powered rifle at someone at more than three hundred yards, uphill and with all the other complications, just to warn somebody," Linda Pasquale observed. "*I* think he wanted to take a shot and then clear the area, whether the shot was successful or not. Too many things could go wrong if he waited around for a second shot. When he saw you fly-dive backward, he thought he had hit you. That's all."

"If he saw that," Torrez said. "Takes a while to get the image back after a shot. He wouldn't have seen the scope fly apart or nothin' like that."

"He just didn't want to take the chance of meeting you face to face, Bobby."

He stretched. "I guess we'll know eventually, even if he has to take another whack at it. Maybe he won't be so lucky this time."

Chapter Eleven

Twenty miles west of Las Cruces, her cell phone came alive, fed through the car's computer system. At 5:02 p.m., her son Francisco should just be…what, in rehearsal? Eating too many strange foods? In conference with his mentors and the Mexican counterparts of the conservatory? She thumbed the button on the steering wheel, *willing* the incoming voice to be that of her eldest son. But the number I.D. flashed her own landline at home.

"Guzman."

"Hey, *Mamá*." The greeting was cheerful enough, but half an octave too high and in the thoughtfully measured cadence of her youngest son, Carlos. "Are you right in the middle of something?" The ten-year-old's adult thoughtfulness always lit a glow for Estelle.

"How about eighty-five miles an hour, lights and siren, escorting *Padrino* to the hospital. Does that count, *hijo?*"

"Oh, but you have the *beast,*" he said, referring to the county car and all its gadgets that allowed hands-free communication.

"I do. Look, *hijo,* I have no idea what time I'll be home. And *Papá* is riding in the ambulance with *Padrino.* So we just don't know. Addy is staying at the house tonight, so give her and *Abuela* a hand, all right?"

"Of course. Will *Padrino* be okay, do you think?" Carlos had long since grown away from the need for simple, black and white answers.

"He has a badly broken hip, Carlos. And maybe some other complications. We'll just have to see. Oh, and Bobby should be home in a little bit, so if you need anything, remember that he's available."

"Ooookay." If the world was coming to an end, and he had no one else to turn to, the boy *might* call "Big Bad Bobby," the man whom young Carlos thought to be the funniest man on the planet. His imitation of the sheriff's beetle-browed, humorless glower was dead-on accurate. "But we'll be fine," he said. "Are you sure *Padrino* will be okay?"

"We're all hoping so. Did your brother happen to call?"

"No. But your uncle did. I don't know him, so…"

"My *uncle?*" Estelle heard a rustle of paper, but it might have been lung tissue as she ran out of air, her heart in her throat.

"*Su tio,*" the boy said. "He said his name was Benedicte Mazón." Carlos spelled it carefully, including the accent. "He said he hasn't seen you in years, but that you would remember him. I didn't know you had an uncle, *Mamá.*"

"He asked for me by name?"

"Yes. And he called me by name, *Mamá*. And he asked about *Abuela.*"

"And he claimed to be my uncle? Are you sure about that?"

"Absolutely, I'm sure. So surprise, surprise," Carlos chirped. "He said you would know. And he said not to worry about the concert tonight."

Estelle's pulse skipped again. "What time did he call?"

"Four forty-one." Of course Carlos would have checked the time down to the minute—a perfect witness. "I asked *Abuela* who Señor Mazón might be. She did not seem to know, *Mamá.*" His voice grew a bit quieter. "But I'm not sure she understood me." Estelle flinched. The ten-year-old knew how to talk to his beloved grandmother, with a perfect understanding of the complications old age imposed. In Spanish or English, his diction and delivery, all with that thoughtful, measured pace, was honed by lots of practice with *Abuela,* with whom he loved to converse.

"Did he say where he was calling from?"

"No, *Mamá*. I asked for his number, and he said, 'There will be a time for that.' That's exactly what he said. I thought that was odd. But you know, I wouldn't be surprised if he was calling from Mexico. There was enough clicking and circuit noise on the phone for that."

"So you didn't get his number?"

"No. But I didn't give him your cell, either."

"That's good." She frowned and repeated, "*Benedicte Mazón.*"

"Benedict with an 'e'," Carlos reminded her. "I didn't know *you* had an uncle. I mean, *Abuela's* Uncle Reuben..." Teresa's uncle, with whom Estelle had lived briefly while she finished her last two years of high school in Posadas, and for whom she'd cared in *his* complicated dotage later on, had been dead for years. Carlos had never met him, but had heard the tales—many from *Padrino,* who was often responsible for keeping Reuben out of various jails, both Mexican and American.

"I didn't know either, Carlos. Listen, you can always reach me at this number, no matter what. You did exactly the right thing to call. Be good company for *Abuela* this evening. And you also did absolutely the right thing not to give out information. Just listen carefully to what they say to you."

"Oh, sure. I have some work I wanted to show her," Carlos said. "And Addy and I are going to make a key lime pie in a little bit."

"Save some for us, *por favor.* I love you, *Hijo.*"

"You bet."

Estelle disconnected, and for a long moment stared at the mesmerizing light show of the ambulance a hundred yards ahead. "Benedicte Mazón," she said aloud, and then repeated the name twice more, engraving it in her memory. Not to worry about the concert tonight, the strange "uncle" had told Carlos. So easily said. A man claiming to be an uncle out of Estelle's past was bad enough. Calling from Mexico with information about her son's concert was breathtaking. She didn't believe in coincidence. Someone claiming to be Tomás Naranjo seeking eight thousand dollars to rescue one of the boys? And now another phantom, another clever invention claiming to be a long lost uncle, telling her not to worry?

She considered swerving across the center median and charging back to Posadas. Airport manager Jim Bergin could have her in Mazatlán in six hours…after a long and hazardous light plane flight across the spine of Mexico. Or she could continue on beyond Las Cruces to El Paso and catch a commercial flight, with any luck arriving in the Mexican city sometime in the morning. But once in the airplane, she would be effectively trapped, no good to anyone. The damn, impotent phone was her only link.

She found Leister Academy's number and dialed again. The phone rang five times before the robot answered with a message menu. Estelle lost patience and disconnected. Of course, no one was manning the offices at Leister…five minutes after six there, and everyone had gone to dinner, the offices vacant. *They* weren't worried. She touched the select to choose her eldest son's cell phone. It rang twice.

"*Óla, Mamá.*"

The wave of relief was a punch in the gut, and she caught the car's swerve before touching the rumble strip. "Francisco, where are you?" Her knuckles were white on the steering wheel, but she fought to keep the desperation out of her voice.

"Right this minute?" She could hear various noises in the background, including odd, single notes hammered on a piano. "I'm helping Dr. Belloit tune the piano. *Mamá*, this is an amazing venue. I didn't come down last year 'cause I had that sucky head cold, but this year is *great*. There's enough gold leaf decoration in this concert hall to shame Fort Knox. It's like playing in the middle of a sunburst!"

"So everything is just fine with you and Mateo?"

"Sure. The Wednesday afternoon host concert went really well, too. This is the one where they have all the school kids for an audience. Anyway, they've got this kid—I think he's ten—who plays a bassoon and makes it sound like an operatic baritone. Oh, and you know who sang with us? You won't believe it."

"Tell me." A hundred questions faded, and Estelle relaxed back in the seat, content just to hear the gush of that beloved voice. He could have waxed eloquent about beach sand, and she would have been captivated.

"Elfego *Durán.*" Francisco said the name as if Estelle would be bowled over by the news. The name was familiar, but Estelle chalked that up to having known a dozen Elfegos over the years, and perhaps a hundred Durans.

"*Ay, caramba.*"

"You've never heard of him, have you?" And before she could agree, he laughed in his grown-up, professional way. "He debuted at the Palacio de Bellas Artes in Mexico City last season. He's a contra-tenor, and just an amazing voice. Have you ever heard one?"

"One…"

"A contra-tenor. They sing up in the soprano range—*really* high. The best thing is that he's going to do a duet with Mateo Friday night, and then again on Saturday at the big concert. They've worked up some of Lloyd Webber's stuff."

"His 'stuff'?" Sometimes—the occasions becoming more and more rare—Francisco Guzman demonstrated that he was still a teenager at heart.

"Yeah. From *Cats.* And maybe from *Evita.* Older modern stuff, but it sounds just dynamic. He does this version of "Don't Cry for Me, Argentina" that gives me goose bumps. I'll bring the concert video home with me next time. They have really good recording facilities in this hall."

"I'm glad that it's going so well, *Hijo.*" Her pulse had stopped pounding in her ears. "No glitches of any kind?"

"Oh," Francisco said airily, "You know, the usual stuff. There was something going on down the street yesterday. I don't know what, but we were too busy to pay any attention. I mean, we *rehearse* and rehearse, and then we take a little break, and rehearse some more. But they were saying that a couple guys got wasted."

"Wasted?" *That's just what I need to hear,* Estelle thought.

"Somebody said they found two guys in an alley about a block from here. Nobody heard the shots, so I don't know what happened. But of course *we* wouldn't, inside the hall. The world could end outside, and we wouldn't know it."

"And you're home when?"

"We'll fly back to Leister early Sunday morning, which is kind of a drag. We have to get up at four-thirty or some such. But not to worry, *Mamá*. We're fine here. And you know, you might be interested in this…the police presence is impressive." She braked for an indecisive motorist, then punched the throttle hard to shoot past. "You're in the car?" Francisco asked, hearing the growl.

"On the way to Cruces, *niño*. Escorting the ambulance. *Padrino* fell and broke his hip. He'll have surgery there in the morning."

"*Ay.* How did he do that?"

"Just a senior moment. He lost his balance in the garage somehow."

"He'll be all right? Does he have a phone in his room?"

"He *will* have, *querido*." She sighed ruefully. "And he'll love to hear from you. But first we have to get there. We had a little trouble with the air ambulance, but we're on the way now. By the time you get home, he'll be eager to talk with you. Not so much right now, though."

"Is *Papá* with him?"

"Yes."

"Well, then," the boy said with "that's that" finality.

"You've met some interesting people during your tour? And what's this 'police presence' you mentioned?"

"The school keeps the circle pretty tight," Francisco said. "They assigned this one young guy—he's actually a captain, I think—to us. He's like a *shadow*. Always there. When we go out on stage, he's right in the wings, and he never watches *us*. He's like one of those Secret Service guys, you know. Watching, watching, watching, scanning the audience. We had a press session this morning, and he was there too, along with three uniformed cops. Serious guys. The session was all right. You know, just the usual stuff."

"Any interesting questions that caught you by surprise?"

Francisco laughed easily. "I wish. No, just lots of the same old stuff. They always want to know how long I practice every day, what's the hardest piece, did I always want to play piano—things like that. And it seemed like they were all trying to figure out how come we're not from big cities, Mateo and me. Only one or two knew where Posadas was, and not a clue about Dos Passos, Texas. I told Mateo he should just tell folks he's from Dallas. Then it might make sense to them. I could say I was from Santa Fe."

Estelle chuckled. "Talented people only come from metropolitan areas, *hijo.*"

"I keep forgetting that. Hey, one of the reporters asked me if the astronomy project was up and running yet. *He* knew where Posadas is. Or at least he'd heard of it."

"I'm impressed. Did anyone try to talk with you after the press conference?" *Like someone claiming to be a long-lost uncle?* But she kept the thought to herself.

"Well, no. Leister likes to keep us quarantined. And we're *always* chaperoned. Always. In fact double. Someone from Leister, *and mi capitán.* Mateo and I thought it would be relaxing just to walk around the city, but that's not going to happen, unless they provide a phalanx of cops to go, too. We might have an arranged visit to one of the beaches tomorrow. Maybe. They worry a lot, these people."

And that's good, Estelle thought. "But other than that, all is well?"

"Seems so. They requested that I play the *Appasionata* tonight. That's a big favorite down here." The powerful, complex Beethoven sonata was a pianist's challenge, Estelle knew. She had heard the twenty-four-minute beast several times in her own living room, and often glanced toward the ceiling to see if the crashing notes had jarred loose the plaster. Her mother routinely listened with her hands delicately covering her ears. But the piece was more than just dramatically loud in places… it was *passionate,* and it always brought tears to her eyes to see her young son interpreting that emotional chaos of the sonata with such depth.

"You'll do fine."

"Thanks. I'd better let you go, huh. Everyone else is okay?"

"Just fine. And you be careful."

"Oh, sure. I have no choice. In fact, *mi capitán* is standing right at the end of the piano, watching me talk to you." The boy laughed away from the phone. "He says hello."

"I'm proud of you, Francisco," she said. "Call often." She disconnected, and with a start realized she had no recollection of driving the last five miles.

Chapter Twelve

Sheriff Robert Torrez often had marveled privately about Bill Gastner's sleep habits. True torture for Gastner would be lying on his back in a hospital bed, any movement more serious than picking his nose impossible. Double that torture when an efficient, well-meaning nurse would bustle into Gastner's room at midnight to check his tubes and deliver "something to help you sleep."

Torrez, on the other hand, had never had a moment's trouble slipping into a deep snooze. Rarely had he lain in bed, staring at the dark ceiling, listening to the sounds of the night, alert for the telephone imperative, chewing at the troubles of the previous day, or concerned about what morning would bring. For years, he had enjoyed the four to midnight shift at the Sheriff's Department for its occasional adrenalin rush, never minding the odd hours. Sleep came easily when the work was done. He had become a master at keeping other people's troubles at a distance, never adopting their misery.

Since his election to the top spot in the department, Sheriff Torrez had avoided working an administratively logical day shift, when he might be available to talk with interested civilians. He avoided the tedium of county commission meetings where he fought the urge to doze off, or confabs with the county manager, or private moments with the press. He even avoided anything remotely resembling electioneering. He didn't speak at service clubs. He didn't grant election year interviews. He didn't trudge door to door with hand-outs. The dedicated band of volunteers who made sure he was elected every four years—now counting three elections under the belt with a fourth coming in only months—worked in a vacuum as far as Robert Torrez was concerned.

Instead, he roamed around the clock and the county, reminiscent of what he considered the most important lesson he had learned from Bill Gastner—know the turf better than anyone else. There was no highway, road, or two-track in the county that Torrez couldn't bring instantly to mind. His understanding of the county, if it could be transferred from his mind to paper, might resemble nothing so much as a detailed topographic map. On top of that, he knew the names, habits, and schedules of every rancher, and where domestic disputes were most likely to erupt. A personal benefit of his prowling was that he had a fundamental understanding of where the game herds were and what the wildlife population levels might be. He did not have to wait for surveys from the Department of Game and Fish.

His hunts were frequent and unannounced, and most of the time legally licensed. And alone, always on foot, never with the snarl of a four-wheeler. He had no "hunting buddies." He never offered to take a friend or relative hunting, and never accepted any of the frequent invitations to do so. In an emergency, if someone needed to bend his ear, the Sheriff's Office dispatcher usually knew where he was. Usually.

Such behavior might have been hard on even the most patient wife. Bob Torrez had solved that challenge by marrying, after a quiet, ten-year courtship, his first passion—the Sheriff's Department office manager and chief dispatcher, Gayle Sedillos Torrez. By the time that ceremony was finally marked on the calendar, Gayle knew her husband's habits well, and was expert at living comfortably with his idiosyncratic behavior.

On this particular Thursday morning, as the clock came up on 3:15, Torrez lay wide awake on his back, staring at the ceiling. Beside him, the whisper of Gayle's breathing was regular as a metronome. From across the room, two-month old Gabe explored the mysteries of his baba, slupping and twisting and shaking his tiny hands, content in the dark. The infant slept in short spurts like a well-fed pup, with stretches, gurgles, and happy little noises punctuating his waking moments.

"What's on your mind?" Gayle's voice was warm breath against his ear. Earlier, he had told her about the day. There was no point in trying to gloss over the details. With intense concentration, she had inspected the shattered remains of his rifle scope, had examined Sergeant Jackie Taber's skillful map of the incident area, had listened to her husband's clipped description of all the rest…temperature, wind velocity, time of day, details of his own antelope shot.

She knew that her husband mulled a fundamental question: did the shooter miss on purpose, or had all the tricks that terrain and weather could play on a high-velocity bullet fired at long range been responsible for the ten or twelve inches deviation from skull to scope.

He had refused even to consider that the shot had been an accidental discharge—perhaps someone reacted to a flash of reflecting sunshine in the distance and scanned the country with a scoped rifle, carelessly doing so with his finger on the trigger. That scenario made sense to Gayle. After the accidental round was fired, the shooter would have fled in panic. Doing such a hare-brained thing was so foreign to her husband's training and expertise that he couldn't imagine anyone else being so stupid—although he wryly admitted that he dealt with stupid people on a daily basis.

Thinking about the day had stirred an awful hollow darkness in her gut, and knowing that her husband couldn't drift off to sleep meant he had no satisfactory answers either.

Bobby took his time answering. "Just thinkin'." Gayle had never heard her husband whisper—she didn't think that he even *could*, but his voice was soft and restrained, just enough to prompt a gurgle and squirm from Gabe.

Gayle said nothing for a moment, choosing her words carefully. "I want to know," she whispered finally, "*how* the shooter knew you were out there. Out there in that one spot, where he must have *known* how to angle around you from the rear, finding a spot for a clear shot."

"Don't know."

"Did you tell anyone at the department where you were headed?"

"Nope. I guess I mentioned it to Miles one time or another. He told Bendix, the foreman."

"And so the grapevine grows. You didn't see anyone following you out?"

Torrez remained silent, loath to admit that he hadn't paid much attention to what was in his cracked rearview mirror. "Keep it simple," was the old adage, and that he'd been followed was the simplest answer of all.

"Did you stop and talk to anyone while you were out there?"

"Nope. Not before. I saw Carl Bendix afterward. That's when he told me that Waddell had mentioned I'd be out there sometime. I never told nobody just *when*."

"Did you see anyone else on the county road when you were driving in to Waddell's place?"

"Nope." Would he have noticed a plume of dust behind him on that busy county road, even if there had been one? Contractors and vendors came and went with a traffic volume long unthinkable in that quiet section of the county.

She let her breathing settle, let the rise of panic settle. "Somebody is an opportunist. He saw your truck, and decided to take a chance."

"Yep. That's what I'm thinkin'."

"That's the connection, then." She rested a hand on his chest, rocking him gently from side to side. "We'll all have to work on that." Her hand paused. "You have a signed landowner's letter of permission from Mr. Waddell."

"Yep."

"So as you said, *he* knows. That's a start."

Across the room, Gabe uttered a little grunt of satisfaction.

"That's his take on the whole deal," Gayle laughed. "Whose turn is it?"

"It'll give me something else to think about," Bobby said, and heaved himself to a sitting position. Barefoot and wearing only his boxer shorts, he swung out of bed and padded across the room. "What you up to, *cachorro?*" The infant gurgled and flailed his arms. "You smell like shit," the sheriff said. "We gotta get you housebroken."

He had unpinned the first side of the fragrant diaper when the phone rang, a muted buzz on the nightstand. "Trade you," he said, but Gayle had already slid across the king-sized bed and picked up the cell phone.

"This is Gayle Torrez."

"Good morning, Gayle. Mike Sands at the S.O. Sorry about the hour, but is the boss man available?"

"He is. Just a sec." Torrez exchanged infant for cell phone.

"What?" Torrez palmed the phone in a huge hand. Sands, who had worked midnight to eight dispatch for only a month, hadn't finished his study course in Sheriff Robert Torrez 101. He immediately assumed the monosyllabic greeting meant he was on thin ice with the sheriff.

"Sir, I'm sorry to bother you." He paused, waiting for some assurance.

"What's up?" Torrez said. His tone was matter-of-fact, almost gentle.

"Sir, we have a situation down just past the overpass. Deputy Sutherland says he has one apparent victim in a parked vehicle."

"Apparent?"

"I mean he is, sir. Dead, I mean."

"Where's he at?"

"Go past the motel, under the overpass, and turn right on that little dirt access road. Maybe a hundred yards down that, Sutherland says."

"One fatality?"

"Yes, sir. He says so, sir."

"Then get everybody on it." Sands had learned in the first week what either the sheriff or undersheriff meant when they ordered, "Everybody."

"I'll be there in a few minutes. Tell Sutherland to keep his eyes open."

"Yes, sir."

Torrez disconnected. "I didn't want to sleep anyway." Gayle had heard the word "fatality" and knew better than to waste her husband's time with questions. She finished up with the infant, who thankfully didn't have a clue about how ugly his world could be.

Five minutes later, Torrez left the house, this time taking the county's Expedition. Two blocks from his home on McArthur, he turned south on Grande, the interstate just ahead. Braking hard, he jolted a hard right onto the dirt frontage road, a narrow lane that allowed service to power lines.

Deputy Brent Sutherland's county vehicle marked the spot with its own lightshow. Parked just ahead of him, half off the lane, was a dark-colored Jeep Wrangler. Sutherland was busy unwinding a yellow crime-scene tape.

Chapter Thirteen

Curled up in a stiff lounge chair tucked in the corner of Bill Gastner's hospital room, Estelle Reyes-Guzman had managed fitful naps, awakened most often when the old man broke out in a string of colorful curses.

At one point, he raised his head slightly, heavy brows furrowed with annoyance.

"What the hell time is it?"

She stretched, taking her time unfolding stiff legs. "A little after three."

"So why are you here? *I'm* sure as hell not going anywhere, but there's no sense in you wasting your time."

"I like hearing you snore, *Padrino*. Anyway, it feels good to sit in one spot for more than five minutes."

"You have something going on? Did I manage to interrupt the flow of justice in Posadas County with my stunt?"

"Yes."

He didn't look especially contrite. "You're holding that damn cell phone as if it's your lifeline to someone."

She touched the screen to wake the gadget up. No new messages. "My mother got a scam call that worries me."

"Teresa did? Hell, I didn't think that she ever answered the damn thing."

"I suppose Addie was out of the room for a minute, and *Mamá* picked up. Anyway, the caller said that the boys are down in

Mexico, in Mazatlán. Supposedly Mateo was in trouble with the law, and needed eight thousand dollars to spring him from jail."

"Oh, for Christ's sakes," Gastner whispered, and cleared his throat. "That one's as old as the hills."

"Not to *Mamá* it isn't. What makes it interesting is that the caller claimed to be Tomás Naranjo. He called *Mamá* by name."

He motioned impatiently. "Come over here for a while. Trying to see you is breakin' my neck." When she stood by the bed, he continued, "So what did the Colonel have to say? Hell, he doesn't even work over on the West Coast."

"Just the point, sir. I can't reach him, and he hasn't returned my calls. I finally got through to Francisco, and he says everything is perfectly normal. But on any level, I can't imagine Naranjo doing such a thing. If the boys needed bail money, he would have called *me,* not *Mamá.* And Teresa's description of the way he talked didn't sound like him one bit—fast, no preliminaries, hard sell."

"Hell, with Naranjo, you could be on the phone for half an hour just with the preliminaries." He closed one eye and said through a horrible Mexican accent, "So tell me, how is the family..." He made sure to give each syllable its full due. "Look, this is one of those things. It's got to be. The scammer hopes to set off an unthinking panic attack. Especially if he can get to an elderly relative."

He patted her hand with the one of his that wasn't a pin cushion. "The jerk saw posters for the concert, maybe read something in the paper, if he can read in the first place. Forget about it." He frowned. "Although you gotta wonder how he knew about your mother, how he knew about Naranjo. The concert is the easy part. That shows a little more effort than usual in these deals." He raised an index finger. "So yeah, sweetheart. I guess you get to worry a little. When do the boys head home?"

"The group flies back on Sunday morning."

Gastner nodded slightly and closed his eyes. "I guess you can hold tight, then. If you're talking with the kid on a regular basis, everything is all right."

"And then Carlos tells me that my *uncle* called." She watched Gastner's broad, bulldog face grimace as he digested that. He knew almost as much about Estelle's unique past as she did, and he'd been involved with plenty of escapades with her great uncle, Reuben Fuentes, now dead for a dozen years. "Have you ever heard of a fellow named Benedicte Mazón?"

He regarded her with half-closed eyes.

"Are you all right?"

"Be patient. I'm marshalling my incredible memory reserves." Estelle could see that what he was actually doing was trying to twist away from the insistent pain in his hip—even with the IV potion dripping in his vein. She slipped a hand into his right, and he clenched hard.

"Benedicte…that sounds like some Latin scholar or monk or something. He's the uncle? If he's related to you somehow, your mother will know. What did he want?"

"Carlos was the one who talked with him. I wasn't home. He left a message that I wasn't supposed to worry about Mazatlán. I took that to mean the eight thousand-dollar episode."

"This is bizarre," Gastner said with relish—admittedly *tired* relish. "You know, I was sort of surprised that you and Francis didn't go down for the concert. I mean, a big deal. Would have made a nice vacation. I was even thinking along those lines for a while. It's been years since I've been there."

Estelle could feel a flush working up her cheeks. "I didn't read the conservatory bulletin carefully enough," she said. "The whole thing took me by surprise. With what that city's reputation has become here lately, I might not have let *hijo* go."

"Oh, come on." He shifted painfully again. "You let the thugs run your life, what's the point?" He took a long, slow breath. "You know, I read *my* conservatory newsletter, and I saw that Mazatlán listing. That's a beautiful place, most of the time. What a time they'll have. And the way those guys will be chaperoned, everything's going to be fine. Trust your son on this one, sweetheart. If he says that he's fine, then he is."

"He talked about all the security efforts," she added. "Apparently he has a police captain who doesn't let him out of his sight."

"That's good, then. But hey, what about the concert in Chicago after Labor Day? Eh?" He nodded at her.

"Camille reminded me. She and Mark are thinking of going."

"Uh oh." Gastner tried to smile. "I'm thinking seriously about that."

"If you go, we'll go," Estelle said.

One finger lifted off the bedding in a slow wag. "No deals like that. You and hubby…don't let these things pass you by." He closed his eyes. "And that's my wisdom for the moment." His eyes sagged closed again. "Go home and get some sleep."

"In a little bit."

"If you're still here wasting time when they trundle me off for surgery in a few minutes, I'm going to be pissed, sweetheart." He closed his eyes for a moment. "What's Roberto say about this scam thing?"

"I haven't discussed it with him. He has his own concerns at the moment." She briefly recounted what she understood of the shooting incident, and Gastner listened with closed eyes. "At the moment, he doesn't know why or who."

For a time, Gastner lay quietly, and she thought he might have fallen asleep. But eventually, when he opened his eyes, they were clear and bright. "Some creep with a grudge saw the chance to remove the man from office."

"For what reason, sir?"

"Who knows what secrets this Robert Torrez person is harboring."

Estelle laughed. "Bobby *has* no secrets, *Padrino*. I thought that when little Gabe came along, he'd soften up some. Not a chance. He treats everyone the same. You break the law, you get arrested. Period."

"Like I said." The half smile held for a moment, and then Estelle realized that the old man had fallen asleep.

Chapter Fourteen

Deputy Sutherland had taped off a hundred-foot radius around the Jeep, and Bob Torrez stopped well short of the yellow ribbon, hands thrust deep in his jacket pockets. He rested a hip against the front fender of Sutherland's SUV. The panoply of stars stretched from horizon to horizon, marred only by the sodium vapor lights along the interstate.

Above them and to the north, traffic on that thoroughfare continued its monotonous drone, punctuated by the loud diesel pounding of big rigs running through the night. The nearest neighborhood was the trailer park two blocks behind them, just off Grande.

"Why are you workin'?" Torrez asked, and Sutherland looked surprised.

"'Cause Pasquale was goin' racing with Mears and wanted to work days for a little bit," the young deputy said. "We traded. But then I was up for court this morning, and thought what the hell."

"You fall asleep on me, and you'll be back in dispatch." He walked to within a dozen feet of the Jeep, one hand catching the yellow tape. "So what do you got?"

"One occupant," Sutherland said. "I'm wondering if it's suicide. Kind of looks like it to me."

"You gave Linda a shout? And Perrone?"

"Sands is rounding up everyone. I haven't called the EMTs yet. Our guy sure isn't going anywhere."

Torrez lifted the ribbon and slipped under. He stopped to play the flashlight back and forth. The dust of the two-track was fine, and captured the detail of the boot prints.

"These yours?"

"Yes, sir. I walked straight from my unit to the Jeep. Nowhere else, except to string the tape."

"The engine was off when you got here?"

"Yes, sir. Key is in the ignition."

"Driver's window was down?"

"Yes, sir. From what I can see, it would be really awkward for someone to reach in to pop him that way." Sutherland looked as if he expected the Sheriff to say, "What way?"

"Maybe so," Torrez said quietly.

"I mean right under the chin like that."

Keeping his flashlight moving, Torrez walked up the right track of the service road. The driver had stopped the Jeep just off the trail, parking in a stand of foot-high weeds, its nose close to an impressive creosote bush. Standing just behind the left taillight, he inspected the vehicle carefully. A rag top, the black canvas was stretched tight, with no damage. However the victim had died, the bullet had not exited through the fabric top. Letting the beam travel down the left flank of the Jeep, he paused and took a step to the passenger side, inspecting the exterior in the same methodical fashion.

Immediately below the passenger door, the scant grass and abundant weeds were bent where someone had walked.

"You came over here?"

"No, sir. To the driver's door, and then back. That's it."

"Okay."

An aging Expedition pulled into the two-track and stopped immediately behind the sheriff's. Linda Pasquale, looking impossibly rested and refreshed, did not get out of the vehicle. Instead Torrez's handheld radio crackled. "You want me to come up?"

"Right to where I'm standin'," the sheriff replied. Sutherland stayed put as the sheriff made his way along the driver's side of the small vehicle. The corpse was belted in, head back against the headrest, both hands and a large handgun in his lap. His black sweatshirt was soaked with blood from chin to lap, a thick puddle that washed out over his crotch and drained onto the seat. Torrez bent carefully, folding his six-foot four-inch frame until he could direct the flashlight. The bullet hole was large, with a corona of unburned powder stippling from one side of the man's jaw to the other.

A Raiders baseball cap had fallen off and lay toward the rear of the center console.

The sheriff took a moment to stretch on a pair of latex gloves and then, reaching into the Jeep, gently placed his left hand on the man's head, his fingertips feeling the skull.

"Huh," he said, and swung the flashlight to focus on the automatic. "Well, that'll work," he said to no one in particular. The gun appeared new, one of the lower-priced, generic clones of the Colt 1911 .45 automatic. Nothing fancy, just large, dependable, and easy to feed.

"No exit wound?" Sutherland sounded uneasy.

"Nope. Not unless it's somewhere we can't see. But no damage to the canvas top." He straightened up and beckoned to Linda Pasquale. "Everything," he said. "Isolate the handgun in his lap, gettin' closeups where you can. Everything else. The wound is under his chin, and I need that, too. And find a way to get me some of that rifle case that's layin' on the floor in the back."

Sutherland's flashlight swung that way. "I didn't see that."

"You weren't supposed to be lookin'," Torrez reminded him. "You were supposed to call it in and secure the scene. That's what you did." He glanced at Linda. "By the time you're done, maybe Doc will be here," Torrez added. "You can open both doors, but protect the latches. Gotta be prints there." He reached out and dropped a huge hand on Sutherland's shoulder. "Prints when Linda's done."

"Did you want me to call Mears for that?"

"No. You know what you're doin'." His gaze had drifted to the Jeep's tires, aggressive tread that left a clear print in the dirt. "Willin' to bet..." Torrez mused to himself.

"Match to the set out on 14?"

"Worth lookin'," Torrez said. "And Linda, when you're finished shootin', I want to check out that rifle case." For a long moment, he stood by the driver's door, looking at the dead man. Olive skin, heavy features, a gaping mouth that showed lots of metalwork, the whole picture held nicely in place by the seatbelt/shoulder harness. The faint snick of Linda's digital camera reminded him that he was standing in the way, and he moved to the front fender and rested a hand on the hood. Stone cold.

"What'd you come up with when you called in the plate?"

Sutherland looked up from his black plastic field kit and dug a small notebook out of his pocket. "The Jeep is registered to a Miguel A. Quesada, 101 Lincoln Circle in Prairie View Heights out in Tucson."

Torrez stood behind Linda as she shot a series of the victim's head against the head rest.

"Pretty ghastly." She reset the camera and took several more from different angles. "Gun in place?"

"Yep. Everything, right from his shoes on up."

"I think he was holding more than the official eleven quarts," Linda said.

"Head shot like that, the heart keeps on pumpin' for a minute or so."

"I needed to know that, sir." She shot a withering glance at the sheriff.

Torrez shrugged. "You're doin' good." He straightened up at the approach of another vehicle, Dr. Alan Perrone's red BMW. The slightly built, dapper physician swung out of the car and closed the door gently. He took a moment to pull on latex gloves.

"How are you folks doing this lovely morning?"

"Okay. Linda's about finished the driver's side."

"Snowbird?" He tipped his head, reading the Arizona license.

"Maybe Tucson," Torrez said.

"He found a nice quiet corner of the planet," Perrone said. "By the way, I just talked to Dr. Guzman. He's happy with the way Bill's condition has stabilized. They expect him to go into surgery in a couple of hours."

"Okay. So we won't know nothin' until mid-morning or so."

"Most likely." Perrone nodded at the Jeep. "I have a clear path?"

"Yep."

For several minutes, the physician looked at the human wreckage from a distance, face locked in a severe frown. Eventually, he reached out and touched the corpse on the neck. "Someone made damn sure." With both hands he worked the head this way and that as Torrez held both flashlights. "Jammed the gun right into the soft flesh under the jaw. Lots of gas damage, stippling, all of that. A contact shot."

He examined the jaw, fingers light on both sides of the face. "Some cadaveric spasm, both here and in the hands. *That's* not so unusual." He straightened up and pointed with his own penlight. "Both hands curled hard, but not around the gun."

"I'm thinkin' that the gun was placed there afterward," Torrez said, and Perrone glanced up at him.

"I'd bet on it. And immediately so. It's right in the center of that blood bath. It just doesn't look as if he was hanging on to it."

"So not suicide."

Perrone made a small grunting sound. "Not likely. *Unexpected,* maybe."

"No exit's kind of unusual," the sheriff said.

The medical examiner nodded. "And *that's* interesting, with a big gun like this one. I mean, a forty-five is no magnum, but from the ones I've seen, there's plenty of power there to disrupt the vault of the skull. Be interesting to see during autopsy."

He examined the victim's body, the flashlight beam brilliant against the reflective blood wash. "No other wounds?" He pulled the seatbelt outward a little. "Somebody got close to him. Surprise, surprise."

He stepped back and removed the gloves. "You can go ahead and call it in," he said. "There's not much I can do with him out here." Torrez nodded at Sutherland, who tended to the radio.

"I'll let you know if there's anything else of interest," Perrone said. "If I had to guess right now, I'd bet on the one wound. There's always room for a surprise at autopsy, but I'll put my money on the one. The blood's starting to crust around the edges of the flow, so a couple of hours at most. The jaw is frozen open from spasm, but the arms aren't showing much rigor yet."

He turned in place. "No neighbors, and parked off the street far enough that no one noticed the vehicle sitting here. How'd Sutherland find it?"

"He noticed."

Perrone smiled at the sheriff. In the distance, they heard a heavy diesel, and the noise echoed and amplified as the ambulance passed under the interstate, then slowed to turn into the lane. The show of emergency lights died.

"I'll let you know," Perrone said. "And you'll call in the I.D. as soon as you have it."

"Yep." But it was another half hour before Torrez was satisfied that the corpse could be moved, and the two EMTs remained at their unit, out of the way. The pistol itself presented a problem, since the slide was fully forward, and the hammer cocked. Torrez snugged a nylon zip tie around the hammer, blocking it. Should the trigger be jarred somehow, the hammer would jam harmlessly against the nylon. He snicked the safety up as well, but otherwise left the lethal pistol alone. With a short aluminum cleaning rod down the barrel, Torrez gently lifted the gun clear of the swamp of blood and eased it into a large evidence bag. Sutherland handed him a large, bright yellow adhesive label that announced "Loaded gun," and the sheriff left the rest of the evidence tag labeling to the young deputy.

"Make sure we find the empty casing," Torrez said. "The way the gun was held, it might have gone right out the window. Or if he had it twisted, bounced off the door."

"Maybe the shooter picked it up?" Sutherland asked.

"Bettin' not. Why bother, and then leave the gun behind?"

"Right there." Linda Pasquale had been leaning in the passenger side documenting the recovery of the gun, and she pointed at the crease between the carpet and the transmission hump where a single brass cartridge case had lodged.

"Huh," Torrez muttered. He made a pistol out of his right hand, index finger extended. Mimicking the assassin, he turned sharply left, ramming the gun hand into the air, barrel upward. "Bang," he said. "Shell kicks out and up if it's held the one way. Gonna bounce off somewhere up above him." He twisted his hand, as if holding the gun upside down, a natural enough position. "Holds it like this, the shell goes down, bounces off his chest, and onto the floor." He bent down and aimed the flashlight beam at the inside of the canvas roof.

As soon as the casing was safe in an evidence bag, he beckoned to the EMTs.

"Before you zip him up…" Torrez said, but Tom Sharpe, a tall and angular man with a shock of white hair, waved him off with an air of impatience.

"I know, I know," Sharpe said. "You can have all the time you need."

Sharpe and his partner, Doug Baca, a morbidly heavy young man whose girth tested his uniform buttons, levered the corpse sideways from the Jeep. Baca studiously avoided examining the victim's face as Sharpe bent to disentangle the uncooperative feet from the pedals. With the black body bag spread out on the gurney, they lifted and swung, settling the corpse on the bag with an undignified thump.

"He's going to want to do the pockets before we zip him up." Sharpe's tone was officious, odd since Baca had been an EMT for ten years longer than the former pastor. He made a point of noting the sheriff's gloves. "Always a smart thing to do," he said. Torrez ignored him.

"No robbery." Sutherland looked at the wallet Torrez retrieved from the man's right hip pocket…the sort of long, slender accessory that would be more at home in the inside pocket of a suit coat than in the jeans. The wallet bulged with money, and the sheriff thumbed through it.

"All right," he said, and pulled out a laminated card. "Arizona. Issued to Miguel Quesada. Tomorrow's his birthday."

"Some present," the deputy offered.

"Yep." The wallet yielded nothing else. "Two grand and a license." With no further comment, Torrez accepted the large evidence bag from Sutherland. Except for a tube of lip balm, the man's other pockets were empty. He handed the bag to the deputy, and gently lifted the tail of the sweatshirt, drawing it up the torso. The fabric was soggy with blood, some of which had soaked through the loose weave. "Linda," the sheriff said, and she stepped forward quickly. "Just one to show there's nothin' there."

No fresh wounds marked the beefy chest, although a puckered scar just below Quesada's right collarbone drew a brief "Huh," from the sheriff. "He collected that one a while ago." With Sharpe assisting, they rolled the corpse over far enough to expose the back, pocked with a far larger scar high up, just below the crest of the shoulder.

"In and out," Sharpe said.

No other wound marked the back of the victim's neck or marred the skull. Blood had gushed from the blasted chin, the mouth and nose.

"You can have him," Torrez said.

"Do you have the State Police Crime Unit coming?" Sharpe asked. His implication was clear, but Torrez instead turned to his deputy.

"You need to call that in to Doc for his paperwork," Torrez said to Sutherland. "He'll want the DOB and stuff when he tags the corpse. And you might as well give Stub Barnes a shout so we can get this thing to impound." He glanced at his watch. "And it ain't long until Taber is on shift, so have her out here. And then...we got two names I want run by the NCIC. This guy, and our friend from this afternoon—Olveda. Let's see what kind of story these Tucson boys can tell."

"And the rifle case," Linda added.

"And that," the sheriff echoed. "Let's see what he's hidin' in there."

Chapter Fifteen

Estelle Reyes-Guzman startled as a hand gently shook her shoulder. She looked up into the concerned face of Blanche Johnson, LPN. "Your gadget is going nuts." The nurse nodded at the little chair-side table where Estelle's cell phone was vibrating itself in a slow circle on the Formica tabletop.

"I don't know what she's got against a nice, comfy motel room," Bill Gastner said. His voice was strong. "Better yet, *home.*"

Estelle drew herself up, untucking her legs. It used to be easy, sitting curled up on top of her feet. It still was, save for the uncoiling. Her watch said 6:10. The phone continued dancing, and she retrieved it, feeling a wash of relief as she viewed the international number.

"Guzman."

"Ah, most fortuitous," the smooth, quiet voice said.

Nurse Johnson had started her morning pre-surgical ritual with the patient, and appeared to be in no hurry to leave the room. Estelle rose from the chair and tried to rotate the kink from her neck. "Colonel, I am *so* pleased that you called," she said. The hallway outside Gastner's ICU room was empty, and she rested her back against the cool block wall, waiting for the knots to release.

"I hope this isn't a nuisance," Colonel Tomás Naranjo continued. "Your officers tell me that you are standing guard, so to speak." He laughed in quiet sympathy. "But this time, our good fellow is not so likely to walk out of the hospital on his own, no?"

"No." She sighed. Gastner once had done just that, albeit with her assistance—perhaps *complicity* was a better word. And of course, Naranjo remembered. He and Gastner had always been neck and neck in the human gazetteer race.

"How is he now? I am told that it is a badly broken right hip, no?"

"Yes, and we can add to that his spending more than a day lying on the concrete floor of his garage, unable to move. But he sounds stronger this morning. He just barked at me for spending the night here."

Naranjo chuckled. "Of course."

"Surgery is here in just a few minutes. They're prepping him now."

"Oh, my. That is such a trial at any age, but at his…Should you have the chance, will you extend my fond regards?"

"I'll do that." She knew better than to push the Mexican colonel toward the central point of his call. With some amusement, she remembered her mother's description of Naranjo in a hurry, speaking too fast for her old ears to follow…and how unlikely that would be.

"You sound tired, Sheriff." His voice was as soothing as a piece of warm velvet.

"An uncomfortable chair for the night," she said cheerfully. "I'm going to go find myself a nice cup of tea here in a moment."

"Ah." The brief silence that followed meant that Naranjo was searching for the open door. She knew it was coming before he said, "And how is your mother?"

"She is well, although I confess that at this moment, she is confused. She had every reason to think that you had called her personally with some most distressing news, Tomás."

"She believed that she was speaking to me?"

"Exactly."

"How puzzling. I *should* call your mother more often, but we know how life's little interruptions keep us from doing those things that are most important." His cadence, his caressing of each syllable, reminded her of the late, great Puerto Rican actor Raúl Juliá. Years before, when she had watched the video, *Presumed Innocent*, she had leaned close to her husband's ear at one point in the film and whispered, as Juliá engaged another character, "He sounds exactly like Tomás Naranjo."

"I was certain you hadn't called, Tomás. Not about this." She quickly told him of the telephone scam and the request for money.

He was silent for some seconds. "But she has not responded to this request?"

"No. She went so far as to ask our bank for a cashier's check. Fortunately, the bank president intervened and discussed the matter with me before proceeding."

"Ay. All of this is most unfortunate. But the most important question, then. Have you heard from Francisco?"

"He called earlier yesterday evening, Tomás. I did not mention anything about the phone call to Teresa because I didn't want my son to start worrying. If he already had reason to think that something was wrong, I know that he would have said so." She sighed. "The news of *Padrino's* injury is difficult enough. He is more than *padrino* for the boys. He is also a close and cherished friend for them."

"I understand that, *Señora*," Naranjo said. "I am told that the first concerts went very well indeed."

Told by whom? Estelle wondered, but she knew that Naranjo's contacts were both efficient and wide-ranging. "They did. Francisco is most excited."

"I should think so. And of course, we send our very best regards to all of our friends north of the border."

"Thank you."

"In addition, I wanted to alert you to a possible situation." He accented each syllable of the word for emphasis. "It appears that two men were killed in Mazatlán yesterday." Estelle heard papers rustling. "The Ortega brothers. José and Hector. I can't imagine that you have heard of them."

"No." Estelle's fingers grew cold holding the phone. "Where and how did they die?" *Two men wasted,* Francisco had reported.

Naranjo paused. "Their bodies were found in a small court-yard not far from the conservatory where your son is performing. Both had been shot once in the head with a small-caliber weapon of some sort. There was no effort made to hide the bodies. They lay on their backs, I'm told, side by side. As if *arranged,* you know. We—actually, let me be accurate. Metropolitan authorities are following several promising aspects of the case."

"Such as?"

"One of the men had in his possession an envelope on which he had written several phone numbers. One of the numbers was underlined. I think you might recognize it." He read off the number, complete with area code—the Guzmans' landline in Posadas.

Estelle said nothing, but realized the crashing she heard was her own heartbeat.

"That would be the telephone that your mother would answer, I would think."

"Yes. She will not use a cell phone. They make no sense to her."

"Something *was* planned, then," Naranjo said. "It appears that way. We—they—do not know who might have interrupted whatever plan was in progress. Perhaps a kidnapping if the phone calls produced no results."

"I don't want to think about that."

"I know you don't, and I don't blame you. But this is a time when we must face all facts, my friend. Security around the venue was doubled and tripled after the discovery of the bodies, let me assure you. It was made very clear...*very clear...* that *nothing* would interfere with concert programs, or with the musicians themselves. Honored guests in our country will remain so, safe and secure so that all may appreciate and applaud their performances."

"Thank you, Tomás. But I must tell you the curious thing. We received a telephone call. Carlos happened to answer and talked with a man who claims to be an uncle of mine. He used the name Benedicte Mazón."

"Most interesting." Naranjo had not hesitated.

"Yes. He asked to speak with no one else, but just called to deliver a message. He told Carlos that there was no cause to worry about Mazatlán. The implication was that if there had been any issues surrounding the concert venue and the boys, they were no longer a worry."

This time, it was the Colonel who fell silent, and Estelle waited patiently. Finally, Naranjo said, "One more time, his name, please?"

"Benedicte Mazón." She spelled it for him, wondering if he was having second thoughts now about recognizing the name— or admitting to her that he did.

"And this Señor Mazón said he was an uncle of yours? *That* is curious." Naranjo had heard the story of Estelle's life journey from the tiny, isolated border town of Tres Santos to her career in the United States, and he had had the opportunity to engage Estelle's stepmother, Teresa Reyes, in conversation on many occasions. Both enjoyed reminiscing about quieter, simpler times in the border country.

A central character of those stories and times had been Teresa's uncle, Reuben Fuentes—a character well known to both Naranjo and Bill Gastner himself. When Teresa had sent her then sixteen-year-old daughter Estelle to the United States to finish high school, the teenager had lived for two years with Reuben, in itself something of a gamble. The sixteen-year-old had prospered, however. Never had Estelle heard the name Benedicte Mazón mentioned.

"We will see," Naranjo said simply. "Kindly allow me some time to pursue this. In the meantime, I will make sure that a contingent of the very best men is assigned to the two musicians and their troupe." He chuckled. "But please…we will be ever so discreet, believe me."

"I appreciate all you can do, Tomás. I really do. I am more in your debt than I can repay."

The dismissal in his tone carried clearly. "You know, over the years," and he paused, "over the years, we have worked closely on so many things." He laughed gently. "I believe we both are beyond counting who owes what debt to whom. To work as one—that is what we must do."

One of the nurses, assisted by a candy striper, pushed a mobile bed silently down the hall toward Estelle, then turned and eased it into Gastner's room.

"They're transferring *Padrino* now, Tomás. I should go."

"Word from us soon, then, Sheriff. And please, rest well."

"Please give my love to Marta."

"With pleasure," the Mexican policeman said. Eschewing the social circles that might seem appropriate for a colonel's wife, Marta Naranjo instead presided over their exquisitely appointed *hacienda* and exclusive gift shop outside the tiny village of Alegre, itself a destination for well-heeled shoppers from both sides of the border. "How do they say… 'when the dust settles,' we must all meet in Alegre. It has been too long."

"I look forward to that," Estelle said.

Chapter Sixteen

With its position photographically recorded half a dozen ways, Torrez lifted the heavy plastic rifle case out of the Jeep. A search had turned up nothing else in the rear compartment—no clothing, no maps, no food, not even a candy wrapper.

He snapped the latches and opened the rifle case. For a long moment, he knelt quietly, one hand on the case cover, the other relaxed on his knee.

"You think that's the one?" Sutherland asked. Torrez didn't reply. He slipped a gloved index finger under the barrel and raised it until he could bend down and sniff the aroma—rich and recent, a tangy odor as yet uncut with solvents or oil. The muzzle itself was threaded for half an inch to accept a suppressor, and that ten-inch black tube lay in its own nest in the foam case liner.

Without touching anything else, he lowered the rifle back in place. He knew ranchers who routinely used suppressors on their varmint rifles—whether the suppressor was legally owned or not wasn't a concern. More effective with sub-sonic ammunition, the suppressors still muted the rifle's report enough that the whole prairie dog town wouldn't dive for cover from a shot fired from four or five hundred yards away. Torrez had heard the one shot aimed at him, however. The shooter hadn't bothered with the suppressor—perhaps saving it for other jobs where the rifle's loud report mattered.

Further lab work might change his opinion, but at first glance, there was nothing unique about the Sako rifle.

Nestled beside the suppressor was a box of premium grade hollow point hunting cartridges. Torrez lifted one corner of the box just far enough to remove it from the case, and using his pen as a stylus, opened the box flap. The Styrofoam innards slid out, revealing nineteen rounds remaining.

"So," he said, and rocked back on his haunches. The Sako was by no means an unusual gun—not a high-priced assassin's tool, but a most competent hunting rifle. Some machinist or gunsmith had taken but a few moments to thread the barrel to accept the suppressor. Chambered in the venerable and common .223 cartridge, ammunition choices were abundant anywhere around the world, military or otherwise.

"Nice rig." He glanced up at both Sutherland and Linda Pasquale. "Get Mears on this," he said. "Every little thing. Might even get some trace DNA off the stock." He lifted his right hand and aligned it close to his nose as if sighting a rifle. "Gonna be something touching somewhere, unless he wiped it down already. Might not have had the time."

With a creak of leather and crack of his right knee, Torrez stood up. "And see what the state can do for us," he said without much enthusiasm. "Adams can call their van down here. Maybe they'll find some fiber or something. Who knows? They ain't going to be happy we got a start already, but tough shit. We ain't got all day."

"You don't want the rifle to go to them, Sheriff?"

"No, I don't. Sign it in to Mears. It and the forty-five both. If there's somethin' there, he'll find it." He turned as an approaching vehicle slowed. The county unit eased into the lane and parked behind his own. Sergeant Jackie Taber's blocky figure appeared. The dawn was just burning cracks through the deep indigo of the eastern sky, and Taber walked carefully head-down until she was within a few feet of the sheriff. She looked up and touched the brim of her Stetson with two fingers. "A perfect morning, sir," she said.

"You find out anything more yesterday?"

She eyed the Jeep with interest. "Well, as a matter of fact," she said. "Linda and I did some scouting. If this is the vehicle, then he parked just ahead of your old heap, disabled it, and then drove on down the road about two-tenths of a mile, right where that rise in the prairie drifts down to join the arroyo. He parked there, and hiked in." She raised both hands and brought them together, like two paths converging. "He flanked you, sir."

"Huh." He turned and flipped his flashlight in Linda's direction. "You didn't tell me about that."

"No, but I would've," Linda replied cheerfully.

"We found the place where he might have taken the shot," Taber added. "Nice little barricade of rocks, a couple of places that made a good rifle rest. Paces out to about four hundred yards, plus or minus." She frowned then added in her characteristically precise, military fashion, "Odd, number one, that he didn't hit you. And odd, number two, that he didn't take a second shot. That giant bush that you used as cover wouldn't have covered much. Had he taken the time, he would have had a comfortable view."

"Yeah, well." He took a step closer to the Jeep, resting a hand on its left tailgate latch. "And then? He spends the rest of the day thinkin', and then come dark, he parks here, and maybe shoots himself in the head. One shot, right under the chin." Torrez abruptly interrupted his narrative, as if embarrassed that he'd talked too much. "Or maybe not," he said after a moment. "Maybe someone was in the Jeep with him, and reached over to jam the gun hard into the flab under his chin. Bang. One shot."

"Which way are you leaning?"

"Why would he shoot himself?" Torrez asked, not expecting an answer.

Taber's shrug was deep and slow. "His grief and remorse were so wretched at missing an easy rifle shot at you earlier that he just couldn't face himself another minute." She kept a straight face, but Linda Pasquale's smile was huge. "That's if we're talking the same Jeep and the same shooter."

"It is," Torrez muttered. "You can match up the tires later, but I know Goodyear Wrangler tracks when I see 'em. There's going to be two Jeeps involved? I don't think so. Got the rifle right here. Maybe the shooter too. Just some leftover questions, is all."

"Such as."

"Why'd the killer leave the .45 behind?"

Taber frowned. "I can think of a couple reasons. Number one, what better way to make sure he isn't caught with it on down the pike? What kind of gun is it?"

Torrez motioned to Sutherland, and in a moment the deputy returned with the bagged and boxed gun. Taber looked without touching.

"Okay. That's pretty generic. A trace is going to be a challenge. But the slug didn't exit, so we recover that and we know a little more."

"Yep."

"So the slug matches the gun, and the killer doesn't need to worry about something as incriminating as that in his possession." She shrugged. "That's my wild-hair, early morning guess, and it's not worth a whole lot." She straightened up, and turned slowly in place. "It's what's outside the yellow ribbon that's interesting." She turned back to Torrez. "Another car? Did the killer drive in here behind the Jeep?"

"No tracks that I saw," Sutherland offered.

"At least none that we haven't driven or walked over," the sergeant said gently. "There shouldn't be anyone parked in here at all, and here we all are."

"I mean, when I drove in to check the Jeep, I didn't know if there was anyone here," the deputy said. "I mean…"

"Gotcha," Jackie smiled, clearly hearing Sutherland's discomfort. "And I would have done exactly the same thing. We pull up behind a vehicle parked along the highway, and we don't cordon the scene off *first,* do we? So we'll see what we can see when the sun comes up." She held up an index finger. "Somebody either *rode* in here with the Jeep victim, then what? Walked away? And to where? Or," and she raised another finger, "they *drove* in behind him in a separate vehicle, had a meeting, did the deed, and then maybe backed out and away he goes." She thrust her hands in her pockets. "Do you have the State Police coming with all their goodies?"

"Yep."

"Do you want the generators?"

"We got morning comin' here pretty quick."

"Have you figured out any new theories about why someone was willing to take a potshot at you, sir?"

"Nope."

"That's a lot of work, for sure. Following you all the way out there, working the location to his advantage, jigging your truck…a creative thinker. Or at least a *determined* one."

"Yeah, well."

"And about three months before the election, too," and she smiled at the dark look Torrez cast her way.

"It don't have nothin' to do with elections," he said.

"I don't know. Maybe Lieutenant Adams has it in for you."

"Yeah, sure," Torrez said, and motioned to Deputy Sutherland. "You want to get them comin'? Otherwise we'll be here all day." If they were able to secure the crime scene investigations unit from the State Police, it would be Lieutenant Mark Adams who would assign it. The Lieutenant's relationship with the Posadas County Sheriff's Department was good-natured and cooperative—if he could call in the rig, he would.

Chapter Seventeen

With a hundred other things that he could, and probably should, have been doing, Sheriff Robert Torrez entered the county commission chambers at six minutes before nine, leaving the crime scene out beyond the interstate to his staff. Had the strange little man from Tucson, Dominic Olveda, not been presenting, Torrez would have had no compunction about skipping the meeting—and wouldn't have much cared if none of the other members of the department had been able to make it, either. He, or someone else from his department, was not so much required to attend as it was *expected.*

Naturally enough, the Sheriff's Department was always the target of those who chronically complained about County services...especially the expense of the sheriff's operations. But as an elected official, the sheriff marched to his own drummer... until voters said otherwise. Try as they might, the county commission could not tell him how to run his department. Paybacks, if necessary, came at budget time.

The meeting would last all day, but guests like Dominic Olveda were prodded to the microphone early on the agenda so they didn't have to wait for all the committee reports, budget minutia, or haranguing citizens.

As he entered the building, Torrez skillfully avoided the foyer, where a couple dozen politicos gaggled. He didn't want to field the inevitable questions about the election three months hence. Twenty people could throw their hats in the ring as far as he cared. He knew that in a county as tightly knit as Posadas, he would probably win.

And if he did not, he was sure that Lieutenant Mark Adams would, even though many voters didn't much cotton to the State Police, or that Adams actually lived in Deming, well outside Posadas County. True enough, he owned a modest home in Posadas that he rented, but was he planning to move there if elected? Adams had implied that he would, but he'd never come right out and said so.

Of more importance, Bob Torrez knew that Adams was retiring from his state job in October, and the two lawmen had agreed that the election loser would become a captain in the Sheriff's Department, replacing Eddie Mitchell, who had left to join the Secret Service, working in Bethesda, Maryland.

It was always possible that a spoiler might come out of the woodwork—possible, not probable. The third candidate, Jerry Steward, had run for sheriff on three previous occasions over the years, his lengthy and often inarticulate diatribes filling the editorial page of the *Posadas Register.* No one took him seriously. For a brief time twenty years before, he had been a deputy in Bernalillo County, and that stint appeared to be his entire foundation of law enforcement, or even administrative, experience. His platform was consistent—the county bureaucracy mismanaged funds to a criminal extent.

Steward was not alone in wanting the top lawman spot. Even the current county manager, Leona Spears, had at one time thought that she did, and she ran for sheriff once, her campaign failing to yield even double-digit returns.

Slipping through the far left of the multiple double doors servicing the chamber, Torrez saw that the audience was going to be SRO by the time the foyer drained into the room. A huge and colorful map of Posadas County was projected on a screen down front, the screen and projector skewed so that the image was visible to both commission and audience.

County Manager Leona Spears, dressed in a conservative and generously cut brown suit, had already taken her seat at the manager's desk near the far right wing of the commission dais. Papers were stacked neatly before her to right and left. She saw Torrez and clapped a hand to her chest as if in cardiac arrest, then favored him with a wide smile and a waggle of her fingers. She bent to one side to talk with the Monica Xavier, the county clerk. Xavier enjoyed the honor of having more relatives in Posadas County, in and out of office, than even the current sheriff, whose list of cousins, nieces, nephews, uncles, and aunts was truly spectacular.

A microphone stand took up aisle space on either side of the center audience section for citizens who wished to vent, and Torrez slipped into one of the seats on the outer aisle, as far from the nearest microphone as he could get. The hall had been built during the flush years when Consolidated Mining promised to make Posadas the industrial gem of New Mexico. With seating for a hundred, the chambers still filled on occasion, and this appeared to be one of them.

Just when he had about talked himself into leaving, a hand dropped on Torrez's left shoulder, and the sheriff looked up into Dr. Arnie Gray's kindly face.

"Sheriff, how's this gorgeous day treating you?"

"That would be a long story, Doc."

Gray, a several-term chairman of the county commission and a busy chiropractor, flashed a comforting smile. "I hear ya." His angular face went sober. "What's this I hear about Bill Gastner? Stroke or something like that?"

"Hip," Torrez said. He squirmed upright in the seat, untangling his boots from the chair in front of him, then stood up. His burly six feet four accentuated Gray's stick figure—six-six and gangling.

Gray's face formed a big O of recognition. "*Hip*," he grimaced. "That's bad at his age. Well, any age. He went to Albuquerque?"

"Cruces."

"Oh, well, *that's* good. He's got someone with him, I hope. I mean family-wise." Gray raised a hand in salute at someone across the room.

"Sure."

"Ah, good." He reached out and patted Torrez's arm. "I'd better get this show on the road, or we'll be here until midnight." He turned, then stopped abruptly. Drawing closer, he dropped his voice. "What do you know about this Dominic Olveda fellow?" When Torrez didn't reply immediately, Gray added, "He's come around to see me a couple times. Very *polished*."

"We'll see," the sheriff said.

Gray apparently took that answer to be as good as he was likely to get. "Leona has spoken with him at some length, I understand. So this should be interesting."

"Yep," Torrez said, not meaning it. Something about public meetings made him itch. Estelle Reyes-Guzman handled the gatherings with aplomb, able to think quickly and eloquently on her feet. When the undersheriff couldn't attend with her succinct monthly report, Sergeant Jackie Taber had filled in on a number of occasions. And Commission Chairman Gray noticed. He paused again and regarded Torrez with a knowing grin. "Are you actually going to do some campaigning this year?"

"Don't think so." Torrez's reply prompted Dr. Gray's smile to grow wider still.

"Lieutenant Adams has lots of friends, you know." He nodded across where the State Policeman, in full uniform, was talking with two of the other commissioners, smiles big, body language buddy-buddy.

"Yep."

The sheriff saw that Dominic Olveda was already seated, managing to enter the hall without causing a caucus of his own. A large briefcase took up a second seat beside him. This time, he was dressed in a conservative dark blue pinstriped business suit.

Airport Manager Jim Bergin slipped down the crowded aisle and Olveda glanced up, then quickly collected his briefcase, nodding to Bergin in invitation. Bergin slid into the seat, looking self-conscious. In the decades that he'd run the FBO at the airport, under contract to both village and county, Jim Bergin had been a steady hand, neither lax nor particularly ambitious to pursue new possibilities. Torrez knew that Bergin found baffling

County Manager Leona Spears' eager politicking on behalf of new runways, taxiways, hangers, and electronics, since he saw no great swell of new business on the horizon. He still chuckled at Miles Waddell and the rancher's *NightZone* development.

Torrez found it interesting that Bergin had chosen to sit immediately in company with Dominic Olveda, thereby at least appearing to support whatever it was that Olveda wanted to develop. He sighed, wishing not for the first time that his undersheriff wasn't tied up in Las Cruces.

Olveda finished shuffling papers just as Dr. Gray rapped the gavel. In the back of the hall, Bob Torrez tried to make himself comfortable, slouching down with one knee braced against the seat in front of him, turned slightly away from the heavy woman who had wedged herself in the seat beside him. She and two companions beamed at Torrez. He couldn't ignore them, since the heavy woman whose elbow prodded his ribs was Veronica Espinosa, née Veronica Torrez, oldest daughter of cousin Milton Torrez and his late wife, Adele.

She leaned closer yet. "You should come to these more often," she whispered. "They're *fun.*"

"Fun" wasn't the description Torrez would have chosen. He muttered a minimally polite greeting, offered a nod and a smile, and let it go at that.

During the prayer that followed the pledge to the flag, Torrez scanned the audience. He knew most of them, always puzzled that people would want to spend a day cramped in chambers, sharing flu germs, listening to the drone of the endless reports. Perhaps they were here to listen to Olveda, or to any of the other seven guests who had reserved space on the agenda.

"It's always a pleasure to see the chambers full," Dr. Gray intoned. He adjusted the microphone. "We have a lot on our plate today, so I'm going to ask that presentations be brief and concise." He grinned. "And we know how that goes." The audience murmured knowing amusement. "At this point, I'd like to recognize Mr. Dominic Olveda, from Development International." He lifted a batch of notes that partially covered his agenda. "From Phoenix, I believe. No—make that Tucson. You've come a long ways to talk with us. Welcome, sir. The floor is yours." Gray leaned back in his chair and laced his long fingers together over his belly.

"Thank you for according me this time." The PA system amplified Olveda's silky voice just enough. The man was no stranger to microphones. The map of Posadas County winked off the screen, replaced by an aerial view of the airport, a view facing west down the length of the runway. "The county is to be congratulated for taking steps to make the astronomical observatory theme center a reality. What is now called *NightZone* will surely attract visitors from all over the world. It will…it *is,* one of a kind." He turned and smiled at the audience. "I have visited several times in the past few days. Again, congratulations. *Most* impressive."

He paused and smiled at the commission as if they'd actually done even an iota of the work involved in the development. "What we propose," and the image changed first to an architect's rendering, and then split to share the screen with a photograph of a sprawling building, "is a sister development of the *Tres Lagunas* hotel complex near Cochepek in Costa Rica." The room was dead silent. "*Tres Lagunas* is a much larger development than what we're seeking permission to build here, of course."

The architect's rendering enlarged to take over the screen. "And don't misunderstand me. What we propose is in no way related to Mr. Waddell's development, nor is intended in any way to be competition. It is only to take advantage of an opportunity that we see. An opportunity that his imagination and courageous development will in its own way, make possible."

Bob Torrez pushed himself up so he could see around a coiffed head. He had not yet caught sight of Miles Waddell, but certainly the rancher would be here to defend his interests.

"First, a modest hotel," Olveda continued, "on the current airport grounds, at the far west end of the runway-taxiway complex. We envision some fifty-two rooms, with all the ancillary features one would expect of such a facility: conference rooms, both restaurant and café dining, and so forth." As Olveda spoke, images of the features wafted across the screen. "This area," and his laser pointer circled an area east of the hotel, "is aircraft parking for patrons. Pilots may taxi right to the facility. And this," and the laser touched a small but elegant building set well back from the taxiway, "is automobile rental. So you see, one can fly in, park, and rent. Or take a shuttle service to the narrow gauge rail facility. It would be that simple. And, as you can also see, we are well removed from the F.B.O., currently operated so ably by Mr. James Bergin on behalf of the village and county."

He paused, and Dr. Gray lifted his pencil. "What you're showing us now is the whole extent of the development that you're proposing at this time? Very ambitious, I must say."

"At this time, yes."

Tobe Ulibarri, a commissioner since the last Ice Age, loudly cleared his throat. Even when saying "Good Morning," he could sound confrontational. "Where the hell is the water for something like this coming from, Mr....?" and he flapped a circle with one hand in lieu of a name.

"That is my purpose this morning, sir," Olveda said. "I am delivering to the commission these proposal packages," and he rested his hand on a pile of fat envelopes, "that will explain the project as we envision it. I wanted you to know from the beginning—in fact, the fundamental purpose of my visit today—that we are not asking the local governmental entities for a single cent of investment. The village water system, for example, was never extended the seven miles out to the airport. We propose," and once more his hand settled on the envelopes, "to develop water resources, sewer resources, and whatever else we may need, funded entirely by Development International."

"On whose land?" Ulibarri snapped.

"I would guess, ours," Gray interrupted. He smiled at Olveda. "Correct?"

The man nodded. "Exactly so. We do not own one square meter of Posadas County lands. All of this is rented, with what we think are generous terms. You will see in this proposal that we are asking only a modest longterm lease to drill two wells, and construct a state-inspected sewer reclamation system north of the development. That is all. A simple lease of the land itself, of the roughly seventeen acres of open prairie." With the laser, he outlined a rhomboid-shaped property that would provide significant cushion around the proposed facility.

"And funding?" This time, Janelle Waters raised both hands in question. "We know something of the private funding that Mr. Waddell enjoys out at *NightZone*, but that's all private property. You're requesting to tie in county and village land through lease."

"That is correct."

"And funding?" she repeated. "I see that you represent Development International. Who are they?" She looked over her half-glasses at Olveda. "Where are they based?"

"I am director of development, based now in Tucson, Arizona." Olveda's heavy accent and modest cadence contributed elegance and dignity to each word. "Our corporate offices are in Cochepek, Costa Rica. The actual corporate office *building* is included in the Tres Lagunas development." He reached across and tapped a computer key. A photo materialized on the screen showing a three-story office complex surrounded by dense vegetation. "This is Development International's corporate office. I'm surprised we get any work done at all." He coughed in self-deprecation. "It's less than a hundred yards from the tee of the twenty-seven-hole golf course."

Ulibarri grunted something and shook his head, but Arnie Gray beat him to the microphone.

"What you're really asking of us is that we join the twenty-first century," he said with a benign smile.

Olveda ducked his head. "I truly believe that your cooperation with Mr. Waddell's enthusiasm and far-sighted world view is helping to make this possible, Dr. Gray."

"And what if it don't work?" Ulibarri asked abruptly. "What if you build all this *stuff*, and nobody comes?" He didn't wait for an answer, but charged on. "Now look, this is pretty simple." He pointed an index finger at Jim Bergin. "Jim, you been with us for a long time. Since this *NightZone* thing started, how much has traffic at your airport increased?" The set of his jaw showed what he expected for an answer, since Jim Bergin's chuckles at Miles Waddell's expense were no secret.

Bergin partially rose, both hands on the arms of his chair. "About three hundred percent," he said, and sat back down. From a seated position, he added, "Last month, with all the corporate traffic, my fuel sales were up seven hundred percent." Ulibarri's face went blank, and Gray took the opportunity.

"Three times?" he said. "That's remarkable."

"They ain't tourists," Ulibarri grumbled. "When the building is done…"

"Nope, they're not," Bergin said, not bothering to stand up again. "Contractors, vendors, big-wigs from the California university that's sponsoring the radio telescope, just whoever. Last group to fly in was some outfit from Switzerland that's making the tramway cable." He shrugged.

"Okay," and Gray held up both hands. "This is all premature. Mr. Olveda, we all look forward to seeing your proposal. That's about all we can say today. We'll read it line by line, and put it on the agenda for next month's meeting. You'll need to be here for that. I'm sure there will be *endless* questions." He smiled, and motioned with his hand to include the audience. "Folks will want to know. But it's far too preliminary at this point to even discuss it. We'll read, and we'll ask Frank," and he nodded toward Frank Dayan, publisher of the *Posadas Register,* "to run a spread in the paper." He smiled again. "Should be quite a meeting."

Several hands shot up, and one man, an area rancher east of town, got to his feet. Gray held up both hands. "Now is not the time." Steel crept into his voice, and then he softened. "At this point, nobody knows nothin'. So we're not going to spend another minute—not today—on this idea. We all need to study first."

He lightly rapped the gavel. "Thanks for coming, Mr. Olveda. We'll be in touch. Mrs. St. Clair, you're next."

Even as the Director of the Posadas Medical Service rose to make her way to the microphone, Sheriff Robert Torrez left his seat and slipped out of the chambers. Evidently Commission Chairman Arnie Gray hadn't heard about the homicide at the south end of town, since he'd not asked questions about it. And since Frank Dayan wasn't dogging him, neither had the newspaper publisher. That was a good start for the day.

As he reached the building's double exit doors, he heard the sharp cracks of hard heels on tile. He glanced back and saw Lieutenant Mark Adams, and the state trooper held up a hand to rein in the sheriff.

"Got a minute?" he said as he joined the sheriff outside.

"Just about."

Chapter Eighteen

As he walked down the hall, Dr. Barry Cushman peeled off his skull cap and ran his fingers through his long red hair, bringing it back to some semblance of order. He laughed loudly at something Dr. Francis Guzman said, and then brightened as he saw Estelle rising from one of the waiting room chairs.

"Long time," he said, and offered a hand. Estelle took it, feeling the long, fine bones and the hard overlayment of muscles. Cushman may have just touched five feet six, but he seemed somehow larger, with his square shoulders and large head.

"Francis was just recounting to me the time that Sheriff Gastner escaped from a hospital room up in Albuquerque. With your complicity, I'm to understand."

"High times," Estelle smiled, and then favored her husband with a ferocious mock frown.

"Well, lemme tell ya, he ain't walkin' out this time," Cushman laid on his west Texas accent a little thicker. "The surgery went beautifully, though. Come on in and I'll show you the as-built."

As they walked across the hall to the hospital's staff lounge, Francis wrapped an arm around Estelle's shoulders. "It really did," he said. "*Padrino* behaved."

Moving to one of the computer terminals, Cushman typed in a password and his request. In a moment, a brilliantly clear X-ray portrait of a hip joint rolled into view. "The trouble with these, Mrs. Guzman, is that it'll serve him so well that he's going to be pestering for one on the other side too. And with the arthritis build up, that may not be so far in the future."

Estelle examined the massive rebuild of William K. Gastner's right hip—new polished socket, new upper titanium femur with a shiny billiard ball nestled into place. "He won't like it, but he'll be on his feet tomorrow." He stroked the image with slim fingers. "The sooner this whole gadget starts to bear some weight, the better it will be."

"What are we looking at, then?"

Cushman made a speculative face. "Mr. Gastner is tough, but we have to be careful. He's had his share of med disasters over the years, so we have to be on our toes when it comes to things like clots in the lower legs. He'll be starting some exercises for that this afternoon, and wearing some nifty TEDs—those fashionable elastic stockings? Those will help. He's also been ignoring his prostititis, so he's going to love that catheter for a while. And a drainage tube or so at the wound site. In short, we're going to insult him just about every way we can for a few days. All that will make him mad enough that he'll be sure to cooperate with the PT folks to get out of here as soon as he can."

"So if all goes well, he may be released by Monday?"

"If all goes well, probably not. My goal is a week from tomorrow. And by then, he'll be shuffling along with a walker. In four months, you won't even know he had the surgery."

"Four months." Estelle looked across at her husband. "Camille might be able to stay for a couple of weeks," she said. "She's on the way."

Francis nodded. "She'll be a relentless coach, that's for sure."

"But the most important thing," Cushman interjected, "is that Mr. Gastner *must*…and I repeat that, *must*…pay attention to his meds. He'll have several, and the ones he was supposed to be taking will all have to be adjusted." He grinned. "I'm told that in the past, he's been something of a hardhead…a bit cavalier with the meds."

"Just a bit."

"Well, no longer. It's this simple. If he wants this whole thing to work, if he wants a normal post-op life, he's the one in charge. I made that very clear to him."

"I think he understands things like that." Estelle slipped her arm through her husband's. "And we'll make sure that he does what he's supposed to."

"And who's this?" Cushman said. The nurse had slipped through the door of the lounge so quietly that neither Estelle nor Francis had heard her.

She gestured toward her companion as if Estelle could see through the wall. "Sheriff Reyes-Guzman, do you have a moment?" The nurse nodded without waiting for an answer, and turned to her companion, still out of view in the hallway. "Have a good visit," the nurse said cheerfully.

"Thank you so much," he murmured. He stepped through the doorway, and they saw a middle-aged man of medium height and astonishing good looks, olive skin, brilliant black eyes and generous mouth, nose sculpted with just a hint of an aquiline curve at the bridge. The cuffs of his chinos broke neatly over dark brown, tasseled shoes, and the expensive golf shirt looked as if it had been pressed. He saw Estelle's startled expression and smiled, his teeth just crooked enough to add character and charm.

Estelle thrust out her hand as he approached. "Joel?" She had met him but once, decades before, but had been so struck then that she had never forgotten him.

"My sister commanded." He wrapped Estelle's hand in both of his.

"Caramba," she whispered. "*Padrino* will be so pleased."

"Maybe so."

"Dr. Barry Cushman and my husband, Dr. Francis." As the three men shook hands, Estelle added, "This is Joel Gastner, *Padrino's* oldest son."

"Ah." Cushman's eyebrows arched up. "Perfect timing, sir. Your father tolerated the surgery well, and is in ICU recovery at the moment." He turned and gestured toward the computer screen. "He's far too groggy to be responsive just now, but this gives you the inside story."

Joel Gastner slipped on a pair of half-glasses from a case clipped to his trouser pocket, and examined the image. "No other injuries from the fall?"

"None whatsoever."

Joel turned to Estelle. "Some sort of episode triggered it?"

"Not that we can determine. His feet just got tangled in cramped quarters and down he went."

"So unfortunately common with the elderly," Cushman added. "And in his case, there was the added complication of a torsional motion…a twisting. He managed to cause some real damage. Here—" He asked the computer something with a few deft key strokes, and a second X-ray image appeared to share the screen.

"This is the before view, and as you can see…"

"Ouch." Joel grimaced. Stared at the image for a few seconds, then reached out to indicate one edge of the shattered hip socket. "A little indication of arthritic erosion, maybe."

"No more than we would expect for a seventy-six-year-old patient." Cushman regarded Joel with interest. "What sort of work keeps you busy?"

"MedArchives International," Joel said.

"The firm out in San Diego?"

"That would be us."

"How interesting," Cushman said, and sounded as if he meant it. "Maybe sometime while you're here, I can corner you for a few minutes."

"Without a doubt."

Estelle smiled broadly, an expression not missed by Cushman.

"What?" he asked her.

"Nothing, doctor. *Sin duda,* he can give you the answers you want."

"Damn good timing, then. What do you do for MedArchives? Sales? Development?"

"This and that," Joel said. "At the moment, I'm president and CEO."

"Well, okay then," Cushman said with delight. "I certainly *do* want a few minutes of your time." He thrust out his hand again, shaking Joel's vigorously. "But, as of now..." He regarded the computer images again. "Mr. Gastner is our immediate worry. When did you last visit with your dad?"

"Well, make it about..." and he hesitated, calculating. "About twenty-seven years ago. We've spoken twice, briefly, since then."

"That's the way these things go, sometimes," Cushman nodded. "In any case, you made good time, and now you're here. You were able to catch a convenient flight?"

"Ah, very convenient. Our Gulfstream is at Las Cruces International. San Diego direct, and rented a car at the airport." He shrugged as if the logistics simply did not matter. "I'd like to see Dad for a few minutes, even if he's not awake."

"Certainly." Cushman glanced at his watch, then at Estelle. "What are your plans now, Mrs. Sheriff?"

"They're changing," she said. "I was going to find myself a room for tonight, unless Camille finds her way down here this evening. But with Joel here...if you're planning to stay for a bit?"

"I am. I have a meeting in Brussels on Monday that I really shouldn't miss, but until then. I really want to talk with Camille, too. She's flying commercial to Albuquerque?"

"And from there to here sometime today, I suppose," Estelle said.

"I'll be in touch with her, then. If need be, to smooth things out, I'll just hop up to ABQ and fetch her. You drove down, or rode in the ambulance?"

"I have my county car. Francis will be coordinating *Padrino's* post op and therapy, so as soon as he's free to go back to Posadas, we'll take my car."

An easy smile lit Joel's features. "Ah, hometown. Interesting stuff."

"May I show you where recovery is?" Cushman intervened.

"Of course." Joel started to follow him, then stopped. "And Mrs. Guzman, please make use of me while I'm here. Anything Dad needs, anything you need, just let me know." He handed her a business card, and pointed at one of the numbers. "That's the one in my pocket."

She nodded her thanks and watched Joel Gastner and Dr. Cushman walk down the hallway, both graceful as cats.

"He looks just like his mother," Estelle said to Francis. "A couple of decades ago, when I first saw him, I thought he was a movie star heart throb visiting town."

"Your heart throbbed, did it?" Francis laughed.

"Oh, *sí.*"

"Should I be jealous, Mrs. Guzman?"

"Ah, no." She smiled at Francis, and then her face grew serious. "I never knew what the original argument was between Joel and his dad, but I know that they didn't correspond much. When *Padrino* retired from the S.O., and we had that big party at the Don Juan? Not a word from Joel. Not even a simple card."

"Buddy came, though."

"Yes, Buddy came. He managed to break loose from the Navy for a week or so and drove here with his son. Camille also came. The other daughter called from Rhode Island with her congratulations. But nothing from Joel."

"At least he's here now, and that's a good start." He watched as Estelle drew out her phone and checked the screen. A deep, calculating frown puckered her thick black eyebrows. "What?"

"I was just thinking…"

"Do I get to know?"

"Joel mentioned that he has a Gulfstream, with a meeting in Brussels next week. So he could have me in Mazatlán in just a couple of hours."

Francis groaned. "And then what? You're going to charge around after all the bad guys with a borrowed machine gun?"

She grabbed him by the shoulder, a grip that softened and slid up to embrace the back of his neck. "Look, Naranjo said two men were *killed* just outside the theater. And *I* have reason to think that they're the ones who initiated the telephone scam with *Mamá*. Something is going on down there, and Francisco is right in the middle of it."

"And so you want to charge in." He raised an eyebrow. "And while you're down there, Bobby is left with a homicide here, no telling what Bill might need, and Camille is abandoned to her own devices?"

"I need to know that my son was safe, *querido*. I can't just *assume* that he is."

"Our son *is* safe. I imagine the *Teatro* is crawling with cops. If Tomás says it is, then it is. And Francisco says he has a personal escort now. So…" He wrapped a big hand around her wrist. "Not to mention that the Mexican police are not going to welcome you as anything other than being a proud mother. They're not going to issue you a rental M-16, *querida*."

"I can be the proud mother. It's just hard to do it from a distance." She felt a pang as the words just made sounds. The Mazatlán gig had been right there, in black and white, in the Leister bulletin. She had missed it.

"I know." He wrapped her in a bear hug. "Do you want me to call him?"

"Call who?"

"Francisco. Let me see if he'll tell me anything beyond what he's told you."

"You'll do that ASAP?"

"Sure. But let me finish up with Dr. Cushman first. We'll make sure Bill is out of the woods."

Chapter Nineteen

"So tell me about your new hobby as a life-sized target," Lieutenant Mark Adams said. He unwrapped a stick of gum, folded it neatly and popped it into his mouth. He offered the pack to Torrez, who declined.

Torrez stopped at his county SUV, parked in the No Parking Zone in front of the county building immediately beside the lieutenant's black State Police Tahoe. The lieutenant rested his forearms on the hood, his pot belly against the fender. He regarded Torrez expectantly. "If I was the target, they missed," Torrez said.

Adams waited, rhythmically chomping the gum. Eventually, the sheriff turned to face the State Policeman. "Here I am, drawin' down on the antelope," and he held his arms like a rifleman. "I don't hear or see nothin' else. Comes the time and I squeeze off a shot, and before I could bring the scope picture back into line for a look, blam. Just like that. The scope blows into a million pieces, one chunk catches me over the eye." He turned his head and pointed at the tiny mark.

"Shee-it." Adams squinted at the scab. "That ain't big enough for a purple heart. He shook his head in wonder. "How long before you heard the shot?"

"I wasn't countin'."

"But you *did* hear it."

"Yeah. I heard it."

Adams worked the gum for a moment. "Shot came from off to the right somewhere? What would that be, to the south? That's what Taber was telling me."

"She found the shooter's spot. Just about four hundred yards south."

Adams played with the wad of gum against the roof of his mouth. "That sucks, you know. You should have called us right then."

"Probably."

"And at that distance, he only missed you by eight or ten inches."

"Yup. 'Cept I don't think he missed. Shooter layin' prone, good rifle, no wind, no distractions? Someone shoots like that don't miss by eight inches."

"Oh, but he could've. I know guys who hunt all year, every year, and can't hit diddly-squat. But he could've. I mean, something like this, he had to be a professional, Bobby. And *they* don't miss an easy shot like that. Now, if the scope was a little bit off, he could have."

"Well, yeah," Torrez conceded. "Then why didn't he shoot again? He had a target. I was tryin' to make myself small under a bush."

"Goddamn, I bet you were. And you never saw him?"

"Nope."

"Taber says the shooter probably either thought you were dead and high-tailed it for his vehicle thinking it was a job well done, or knew you *weren't* but just wanted out of there without taking time for a second shot or being seen. Which means he wanted you alive."

"Seems so."

"Which means it was either a stupid spur-of-the-moment prank, or a warning for you. Which do you think it is, Sheriff?"

Torrez turned and rested his back against the fender, hiking up one boot to rest it on the tire. "If he wanted to kill me, he would've. And if he wanted to kill me, he wouldn't have bothered taking the coil wire off my truck."

"Taber didn't tell me about that."

"Yeah, well."

"You're confident that the dead guy your man found this morning down at the underpass is your shooter?"

"Yep. Good rifle for what he was doin'. Been fired. Has a suppressor fitted, although he didn't see the need to use it. We'll check the accuracy of the scope sight-in when it comes to that."

"Mears doing the run-up for you?" The lieutenant sounded perfectly content with not having the rifle in his department's possession.

"Yep. On both it and the forty-five."

"And look, I'm sorry that the crime scene van wasn't available, but there's a triple suicide-homicide thing up near Fence Lake for the one unit, and the other is stuck up north of Farmington. But the two guys that we were able to spring loose should be some help for your folks."

"'Preciate it."

Lieutenant Adams regarded the macadam parking lot. "You'll keep me posted?" It was a request, not a command. As the top law enforcement officer in the county—the *only* elected cop, the county sheriff didn't answer to the State Police, or any other agency. They could ignore him, certainly. But Adams knew that the Posadas County Sheriff's Department, under first Bill Gastner and now Robert Torrez, was an invaluable resource for his own desperately understaffed organization. Turf wars and pissing contests accomplished nothing. Providing a state escort for Gastner's ambulance the day before had been a natural thing for Adams to do, a natural tip of the hat to an old friend and ally.

"Sure," Torrez said.

"The thing that bothers me is the 'why', Bobby. You've pissed off somebody enough that he wanted to kill you? Couldn't do it face-to-face? Or if it's a warning—*why?* Warning you for what?"

Torrez shrugged. "Don't know."

"The only reason I can think of for a long-range warning like that," and the lieutenant paused to give his gum a series of quick chews with his incisors, "is that it's important that you *not* see who the trigger man was. Why the warning, I don't know. But I can understand doing it from a distance…anonymous, so to speak. The last thing the bastard wants is to confront you face-to-face."

"Could be."

Adams smiled at Torrez's refusal to jump in with conjectures, wild or otherwise. "I was surprised that Miles Waddell wasn't at the meeting this morning to hear that Olveda guy's presentation. I'd think he'd be mightily interested, considering what Olveda's outfit is proposing. Maybe even some competition for Waddel's own development."

"Maybe so." Torrez glanced at his watch and pushed himself away from the truck fender.

"Huh," Adams said in puzzlement, wishing that Torrez had an opinion that he cared to voice. "By the way, what's the latest on Bill?"

"Out of surgery, doing well in recovery."

"Estelle going to be down there for a while?"

"I would guess so."

The lieutenant smiled broadly, both at Torrez's taciturn replies and at what he was about to ask next. "You're still holding the captaincy open until after the election?"

"Sure. The job's yours the day you retire from the state— the day after the election." A trace of a smile lit his handsome features.

"No, no, the job's *yours* then," Adams laughed again and glanced at his watch. "Where you headed now?"

"Waddell's the guy I want to talk to. He's got this big-time security outfit workin' for him now, and I want to find out what *they* know."

"And you already know who they got workin' the gate, Sheriff."

"Yeah, I do."

"Why don't you ride up with me? Just leave the bus here. If you don't mind, I'd like to hear what Waddell and his gang have to say."

Torrez hesitated, then shrugged. "Hell, yes. I'll help you waste state gas." A quick reaction of surprise crossed Adam's face. The lieutenant would have wagered that Torrez would refuse the ride, more comfortable in his own vehicular office.

As they settled into the SUV, Adams glanced at his passenger. "Promotion list came out the other day."

"Okay."

"Captain's list is pretty short. I'm not on it."

"Huh. Their mistake."

"Maybe so. All politics. You got to kiss the right ass. Thinking about it now, I'm not sure I want the job. You don't see too many captains out on the road, havin' fun. They push papers mostly."

"Not *my* captain," the sheriff said. "We ain't got time for paperwork."

They rode in comparative silence for a while, the radio chatter intruding at regular intervals. Adams chose to take the southern route on State 56, and twenty minutes later, as they turned onto County Road 14 and headed north toward the observatory development, he glanced at Torrez.

"You got the antelope, though."

"Yep."

"Well, that's the important thing."

"I guess." It didn't appear that Torrez understood that Adams meant the comment as a joke.

"If the shooter hadn't left by then, weren't you taking a chance? He could have shot your ass off while your fiddling around field dressing that carcass."

"Not much of a chance. He was gone by then."

"How do you *know* that?"

Torrez didn't respond for a moment. "Just do," he said finally. Shifting uncomfortably in the cramped seat, he added, "I covered the top of the hill, where I could look down at the road. Got there in time to see a truck leaving the area, and we stopped 'em down on Fifty-Six. Turns out it was this Olveda guy."

"That's what Sergeant Taber was telling me. The kid stopped him. Young Parnelli Pasquale."

Torrez nodded. "Olveda said he was out there just cruisin'. Looking the development over. He says he drove by on the county road, even noticed that the hood of my truck wasn't latched. That's when I seen him."

"He never got out of his truck?"

"Nope."

"I'll be damned. And the shooter, now…he found you even though not a soul in this county knows that old truck belongs to you…" The crow's feet around his eyes twinkled. "Does Waddell give lots of locals permission to hunt out here on his property?"

"Not lots. I don't know. Maybe not anybody else. I never asked him. I don't see nobody when I go out, though."

"So just you?"

"Well, probably. Once in a while a Texan trying his luck, but he's usually lost."

Heading north, they followed three dust clouds spaced a quarter of a mile apart, big yellow belly-dump ore trucks headed toward the mesa. "What's your bet?" Adams leaned forward, looking up toward the mesa. "They heading for the top, or down below?"

"Last I was up there, they were workin' on one of the big sewage treatment fields out behind where the hotel is gonna be. So I'd guess top."

"Then I don't want to be stuck behind 'em," the trooper said, and punched the gas. Within seconds he had pulled closer to the third in train, and lit the roof light bar. The ore truck eased toward the narrow shoulder when the road swept around a dense grove of scrub, and they shot through the red cloud of dust. All three trucks were running heavy, and with little wind, the red billow hung tight over the road.

"They're running over from McInerney's." Adams made a face and squinted against the dust. "Hell of a contract he landed himself."

"Yep."

"That's one thing I'll give Waddell. He's sure keeping to his promise to shop local."

"Much as he can."

Adams waited a moment before a stretch of road straight and wide enough presented itself, and then he shot past the two lead semis. About six construction projects were going on in and around the huge lower parking lot, now sporting its fresh black coat of macadam. A large visitors' and registration center was wrapping itself around the jumble of house-sized boulders at the base of the mesa, along with what would be the gift shop, rest rooms, office complex, and the infrastructure for the tram car up the nearly sheer side of the mesa.

Even the small station for the narrow gauge locomotive was staked out on the east side of the lot. Since it functioned as efficiently in either forward or reverse, there was no point in turning the locomotive around—it would pull from Posadas to *NightZone*, and push on the return trip.

What had been an informal gate at the bottom of the mesa highway—the wide, spectacular access that wound up the side of the mesa to the 700 acres of the *NightZone* facility itself—was now a hi-tech archway with a gatehouse that reminded Torrez of a national park facility. None of the architecture spoke Old West—a look that Miles Waddell had been adamant about avoiding. Even his narrow gauge locomotive avoided the look of the rest of the state's narrow gauge offerings. At first he had investigated the purchase of a replica 1880s steam engine, but had quickly changed his mind. The propane-electric engine whose photo had been in the Posadas newspaper more than once was as modern and sleek as the Amtrak locomotives.

None of the park's design spoke of the modern West, either, full of howling, kerchiefed coyotes or out-of-place saguaro cacti. Rather, everything reminded visitors that, if mankind was going to observe and probe the universe, the world of hi-tech science and engineering was going to lead the way.

A small parking area at the gatehouse could accommodate half a dozen vehicles, and at the moment, only two were parked there—a small, tan Jeep and an older model sedan that Torrez recognized. The brown Chevy Impala was showing signs of a hard life. One spot light remained on the driver's side, the other just a hole in the windshield post. Two men stepped out of the gatehouse, one holding a clipboard and wearing work boots, chino trousers, and a short-sleeve shirt with crossed golf clubs over the left pocket. His companion, not yet over the thirty hump, wore cargo shorts and matching shirt. He also wore stout boots with colorful socks reaching halfway up his calves. If he had a fanny pack with water hanging from the belt, he'd be just another fashionable hiker. A black baseball cap scrunched blond curls. He raised a hand in salute to Torrez.

"The kid in hikin' duds is Rick Bueler, one of the USR chiefs," Torrez said.

"You're kidding."

"And that's himself." The lieutenant slowed the state Expedition and lowered the window. "Hey, Jer. I almost didn't recognize you in your work clothes."

Jerry Steward, looking a little more apprehensive than welcoming, stepped up to the vehicle door. As he did so, he glanced back, as if to make sure that Bueler was at his side.

"Gents," he greeted. The grin spread across his face. In person, Steward was Mr. Affability himself. That good nature didn't wash over into his hobby of editorial writing, or to his political adventures. In his run for sheriff, he'd accused the department of financial profligacy, irresponsibility, and general incompetence—charges that Torrez had ignored, or, perhaps since the sheriff rarely read the local paper or listened to grapevine gossip, he hadn't even heard. Somehow, Steward had managed to win the endorsement of the Posadas Democratic Party, vacant since no one wanted to spend money being a sacrificial lamb against Torrez, an independent candidate who couldn't be beaten. No one gave Steward a snowball's chance of winning.

Sheriff Torrez wondered how Steward had gotten through the interviews with United Security Resources. He had somehow impressed Rick Bueler enough to win his new front gate job. Maybe affability was the criteria. His clothing bore nothing indicating his association with USR. That also was a Waddell criteria for his security team. No black Suburbans, no intimidating uniforms, no show of weaponry.

"Good morning to you both." Steward leaned against the door, the grin spreading. His wide, round face was sunburned, his pug nose peeling. Bright blue eyes regarded the two officers, first one and then the other, as if he was having trouble figuring out who was in charge of the field trip. Then he leaned back and eyed the State Police SUV with admiration. "We could use a few rigs like this one, L.T." He patted the door. "You know, I think this is the first time I've seen the two of you together, come to think of it. Which one of you is in trouble?" He turned to make sure Rick Bueler had heard his joke.

Mark Adams, not to be outdone in the affability game, reached over and shook Steward's hand. "Things going well for you?" Although Steward might have been interested in their presence, Bueler apparently was not. He'd walked away far enough that he could talk uninterrupted on his cell phone, and watched the progress of the incoming ore trucks as he did so.

"Busy," Steward said. "This place is a whirlwind."

"We're going up top," the lieutenant said. "We got some big rigs trucks coming up behind us, so…" He let the SUV idle forward. "Is Waddell in the neighborhood?"

"I just talked to him," Bueler offered, and nodded toward Torrez. "He's topside. Sheriff, how's your world today? Is there something specific I can help you with?"

"Nope. Just Waddell."

Steward turned the clipboard toward Adams. "You gents want to sign in?"

Adams smile cooled just a touch, but he winked at Steward. "Nah, I don't think so." The deep, guttural sound of a big diesel's Jake brake echoed off the mesa side, and Adams glanced in his rearview mirror. "We'd best git."

As the Expedition eased forward, Steward looked at his sign-in sheet as if the names might appear there by magic. "Mr. Waddell was over at the reclamation site a bit ago."

"Thanks."

Looking back, Torrez saw the first of the three trucks round the curve past the parking lot. "That guy has a handshake like a dead fish." Adams grinned at Torrez. "First thing you know, we'll have to show a warrant to get up here."

"That's comin'," Torrez muttered. "Or a damn window sticker."

The road ahead appeared to offer direct travel to an endless horizon. Startling vistas marked every foot of the way, unmarred by signage. In the European tradition, the developer had adopted road markers painted on the highway itself. In fact, the road, smooth and well marked and guarded as it might be, was not intended for general tourist use. Work on the reinforced concrete root system for the center tramway tower had begun. When *NightZone* actually opened for visitors, access would be restricted to the tramway—both to avoid congestion or accidents on the mesa road, and to limit light pollution from automobiles.

"It's the aerie principle," Waddell had once said in a newspaper write-up. "If it *seems* inaccessible, it adds to the mystique. The tram access will be a convenient delight for visitors."

In the middle of a sweeping left-hand curve toward the south, Torrez's cell phone vibrated urgently, and he fished it out of his shirt pocket.

"Yep."

"Sheriff, this is Mears. Did I catch you at a bad time?"

"Nope."

"Okay. We fired the rifle, both with the suppressor and without. The windage is off by just about a foot to the right at three hundred yards. That's the best we could do."

Torrez mulled that in silence for a moment, then asked, "You used the machine rest?"

"Yes, sir."

"Consistent?"

"Yes, sir. I grouped it at a hundred yards first. Shot five rounds that measured under three-quarters of an inch. But…to the right. Tried it five different groups, same results each time."

Torrez stared out the window, the silence heavy. "Okay. Thanks." He was about to switch off, but added, "Any word from Las Cruces?"

"No, sir."

He ended the call. Adams looked across expectantly. "The rifle prints to the right." Torrez held his hands a foot apart.

Adams shuffled his gum around with his tongue for a moment, squinting at the road ahead. "So if that's the case, he held the crosshairs right on your ear."

"Looks like."

"Comforting thought, Roberto. Who did you piss off, anyway?"

Chapter Twenty

One tired blue eye opened a quarter of an inch, and wandered a little as the patient focused on Estelle's face. His cheek twitched as he tried for a wink.

"You can't imagine…what they told me…this morning." His raspy whisper came in three short spurts, each one requiring exhausting concentration.

"What was that, *Padrino?*"

"They said…that I'd be on my feet…later today."

"That's amazing."

His eyes brightened as if some internal switch had decided to work. "It amazes me, all right. With a quart or two of morphine…I can probably do anything." He reached across and palmed a small gadget. "They said…I could give myself a fix…whenever I needed it." He winked again. "They lied. This damn thing…is useless."

"I think it has a limiter of some kind, sir. So you don't over-do it."

"Jesus. Who the hell wants limiters?" He paused for a long moment, fingering the gadget. "That's missing half the fun."

"They want you to hurt *a little* bit, *Padrino*. Otherwise you'd loaf around all day and become a hopeless slug-a-bed. What *Mamá* calls a *flojonazo grande*."

"That sounds good." He raised his head a little. "Where are the hoodlums?"

"Carlos is home, and Francisco is enjoying Mexico."

"How is that going? The Mexico gig."

Estelle had told Gastner about the phone scam, and about the two dead men found in the alley in Mazatlán, not because he could do anything about it, but because he would chide her later if she *didn't* tell him. How much he remembered of what she'd told him was another issue.

"The concerts are going fine. They may go to the beach. They'll be home Sunday. Until then, I get to play the worried mom."

"Well, *don't* worry. Worry is a waste of time." He took a long, slow breath. "Easily said, huh."

"Oh, yes."

"What's Naranjo…?" Gastner stopped, his eyes drifting toward the door. He frowned, squinted, then closed one eye and squinted again. He reached up in slow motion to adjust his glasses. Estelle turned and saw Joel Gastner standing patiently in the doorway. Slowly, as if someone were turning up a rheostat, the old man's face wrinkled in puzzlement. "Well, son of a gun."

He held out a hand, a little shaky, and Joel advanced to the bed. He gripped his father's hand in both of his.

"What a goddamn time to chose to visit," Gastner said without a trace of accusation. "My God. Estelle, do you remember my son Joel?"

"I do indeed."

"That's good, because I almost don't." He lifted his head a little, scrutinizing his son. "My God, look at this guy. You look as if you should be the President of the United States or something." He relaxed back, closed his eyes in a long blink, and reopened them, relieved that the vision hadn't vanished. "When did you get in?"

"Earlier this morning." Joel turned and slipped his arm around Estelle's shoulders—a brotherly hug. "Caught up on some old times."

Joel's gaze turned to the bank of monitors, and then he leaned down close. "Are they managing your pain all right?"

A slight shrug sufficed. "The hell with that. What's the occasion?"

"I flew in earlier this morning." He nodded across at the post-op X-ray that hung on the viewer. "I had to see the pretty pictures for myself, you know."

Gastner nodded. "That's me, in all my glory. Pretty fancy, huh? Is this all Camille's doing?"

"She called me...yes." He rested a hand on his own chest. "Her command is my wish, or something like that." He concentrated on the X-ray image, then nodded in approval. "You know, Dad, I know about this Cushman guy who carved up on you. In fact, he's one of our clients." He stood with head cocked, gazing at the image for a long moment.

"You have any idea...how much that thing costs?" Gastner wheezed. "All that hardware?"

Joel smiled again. "Actually, I know *exactly* what it costs, Dad."

"Seems like kind of a waste to me."

"Well," the younger man said thoughtfully, "it beats a wheelchair, or walker, or even a cane when all is said and done. I guess they could just amputate at the neck."

Gastner watched his son for a moment, then glanced at Estelle as if she had the answers. She remained tactfully quiet, but understood the source of Gastner's question. He had enjoyed a hospital bed for heart attacks, strokes, gunshot wounds—any number of interesting episodes. His eldest son hadn't visited during those times. "So tell me...what's the occasion?"

Joel turned away from the X-ray and regarded his father. His expressive, dark eyes were gentle. "All the planets and stars aligned, Dad."

"Convenience is a wonderful thing," Gastner said gruffly. "I'd like to see you sometime when I'm on my feet." Despite the grumble, he made it sound not like a complaint, but instead a hopeful request.

"Count on it," Joel said without hesitation. "And if you think you're strong enough, the other news is that I'll head up to Albuquerque here in a few minutes and fetch the dragon lady. Her plane is about two hours out."

"Oh, my God. I'm finished." The two Gastners fell silent, eyes locked. Estelle watched from near the end of the bed, hands thrust in her trouser pockets. Besides one standing and one prone, the two men could not appear any more different. When on his feet, the seventy-six-year-old Gastner was two inches shy of six feet, less obese now than he used to be, but still compact and burly, hair buzz-cut close to his big round skull as a left-over habit from his Marine Corps days, blue eyes that could go from the warmth of a summer sky to flinty to ice cubes as the mood warranted.

An even five-foot eight with an elegant, slender build, his son favored his mother's dark Peruvian ancestry. The last time Estelle had seen him, Joel was an impossibly handsome teenager on his way to college, a kid whose eyes smoldered like a character from a pulp romance novel. He'd smoldered her way on an occasion or two, and she'd probably smoldered back. Too much water had slipped under the bridge since then.

She knew that twenty years had passed away without conversation between the two men—she was not privy to the reasons, but could guess that the passage of time had made petty whatever those reasons were. It was *Padrino* who broke the silence.

"Are you on a tight schedule?"

"Whatever we want it to be, Pop." Joel grinned. "I'm blessed with having a wonderful secretary, and an ambitious, take-charge vice-president. They assure me that MedArchives will get along just fine without me. My crew on the Grumman is content to rent a car at the airport and find all the good Mexican food restaurants in Las Cruces."

"Crew, yet."

"It's not a single-seater," Joel said.

"So you fly?"

Joel ducked his head. "I do, but not this one. Little puddle-jumpers are more my speed, not intercontinental. We took the Gulfstream because I have a meeting on Monday in Brussels; that's one I can't miss. Then I'll drop back for a few days, probably about Wednesday."

"Watch out for the antelopes on the runway," Gastner said.

"That's for sure. I heard about that." Joel Gastner puffed out his cheeks, surveying his father's white-sheeted form. "So, tell me how you managed all this."

"A clumsy fall is all. It's just that when you're old and fat, things break at the damnedest times. But now I'm all new— bionic, in fact." He reached over and squeezed the morphine button. "Better than ever. They're going to get me up today. I can't believe it." He frowned suddenly. "But my God, you've got better things to do than watch a stinky old man try to heal himself. It was great of you to stop by, though."

Joel turned to Estelle. "I feel as if I'm being dismissed," he chuckled. "Actually, I didn't just 'stop by.' What I'd *like* to do is enjoy your company while I have the chance, Pop. And it's been a while since I've had the opportunity to talk with Camille." He held up a hand. "Amend that. Since I was *talked to* by Camille."

"Put on your flak jacket, son." Gastner rested his left forearm carefully on his forehead. "Better she talks to you than to me, anyway." He moved his arm so he could see Joel more clearly. "So how long has this new company been keeping you busy? MedArchives? I haven't crossed tracks with that one."

"We launched twelve years ago. Basically what we do is archive medical records. In electronic form, of course."

"Huh. For whom?"

"Well, it started in Peru, believe it or not. And then one thing led to another. I guess you could call us global."

Estelle, quiet in the corner, wondered if the Peruvian connection had come about after the years Joel had spent in that country, the land of his mother's birth, working first for the Peace Corps, and then for a Catholic mission near the very town where his mother had been born. His mother had been proud of his field work, but a thunderstorm's wind sheer had smashed the airliner on which she was a passenger into the turf at Dallas-Fort Worth before Med-Archives was realized.

Gastner adjusted himself again so he could look more directly at his son, and then at Estelle. "You know, sweetheart, the last I heard, this guy was working…in some tiny village in the Andes that didn't even have a McDonald's."

Joel grinned. "True. My partner was the one who had the original idea. I can't make that claim to fame. He was the physician at the mission clinic, and his chief complaint was that there was no practical way of keeping medical records secure and available." Joel shrugged. "When you live with the 'Government of the Month Club,' things can get dicey. It turns out that saving records to another location far removed from the clinic itself was just what was needed. So that's what we do. Minimal equipment, and satellite contact for Internet, and there you go. Just an electronic cloud thing. It doesn't matter if the X-rays you want to save are in Las Cruces or a hut for a clinic in the Andes." He smiled at Gastner. "As long as there's a satellite going overhead once in a while."

Gastner regarded his son with mixed amusement and curiosity. "And he works for you, now. Your partner, I mean."

"Yes, he does. And about seventy-five other folks as well."

"So what's in Brussels?"

Joel's handsome face broke into a smile at the blunt question. "Well, it's about as preliminary as you can get. There's a group of bureaucrats who want to organize records for professional cyclists—it's all an outshoot of the doping mess. Press a key, and there are all the records for any rider. *Any* pro rider." He shrugged. "We'll see."

Gastner turned to Estelle. "What do you think about that?" But before she had a chance to respond, the old man added, "Well, if it's all the same to you folks…a nap is calling. If they're going to make me do any kind of work, I need my beauty sleep." Even as he finished the sentence, his voice had sunken to a slurred whisper, the morphine taking hold.

Joel Gastner watched him for a moment, then reached out and touched his hand. In a moment, he turned away and escorted Estelle back out into the hall. "What do you…?" He chopped off the sentence as Dr. Francis Guzman approached. "Here's the man to ask." He thrust out a hand and shook the physician's enthusiastically.

"Any surprises in the surgery, Doctor? That X-ray looks good."

"The best thing he has going for him is your visiting, Joel," Francis said. "He's an amazingly tough old bird, as we all know. And at this point, a positive attitude is number one. My guess is that he's going to get through this preliminary bout without the complications of pneumonia—he got lucky there. It's my understanding that his daughter is on the way, so *that* will help."

Joel looked at his watch. "I've alerted my crew, and the most convenient thing is for me to fetch her back here. Easier on everyone. And it gives my flight crew something to do."

"That would be good of you. The most important part of all of this is after the immediate post-op. When we're outlining his therapy schedule, trying to make it work with the way this old badger lives. We can't have him just ignoring his regimen." He grinned again. "'Cause you *know* that's exactly what he'll do."

"I'll help any way I can."

Francis turned to Estelle. "What are *you* going to do, *querida*?"

"I thought that as soon as Camille gets here, I'd head on back to Posadas. I'll stay here at the hospital until then."

"Smart lady, this," Joel chuckled.

"Come on. Be kind. Camille is a treasure, and I hope she is able to visit for a long time." Estelle reached out and linked an arm through Joel's. "And you too, *hermano*. Get this Brussels thing over with and come back for a decent visit."

"We'll see. I'll try to do that. I really will."

"The problem is that we have a couple of issues at the moment with the S.O.," Estelle said. "If *Padrino* has lots of company, it'll be a good time for me to slip away for a bit."

"I should ride with you back to Posadas, then," Francis said. "Cushman's got his team all lined out here, and they have their own way of doing things." He smiled. "I can buzz down now and then to make sure *Padrino* isn't hatching some escape plan." He watched with some amusement as Estelle turned on her cell phone. "Depending," he said as Estelle held up a hand to cover one ear.

"Guzman."

"Ah. I hope I find you well," Tomás Naranjo said, his voice barely a whisper.

"Colonel, it's good to hear from you." She turned to her husband and mouthed "Mexico," then walked over toward the window. Each time she heard the Mexican policeman's calm voice, her pulse hammered with anxiety. "I'm still at the hospital with *Padrino*. He's out of surgery, doing well, and the best news is that his oldest son Joel is here. I don't believe you've ever met him."

"That is good to hear. You are correct...I have never met the son. But I know that they have not been on the best of terms."

"That's true." Estelle wondered what little tendril had brought that bit of Gastner's family history to Naranjo's attention.

"And I have some news for you." Naranjo's said with uncharacteristic bluntness. "Does the name Hector Tamburro mean anything to you?"

Estelle frowned hard, blocking out the quiet conversation behind her. "Tamburro..." She spelled it aloud.

"That is correct."

"Then no. I don't think so."

"It would appear that is the name, the alias, if you will, used by this man Benedicte Mazón, from time to time. No one in the prison where he was incarcerated," and Naranjo added an elegant emphasis to the five syllables, "knew him by this name. By Mazón. To them, he was—is—Hector Tamburro."

"This man who claims to be an uncle of mine—he was in prison?" Like small pebbles that begin an avalanche, the incidents in Mexico gathered while she stood helpless, out of reach. She turned slightly and watched Joel Gastner as he chatted with her husband. *Padrino's* son had a jet that could whisk her to Mazatlán in two hours—the drive to the airport on the mesa outside Las Cruces would take nearly half as long as the flight deep into Mexico. Tomás Naranjo would clear the way through Mexican customs, he would have a car waiting. She realized he was speaking, his soft voice intruding on her thoughts.

"...it would appear so. Until a few months ago, in any case. We have only just established that Mazón and Tamburro are one and the same. Sometimes, the intelligence efficiency of these... *families*...is far superior to ours. The people we pursue set the rules, or so it sometimes seems."

"He escaped?"

"No. He was released. Let me ask you something." He cleared his throat, and Estelle heard the snap of something that sounded like a cigarette lighter. "You have no recollection of a *Tamburro* from the early years—or a Mazón, for that matter? I mean, of course, when you were a child. Or perhaps Teresa spoke of him."

"Tomás, I have no recollection of *any* uncles, except Reuben, who was a *great* uncle...Teresa's uncle." She shook her head in desperation. "And Teresa *isn't* my mother, as both you and I know. But I never heard who my parents were, and if she knows, she chooses to keep the information to herself, for whatever reason. For all purposes dear to me, Teresa is my mother, in all respects except the biological act that created me. I am satisfied with that."

Naranjo sighed. "Well, no matter. We may never know, or we may know shortly." Estelle wished she could adopt the calm, philosophical air of the Mexican policeman. "In any case," Naranjo continued, "the police in Mazatlán have gathered information that clearly this *Tamburro*, this Mazón, was directly involved in the death of the two men near the Teatro Angela Peralta. "

"*He* killed them?"

"That would appear to be the case."

"I want my son out of there."

"I understand your concern," Naranjo said, his voice now little more than a whisper. "But I would not advise you making a precipitous journey to Mazatlán at this time. As it happens, I am but moments away from that city myself, and I assure you it will give me great pleasure to contribute to the security surrounding your son. He is, after all, not only an international treasure now. He is the son of an old and dear friend."

"I prefer to think of him only as my son, Tomás."

"Of course. Of course. But let me share with you one other item of information."

"Sometimes I wish you were from New Jersey or some place like that, Tomás, so you would just blurt out exactly what you have to say."

He chuckled. "I apologize, my friend. Sometimes…" He stopped abruptly. "There is information that Señor Tamburro, or Mazón, has now fled the country."

"Fled to where?" *Let it be Argentina, or the Antarctic. South. Far, far south.*

"North, we are told."

"You don't mean just generally *north*, do you. Are you telling me that he's headed here?"

"I am afraid so. That is what our sources think. He does not work alone, you see. For a man who has spent so much of his life in prison, he has connections that are most impressive. Maybe his prison experience is exactly *why* he does have those very connections."

"Why…"

"I don't know, my friend. But it would be prudent to remain watchful."

"I want my son out of Mexico, Tomás."

"Will you give me just a couple of hours? I have the word of colleagues in Mazatlán that all is well. In just moments, I will check for myself, and be in contact with you. Can you wait that long?" When Estelle didn't answer, he added, "I would hate to think that we are not capable of providing adequate security for such an important event."

"When will you see him, exactly?"

She once more looked down the hall, and saw that Joel was following Dr. Cushman and two nurses into Bill Gastner's room. Her husband was lingering in the hall, watching her. Estelle caught his eye and held up a hand. "Two hours, you say?"

"Yes," Naranjo replied. "No more."

"I will be making preparations to arrive there myself. I have access to a plane that will make the trip in no more than that."

Even as she said it, she had second thoughts. Joel had not visited after all these years to provide air-taxi service.

"I would treasure seeing you again," Naranjo said smoothly. "But may I make a suggestion?"

"Of course."

"I haven't spoken with the sheriff about this matter. The sheriff should be apprised."

"Of course he should."

"Of every detail, my friend. There could be so many complications in times like these. Have you spoken with him recently?"

"No," Estelle replied, and her answer prompted a pang of conscience. Bill Gastner's surgery and her son's Mexican adventures—she hoped they were only that—had monopolized her thoughts, with Posadas County left to fend for itself. More doubts joined the chorus. It had been so easy to imagine Joel Gastner's agreeing to fly his handsome corporate jet to Mazatlán at an instant's notice. How convenient. How simple to ask. And Joel would probably consent, possibly without giving it a second thought. And what then?

Instead of being at his father's bedside, with the possibility of a heartwarming reconciliation, Joel and his crew would sit at the airport in Mazatlán for who knew how long, while she played out the scenario of the worried mother. And she wouldn't be allowed to play much more than that, for Mexico didn't embrace armed cops arriving from across the border, interfering with what the Mexicans themselves could handle with aplomb. Colonel Naranjo had said so himself, in so many gentle, tactful words.

She palmed her cell phone and pushed the button. Sure enough, in a moment her eldest son's voice answered, and she detected a note of impatience in his tone after the caller I.D. flashed its message.

"Yeah, *Mamá*." In the background, she could hear voices and a single flute running scales and arpeggios—Mateo Atencio, she assumed.

She felt as if she had barged into the concert itself. "*Hijo,* do you remember a Mexican policeman named Tomás Naranjo?"

"Sure. I mean, I remember you talking about him a lot. I think I met him once when I was little. I remember I was impressed with his uniform."

"Well, even more so now," Estelle said. "He's a colonel. Anyway, he's headed your way. He should be at the theater in about two hours."

"Cripes, *Mamá*, we won't have room for an audience." He laughed. "There are so many cops around now that it's funny. Can you believe that they swept my piano *twice*? Who's going to put a bomb in the Steinway, for God's sakes?"

"Well, stay amused, *Hijo*. That's part of the price of being who you are."

"*Aye.*"

"Oh, *sí, aye*. When Tomás gets there, I want you to trust him. Do exactly what he says. Okay?"

"Sure. But me and Mateo are going to break out of here and go downtown in a few minutes, pick up some chicks, and do the local bars and stuff."

"Stop it, *Hijo.*"

He laughed loudly, and several voices babbled in the background. "It's my mom," he said without bothering to cover the mouthpiece. "She's worried." Directing his conversation once more to her, he added, "*Mamá*, I'm fine, Mateo's fine, the concerts are going to be fine, and we'll be careful, all right?" This time he covered the receiver, but she could still hear his voice. "*Mi mamá, Dona angustias.*"

"Yes, I'm a worrywart," she replied. "Call often, *Hijo.*"

"Sure. How's *Padrino* getting along?"

"Remarkably well." She wanted to settle into a long, warm conversation with her son, but she settled for, "We'll see you soon, *Mihijo.*"

Chapter Twenty-one

"How many miles is that?" Lieutenant Mark Adams asked. He stepped to the very edge of the rim rock, able to look down at the activity in the parking complex and the crews working on the base station and first tower of the tramway. Sure of his footing, he looked out once more toward the northeastern horizon, toward where Torrez had been hunting.

"That ridge along the county road, and then to the other side," Torrez replied. "I was parked just about where that dump truck is comin' up on…right *there.*"

Adams scanned the prairie with his binoculars. "So two or three miles from here."

"'Bout that."

The state officer fell silent for a moment. "Lots of places the shooter could have gone," he said.

"Taber found the Jeep tracks on down the road about a quarter mile." The sheriff swept his arm in an arc. "Parked over there where they're storin' those culverts. He parked right there, then cut around the south end of the ridge."

"How the *hell* could he have known where you were, though?"

"Don't see how. But that's what he did. He hiked around and then found his spot. Saw me out there, somehow. If you look back up the county road, there really ain't no place to go *west* of the road without gettin' tangled up with all the construction. So east makes sense. He guessed good."

"'He guessed good.'" Adams sounded unconvinced. "A man with a powerful set of binocs could have watched the whole thing from right here, Bobby. Played spotter. But then the logistics of calling in the rifle man at just the right time? Nah." He cocked his head. "Of course, anything could have been going on, and old numb-nuts down at the gate wouldn't have seen a thing." He turned at the sound of a vehicle. "It's himself."

Miles Waddell's diesel one-ton pickup idled to a stop behind Adams' state SUV. Riding with Waddell was the security chief, Rick Bueler. Carl Bendix, the contractor whom Torrez had talked to the day before, was wedged in the backseat. Bueler, small and lithe, slipped out and deferentially held the rear door as Bendix worked his bulk out. Waddell, neat as always in his pressed shirt and spotless jeans accented by his trademark purple scarf, unconsciously patted the front of the truck as he walked around it.

"Mornin', gents," he called affably. "I had a brilliant idea."

"You have plenty of those," Adams said.

"No, really." Waddell extended a hand to Sheriff Torrez. "You're lookin' good today, my friend. And Lieutenant." He released Torrez's hand and clasped Adams'. "Is this a new strategy in election politics now? You guys roaming around together? You have impromptu debates going, or what?" He waved at his companions. "You both know Rick Bueler, here? He's down from Colorado, doing a stint as my security chief until he finds us the best man for the permanent position. And Carl Bendix here is head man with Stout Construction Logistics." Waddell waited a few seconds while the round of handshaking finished. "Carl is the man who's going to make sure the tramway is the smoothest ride in the hemisphere." He twisted at the waist and looked down hill toward the activity.

"No, really," he said again to remind the men of his brilliant idea. "We got old Jerry Steward down below minding the gate. Now here you two are. We could have an impromptu press con-ference with the three of you sheriff candidates—a mini-debate." He glanced at his watch. "First time in the history of Posadas

County such has ever happened! See, I got Frank Dayan comin' out in a few minutes. Watts Helicopter Service is setting the first section of the tramway tower today if the wind doesn't pick up, and Frank wants pictures." Waddell's development at first had been an effortless bonanza for Dayan's *Posadas Register,* but the publisher's efforts at journalism had doubled and redoubled as the competitive pressure from larger media sources increased.

"You're so thoughtful, Miles," the State Police lieutenant said with exaggerated courtesy. "Fortunately, I have to be in Deming in a few minutes." He reached out a hand toward Torrez. "I'm sure the sheriff here will be happy to talk to Frank and Jerry both, though."

"*That's* gonna happen," Torrez muttered.

"Mr. Campaigner," Waddell laughed. "Carl tells me you had some luck out east with the antelope."

"Yep. One little guy."

Waddell turned and surveyed the laser-flat mesa top. "I think it's interesting. We still get 'em up here on top once in a while. Hell of a climb. I think they come up on the east side where there's some cuts in the rock. I never knew pronghorns favored that rugged country, but maybe they know something we don't."

Torrez thrust his hands in his back pockets. "Do you know a guy named Dominic Olveda?"

Waddell frowned, the sudden change of subject forcing him to take a moment to find the new mental tracks. "Sure I know him. Well, actually…" he waved a hand in dismissal in the general direction of Posadas, twenty-five miles off to the northeast…"he's the one who wants to develop the village's land at the airport, so he's over the horizon as far as I'm concerned. But look," and he included all the other men in his gesture, "this is how I see it." He patted the knot of his kerchief into perfect position. "The more we all work together, the better it's going to be for *everybody* in the long run. A hotel at the airport makes damn good sense to me. In fact, I don't see any reason why the train couldn't include that development as an official stop. I mean, how neat is that?"

"Hot stuff," Adams said. Bob Torrez remained silent, still scanning the country below.

"Olveda wants to do car rentals, and that's a good thing, since I *don't*," Miles Waddell said. "He's going to provide additional facilities for air traffic, and that'll benefit Jim Bergin. And see, that's something I can't do, short of building a whole new airport out here somewhere, which isn't going to happen. But see, you can't ignore air traffic when you're working out visitation figures. So the facility at the airport makes great sense, no matter who owns it. Everybody wins."

He smiled at the sheriff. "Now I know there are *some* folks who would rather see the country stay undeveloped, am I right? And I'm in sympathy with that. You can see here, I'm limiting what I'm doing to this mesa top and a small area down below. That's it. No housing, no malls, an absolute bare minimum of lights. This is an attraction that is a destination in itself. And it'll be so damned dark, you won't even know it's here come night-time. Olveda's plan just tags on to that. He'll make it easier for tourists who use air travel." He held up both hands, palm up. "Win, win." If he was fishing for a comment pro or con from Robert Torrez, he didn't get it.

"I saw him on the road yesterday." Torrez pointed at the county road down below with a jerk of the chin. "Has he come out here a lot?"

"Once or twice," Waddle nodded. "I toured him around both down below and up here. The day before yesterday, he spent about three hours with Jerry, seeing the sights. I was in Albuquerque."

"All this stuff Olveda plans…it seems like considerable risk," Adams said. "Lots of money in, without much of a guarantee of money out. You have a head start on him, but I guess the same could be said of this place."

"Sure," Waddell said easily. "That's the way of these things. But I look at it this way." He turned and encompassed the mesa top with both arms. "I have something here that no one else *in the world* has. No one." He pointed to the southwest, toward the area designated for the California university's radio telescope project that had already tied in with Waddell's vision. "Where else are the aficionados going to see something like the big dish? Visitors can sit in comfort and listen to deep space microwave background noise to their heart's content."

"Keeps folks like Steward employed," Adams laughed.

Waddell raised his eyebrows. "I hope it does more than that. And you know, he's done a good job for me. Turns out he has a useful talent." He glanced sideways at Bueler. "He's a statistician of some merit. I keep laying more on him in that regard. When some tourist wants to take a bird walk and asks if we have bifurcated needle-nosed cactus warblers, I want our bird pamphlet to report accurately—how many seen, where seen, and so forth. Ditto for coyotes, antelope, comets, you name it."

"Illegal aliens," Adams jokingly added.

"Well, that too. Steward is good at keeping track of stuff. Isn't he, Rick?" Bueler, whose personality didn't just bubble to the surface, nodded without much enthusiasm.

"You've probably heard we're investigating a homicide in town," Adams offered, and Torrez grimaced. He hadn't planned on mentioning the hunting incident, or his talk with Olveda, and most certainly not the homicide of the Jeep driver. There were too many loose ends to be snarled by lots of loose lips.

Undeterred, Adams added, "A fellow named Miguel Quesada, probably from Arizona by way of south of the border. Execution-style, over on that little piece of property just south of the interstate. If you hear anything you think we ought to know, we'll want to hear it."

"Miguel who?"

"Quesada." Adams spelled it for him.

Waddell's eyebrows drifted up. "Ah."

"Miguel Quesada," Adams prompted again.

"You know, that might have been the guy who was with Olveda a day or so ago. He never said a word...in fact, I'm not sure the guy even spoke English. When Olveda introduced him to me, he just nodded. I remember that."

"What'd he look like?" Torrez asked.

Waddell studied the ground. "Burly guy. Thick black hair with more pomade than I use in a year. I don't remember what he was wearing, except it was dark-colored." He shrugged. "That's as close as I can get." Waddell shook his head. "Our little town doesn't need anything like that," he said. "When you say 'execution-style,' what do you mean?"

Adams put his index finger under his own chin, cocked and released his thumb.

"Ugg. But what's the connection with out here?"

"I didn't say there was one," the state officer replied.

"No, but why else would you mention it to me, or be nosing around my doorstep?"

Torrez took a deep breath. He liked the State Police lieutenant most of the time, although the sheriff was acutely aware that he himself lacked the glad-handing skills Adams so effortlessly employed. But his philosophy of law enforcement public relations procedures differed radically. He had no trouble embracing the "need to know" rule. He knew others found him beyond taciturn, beyond tight-lipped. That, Sheriff Torrez had told his wife, Gayle, on more than one occasion, was their problem, not his.

Now a little irritated that Lieutenant Adams had so effortlessly gushed information to Waddell, Bueler, and Bendix, the sheriff chopped the conversation off. He didn't want the conversation to drift on to the next logical target—the single shot fired at him while hunting on Waddell's land.

"If you hear something you think we should know, holler," he said.

"Kind of a coincidence," Waddell added.

"What is?"

"Mr. Olveda is in town, talking up his projects. *He's* representing interests from down south. And then this Quesada fellow…*he's* evidently an associate of Olveda's, they're kickin' around together… we know what Olveda wants, or at least we think we do, but who the hell knows about Quesada. Maybe he's just a sidekick."

"One thing." Torrez's heavy-lidded eyes regarded Waddell evenly as he considered what he wanted to say. "You have lots of publicity out there now." He ticked off fingers. "You got newspaper. Radio. TV. Probably Internet…who knows. Lots of interest."

"All true," Waddell nodded. "And it's all workin' for me so far."

"So far." Torrez hesitated, and Adams jumped into the breach. He held up both hands, making a beckoning motion with all ten fingers.

"It's like attracting a bunch of Africanized bees from down south," he said. "You're attracting interests from south of the border, and I'm not saying that's a bad thing. If I were to guess, I'd have to say that it would be foolish to put roadblocks up to prevent international tourism." He reciprocated Waddell's nod. "But my suspicion is that you're getting more than that. Olveda represents international investments. I mean, you should have seen his presentation to the county commission. What he's planning?" Adams flashed a smile. "He's got as much backing as you do. But—we need to know who the hell this Quesada is…was…and who the hell he represents."

When Waddell didn't respond, Adams added, "Who's got vested interests in what. And where the money's coming from."

"What's Olveda say? I assume you've talked to him, now. About Quesada."

"That's comin'. He don't need to know we was up here, askin' about him," Torrez said.

"Well, in the 'for what it's worth department,' nobody has invested in this project other than me," Waddell said. "And the group from California with the big radio scope." He nodded with satisfaction. "Not that I haven't been asked, mind you."

"By who?" Torrez's question was blunt and Waddell took his time.

"Nothing serious. A couple of industrial firms were thinking of pursuing relocation to this property. I said no, even though the funds were solid."

"Miles, we're not talking about money on the table to help you build all this," Adams said. "We're talkin' about other people with other plans. Whoever Olveda and Quesada represent."

"The Development International group?"

"Maybe that. If you don't think they represent big money, big *international* money, then you're more naive than I thought," Adams said easily. He reached out a hand, ushering Waddell to one side. "Excuse us, gents." He beckoned to Torrez. He led them eastward until they were fifty yards from the trucks and the other two men.

Adams stopped, his back to the security chief and the contractor.

"Miles, you got to ask yourself why Quesada would take a long-range shot at the sheriff."

"You're shitting me." Waddell's surprise was not feigned.

"No. Our antelope hunter damn near got bagged himself. One rifle shot, from three or four hundred yards out. Missed Bobby's head by inches. Then the shooter takes off. Later, the S.O. finds the shooter dead, executed with one bullet through the head. The victim is our friend, *Señor* Quesada." Adams clamped a hand on Waddell's shoulder. "*None* of this goes any further than the three of us here. We know *who* fired at Bobby. We don't know *why*. But later that morning, here's the victim's buddy, Olveda, at a county commission meeting, cool and collected as you please. Either he didn't *know* that his associate is in the morgue with his head blown apart, or he's about the smoothest act this side of any border."

Torrez watched Waddell's face, and saw nothing but incredulity twist his features.

"Jesus. But you're okay?" He looked anxiously at Torrez.

"Yep."

"And you think the shooter was this Quesada fellow?"

"Most likely. About ninety-five percent likely."

"But why?"

When Torrez didn't respond, Adams said, "That's why we're here, Miles."

"We should be talking with Rick Bueler." Waddell glanced back at the truck where the two men waited.

"Nope," Torrez said quickly. "Not yet. Bueler works for a private security company, and we don't know yet what *he's* up to."

"And double that for your contractor, and *triple* it for your guy down at the gate," Adams said.

"You mean *Steward?*"

"That's who I mean. Until we know some agendas in all this," and he mimed a button-the-lip gesture.

"So what now? Christ, Sheriff, *this* is the sort of thing I can't afford."

"Just keep your eyes open." He took a deep breath. "And we need to know exactly when Olveda was here the past few days. Exactly. Steward keeps a log sheet, right?"

"Right. He does meticulous work."

Torrez nodded.

"So you think that Olveda and this dead guy are in this together somehow?"

"Got to be. Why would they drive out here together if that wasn't the deal?"

"Well, sure," Waddell nodded. "Of course. You're telling me that this Olveda isn't exactly who he seems to be, then. Not if he's traveling around with some heavy muscle body guard or something. Some hit man sort of deal."

"You said that, not me," Adams said easily.

"Well, that's how it looks. Is that the direction you're going with all this?"

Torrez almost smiled. "If I knew what direction I was goin', I wouldn't be standing here in the hot sun talkin'."

"Look," Waddell said. "I'll talk to Steward. I'll be discreet."

"Don't bother. I'll just look at his log on the way down the hill."

"That shouldn't be a problem."

"It ain't gonna be a problem," Torrez said.

Waddell started to turn back toward the truck. He stopped abruptly. "Bill is doing all right?"

"Far as I know. He's got a phone in his room. Give him a call."

Waddell nodded. "I'll do that today."

"Give him something to think about," the sheriff said.

"You bet."

To Torrez, it sounded as if Waddell thought that an old broken man in a hospital bed a hundred miles away was just the ally he needed.

Chapter Twenty-two

"How does a medical records company make enough money to afford a transcontinental corporate jet?" Bill Gastner's eyes were closed, but obviously his brain wasn't. Face ashen after a "therapy" session commanded by a jovial young man intent on torture, a session that included nothing more than stretching the patient's toes, foot, and knee through a narrow, careful range of movements, Gastner lay quietly with his hands folded on his belly.

Estelle Reyes-Guzman pushed herself out of the chair in which she'd been curled for the past hour, and the patient opened one eye.

"What are you still doing here?"

"We can't afford an officer posted in the hall, sir."

Gastner grunted. "You didn't answer my question."

"About the jet?"

"He stores medical records for people, and that earns enough to be a jetsetter? Enough to have a flight crew on stand-by out at the airport? To run a whole Goddamn company?"

"Yes, yes, and yes, *Padrino.*"

"I find that hard to believe." He finally opened both eyes and regarded the ceiling, his heavy brows frowning. "What's this fancy hip going to cost me…fifty grand?"

"If you're lucky."

"If my insurance is lucky, you mean." He reached back and bunched his pillow forward. "They're going to give me hell for not going to a VA joint, you know." He waved a hand in dismissal. "So if this hospital sends my records to Joel for safe-keeping, stored away in that great cyber-file in the sky, what do you suppose they have to pay for that privilege?"

"It's certainly not eleven ninety-five plus tax, *Padrino*."

He huffed a laugh. "That fancy jet sucks that much jet fuel in thirty seconds."

"If his firm has contracts with hundreds—maybe thousands—of medical centers around the world, and an equal crowd of physicians, dentists, maybe even veterinarians, then the jet will dine well."

"Remember the days of those nice long brown lines of patient file folders in the doctor's office? How simple that was."

"Until the doctor dies, or moves, or retires," Estelle said. "Or until there's a fire or flood or who knows what that destroys the files. Then it would be pretty nice just to click a button and draw on that cyber-library."

"Sure...until *that* all collapses. Does Francis do this cyber stuff at the clinic?"

"He has cloud storage—I don't know with whom."

"Now I'm curious," Gastner said, and Estelle was pleased at the color that was creeping back into his cheeks. "Maybe he'll tell me what he pays for that archival service, and we can extrapolate from that."

Estelle stepped close to the bed, rested a hand on Gastner's pillow and leaned down until she was looking him square in the eye, their faces six inches apart.

"*Padrino,* why not just talk with Joel?" she whispered. "I'm sure he'll tell you anything you want to know."

Looking vexed, Gastner examined the IV feed in his arm. "I can't do that."

"Whyever not ?" She straightened up, drawing back a little.

"Has Francisco or Carlos ever asked you questions that you can't—or won't—answer?"

"Not yet."

"Then you're a lucky lady, sweetheart." He nodded at the nurse who had appeared in the doorway. "And I know I should be smarter than I am about all this. He's my goddamn son, after all. I should be able to ask him anything." He beckoned to the nurse, adding as an aside, "Even about his 'partner.'"

"I know you, *Padrino*. And I know you haven't made an issue of that. You wouldn't."

"So you're saying that I'm a goddamn closet liberal?"

The nurse hovered near the end of the bed, and Estelle lowered her voice to a whisper. "Just talk to him, *Padrino.*"

"Sheriff Guzman?" The nurse sidled around to the side of the bed, uncharacteristically reticent about intruding on a private conversation.

"Yes, Melina?"

"Sheriff, there's a gentleman who would like to speak with you. He asked if he could meet with you down in the Coffee Corner?"

"Right now?"

"Yes, ma'am."

"I'll be right there." She patted the back of Gastner's hand. "Naps are good, *Padrino*. Indulge yourself.*"

He grunted in mock desperation. "Especially with Camille on the way. I want to be running laps by the time she gets here."

"*Sin duda, Padrino.*"

Down the polished tile floors beyond the ICU waiting room, past radiology, beyond a fleet of other offices and departments, the Coffee Corner nestled in a corner room with enough space for four small tables, a counter, and a rack of ultra-smarmy post cards. The smell of coffee that had been on the hot plate for too long overpowered any fragrance that might have escaped the wrapped baked goods provided by the hospital's auxiliary. An elderly hospital aide in pink stripes worked the counter, at the moment refilling the coffee cup dispenser, her back to the door.

The sole customer at the moment was a middle-aged man who sat at the table nearest the single window, hands cradled around a paper cup. Estelle watched him for a moment, his profile softened by the window light. He did not look up. Unbidden, a flood of intuition played games. *I know this man,* she thought, then immediately dismissed the notion. And although the man was alone in the coffee shop, he might not have been the one who had sent the messenger.

Whatever remained in the man's cup held his interest. Simply dressed in a white linen shirt with dark brown slacks that molded over a small but powerful body, the man peered through scholarly wire rim glasses. A physician on holiday? One of surgeon Barry Cushman's associates, perhaps, although he didn't favor those two ubiquitous badges of office—a white lab coat or a stethoscope around the neck.

He picked up the cup and gently swirled the liquid, his manner not the least bit animated or impatient. His hair, most likely jet black years ago, was neatly trimmed salt and pepper, zipped cleanly over his ears and at the back of his neck. Although clean shaven, the ghost of pale skin remained where a full mustache had once shaded his face.

The motion of drinking from the Styrofoam cup drew attention to his aquiline nose, the gently arched, almost bushy eyebrows, the slight pursing of his full lips. Estelle sucked in a ragged breath, realizing that she'd been frozen in place. She was wearing a trim, summer weight pants suit, and her left hand loosened the last button on the tan jacket, her right hand sweeping the jacket back. As her fingers touched the holstered Sig-Sauer, an electric shock ran up her arm, raced across to her neck and twinged through her jaw. There must be no confrontation in this quiet place.

She let her jacket fall back into place and touched the door with her left hand. Although she had made no noise, had not actually moved the partially open door to enter the shop, the man looked up as if the wild thudding of her heart had roused him. The coffee cup returned to the table. His bottomless eyes locked on hers, and the flicker of what might turn into a smile touched his lips. He rose slowly, as if intentionally giving her time to watch his every move.

"Sheriff Reyes-Guzman," he said, and bowed his head deferentially. He did not extend his hand. Estelle did not reply, but forced herself to take the time to inventory his person from head to toe. If he was armed, the weapon—knife, pistol, who knew—most likely would be concealed in the small of his back, easily covered by the loose shirt. His hands, a deep smooth olive, were unmarked, and she saw no tattoos on his neck or revealed by the V of his shirt.

Amused by her scrutiny, he set the coffee cup aside and spread his arms and hands out wide. He turned a full circle in place as if to say, "See...look at me. I am harmless." At that, the aging hospital volunteer behind the counter looked up. Unsure about what this strange ballet of body language might be about, she settled on hospitality.

"May I get something for you, honey?"

"Not just now. Would you excuse us for just a moment?" Estelle swept aside the tail of her jacket just far enough to expose the heavy county badge that rode on her belt.

Not slow to put two and two together, the lady had a heroine's streak. She lowered her voice a notch, but remained cheery. "Should I fetch someone?"

"No. No one. We're fine." A crinkling around the man's eyes reminded her of the same expression she'd seen not long ago when she'd examined her own tired features in the restroom mirror, and then laughed at the image. She'd washed her face then, but the crows' feet hadn't disappeared.

But she refused to acknowledge what she already knew—what she could feel running rampant through her emotions. This man whom she was sure that she had never seen before had called her by title and name. And his features called out to her. The coffee shop volunteer waddled out a side door, closing it silently behind her. She would mention the encounter, surely. Perhaps they had five minutes of privacy.

"How may I help you, Mr....?"

He didn't move from his spot by the table, didn't offer a hand. When he spoke, it was in Spanish, his rich accent combined with rapid, sharp-edged delivery completely devoid of the Spanglish so common along the border. "You do not know me," he said.

"We have never met, I regret to say." He smiled gently. "Actually, that's not true. We did meet, once—a lifetime ago. You a newborn, myself an impressionable twelve-year-old."

He appraised her frankly from head to toe, shaking his head as he did so. "Amazing." He held his hands an infant's length apart. "There you were, crying with all the lusty strength of a newborn, bathed in rain, naked and bloody and battered—but still astonishingly beautiful. So perfect."

Estelle remained silent. The man lifted his hands as if in appeal. "And now look at you. As beautiful a woman now as you were a perfect infant then."

When she again did not reply, he added, "I did speak briefly on the telephone with your younger son, Carlos. Perhaps he told you? Just in the few seconds we conversed, I could tell that he is a remarkable child." He ducked his head and extended his right hand. "My name is Benedicte Mazón."

The undersheriff regarded the man as her emotions ran the gamut. She ignored his offered hand, keeping the round table between them. Since old enough to think on such matters, she had come to regard Teresa Reyes as *Mamá*. Once old enough to understand, Estelle had known that she had been adopted by that gentle, childless widow, but that at some point in the distant past, of course she had had another family. If this man now facing her was somehow a part of that distant past—and worse, if he had some odd connection with the possible threat to her son in Mazatlán…

Her words felt as if she were forcing them through molasses. It seemed somehow important for this man to know that she had not been taken completely unaware by this encounter.

"Colonel Naranjo knows you as Hector Tamburro. Which am I to believe?"

The man smiled. "Ah, the good colonel. He is something of a legend, you know. A force of nature. It is astonishing that he has survived so long in these turbulent times."

"That could be taken as a threat."

"By no means," he said quickly. "Just an observation. The colonel is the reason I must be so careful now. He is a shadow in so many respects. But now I am here, safe in your country, and you are my concern." He lifted an instructing finger. "This *Tamburro* business—it is just a convenience. If you were to…to *mine* the records of Our Lady of Sorrows in Janos, you would find an entry for Mazón—Hector and his good wife Dulce, and their two children, Bernice and Teodoro. Their third child had yet to be born…but was promised in a matter of hours on that tragic day." He beckoned toward one of the white straight-backed chairs. "Will you consent to join me? Please." He remained standing until she had taken her place. She sat askew, right hand resting on the holstered handgun.

He once more folded his hands. "Would you care…?" and he nodded at the snack bar. "I know she has left us, but…"

She shook her head, refusing to be baited.

He regarded her, eyes bright. "You have grown into an astonishing young woman." When she did not reply, he continued, "I have caught sight of your husband, but only fleetingly. He is a busy man. A handsome man. Your children as well, I would wager. I have only seen Francisco in photographs and most of the time, those are taken from a considerable distance. But a few…"

"What do you want, *Señor?*" *Do not take the plunge,* she told herself, and let the blunt question suffice. She could feel the weight of the handcuffs, now looped over her belt behind her jacket. She knew that's what she *should* have done—taken this man into custody immediately, and let all the questions and revelations follow. He was certainly wanted by Mexican authorities—Naranjo had warned her about him. But she sat quietly. Mazón leaned forward, both hands still clasped together, the right cradling the left.

"Do you remember a man by the name of Guerrero from Tres Santos? Juan Guerrero?" Estelle said nothing, which Mazón took as assent. "He was a man of modest means, as are most in that village. A good wife, seven children. He still lives, although he is now in his late eighties. Perhaps older. His wife has long since passed, the children have moved away, save for a son who earns a living as a laborer and takes care of his father. His son and I were close at one time."

"What do you want, *Señor?*" She forced her tone to stay abrupt, official, disinterested. But her curiosity wanted to pull her into this strange man's story, a man who obviously knew something of her past that even she had never probed. And, in one of those rare moments of crystal-clear intuition, she recognized the electricity between herself and him—two people destined to meet. She forced up a wall of stiff authority, even though he was trusting her at this moment simply to *listen.*

Without answering, he watched her struggle, watched with interest as she withdrew her cell phone. "*Un momento,*" she said to him, and clicked the appropriate directory entry. The phone rang five times and automatically connected to her older son's voice mail.

"Call me ASAP," she said, and switched off.

Mazón could not have known whom she called—he could not see the face of her phone, and heard her mention no name. And yet he raised one hand as if to soothe. "Your son is safe, *Señora.* Trust me. He is well-protected now."

"Trust you?"

"You can, you know." He watched her settle into the chair, then leaned forward to clasp his hands together near the middle of the small table. He repeated slowly, this time in English, "You *can* trust me."

"I've heard that often enough from all kinds of people that I could *not* trust," Estelle replied softly. It would be easy to slam the handcuffs on his unprotected wrists…they lay on the table as if presented to her for just that purpose.

"I do not know what the colonel knows, or what he has told you. But what if I were to tell you what *I* know?"

"There is not much time." And then she held up a hand as she pulled out her vibrating phone. She instantly recognized the number and connected.

"I won't keep you, *hijo*. Just tell me. Is everything still all right down there?"

"Sure, Ma." Francisco had dropped the *Mamá*, settling instead for the teenager's abbreviated lingo as if that would assuage her worries, as if she were being so *silly* to worry. "But how is it with *you?*"

"A snarl," Estelle whispered. Her son knew better than to ask for an explanation.

"And *Padrino?*"

She heard a sea of voices in the background. "He's recovering nicely. His son is here."

"Buddy? The Navy pilot?"

"No. The older one. Joel."

"I've never met him."

"Maybe someday you will. Listen, *hijo*. Everything is as it should be?"

"Spectacular. You called me only a couple minutes ago, and I didn't have a chance to get back to you."

"I just need to know," she said. It would be such a luxury to settle into a long conversation with her son, a luxury neither of them could enjoy at the moment.

"We are fine." He laughed. "We are *fine*. We're about to rehearse with *Maestro* Durán. He's the counter-tenor I was telling you about. Just super cool stuff."

"And Mateo?" She wondered if the flute prodigy's parents, nestled in their little village in Texas, were as much a basket case as she was. Perhaps they had found a way to travel to Mexico to watch the performance.

"He's the *we,*" Francisco laughed. "Mateo and I, and the maestro. It's kind of a churchy piece by Handel for flute, piano, and voice. The audience tomorrow night will love it, even if they don't understand Latin."

"I wish I could be there."

"Well, I wish you could be, too. And, hey, every time we talk, I forgot to ask. How is Big Bad Bobby's baby doing?"

"Thriving," Estelle said, trying to sound lighthearted. "Gabe is just a wonderful little boy." As she spoke, she never let her gaze leave Mazón's face. Now just a white ghost remaining, at one time his drooping mustache had nearly hidden his mouth. Thick black eyebrows framed disarmingly expressive eyes. His nose, though broken at least once, added to his attraction.

"Yep," Francisco said in fair imitation of Bob Torrez. "Look *Mamá,* I really have to cut away. Somebody said the Maestro has finished his warm-ups, so here we go."

"Take care, *querido.*"

"Sure. Love you, Ma."

She switched off, irritated that Benedicte Mazón had made no effort to grant her privacy. He had listened to her half of the conversation with interest.

"So," he said. "All is well." It was a statement, not a question. "As I said."

"Why are you here?"

Mazón looked down at his hands. "I should tell you that I have just been released from prison after twenty-one years of incarceration." Despite the rapid cadence of his speech, his diction in English was fluent and clear. His eyes rose slowly to Estelle's. "I am fifty-three years old. I have spent thirty-six of those years in places too horrible to contemplate, *mi sobrina.*"

"Do not call me that," the undersheriff whispered.

He offered a small shrug. "Who can blame, eh? Suddenly," and he leaned back and spread his hands wide, "here I am, face-to-face with a niece until now merely a mystery to me. You have never seen me before, you do not know me." He leaned forward quickly. "Let me ask you this. Have you spoken with *Señor* Guerrero recently?"

"The old man in Tres Santos? No. I have no reason."

"No recollections?"

"None that are clear. I remember seeing him now and then when I was a child. I remember his wooden pushcart. He offered to give me a ride in it once, and I ran away. He would hardly remember me now." *Por Dios,* why was she telling a stranger this?

"*Señor* Guerrero will remember you as clearly as if it was yesterday. *Salvaste por los Ángeles* is what he calls you. *Saved by the angels.* To a simple man such as him, you are…" and this time he groped for the word. "That night—it is hard for him even to talk about it to this day, his heart was so charged by what he saw." He paused. "Tres Santos is but an hour's drive. You have but to talk with him. I imagine he will find it difficult, but it is a thing that should be done. You know…" and he stopped abruptly, staring at his hands. "He never talked with the woman who later adopted you about that night. He could not bring himself. In such a small town, of course, your mother knew the story well. Yet she did not tell you?"

Do not go there, she told herself. "So far, you have told me nothing, except that you've spent most of your life in prison, and that you know one or two people from my childhood."

"Ah," Mazón said, and twisted as he withdrew his wallet from a back pocket. The photograph that he fished out was a battered one, eight by ten and folded in quarters, a digital photo enlarged as big as the cheap paper would allow. He passed it to Estelle. "I have one of the prison guards to thank for this," he said. "A young man with more than his share of humanity who has aspirations for a book someday."

Estelle studied the photo carefully. It was bleak, in color so stark and muted that it could just as well have been black and white. The photographer had stood back from the iron bars and shot through them into the tiny, stark cell without the harsh shadows of a flash. Benedicte Mazón stood just left of center in the photo, head down, hands clasped behind his back, half glasses sliding down his nose like an old scholar lost in thought.

Two cell walls were visible, and both were papered with magazine articles and photographs. Without a magnifying glass, she could not assess the entire collection, but she could see enough. Light streamed in from a high, barred window on the left, casting the prisoner's face in the shadows. But the walls were illuminated, and presented a heart-wrenching record of her son Francisco's incredible career—solo in concert at age seven with the gigantic nine-foot long grand piano stretching away from his knobby little knees like a vast, black ocean; in concert with various orchestras; in impassioned duet with the child flutist, Mateo Atencio. Several publicity portrait shots also graced the wall, including the formal black and white study of him that had been used the past year for his concert in Posadas, New Mexico. Someone not intimately familiar with the photos would have had a hard time understanding the images, but to her, they were all achingly familiar.

"You may keep that, if you wish," Mazón said.

"No." She laid it on the table in front of him. "It's yours. I'm surprised that the prison guards allowed you this collection in your cell."

"Some were understanding. What harm in photographs?"

"And I repeat…so what? You have obviously followed my son's career closely for some time. That alone makes me nervous. And you have yet to say how all of this concerns *Señor* Guerrero in Tres Santos."

"Besides my twelve-year-old self, the old man is the only witness to the accident that killed your parents and your two siblings, *Señora* Guzman."

Chapter Twenty-three

"The fact that he hiked *around* the south end of the ridge to get you in his sights tells me that he was familiar with the country."

Torrez tried to stretch his long limbs in the confines of the state SUV. "That part ain't hard. I mean, it's obvious what the ridge does. But I wasn't lookin' behind me."

The sheriff fell silent, thinking through the previous day minute by minute. Miles Waddell had known the sheriff was hunting, but not when or exactly where. Had the developer seen the sheriff's aging pickup, he would have recognized it. Torrez had not told the Sheriff's Department dispatcher where he was. He had not told any of his staff, including Undersheriff Estelle Reyes Guzman. The hunt had been more a spur of the moment thing, prompted by perfect weather, mood, and no pressing engagements. Robert Torrez had had the time, and took advantage of it. The hunt wasn't a grand secret of some sort. He simply didn't *care* who knew. When he had left the house that morning, he hadn't even told Gayle what his plans were. She was used to that.

He tapped his knee impatiently as the State Police lieutenant guided the SUV down the hill at a conservative pace, closely followed by Miles Waddell's pickup.

At the bottom, Steward had already opened the gate, and stood expectantly on the right side of the road, trusty clipboard in hand.

"How well do you know this guy?" Adams asked.

"Little bit. He's been around for a long time."

Adams glanced in his rearview mirror. "Bueler didn't have much to say."

"Nope."

"I'd like to know what's on his mind."

Instead of driving through the gate, Adams pulled hard to the inside curbing, giving Waddell room to pass. The developer did, and parked just beyond the small security building.

"This ain't the best place to park," Steward said as he approached the State Police unit, but Adams was already out, letting the SUV's door swing closed behind him. The security guard added, "We got some big rigs that come through here."

"We won't be long," Adams said easily. Torrez joined the caucus, and Steward looked a little uneasy as Waddell and Bueler walked around the end of the gate.

The representative from United Security Resources had been quiet, Torrez thought, but what did he need to say, with the loquacious Waddell and Mark Adams leading the conversations?

"We need to see your log," the sheriff said to Steward.

Clearly uncomfortable with the request, the man looked down at the aluminum clipboard as if to say, "You mean this?"

"Anything they want, Jerry. Anytime, anything," Waddell said, and it wasn't a suggestion.

Steward passed the clipboard to Torrez, who studied it for a long moment. Another bottom-dump semi swung off the county road in a cloud of dust, and the lieutenant stepped out on the pavement and judged the clearance between the SUV and the guardrail.

"Lots of room," he announced.

"So who *doesn't* sign in?" Torrez asked.

Steward reached out and thumbed the thick sheaf of pages behind the cover page. "Everybody who comes up here signs in," he said officiously. A second semi appeared, the driver riding his Jake brake as he swung the monster off the county road, following the first one across the vast acreage of the parking lot. Both units slowed a bit as they neared the gate, but it was obvious they weren't stopping. Torrez waited until they passed, trailing clouds of residual dust and diesel fumes.

"Almost everybody," he said.

"Well, I mean *visitors,* you know," Steward said.

"When was the last time Olveda was here?"

"Who?"

"Dominic Olveda," the sheriff repeated.

"The guy from Tucson who wants to build out at the airport," Waddell prompted. "He's been here a couple times." He reached across for the clipboard, rifled through the pages, and then paused, holding the sheet out toward Torrez, thumb marking a signature, a classical flourish unlike any of the other scrawls on the page.

"That's him, there. Came out last Thursday. Last week."

"That's the only time?"

"I think," Waddell said, shuffling more pages, "it's the only time he signed."

"You know, we get busy," Steward flustered. "Sometimes there's a line here, and if I know 'em, well, on they go."

"And you know *him.*" Torrez studied the man, and Steward shrugged uncomfortably. "You spoke to him?"

"Oh, sure."

"He ever have anybody with him?"

"No, just the once."

Torrez's brows twitched with a mix of amusement and exasperation. "What's that mean?"

"No, I mean this Olveda fellow has visited a couple of times, and at least once, he had this other guy with him. Some Mexican guy." Steward's eyes flicked to Torrez and then away, as if he'd stepped in it. "I mean he…"

"What was his name?"

Steward took the clipboard back and scanned the signatures. After a moment, he flipped the pages and started the search all over again. "I don't guess that he signed it. Appears not."

Mark Adams looked across at Waddell, making no effort to conceal his grin.

"Good system you got going here," he said.

"You'd remember what he looked like?" Torrez asked.

"Oh, sure. Least I think so."

"I'll drop by with a photo today or tomorrow." The 'after' shot of the assassin that the medical examiner would produce after a little clean-up wouldn't be pretty, but the .45 slug had left his face more or less intact as it rattled around inside his skull.

"You got it," Steward said eagerly. "Now what's the deal, anyway?"

"Just curiosity," Adams said. "You know, it's quite a place you have here." He reached out and nudged Steward's arm. "Quite a responsibility for you."

"Oh, yeah," Steward said, the self-aggrandizement surfacing effortlessly.

Rick Bueler stepped closer to the sheriff as the group separated. "I'd like to see that photo when you have it. If you want me to come into the office, I'll be happy to do that."

Torrez regarded the man for a moment. "No problem with that."

"I've talked to Mr. Olveda twice up on top," Bueler added. "And once he did have company with him."

"What did they want?"

"Olveda was waiting to talk with Mr. Waddell. Actually both times. The other gentleman, I don't know. He was impressed with the view, I know that. He had binoculars, and spent some time just looking."

The sheriff nodded and started to walk across the highway, beckoning Bueler to follow. On the far side of the pavement, Torrez stopped, his back to the group. "What did Olveda want?"

"I don't know, sir."

"You didn't talk to Waddell afterward?"

"A little. I asked if there was anything I needed to know, and Mr. Waddell shrugged it off. He said that Olveda was scouting out opportunities for the guests at that hotel he's building at the

airport…things that would be available on *NightZone* property."
Bueler linked his fingers together. "He's thinking along the lines
of some sort of cooperative venture with Mr. Waddell."

"Like?"

"I don't know for certain. We have thousands of acres here,
though. And I know that Mr. Waddell is cranking out one idea
after another. I know that he was talking about earmarking the
arroyo wash area to the northeast for a bird-watching sanctuary.
And maybe the BLM caves to the west for spelunkers. I don't
know what Olveda wanted to suggest."

"When was all this?"

"He and the other gentleman were out here earlier in the week."

"Just this week, you mean?"

"Yes, sir. In fact, it was Monday. I'm certain of that."

"Describe him for me."

"Olveda, you mean?"

"His buddy," Torrez said patiently.

Bueler looked down at the ground. "Five-six or seven, maybe.
A real stump. Burly." He held his arms out to encircle a barrel.
"I'd say maybe he went two thirty, two forty. Not fat, but solid.
That day he was wearing blue jeans and kind of a fancy shirt."
He laid his hand on his chest. "Fancy stitching in the Mexican
style. Long, wavy hair combed back, heavy on the pomade.
Heavy features. No mustache, no beard, but sideburns down
even with his earlobes."

"He say anything?"

"Not a word. A nod for greeting, but that was all. In fact I
never heard him speak. I don't even know if he spoke English."

"Did Olveda ever call him by name?"

"No, sir."

"When Waddell arrived, you didn't stick around to hear the
conversation?"

"No, sir. I had things to do. Lots of bugs to work out. And
Miles Waddell is the boss." Bueler grinned. "What he says goes.
He does what he wants to do. The rest of us just try to keep up."

Torrez almost smiled and glanced back at the others across the road where the flustered Steward was engaged in conversation with his boss and Lieutenant Adams. "I can see that."

Chapter Twenty-four

"So long ago," Mazón sighed. "I was but ten years old that night. My brother was but twenty-two." He bowed his head slightly in deference. "You, *mi sobrina*, were but days away from entering this world had circumstances not interfered."

"I have no desire to relive ancient history," Estelle snapped, but even as she formed the words, she knew they rang false. How could she not be drawn into this?

But one issue, of even greater importance, loomed. "What do you *want*? Here and now...what is it that you want?"

Mazón took a deep breath and did not reply, perhaps searching for a strategy to draw her into his story.

"You are wanted by Mexican authorities on at least a double murder charge, maybe other charges as well," Estelle persisted. "You are obviously a fugitive in this country. I could arrest you now, and in short order, you would be in the hands of Mexican police. So." She paused expectantly. "I will do this one favor and grant you about thirty seconds. What do you want?"

Mazón looked pained. "The two men who died near the theater in Mazatlán," he said softly. "I knew them in prison." He grimaced and looked down at the table. "I talk too much there, to anyone who would listen. My pride is..." and he sat up straight, swelling his chest and holding his hands out as if presenting his heart to her. He lowered one hand to touch the folded paper, then both as he smoothed it out. "Of course you realize what a *gift* this young man, your son, brings to the world."

"I realize it very well. What do *you* want?"

"As worthless a life as I have led, still I recognize the treasure that *mi gran sobrino* represents. I do. And over some time, I came to understand that I had done a dreadful thing." He rested his hand on the pictures. "Displaying all this, talking with such pride…" He closed his eyes, hand still protecting the photo. "I provided a target for the unscrupulous predators."

"The men who tried to coerce money from an old woman?"

"That was one silly plan, and I told them so—these two silly Costa Ricans. An opportunity presented with this concert is all it was, and they jumped at the chance." Mazón fell silent for a moment. He had turned the photo and examined it. "When money wasn't immediately forthcoming, they began thinking. *Conspiring.*" He sighed heavily. "Do you recall when the prominent woman reporter came and interviewed you a couple of years ago?" He bent forward, squinting, and touched the photo near the upper right. "Here is the very article. The reporter talks about Teresa, that remarkable woman. And here…" He moved his finger to another larger photo. "This concert was in your village of Posadas just this year, and one of the portraits of the audience, enthralled, shows you and your family." He looked up at Estelle. "A glorious time. And I could not keep it to myself. I *reveled* in the experience, even though I could not be there. And I certainly talked to the wrong people. For that, I must make amends."

"And your cohorts hatched a plan when it became clear that extorting money from us, through Teresa Reyes, obviously wasn't going to work."

"That is correct. We were never sure, of course, when our release would actually happen." He smiled with resignation. "Perhaps you know something of the administration of Mexican prisons. But first thing you know, the three of us are free once again. And so the plan went forward. Although I beseeched them to abandon the conspiracy, I remained close. I saw it as the only way open to me to protect the artist."

"This kidnapping never would have worked either."

"As I said, that much became obvious very quickly. But they had heard of it working before, in other times, other places, this telephone game. Sometimes just for a thousand or two... trifling amounts. In their greed, they settled on a larger sum. As I said, a silly plan. Equally obvious was that there might be far more money to be gained by holding your son for some sort of ransom. They came to believe that. The Mazatlán experience provided the opportunity. I could not let them pose such a threat, so I..." He shrugged.

Air froze in Estelle's lungs. "When they first contacted my mother, they used Colonel Tomás Naranjo's name."

"They spoke of that scheme. At least one of the photographs includes the colonel's image as a family acquaintance, so I suppose they assumed..."

Two hospital employees entered the snack bar, and he fell silent. The men took their time pouring coffee and selecting just the right pastry before heading for a two-top in the corner. No matter how quietly Estelle whispered, they would be heard. And if Mazón had plans other than conversation, they could be at risk.

"Come outside with me." She kept her voice pleasant.

"Of course I would rather not do that," Mazón said.

"It was not a choice."

For a long moment he regarded her, and then smiled as he glanced over at the two other men. "I see so much of my brother in you." He shrugged. "As you wish."

In the relative anonymity of the hallway, Estelle dialed quickly and in a moment Naranjo's voice came on the line, overlaid with static and the click of other circuits.

"Can you hear me clearly?" she said, avoiding using his name.

"Let me call you back, my friend. I am at the airport in Mazatlán right now. Be patient but a few moments."

"I'm waiting with one in custody." She switched off before Naranjo could reply. She led Mazón out one of the staff exits that was prominently marked Authorized Personnel Only. The small courtyard fronted on utility parking, a chain-link fence defining the perimeter. As Mazón passed, she nudged a fist-sized rock between door and jamb.

"This looks like home," the Mexican said wryly.

"It'll work for some privacy," Estelle said. "Before anything else, give me a simple answer. Did you kill the two men in Mazatlán? The two found near the theater?"

"Yes. I had no choice. They were armed and determined. Most dangerous men. I was forced to act quickly, without mercy."

"And Mexican authorities know that you killed both men?"

"Yes." He grimaced. "Unfortunately, there was a witness who provided them with a useful description. The Mexican police can be most efficient when they want to be, what Hollywood says not withstanding."

Her phone vibrated, and she saw the international number. "Guzman."

"Everything is secure in Mazatlán," Naranjo said. "That was first and foremost my major concern. One of the officers assigned to the *teatro* happens to be an aficionado of performance music, and is aware of your son's astonishing career. Francisco's safety is now a personal crusade with the captain." Estelle's heart pounded. "But tell me…I wasn't sure I understood your message. We were somehow cut off."

"Mazón is here," she said. If Mazón felt threatened, he gave no indication. In fact, he walked over to the chain-link fence with its locked exterior gate and curled his fingers in the fencing, gazing out at the empty space beyond.

The phone was silent, and Estelle kept her eyes on her companion as she waiting.

"I had information that he was headed to New Mexico for other reasons," Naranjo said carefully. "It surprises me that he has found you in the hospital. Be very careful with this man, my friend. He is most resourceful and can be a dangerous adversary. He will almost certainly be armed."

"He admitted to killing the two men outside the theater. He claims self-defense."

"You mentioned custody just as the connection was broken. Is that the case?"

"In a manner of speaking."

"If he is *not*, then he should be. We have discovered that he has other business. Have you heard of a man named Miguel Quesada?"

"No."

"He was a companion of the two men who were murdered. In fact, I have a photograph, of less quality than I would like, of all *four* men photographed by a friend shortly after the brothers and Mazón were released from prison. The fourth man in the photo is Quesada. None of them are Mexican nationals, you know."

"Mazón mentioned something about Costa Rica."

"That is a possibility."

Mazón appeared to be occupied tracing the perimeter of the chain-link square with his index finger as he gazed at the parking lot beyond.

"This Quesada…do we know where he is?"

Naranjo didn't reply for a moment. "You haven't been in communication with Sheriff Torrez?"

"No."

"Ah." Naranjo let out a small breath, almost a chuckle cut off before it formed. "It is a challenge keeping track of both of you," the Mexican colonel said. "I have information that Mr. Quesada may have also headed north. It is interesting that both he and Mazón should do that."

"And Bobby knows this?"

"He does now, my friend. Your office faxed mine a gruesome photo of an apparent homicide victim. This Mr. Quesada, it would seem. He has run afoul of someone more dangerous than himself in your quaint village of Posadas."

"Mazón, you mean?"

"That is exactly what I mean. I do not believe that this man who claims to be your uncle is in the United States to attend a family picnic."

"I'm out of that loop at the moment," Estelle said. *Bobby doesn't talk, and apparently I don't listen.*

"Our belief is that Mr. Mazón may be responsible for Quesada's murder. A falling out among thieves, so to speak. When two rival groups argue, there is often a single man who *mediates* the problems, whatever they might be."

She avoided looking across the courtyard at the man who claimed to be her uncle. If what the Mexican colonel said was true, Mazón had been busy man—he would have had to travel from Mazatlán first to Posadas, then to Cruces. And his plans now?

"Please follow my advice, *Señora.* Take Mazón into secure custody right now, if you can do so safely. Call for assistance, I beg of you. And then we will find out all of the connections."

"All right. I'll be in touch."

"Be careful. I will be there late this evening or in the morning." *Let no border be a barrier,* Estelle thought. The colonel's red tape scissors was legendary.

"I'll let you know." She switched off and took a deep breath. Mazón turned away from the fence, his left hand lingering on the chain-link.

"So…" he prompted.

The sun was hot, bouncing off the plastered cinderblock walls, and Estelle unfastened the last button of her light jacket. She walked over to Mazón, her hands relaxed as she slipped the phone back into her pocket.

"There is so much…" the Mexican started to say, but he was totally unprepared for the speed with which Estelle moved. His right arm was vulnerable, and she drew the cuffs and smacked them over his wrist in one fluid motion, then slapped the other side through the chain-link down low, pulling his hand hard below waist level. As the cuff's lock ratcheted closed, she was already stepping back. Mazón made no move to test the strength of the handcuffs. Instead he regarded them with bemusement, tugging just enough to flex the fencing toward him a bit.

"This is so unnecessary," he said softly. His dark eyes held only puzzlement, and then darted toward the entranceway. Estelle heard the door swing away from the rock, and she turned to see a white-shirted security guard, half shielded by the heavy door. He hesitated to step outside.

"Everything all right here?" An older, stout fellow who at one time would have been powerfully burly, gave Estelle a quick once-over, his eyes then flicking to the fence.

"I need to borrow your cuffs," Estelle said.

"You want me to call someone?"

"Right now, I want your cuffs."

He withdrew them slowly from the leather belt holster, but hesitated. "You have some I.D.?" His eyes strayed to the badge on her belt. Slipping the small wallet from her hip pocket, she held it out so he could see the certification card.

"Posadas County," he said. "Huh. Your legendary old sheriff is in ICU."

"Yes, he is. The cuffs?"

"Oh, sure." He looked as if he wanted to say, "They cost $29.95, you know." He handed her the cuffs, and then backed up a step, once again commanding the door. "What's the deal here? I seen this fellow earlier, come to think."

"If you'd just secure the door, sir."

"You want backup? I should be calling the city."

"No. That's not necessary. This man is wanted in Posadas County, and that's where he's going."

"If you're arresting him, Las Cruces PD ought to be here, you know. This sure ain't your turf."

"He's not under arrest. The cuffs are preventative only—for his own safety."

The security guard looked puzzled, and watched as Estelle approached Mazón.

"Back up to the fence," she ordered. Docile and cooperative, Mazón swung his right arm back so she could easily cuff that wrist, and then secure it to his left. With him properly restrained, she keyed the second pair from the fence and snapped them closed on both wrists, freeing the security guard's set. "Do you have a key to this gate?" she asked as she tossed the extra set of cuffs back to their owner.

"Sure." Steering well clear of Mazón, the man fumbled out a large wad of keys and selected the wrong one. Estelle waited patiently, a hand on Mazón's locked wrists, while the search for the proper key continued. Finally, the lock clattered free and the gate swung open with a dry howl.

"Thank you." The parking lot was sizzling in midday. Her car was parked around two building wings, not far from the Emergency Room portico, and by the time they reached it, her hands were sweaty.

"Turn around and lean against the car, feet spread," she ordered.

Mazón vented a mighty sigh. "This is so unnecessary. I am no threat to you, *mi sobrina.*"

"Your record says otherwise, sir." She pushed him tight against the car, then frisked him, running her hands up his sides under the loose shirt. With one hand hard against the small of his back, she knelt and none-too-gently continued the search. The slender knife was in a sheath on the inside of his left thigh, two sheer straps binding it in place, so thin that the weapon would remain well concealed by the loose khaki of his trousers—doubly hidden since the handle would not show if he bent over.

With a flick of her wrist, she snapped open her own knife, pinched taut the fabric of his trousers, and sliced the fabric with a single stroke. She fished out the knife, a slender weapon with a white ceramic blade…a chef would have cherished it. "I see. Absolutely no threat at all." She opened the car's back door, using it as a shield between herself and Mazón. "Kick off your shoes."

"Ah," he exhaled loudly. "A strip search right here in a public parking lot?"

"It could come to that. The shoes."

He toed them off, stepping gingerly on the hot asphalt. Estelle ignored the footwear, but held the door securely. Mazón himself drew up as if he might refuse to duck inside the car.

"I will just vanish," he said. "The men in Mazatlán are dead. They were not even Mexican citizens, Sheriff."

"And so certainly worthless."

"Their account has nothing to do with you. Release me, and you will never see me again. You have my word."

"That's not the way it works." Rounding the door, she grabbed his right shoulder hard and spun him around, forcing his head down. He slid inside and she slammed the door. Picking up the shoes, she gave them a cursory inspection, including ripping out the sole pads. The shoes were just that—shoes, hiding nothing.

After sorting through the trunk to find what she needed, she slipped the shoes into a plastic evidence bag, and placed them in a cardboard box. When she returned to the cab, she started the engine and pushed the air conditioning to maximum. Mazón leaned forward. "Your mother gave birth to you on the bank of the river. It was Juan Guerrero who tried to save her, but the injuries were too great. He managed to save the newborn daughter. That was you."

With a sigh, Estelle twisted in her seat, looking long and hard at Mazón through the heavy-gauge security screen. "That's supposed to give you a free ticket to kill two men, maybe more? That's supposed to make me embrace you somehow, welcome you back into my life, protect you from the other men who no doubt are going to be coming after you?"

Mazón shook his head. "You misunderstand me, *mi sobrina.*"

"I don't think so."

"I had to do what I did to protect *mi gran sobrino.* That is my sole ambition. You must understand that. I'm not sure you appreciate the…" He sucked in a deep, shuddering breath, pressing back hard against the seat and the headrest with his eyes closed. "The *magnitude* of your son's accomplishments. The accomplishments that now bring such…such *pride,* such *honor,* to the family. I have ruined my own life. But now, please understand my motives."

"Oh, but I do. And he's safe. Thank you. I owe you nothing."

"Ay, you are a hard woman. So like your father in so many ways. Listen to me. That night is carved into my memory. A road crossing washed away, the mud so slick and impassable. He and the townspeople—myself included—stood on the bank the next day, looking at the wreckage down below."

He brought his hands up to his face, and the cadence of his speech increased until the words gushed in a torrent. "You see, I had been living in Ganos with my aunt since the loss of my parents...your grandparents...to the influenza. We were poor, you see. Desperately poor, as most of the families there are. After the crash, after your miraculous birth and rescue, as the only survivor of the tragedy, you were delivered to the church, to the convent. My aunt, in failing health herself, could not take you. A year later, just before her death, I heard my aunt say that you had been adopted by the school teacher, the widow. *Señora* Reyes."

Estelle sat quietly, watching him struggle with memories.

He shook his head with impatience. "You may want to know more about the years that followed, and your foster mother— the *Señora*—can certainly tell you. Yet there are other threats as well to your life here...to the life of your family. I have done what I can." He managed a wan smile. "There is some satisfaction for me in just the knowledge that your family now knows about me. I am alone now, you see. The *knowing* is important to me."

"You will be going to prison, you know that. Either here or in Mexico. For the rest of your life."

"You do not need to tell the authorities, *mi sobrina.*" He held up his cuffed hands, then amended his remark. "The *other* authorities."

She didn't reply, but turned around to face front. Pulling the car into gear, she maneuvered the cruiser to a spot under the Emergency Room portico, in the deep shade. Her husband answered his cell phone on the second ring.

"*Oso,* I need to head back to Posadas right now."

"Did something come up, *Querida?*"

"Oh, *sí.* Did you still want to ride back with me?"

"I think...well, maybe. Are you going to be able to visit with *Padrino* before you go?"

"I'll call him. I really need to be on the road. I have a passenger in custody." She glanced in the rearview mirror at Mazón, whose gaze seemed to be trying to bore holes into the back of her skull.

"In custody? What, did somebody back into your squad car, or what?"

"I wish it were that simple."

"Where are you?"

"Under the ER portico, ready to go."

Frances let out a long sigh. "I need a little more time than that. Look, I'll find somebody to run me back. Okay?"

"Call me when you're ready, *Oso.* I'll come and get you. Maybe bring Carlos to see *Padrino* this evening."

"That would be perfect. Hang on just a second, though. I'm almost there."

Estelle ducked her head and saw Francis Guzman's large blue-scrubbed figure approach the automatic doors. In a moment he was circling the car, and bent down at the driver's side window. "Does Bobby know you're headed back?"

"He will shortly, *Oso.*"

Unable to see clearly through the tinted rear windows, he bent down further and looked through the security grill.

"I have never had the pleasure," Mazón said.

"And now's not the time," Estelle snapped, and then added for her husband's benefit, "A Mexican national who shouldn't be here."

"And he goes back to Posadas?" Francis continued to stare at the prisoner, and Estelle wondered if he had made the connection. The family features were strong.

"As I said, it's not a simple matter." She patted the back of her husband's hand, and with considerable contortions they managed a kiss. "Things are going well with Francisco, *Oso.* Naranjo is with him just now. I don't know how he managed that."

"Maybe it's one of those 'don't ask' things, *querida.* But that's good news. Stay in touch." Francis straightened and took a step back from the car. "See you this evening."

By the time she guided the car out of the hospital's parking lot, she had dialed Naranjo, missed him, and left an urgent message to return the call. As she headed up the interstate ramp, she had informed Posadas dispatch that she was inbound with a prisoner in custody. She had driven no more than ten miles westbound on the interstate before a State Police cruiser pulled within five car-lengths behind her and stayed there all the way to the Posadas exit. Through it all, Benedicte Mazón uttered not a word.

Chapter Twenty-five

Estelle slumped in the chair and stared at the large schematic of the prairie, neatly drafted in colored markers on the white board. Straight lines marked the trajectories of the two bullets fired—one from Bobby Torrez's hunting rifle eastward to the small cartoon representing an antelope, the other another perpendicular, coming up from the south. No extraneous detail cluttered the artwork—just small numerals indicating the distances, each lettered in Sergeant Jackie Taber's draftsman's hand.

"Those are both *very* long shots," she said.

"Yup."

She glanced at Torrez, who lounged back, feet up on the conference table, chair tipped on its hind legs. "We're glad he's not as skilled a marksman as you are." The sheriff didn't reply. "You heard the shot?"

"Yep."

"And saw no one running afterward." He settled for a shake of the head. "And you saw no one following you out there."

"Nope."

"But you did see a pickup truck that turned out to be driven by Dominic Olveda shortly afterward?"

"Yep."

"And nothing to connect him in any way to the shooting."

"He ain't the type."

"He had some reason to be in that area, as I understand it."
The schematic showed the snake of the county road, and the

sheriff's pickup truck parked on the shoulder, and farther down the road, a question mark where Sergeant Taber had found tracks from a vehicle that could have been Miguel Quesada's Jeep. To the west, a dotted line marked the boundary of the Miles Waddell's astronomy park development.

"Olveda has been there a number of times."

"He's staying at the Posadas Inn?" The sheriff nodded. Estelle fell silent, hands clasped in front of her mouth. "Where you found Quesada is not far from there…just through the underpass."

"Little more than a tenth of a mile walkin' it."

"I wish you'd called me," she said after a moment.

"I didn't miss nothin'."

"That's not what I meant. I just should have been here. Another set of eyes. With some freak out there with a rifle…"

"Not anymore."

She laughed in spite of herself. "Front door, back door," she mused. "Do you actually have anything that directly links Quesada with the shot fired at you?"

"Just the sniper's rifle in his possession."

"No captured bullet, though."

"No."

"Lots of folks own what could be considered a sniper's rifle, Bobby."

"Costa Rican nationals on U.S. soil? With a suppressor?"

"*You* hunt prairie dogs with one." She smiled at Torrez. "Did you find any paperwork with Quesada that registered the suppressor?"

"Yep. He had it folded up in the rifle case with the gun. He was legal for that, if the paper's good. Don't know why he'd bother with it, kind of work he's in."

"Interesting rig for a Costa Rican national to be lugging around the states. How odd." She once more cupped her chin in her hands and closed her eyes. Torrez waited silently. "Why would Quesada shoot at you?"

"I got no idea."

"And out there in the middle of the prairie? If he wanted to take you out, there are lots easier places to do it. You're not exactly a shadow player in Posadas County."

"Yeah, well…"

"What if," Estelle said softly. "What if…?"

"What if what?"

She opened one eye and regarded the sheriff. "What if he didn't?" Torrez didn't reply. "It seems to me that you have nothing that links him to that shot, Bobby. Not a thing. No bullet, no shell casing, no clear vehicle tracks, no witnesses. The same goes for Olveda. He was out there, too, true enough. But he didn't make the shot, and why would he? You're at the top of the list of people with whom Olveda would have to work carefully and closely with that airport development of his."

She straightened up a little and placed both hands together on the table, then moved them to one side as if pushing something out of the way. "What if Quesada and Olveda have *nothing* to do with the attempt on you?"

Torrez pursed out his lips in thought. "You see your man involved in this?"

"I don't know. Naranjo thinks that Mazón is most likely linked to Quesada's killing, but he hasn't admitted to that. And if he did, we sure don't know the *why* of any of it."

"But he *does* admit to killing the two guys outside the theater in Mazatlán."

"Self defense, he claims. And to neutralize the threat against the boys."

"Maybe so. And you brought him in without a SWAT team's help." Torrez actually smiled, then piled a frown on top of it. "Two down in Mazatlán—the Mexican authorities are going to shout for extradition, you know." He studied Estelle for a moment. "So what do you want to do with him? Our guys will be finished processing him here in a minute. Possession of a concealed kitchen knife ain't much to hold him on."

Torrez pushed himself out of the chair, stretched, and then sat on the edge of the table, the fingers of his right hand idly pulling at a loose bit of stitching on his black boot. "We need to play this just right."

"You know," Estelle said, "what I'd like to do is meet the colonel at the airport and hand Mazón over, no fuss, no bother. That's what I *want* to do. The Great Wheels of Justice might have other ideas. Especially until we clarify any links he might have with the events involving you."

Torrez's eyes appeared to be closed, but after a moment he shrugged. "Did you get all the family background you wanted for yourself?"

The muscles along Estelle's jaw tightened, and she didn't answer for a long moment. "Right now, I don't know what I want, Bobby. First, I need to hear everything that Mazón can tell us. What his role in all of this might be. If he assassinated Quesada, I want to know why." She took a deep breath. "I don't have a sense of him yet, Bobby. I don't know if he did what he says he did—I don't know anything about his motives." She straightened up in the chair. "Why, why, why?"

"We're going to find out." Torrez frowned and looked down at his hands. "And if this guy *is* your uncle, what then?"

"It doesn't matter if he's my long-lost uncle or not. He goes to jail forever, regardless."

"After we pump him dry, you mean."

"Well, sure. I'll find out what I want to know. He's a blabby son-of-a-gun, and he has his own ulterior motives. He claims a large dose of family pride. Maybe. Maybe not. Who knows what he's been planning all these years, as he collects picture after picture? I'd like to know who's feeding him that material from the outside. I can't imagine that most Mexican prisons maintain a lending library and clip service."

Torrez stood up as the conference door opened. Lieutenant Tom Mears stuck his head in, and behind him, Estelle could see Mazón escorted by Deputy Tom Pasquale.

"Give us a minute, L.T.," Estelle said, and the door swung closed again. "He claims that he's been following my son's career for years, from inside prison. I don't know what he wants, other than playing the part of a proud and protective relative. I don't know, Bobby. Like I said, I can't get a sense of him yet."

"Is anything he's told you about your family true?"

"I don't know." She stood up and straightened her suit. "Maybe something is wrong with me. You know, some people spend their whole lives trying to track down relatives. I know I lost my family somehow. I could have pressed Teresa for details years ago, but I didn't…there was so much else to do. My life was on this side of the border, and I understood that early on. I have my own family, and Teresa is very much a part of that, and always has been. She's ninety-nine now, and I can't see upsetting her by pushing for painful details." She smiled. "You know, with his sense of historical detail, I think *Padrino* would be more anxious than I am to dive into the genealogy."

Torrez frowned and held up a hand. "When are you goin' back down to Cruces?"

"I thought I'd run down this evening, if things break loose."

"I want to talk with Gastner myself. Let's make it one trip."

"You got it." She touched his arm. "And it's not that I'm not curious, Bobby.

"Along with Teresa, Bill Gastner is as close to a grandparent as Carlos and Francisco have. My husband's parents are long gone, and that leaves just his Aunt Sofía. That's it. It would be appropriate for the boys to know a little something about their lineage."

Lost in thought, she looked out through the window at the blocks of the annex next door. More than four decades had slipped by since the old pickup truck had been swept off the dirt crossing and into the torrents. She knew that much of the legend now, and the rest she could imagine—the Mazón family (was that actually her family name?) wiped out in the roar of chocolate-colored water. One bloody, limp body pulled to shore, the rain pounding the woman's simple cotton dress hard against her awkward belly. Convulsions as death approached, and in one desperate, instinctive act, her body trying to save what it could.

Old Juan Guerrero—Estelle had only known him as 'old,' even though at the moment of her birth he would have been but forty himself—stood drenched and terrified less than a hundred yards from the warmth and safety of his own home and family. A half mile up a dirt lane, well away from the choked arroyo, Teresa Reyes may well have been wrapped in one of her treasured afghans, rocking beside a small reading light, oblivious to the events outside that would change her world.

Estelle knew that she would find Juan Guerrero, that she would talk with Teresa Reyes about that night, about the events during the year following, about Benedicte Mazón.

She took another deep breath and pushed herself out of the chair. "Let's get started."

Chapter Twenty-six

"I will cooperate completely," Benedicte Mazón said. "This is so unnecessary." Still, he didn't resist as Sheriff Robert Torrez loosened the cuffs from Mazón's left wrist and transferred the shackle to the heavy steel bar that ran under the rim of the table.

When Estelle had first seen the man who called himself her uncle, he had seemed wiry and strong...vital and sure of himself. Now, compared to Torrez's imposing physical presence, Mazón appeared frail, his olive skin sallow.

Earlier, he had grimaced with impatience when Estelle had presented the written Miranda form, reading it for him, indicating each box for an initial. His signature had been precise, even old-fashioned in its penmanship. He had handed the signed paper back to Estelle with deference, and now sat composed, his free left hand flat on the table surface.

Torrez ignored the man's comment and instead said to his undersheriff, "Naranjo says he's on his way?"

"He has a Beech Baron at his disposal, so he's already en route."

"Let's get some preliminaries out of the way before Schroeder shows up and complicates things." The district attorney, busier than usual with a full week of district court, would be nervous in Colonel Tomás Naranjo's presence. A born self-aggrandizer, the district attorney spent a good deal of energy trying to appear relaxed and in charge. But he was not as adept at cutting red tape as the Mexican colonel. Still, budgets being what they were, the district attorney might be willing to see this suspect released promptly into Mexican custody.

"What are you calling yourself now?" Torrez's eyes were heavy lidded, disinterested, almost bored. He looked as if he'd rather have been taking a nap. Estelle had briefed the sheriff in detail, relating the events that allegedly had taken place in Mazatlán, and even Mazón's version of the death of Estelle's family.

"My name is Benedicte Hernando Mazón." He bowed his head slightly.

"Colonel Naranjo informs us that you go by the name of Hector Tamburro."

"Well," and the man shrugged his shoulders.

"So which is it?"

"My name is Benedicte Hernando Mazón. I suppose there are times when another name is of some convenience."

Torrez regarded him silently, and Mazón met his gaze without flinching.

"And Miguel Quesada?"

"That is *not* a name I would use." He smiled faintly at his jest.

"Did you kill him?"

"This Quesada? I think *not*, Sheriff. I did not know that he was dead."

"Did you know him?"

Mazón shrugged. "Yes, I knew him."

"From where?" Estelle asked, and he turned to look at her, taking his time as he examined her face as if seeing her for the first time.

"From prison." He smiled tightly. "It is a place where you meet the most interesting people."

"Why were you in prison?"

Mazón looked amused. "For violating the laws of México, Sheriff."

Torrez raised one hand and turned it palm up, as if to say, "And?"

"They accused me in the death of another man."

"So you were in for murder."

"And never proven. But long ago, without what you might call an alibi? I enjoyed Mexican prison hospitality for a good many years."

"The four of you," Estelle said, her pencil pausing. "You, the Ortega brothers, and Miguel Quesada—the four of you hatched this plan to kidnap my son. And then…"

Mazón had already begun shaking his head vehemently, even before Estelle had finished the question. "What part of that is untrue?"

"I did not plan to kidnap my grand nephew," he said, this time using the English term. "I went along, perhaps, so I would know what the plan *was*. You see, I had to know. There was a good chance that the Ortegas and I would perhaps be released at the same time…or nearly so. If I could not dissuade them, then I would do what I could to *prevent* them from carrying out the plan. To do that, I had to know."

"What was Quesada's role in all this?"

"He…" and Mazón stopped short.

"He what?"

The Mexican stared down at the table, brow furrowed. "The man has certain skills, certain connections both in Mexico and his homeland. In fact, I came to know him far better than the brothers did. I knew that in all likelihood I would want to cross the border, perhaps permanently. Quesada had ways…"

"He was in prison with you all?"

"Yes. Before the Ortega brothers themselves were incarcerated, they worked for Quesada from time to time. Opportunists, you would call them."

"Do you know why Quesada was shot?"

"I can guess."

"And?"

Mazón hesitated, sliding the handcuff back and forth on the bar. "This is information that might have value to you."

"Yep."

The room fell silent.

"I do not wish to be turned over to authorities from my country."

"I suppose not."

"If you would help me avoid that…"

"Nope."

Mazón shifted in his chair and looked across at Estelle. "If I go back to México, I will never again see the outside of prison… and that is if I lived long enough to be arrested." He waited for a response and then added, "If I had not confronted the Ortega brothers…had I not responded the way I did, they would have kidnapped your son. I knew that they were planning to do that, but I had hope that something would interfere with their plans at the last moment. It did not."

"And so you shot them."

He sighed. "Had you been in that alley with me, you would have understood. These two brothers, they saw your son as the perfect opportunity. They tried the…" he hesitated, searching for the words…"the telephone business. That has become popular, and in some few cases, successful when the target is elderly and confused. I told them it would not accomplish what they thought, because *you, mi sobrina,* would be aware. As it turns out, I was right. Their plan was the foolish notion of amateurs."

"So you shot them, and left the country."

"I had to stop them that night. Here they were poised to slip into the theater and grab the boys. At that point, there had been no hints of trouble, and the theater's security, I confess, was not what it should have been. And the two brothers were armed. The risk was…" He shook his head and closed his eyes. "I had to do something."

Torrez grunted with impatience. "Afterward, you drove? Flew? What?"

"I flew to Juarez. I was fortunate. The police at the airport had not yet been alerted—and of course, even if they had been, they would not know who to look for. A simple what do you call it…a *commuter* flight. From Juarez, I drove across the border in a car borrowed from an old friend."

"Where's the car now?"

Mazón held up both hands in surrender. "It is parked in the hospital parking lot in Las Cruces. A rather nice little Miata. *Azul,* like the robin's egg. It has been my experience that the gentlemen who work at the border crossing have little interest in them."

"You've done this before."

He smiled and didn't answer.

"How did you learn that I was at the hospital at Las Cruces?"

"Young master Carlos so informed me." He held up a hand when he saw the anger flash across Estelle's face. "He is too young to be blamed, *mi sobrina,*" he added quickly.

"You were in Juarez when you called my home and talked with my son?"

Mazón hesitated just an instant, then nodded.

"So you drove from Juarez to Las Cruces?" Torrez's voice was nearly inaudible.

"Yes."

"To meet with who?"

The Mexican took a long, deep breath. "I had hoped to speak face-to-face with my niece."

"What for?"

Mazón looked puzzled at the sheriff's question, and he raised both hands as far as the cuffs would allow.

"After a lifetime, you want to know why I wished to speak with my only living relative?" He reached out and touched the corner of the photograph of his cell. "After all this time, this is the only proof I have, you see. I am hoping that Señor Guerrero might have memories of that night, the night of the tragedy that orphaned…" He shook his head. "So you want to know *why?*"

"Yep."

Mazón's laugh was sharp and cut off abruptly. "You are an amusing man, Sheriff. I assume you have no family of your own?"

"We ain't talkin' about me," Torrez snapped. "Tell me how you know this Quesada guy."

"At first, only in passing. He was more an acquaintance of the brothers' than of mine, and I will say that he wasn't a conversational man…not the sort with whom I might spent long moments in pleasant exchange. But later, we talked. I gathered that from time to time, he worked with *Señor* Olveda, a fellow Costa Rican—a man with grand plans for your country, I am told."

"Why was he in prison?"

"Quesada?" Mazón frowned. "As strange as it may seem, I do not know."

"When was the last time you saw him?"

"He was with the brothers briefly in Mazatlán. We met at a restaurant there, celebrating the good life *outside* of prison. That is when I tried to talk the brothers out of their plan to kidnap the two boys. Even Quesada told them that it was both foolhardy and dangerous to consider such a thing. I know they had asked him for help." Mazón shrugged. "He refused."

"They went ahead anyway?"

"Yes. I finally agreed to help them. But only as a way to find a way to stop them."

"You came to this country because?" Estelle asked.

"I have said, and it is obvious. In Mexico, I am a wanted man. But more than that. I came to meet you, perhaps to see the family. And if I can find a way to avoid returning to Mexico, I will do so. With my record…it is easier for the authorities to look at the two killings as murder rather than self-defense."

Estelle relaxed back, her eyes never leaving Mazón's face. "Especially when the Ortegas both died after being shot from behind. One of them had a gun, but never had a chance to use it. You must think the colonel is a gullible man."

"That is where I need your help, *mi sobrina.*"

"I have only your word that you are my uncle. Whether you are or not," and she paused. "There will be ample chance to discuss your case with Colonel Naranjo."

Torrez rose and thumped the table with his knuckles. "NAA test is going to tell us a few things," he said to Estelle. "And we got us a lot of prints to process. You're going to call the Las Cruces PD about his car in the parking lot?"

"You bet. There might be some interesting prints we can lift off of that, too." She thought of Mazón's filleting knife that was now safely tucked in an evidence bag. "We'll see what other surprises we can find."

Chapter Twenty-seven

Colonel Tomás Naranjo relaxed in one of the plastic-padded group chairs in the hospital waiting room, hands hanging off of each of the chair's arms, legs crossed at the ankles. The room was early evening quiet, not yet geared up for the nighttime rush, a rush that reached its peak about the time the bars and saloons closed. Naranjo had traded his uniform for an immaculate linen suit with a muted blue patterned tie against a soft yellow shirt. The moment he saw Estelle, he rose and spread both arms out wide, then brought them together and grasped the undersheriff's right hand in both of his.

"How wonderful to see you," he said, his cadenced voice favoring each syllable. "And you as well, Sheriff." He pumped Bob Torrez's hand in turn, then relaxed back with his hands on his hips, spreading his suit coat as he beamed at the two officers. He lifted his right hand then, index pointing heavenward. "First, let me tell you—your son's concert series at Teatro Angela Peralta is *magnificent.* Such a triumph." He glanced at his watch. "The one remaining concert, and then he flies home on Sunday, I'm told."

"None too soon," Estelle said.

"I'm sure it has been a worry for you, but no need. No need." He raised the index finger again. "You know, should we be so fortunate as to finish our work efficiently, there would be yet time for you to attend the final concert tomorrow. I would be pleased to offer you that."

"Don't tempt me." Estelle glanced down the hall that led toward intensive care.

"Ah, but I will," Naranjo said.

"I'm sure that the powers that be in the *Judiciales* might question me cavorting about Mexico in their aircraft, simply to attend private concerts."

"But you see," Naranjo persisted, "number one, you are vital to the *security* of this concert. You can't imagine how proud we are to have such an event in what is essentially a *regional* theater, however grand its stature. But perhaps more important, it is *my* aircraft, not my government's."

Estelle regarded the Mexican policeman with amusement. Over the years, his invitations had been frequent and persistent for Estelle to accompany the colonel here or there, to restaurants or concerts or even his own home. Estelle had never accepted them, much as she was amused by his suave manner, much as she even *enjoyed* the colonel's presence.

"I would treasure attending the concert myself," Naranjo added. "But first—you have had the chance to talk with this man of mutual interest to us?"

"At some length." She was surprised that Naranjo had come to the point so quickly.

Naranjo nodded and bent down to retrieve a slender attaché case that was resting against the leg of his chair. Opening it, he retrieved a single document and handed it to Estelle. "Forgive me for not faxing this to you, but your office said you had come here, and I thought it simpler to hand-deliver it."

Estelle turned slightly so that Bob Torrez could see the paper. Naranjo allowed a couple of seconds to pass, then asked, "I am so curious. Were you aware that Mazón was your family name?"

"No. I lived with the Sisters of Charity orphanage for the first year of my life. I've been told that. Then Teresa Reyes adopted me, but the sisters never divulged my past." Estelle smiled. "That Teresa *wouldn't* know, in such a tiny town, is a little hard for me to believe. But the fault is as much mine as hers. I never pressured her to tell me. My home, my heart, was with her."

"For whatever reason, *Señor* Mazón saw fit to adopt the Tamburro name more then thirty years ago." He wagged his head. "Off and on, you see." He touched one of the information boxes. "No *AKA* until this past incarceration. He will go back to prison for the rest of his life, no doubt. And he will do so as Benedicte Mazón." The colonel smiled gently. "I'm sorry if that somehow causes you any discomfort."

"Not a bit," Estelle said. "He's done what he's done. My concern is what he *intended* to do. He killed the two amateurs who were trying to get to my son. Then what?"

"You mean by coming to this country?"

"Exactly. The risks are huge for him. And he wants me to believe that he took those risks just to see family?" She scoffed. "He claims that he saw the very moment when I was born. The first and last time that he laid eyes on me. And during brief moments when he was out of prison, he never chose to visit, to make himself known to me? How convenient that now he's captivated by the thought of his great nephew—if that's what he really is—when the boy has achieved some international acclaim as a concert pianist? Believing that his familial pride runs that deep is a stretch, Tomás. If he's playing with some kinky fascination, some sick preoccupation, then I don't want him within a thousand miles of my family."

"We shall see." Naranjo saw that Sheriff Torrez might be growing impatient, and the Mexican shook his head as if to clear it. "You've come to the hospital tonight to visit with our mutual friend," he said.

Estelle pointed down the hallway. "He's been moved out of ICU. Next floor up, three eighty-two."

"Well, then, maybe we should…" Torrez started to mutter, and Estelle slipped her arm through his just long enough to turn him away from the exit. "Yeah, okay," he added.

They shared the elevator with a young man pushing a cart loaded with fresh blankets on the top and various toiletries on the bottom. Jet, if his name tag was to be believed, looked first at Estelle and offered a self-conscious smile, then glanced

sideways at Bob Torrez. Although not in uniform, the sheriff's
gun, cuffs, and other paraphernalia were clearly evident. As the
elevator lurched to a halt, Naranjo held the door for the cart
boy, and Jet scooted off without a word.

"His name is Anselmo Trujillo," Naranjo said calmly. "Anselmo
'the Jet' Trujillo. I'm glad to see that he is trying."

They turned right toward the nurses' station. "How do you
know him ?"

"For one thing, his name was on the clipboard schedule on
the side of the cart. But in this small world, nothing surprises
me anymore. He was seven when I arrested his brother—and
his only guardian, I might add—in a sad incident in Juarez.
Anselmo was sent to live with a cousin in El Paso. I haven't seen
him again until today."

"And yet you remembered him," Estelle marveled.

"That is my curse," Naranjo laughed. "Faces and names come,
but they never go." He laughed gently. "A curse I share with the
gentleman in three eighty-two, it seems to me."

They stopped at the nurses' station where a physician and
nurse were conferring at a computer. The physician glanced up
at the trio. He offered a tight smile that didn't crack the smooth
mahogany of his face. Dark eyes centered on Estelle, and he
nodded. "Undersheriff," and his Indian accent buzzed both 'r's.
The nurse turned around at that, frowning. Estelle folded her
hands on the maple counter.

"We need to see Mr. Gastner for a few minutes if he's not
asleep yet. I hope now is a good time."

"The patient is most definitely *not* asleep," Nurse Schuyler
replied, glancing back at the computer. "He wanted to sit up for
a while." She smiled brightly. "Such a determined gentleman."

"And you are…?" Dr. Patel offered his hand to Bob Torrez.

"Sheriff Torrez, Posadas County."

"And…" The hand was withdrawn before any lasting damage
was inflicted by the vise-like grip, and offered in turn to Naranjo.

"Colonel Tomás Naranjo, a brother from the other side of
the border." He smiled indulgently at the physician.

"Ah," Dr. Patel said, "well, then. Let's see just what's going on with our friend." He adjusted the stethoscope around his neck, scooped up an aluminum clipboard, and nodded down the hall. "Just this way."

The door of three eighty-two was ajar, and they could hear laughter interspersed with grumbles and the coaxing voices of nursing staff. Patel eased the door open, and saw Bill Gastner sitting on the side of the bed, both hands flat on the mattress at his sides. An aluminum walker stood just a tantalizing step away. One nurse stood at his right side, a hand on Gastner's shoulder, watching the second hospital staffer, a physical therapist, with hawk-like eyes.

"Just from the knees, now," the swarthy youngster was saying. He had one hand on Gastner's left knee, the other on the older man's hip.

"My God, *flagrante delicto*," Gastner quipped as he looked up at his visitors.

He nodded at the aluminum walker that was parked nearby. "You see the torture that they're planning? They promise that tomorrow I have to actually reach out and touch that damn thing." He glared at the walker, then his face relaxed. "But my God, it feels good to be upright again."

"Donald, perhaps you can give us ten minutes or so?" Dr. Patel asked, and the therapist stood and offered a radiant smile at Estelle.

"We're making such *good* progress," he said. "I'll be back, sir," he added, and Gastner grimaced.

"That's what I'm afraid of. That guy said he's going to charge me overtime for making him work in the evening." He adjusted the hem of his gown daintily with thumb and index finger. "And here I am, held up for all the world to see, just in my fashionable nightie." The nurse hovering at his side straightened an imaginary wrinkle in his gown. "Camille should be here any minute," Gastner added. "You staying to see her?"

"You might be more comfortable resting back," Dr. Patel suggested, but Gastner shook his head.

"Nah. I'd just have to sit up again when Torquemada comes back. I'll just perch here." He patted the mattress. "I'm fine." With care, though, he lifted his right hand and Naranjo stepped close to clasp it in both of his.

"It is good to see you," the Mexican said. "Not here, of course…"

"A minor hiccup," Gastner shrugged. "I have plans." He winked at Estelle and traded grips, and as the nurse turned away, he let Estelle fuss over the tie of the gown that appeared to be digging into his neck. "And Bobby, what brings your ugly mug to Cruces tonight?"

"Couple things we need to check out," Torrez mumbled. He turned to Dr. Patel. "Give us a few minutes?"

"Please assure that he does not move an iota from that position," the physician said. "I will be just down the hall at the nurses' station." He closed the door as he bowed out of the room.

"So, who brought the coffee and donuts?" Gastner said. "I don't know how they do it, but the coffee here is enough to trigger a relapse." He frowned at Naranjo. "What pulls you away from your home turf?"

The Mexican, ever politic, looked first at Bob Torrez and then at Estelle, giving them a chance to lay the boundaries.

"Sir, a man has showed up who claims to be my long-lost uncle." She quickly outlined the case, and Gastner sat quietly, his brows furrowed.

"And this Mazón character admits that he killed the two men outside the theater?" He turned to Naranjo. "This isn't just a friendly visit across the border for you, then. You want Mazón back."

"Exactly so."

Gastner reached out a hand toward the sheriff. "You think he had something to do with taking a shot at you?"

"Don't know for sure," Torrez said, and that prompted a smile from the older man.

"'*Don't know,*'" Gastner mimicked with amusement. "You found the shooter with his brains blown out and now with all this, you're starting to think Mazón is linked in somehow?"

"He could be." Estelle held up both hands, and joined the fingers. "So much going on, I don't like the coincidence of Mazón surfacing on this side of the border."

"And all the principals know each other," Naranjo observed. "What's your uncle say?"

"That he killed the two thugs in Mazatlán, and that he fled north to re-establish family ties."

Gastner snorted and pushed himself more upright. "That's goddamn likely," he said derisively. He settled some, and shrugged philosophically. "He ducked out to avoid the Mexican cops, you mean. But who the hell knows. He's either a totally infatuated stalker, or he's willing to do anything necessary to protect *la familia.*" He shrugged again. "Or he's up to something else." He smiled quickly. "How's that for narrowing it all down?"

"What do you remember about Jerry Steward?" the sheriff asked, and the question was such a non-sequitur that Gastner sat like Buddha, gazing at Torrez as he worked to switch gears.

"*The* Jerry Steward we all know and love?" Gastner said finally. "The one who's working now for Miles out at the mesa project? The one who's running for sheriff this time around?"

"He's workin' gate security," Torrez said.

"Good place for him. Give him a clipboard and a walkie-talkie to keep him happy."

"He started out with Bernalillo County?"

Gastner turned his head and squinted into the distance. "Tried to. He never was a certified officer with them. Worked the Sheriff's Posse for a while. He moved down here to work with the mines, but *that* didn't work out for him. He tried to get on with Posadas PD back when they were active, and *that* didn't work out either." Gastner sighed. "Poor old Jer. Kind of the village idiot in a lot of respects. For a while, it looked as if he'd get on with the Sheriff's Department—for some reason, Eduardo liked him. I didn't." He grinned at Torrez. "Sheriff Salcido *often* liked people I didn't. You probably remember Steward better'n I do. He worked dispatch for a little while when you were a road deputy."

"Yup."

"So…what's the deal with him, anyway? Is the campaign heating up or something?" Pointing an accusatory finger at Torrez, Gastner said to Naranjo, "You know, it's really hard to get this guy off the campaign trail long enough to take care of business. A real *politico,* he is. "

Torrez managed a brittle smile.

Gastner's shaggy right eyebrow lifted as he regarded the sheriff. "Steward's a point of interest in all this somehow?"

"I'm thinkin' maybe, is all. Somehow."

"That's some precise thinking, Bobby." For a long moment, Gastner sat silently, gazing down at his toes. "Then talk to Miles, Bobby. He's discreet, he minds his own business, but he's also observant. If something is going on that involves his project, he's the one to talk to." He looked askance at Torrez. "Not that it's any of my business, but what's your interest in Steward? What's got you thinking down those lines? I never thought him to be much more than a harmless wannabe."

"Just thinkin'," Torrez said.

"About?"

"Olveda has been out to the mesa a couple of times, and at least once he brought Quesada along with him. So they know each other."

"And Quesada is…remember you're dealing with my failing post-op memory, Bobby."

"The sniper."

"The *dead* sniper."

"Yup."

"And so…Steward? What's the bee in your bonnet about him?"

"Olveda has talked with him. At one point, they were together out at Waddell's. Quesada, too. I've been tryin' to think who would be in a position to know if I was out there on that property. Who would know that I was huntin'."

"Half of Posadas, most likely." Gastner heaved a careful sigh, shifting position ever so slightly. "I'd say you were grasping at straws, Roberto. Except," he nodded in resignation, "we know how the tendrils wind around," and he flashed a smile at Estelle. "And isn't *that* goddamn poetic? But *somebody* knew. You're absolutely right on that. That somebody flanked you, took a shot, and high-tailed it out of there. So—*somebody* knew." He looked up sharply. "What's the kid Bueler say?"

"Ain't talked to him much, but he keeps it to himself."

Gastner made a wry face. "Well, you *should* talk to him. Somebody as quiet as he is—he's spending time *thinking*. Like some other people I know. And listen to me, now. Such a big help." Shifting again on the bed, he patted Estelle's hand, still clamped on his right shoulder. "How's the kid doing with his concert?"

"He comes home Sunday."

"You're sorry about that, huh?"

"Oh, *sí*."

"I am trying my best to convince her to go to the final concert tomorrow night," Naranjo said. "She and Francis would be welcome guests."

"There you go," Gastner nodded. "Don't let that opportunity slide by."

Naranjo held up both hands. "And if you wish, if *he* wishes, the young virtuoso can come home with us. He, as well, more than welcome. I…"

Torrez took a step backward as he pulled his phone off his belt, and at the same time, Estelle felt the familiar vibration in her jacket pocket.

"Torrez," the sheriff answered, and he opened the door, pausing with his hand on the knob. Estelle saw that her message was from Sergeant Jackie Taber, and she said only, "Hold on a second, Jackie."

Torrez listened intently, his face expressionless. "Yup," he said finally. "I'm on my way. Shut things down. Get the SPs workin' the interstate." He snapped his phone off.

"The sheriff just got the message," Jackie said to Estelle. "You're both at the hospital?"

"Yes. Colonel Naranjo is with us."

"Might as well bring him along. You might need him," Jackie said.

"And find Olveda," Estelle said. "Wherever he is, find him."

Torrez was already out in the hall, hands on his hips, his face now dark and furious.

"Ride with us?" she asked Naranjo. "We'll make sure you have a ride back."

"Absolutely. I am most interested."

He nodded and turned toward Gastner, holding out a hand. "I'll visit again, old friend. Sometime when the world is not coming down around our ears." His smile was sympathetic. "It is hard to be…what is it that the sports announcers say? Benched?"

Estelle took time to give Gastner a quick hug. "Don't go away," she said.

All three had cleared the room as the nurse returned, along with Dr. Patel.

"Hell of a deal," the old man muttered, reflecting with some irritation that the substance of the phone call had never been mentioned. Even Tomás Naranjo, who had not been privy to either call, seemed to know what the emergency was…either that or his magnificent patience was in tight control as he left with the others.

"It's nice to have such good friends, isn't it?" Patel said cheerfully.

"I don't know about that," Gastner said. He watched with resignation as the physician read his chart, concentrating as if he'd never set eyes on it before this moment.

The hospital room door opened without a knock, just far enough to allow Estelle Reyes-Guzman to slip in. "Excuse me again, for just a moment," she said to Dr. Patel, and he backed up a few steps, still chart hopping.

Estelle put a hand on each of Gastner's shoulders and lowered her voice to a whisper. "I'm sorry, *Padrino*. I should have told you. Mazón has escaped." She nodded in resignation. "I'll get back to you as soon as I can." And then she was gone.

Chapter Twenty-eight

The drive west to Posadas—a mere forty-eight miles from exit to exit—took hours…or so it seemed to Undersheriff Estelle Reyes-Guzman. With all his opportunity before Estelle had taken Benedicte Mazón into custody—and even afterward, if he was as quick and strong as he appeared—the prisoner had chosen his time with exquisite care, and likely with clear purpose.

Why hadn't he simply taken a walk in Las Cruces, when he had ample chance? His behavior was too easy for a desperate man. He had *allowed* himself to be arrested. A calculated risk—but calculated for what? The logical conclusion was that the man had unfinished business in Posadas. He couldn't be so naive as to expect that the undersheriff would run interference for him with Mexican authorities, no matter what tall tale of familial relationships he relied upon.

Torrez and Naranjo remained silent during the forty minutes on the interstate. Estelle wanted nothing more than to plant the Charger's accelerator pedal flat to the floor, but she forced patience, keeping below a hundred. Despite the blur of guard rails and the other traffic that stood still, the wait was agony.

Estelle hadn't asked, during her brief telephone conversation with Jackie Taber, *how* Mazón had managed to escape. Granted, the Posadas County lockup was no high security Leavenworth. Still, the renovation of the county building a dozen years before had included upgrades—cameras, new doors and hardware. No amount of digging with an old spoon, or sweating with a hacksaw blade would do the job. Mazón was smart enough to know that. The last escape from Posadas custody had been in 1952, long before mandated renovations, when Bobby Barton had simply walked out through an unlocked door. Nothing that simple could have presented itself to the Mexican.

Within the hour, Dispatcher Mike Sands faced the sheriff, undersheriff, and a colonel of the Mexican *Judiciales,* and tried his best to explain exactly what *had* happened. At 8:16 that evening—just about the time the undersheriff, Bobby Torrez, and Tomás Naranjo had been greeting Bill Gastner back at the Las Cruces hospital—Mazón had been the only guest in the Posadas County jail, awaiting a decision by the ponderous wheels of justice that would not come until the next day.

Earlier, Estelle had deliberately stayed clear of the man during the initial processing and incarceration—Mazón was too good a salesman, his tales of tragedy in the river too compelling.

The county itself was quiet at 8:16, still several hours away from the predictable Friday night witching hour when the bars turned up the volume.

The young dispatcher, just turned twenty-two and now, as he faced the grim trio of officers, so nervous that his lower lip seemed to have a life of its own, tried to stand still as he recited the events leading to the prisoner's escape. They stood just outside the cell door, the aroma of the incident strong.

The young man's first thought, naturally enough, was fault—regardless of how it happened, the escape had occurred on his shift. A single corrections officer, Benny Montoya, had been on duty upstairs, no doubt preparing for increased Friday night business. Benny was now downstairs, typing up his version.

"Everything was quiet, and Benny was in the john. I went upstairs for just a minute to check on the prisoner," Mike Sands related. "I get here and Mazón is half out of bed, as if he had been crawling across the floor and then tried to pull himself back up on the cot."

"And in distress?" Estelle asked. Bob Torrez rested his shoulder against the steel doorjamb, eyes riveted on Sands' pale face.

Naranjo stood silently, hands folded at his waist, managing to project an air of authority even though this was not his department, not even his country.

"He looked awful," Sands said. "He'd soiled himself, and I could smell the urine, you know? His left arm was clamped across his chest, with his fist tight up under his chin." Sands mimicked the motion, and Estelle felt a turn—the gesture was exactly the one that her youngest son, Carlos, adopted when unsure of himself, or worried, or frightened, or even delighted beyond endurance. "His right hand was grabbed onto his left elbow."

"Did he speak to you?"

"No. I don't even think he knew that I was there. Just gasping, I mean long and shaky, almost like sobs. Like he couldn't get enough air. He was just staring at the floor, and I could see he was bleeding from his right nostril."

"Actively bleeding, or just some blood smear?"

"No…it was running down over his upper lip."

"You did the right thing," Estelle told the shaken young man. Sands, on the job for less than two months, had indeed known what *not* to do. He did not open the cell door. Instead, he pounded on the bathroom door, yelling for Benny, then dashed downstairs and called for an ambulance. Without a pause, he then radioed the only deputy on duty in Posadas County, Thomas Pasquale, for assistance. Pasquale was cruising contentedly twenty-six miles south on State 56, enjoying the final cup of coffee from his Thermos and waiting for drunks to start leaving the Broken Spur Saloon.

Still feeling adrift, even as Pasquale's patrol unit hurtled northbound toward the village, Sands called his shift sergeant, Jackie Taber, and Lieutenant Tom Mears.

Before Sands could question Mears' emphatic instructions *not* to try first aid, *not* to enter the cell by himself, the ambulance arrived with Matty Finnegan and Barbara Carl on board. By then Benny Montoya *had* entered the cell, and was in the process of assessing the prisoner's condition.

Because the cheerful Matty was the senior EMT of the outfit, Ms. Carl, fiftyish and a good, solid rookie, was gaining experience behind the wheel. She took the time to off-load the gurney while Matty sprinted inside.

"I could tell he was in a bad way," Sands said. "Benny wasn't making any headway with him, and it looked like he was starting to convulse. When the EMTs got here, I stayed outside the cell to secure the hallway. His breath was all choppy-like, and I heard Matty say something about 165…his pulse, I guess."

"What did you think was happening?"

Sands wore the first aid responder patch on the shoulder of his uniform shirt, so he'd completed the first step in his training process, and should have been able to begin the patient evaluation.

"Heart attack maybe, blood clot. I wasn't sure, 'cause his lips weren't blue. The blood from his nose? I didn't know about that. Maybe he just whacked his face against the frame of the cot. I knew they were going to transport, though. Matty got the IV for saline in quick and easy, and then we strapped him down and shot out to the ambulance."

Estelle remained silent and let Sands fidget. So far, his recitation of events had matched Benny Montoya's perfectly. What had been Mazón's plan at that point? She remembered his calm, polite demeanor in Las Cruces earlier in the day, even his patience in the Posadas cell after he was locked up.

And then he had ample time to think and plan. Even if he had never visited the facility, he would have known that, in a village as small as Posadas, the modest hospital would be just a few blocks at most from the county building. The ambulance ride would require but a minute or two.

"Was there ever a moment when it appeared that the prisoner was resisting the EMTs?"

"No, ma'am. I mean, he was *out* of it."

Estelle turned to Torrez. "Mazón would know that the saline IV was standard," Estelle said. "It wouldn't hurt him a bit. He might have guessed that the EMTs would administer nothing more risky until the hospital's ER staff had done some kind of emergency workup." She stepped farther into the cell, avoiding the mess on the floor near the cot, and then turned to Sands.

"During all of this, did the prisoner say anything at all? Anything at all?"

"No, ma'am. He didn't look like he *could* talk."

Estelle thumbed back a page or two in her pocket notebook. "Deputy Pasquale arrived at the hospital about seven minutes after the escape," she mused, "just moments after the ambulance reached the hospital." As she read her notes, she knew that the only two officers *not* scouring the neighborhood for the fugitive were herself and Bobby Torrez…every deputy in the department had been pulled in, along with calls to State Police, Border Patrol, and Customs—even the sole Game and Fish officer in the district. But Estelle was not optimistic. Mazón had chosen the cover of darkness, and that escalated his chances. Logically, he would head south, since he knew his nemesis, Colonel Tomás Naranjo, was now in the country.

"Why now?" Torrez straightened up, surveyed the cell once more, and then jerked his thumb at Sands in a brusque "out" command. "Soon as Linda has all this documented, you and Martinez can go ahead and clean up."

Mr. Soft Touch, Estelle thought. To make sure the young dispatcher understood, she added, "You did everything you could have, and everything you *should* have, Mike. Nobody was hurt, and the rest will take care of itself. That's the important thing now. Get your written deposition finished today."

"You bet. Right now."

"So…why does he pull this stunt now?" Torrez repeated as the stairway door closed behind Sands.

"Mazón must know," Estelle said slowly, "that the odds are good that if he stays in our custody, we'll turn him over to Colonel Naranjo, one way or another. At the moment, we have nothing concrete to hold Mazón here, other than illegal entry, and what's the penalty for that?"

"Nothin' yet," Torrez added.

"He doesn't know for sure what he's facing here, but in Mexico, he's up against two capital charges, going up against those carrying a lengthy prison record. Not good. That's not a gamble he wanted to take when it became clear to him that I wasn't going to cooperate with him in any fashion. That's why he didn't just duck out in Las Cruces. There was always the slim chance that I'd cave, that I'd cover for him in some way. Then he saw that wasn't going to happen. He saw a good chance when we decided to return to Las Cruces."

"Yep, but it takes a while to arrange an extradition, and who knows what might happen in the meantime. Be nice if we could just dump him over the fence." He glanced at the colonel, who remained a silent spectator, then regarded Estelle as if she should have all the answers. "So where's he goin'?"

"I don't know. He's smooth, Bobby. He made it into this country without a hiccup. Maybe drove to Posadas, found Quesada. Then he decided to meet with me on neutral ground—the hospital in Las Cruces, and at that point, who knows what he thought he could accomplish. Sanctuary after a fashion?" She flashed a quick smile. "Did he think I'd say, 'Hey, beloved Uncle…at long last! Don't worry—I won't tell the good colonel that you're here.'"

"So where's he headed?" Torrez persisted.

"I don't know. All I can say is that I'd be *very* surprised if *we* catch him. This is not a man who makes clumsy moves. He's just thirty miles from the border at this point, and I can't imagine that's much of a challenge for him."

"Don't know about that," Torrez grumbled. "The Mexicans had him in jail for twenty years or so. He got clumsy somewhere along the line."

Naranjo chuckled. "I like the way you put things in focus, Sheriff."

Estelle shuffled pages in her notes and scanned the interview with Matty Finnegan, loathe to waste another moment pondering what *had* happened, instead of being out in the night, probing the shadows. But there might be hints.

An IV for saline was quick and easy, and Mazón was strapped in and transported downstairs and out into the ambulance. That's what dispatcher Sands and jailer Benny Montoya related, and the EMTs corroborated. It was simple, really. Mazón couldn't break out of jail. But an ambulance was far from high security, even though, now without any other prisoners to supervise, jailer Montoya had gone along for the ride. The ambulance reached Posadas General Hospital: Benedicte Mazón did not.

EMT Matty Finnegan had been stunned. One moment she was working every angle she could to keep her patient alive during five blocks of transit, and the next she was caught around the neck by one of the cables yanked from one of the monitors, Mazón's saline drip swept to one side, a free hand popping the clasps of the gurney restraints. Both Matty and Barbara Carl remembered Mazón's single line clearly as he twisted the cable, speaking directly into Matty's left ear.

"Stay off the radio and the phone." It was spoken with such polite command that Barbara almost collided with one of the portico pillars outside the emergency room doors. With a certain amount of loyalty, no one wanted to discuss Montoya's performance. A small, chubby man, Montoya had frozen—and maybe that was a good thing for Matty's welfare.

And then, moments before Deputy Pasquale arrived, only minutes before Sergeant Taber and Lieutenant Mears had responded as well, Benedicte Mazón was away into the night.

"Did he have any other weapon in his possession?" Estelle had asked, and Matty shook her head. She had been close to tears, but more angry than frightened.

"I remembered what you guys always say," she had whispered. "What's important is to be able to go home at the end of the shift." Her eyes were steady as she met the officers' gaze. "I'm no hero and neither are the others. If he wants to run off into the night…" Matty Finnegan shrugged. "He convinced me that he was sick, I mean *really* sick. That's why I didn't wait for Tommy to arrive with cuffs. I *really* thought there was a better than even chance that we were going to lose him. And you know, I still do. It wouldn't surprise me a bit if we find him in a puddle on the sidewalk just a few blocks from here. If he was faking it," she shrugged, "then he's a hell of an actor. But where's he going to go?"

If Mazón was unlucky, officers would be able to follow the trail of barking dogs as the escapee worked his way through the village. So far, that lucky break hadn't materialized.

Because it was the one of only two logical connections, Deputy Thomas Pasquale had been assigned to the Guzman home on Twelfth Street. It was hard to imagine that Mazón would escape jail only to settle in the Guzmans' living room, to chat amiably with Teresa or Carlos, waiting for Estelle to return home to slap the cuffs on him once again. But it was one obvious connection, and Lieutenant Mears had made sure that doorway of opportunity was slammed shut.

On the off chance that some unfinished business remained between Mazón and Olveda, Deputy Brent Sutherland, inconspicuous in jeans and t-shirt, was dispatched to the Posadas Inn near the interstate where Olveda had taken a room.

The murdered hitman, Miguel Quesada, had been an associate of Dominic Olveda, the developer. If Mazón had popped Quesada, there Olveda himself might be in danger.

Deputy Sutherland caught sight of Dominic Olveda in the Inn's modest dining room, sharing a late dinner with county commissioner Tobe Ulibarri and county manager Leona Spears in a booth toward the rear of the restaurant. Leona's laugh boomed out, and Ulibarri leaned forward as if to repeat the hilarious punch line. Sutherland could not see Olveda's face, but the man turned slightly sideways in the booth, one arm companionably draped over the back of the booth behind Leona. The lateness of the hour was a nod to Olveda's habits, no doubt—not to mention Leona's love of the continental good life.

Sutherland slipped back out of view, and a moment later, the sheriff answered the deputy's cell phone call.

"Olveda is here, sir. He's having dinner with the county manager and one of the commissioners."

"Keep him in sight. We'll be down in a minute. If Mazón shows up, shoot his ass."

The deputy settled in a booth on the other side of a center island that had become a plant jungle, more than a little nervous after the sheriff's blunt instructions. Out of sight, he could see the back of Commissioner Ulibarri's head, and a vague shadow of the other two. He had a clear view of the motel entrance.

Sutherland had time to relax and take two sips of iced tea when he heard Olveda say, "No, really. There's more square footage on that site than you might think." They weren't whispering in conspiracy, that was clear. Olveda slid out of the booth and stood up, and Sutherland could see his face through the fronds. "You know, I have an architect's rendering out in the truck. Give me but a moment. You will be *astounded.*"

The deputy waited until Olveda had reached the restaurant's double doors before rising himself. By the time he reached the lobby, Olveda was just stepping outside. As he stood just inside the entrance by the small Community Attractions bulletin board, Sutherland could see the dapper little man walk diagonally across the parking lot. The destination was a white Ford F-150, and a kaleidoscope of lights flashed as Olveda clicked the remote. His movements now shielded by a large van, Olveda opened the driver's door, and then the back "suicide" door, effectively blocking what little view Sutherland had. Moving shadows hinted that he might be sorting through the documents on the backseat. For a heartbeat or two, Sutherland could see the man's right hand on the door frame.

A young couple slipped out the front door past Sutherland, the girl giving him a pleasant smile and nod of greeting. "Waiting on a hot date?" Tory Hastings had been in several of Sutherland's community college classes. He had always thought her too pixyish for a career in law enforcement, and sure enough, she'd switched to cosmetology, finding happiness with her current boyfriend— who gave Sutherland a quick, dismissive up and down glance.

"Long wait," the deputy replied. Their walk across the parking lot took them to a dark blue Camaro several spaces down from the van and Olveda's truck. On a weekend evening, the lot was gratifyingly full, and Tory, who was driving the flashy Camaro, had to wait for an incoming Toyota sedan to pass by. The Toyota headed for the modest entrance portico. As the car parked, Sutherland shifted position so he could keep the tailgate of Olveda's pickup in view. Five or six spaces down toward the lot entrance, an older model sedan backed out. Its taillights winked as it reached Grande Avenue and turned left.

Olveda's cab lights still glowed, but it wasn't obvious where Olveda was. Toyota man, looking road-weary and scruffy, entered the motel without so much as a glance at Sutherland. The deputy ducked outside, taking the sidewalk that paralleled the building. From across the tarmac, he could see no sign of Olveda. His heart started to pound.

Sutherland's own vehicle was parked ten spaces down, nosed in toward the building. One of the older, unmarked Crown Victorias, it looked exactly like what it was. Staying clear of it, Sutherland ambled across the parking lot, aiming for a battered Suburban to the right of Olveda's truck. The white Ford now appeared to be empty.

The Posadas Inn parking lot fronted the interstate right-of-way, in this case the westbound entrance ramp. The pavement of the parking lot angled upward to the concrete bumpers, and then the prairie beyond was cut in a moderate drainage channel, completely weed- and litter-choked. Seeing no sight of Olveda, Sutherland crossed quickly to the Ford. The cab was empty.

"Oh, shit," Sutherland whispered. He snapped on his flashlight and swept the area ahead of the pickup—had Olveda moved toward the rear of the truck, Sutherland would have had a clear view of him. The harsh beam probed the litter of plastic bags, beer cartons, diaper wraps, and drink cups in the small field across the concrete bumpers. It was Dominic Olveda's silver belt buckle that caught the light first. A few steps brought the deputy close enough to see the surprised but dead eyes staring up into the heavens.

Chapter Twenty-nine

The lone figure stood out of the circle cast by the generator-powered spotlights, away from the swarm of people who had reason to be inside the yellow tape or who *wanted* to be. A group of several people, including the county manager and the county commissioner, stood by the motel's front door, all trying to talk at once.

Estelle Reyes-Guzman set out across the parking lot after exiting through the motel manager's outside office door, accompanied by Colonel Tomás Naranjo. They had managed to sidestep the ebullient and now white-faced county manager. Estelle had also avoided Frank Dayan, the publisher of the *Posadas Register.* Frank had parked on the other side of the building, and blended with shadows until he worked his way close enough to include himself.

Earlier, Estelle had grilled Deputy Brent Sutherland, as had Bob Torrez—the sheriff's brief encounter with the deputy guaranteed to contribute to a sleepless night for the young man.

Even as the search for Benedicte Mazón intensified, even as two State Police helicopters headed toward Posadas and ground troops established roadblocks on both the interstate and State 56—and even as Mexican police tightened security at the border crossings, Estelle had sent Deputy Sutherland off by himself, to seek a quiet corner, and *think.* That had been forty minutes ago.

In that time, she'd examined Dominic Olveda's corpse, and listened to Coroner Alan Perrone first pronounce him dead, which he obviously was, and then attribute death to two wounds.

One was a disabling upward knife thrust deep through the diaphragm, immediately at the base of the sternum. Olveda could have managed a gasp, even a few seconds of consciousness and perhaps a feeble cry as severed great arteries gushed blood into his chest cavity. He would not have been able to lift his hands to ward off the second wound, a smooth, deep slash across the left side of his throat forward from under his left ear almost to the tip of his chin.

Copious blood splatters on the inside of the truck cab indicated that Olveda was either sitting in the truck, or standing beside it with the door open, when attacked. Then, perhaps to gain a few precious seconds, Olveda's body had been dragged away from the truck, off into the ditch. Both the little "suicide" door and the van parked alongside the pickup had blocked the deputy's view.

And Benedicte Mazón—for that's who Estelle was sure had orchestrated the attack—had slipped away into the night. Like the two murders in Mazatlán, the killer had struck with confidence and precision. Mazón. If he was indeed the killer, he'd made the most of brief moments after his escape. Where did Mazón find yet another knife? A steak knife from the motel's dining room? A quick stop at the HandiMart? There were any number of possibilities. The knife had yet to turn up. After racing half a mile through the darkened village from hospital to Inn, how long had Mazón waited at the motel for an opportunity to strike? The questions swirled.

"Are you doing all right?" She waited until she was whisper distance from the young deputy. Sutherland looked over at the crowd, his fingers latched onto his belt. He watched apprehensively as Sheriff Torrez and the Mexican colonel conferred near the bloody pickup truck.

"I'm fine," he said. "I ought to be over there, workin' the scene."

"You are needed here, Brent," Estelle said gently. "We need to know what you heard, what you saw. Everything. That's why I wanted you isolated and reviewing everything that happened in your own mind. Without distractions."

"I've thought it through a hundred times, ma'am." He grimaced. "I couldn't see what was goin' on, so I shouldn't have waited. I should have run over there." He shook his head in disgust. "The sheriff's going to have my ass."

"I'm sure you *have* thought about it, and that's just what we want. You arrived at the motel at 9:20. That's what you told me before."

"Yes, ma'am."

"And…"

"I walked in, glanced in the restaurant, and saw Mr. Olveda having dinner with Ms. Spears and the commissioner."

"So 9:21 or so. Maybe 9:22."

"Yes. After a couple of minutes, Olveda stood up and said something like, 'No, really, there's more square footage than people think.' He said he wanted to go out to the truck to get some map or something."

"He never saw you?"

"No, ma'am. Then I followed him out. I waited out of sight in the foyer. I saw him walk to his truck, but that big van there? Parked beside his like that, it blocked my view. That and the way the doors are?" With both hands, he imitated a clam shell opening. "It's a 4x4, and he wasn't very tall, anyway. See, I should have gone over there right then. Right then."

"The vehicles that left the parking lot around that time… you're sure what they were?"

"Yes, ma'am. A brown older model Chevy Caprice with a spotlight on the driver's side windshield post, like an old cop car. The sheriff said that he knew who it belonged to. He was going to go check it out."

Estelle turned and surveyed the crowd. Sure enough, Sheriff Bobby Torrez had shifted into his normal hunting mode, sinking into the shadows, leaving the talk and the confusion behind. Colonel Naranjo stood beside Leona Spears, his hands in his back pockets. Leona was animated, Naranjo listening politely.

"That guy left just about the time that Tory did. Tory Hastings and her boyfriend. They were driving her fancy Camaro."

"And the older sedan…you're sure about that one?"

"Yes. A dark Caprice. Brown, I'm pretty sure. A cop Caprice."

"At that distance?" and she turned to gaze down the lot toward Grande Avenue.

"Yeah, I could tell. They're all roundy, you know. The old chief of police used to drive that custom black one, the one with the chrome wheels. The sheriff knew who it was. Probably."

"Okay." Of course Torrez hadn't mentioned the owner to anyone else, but the information wouldn't be long in coming.

"Who drove out first, Brent? The young lady in her Camaro, or the Caprice?"

"Ah…she was second. The Caprice backed out, and was close enough that Tory had to tap the brakes. Then she went out. And there was a Toyota comin' in. It's that one parked over by my unit."

"She may have had a look at the driver." She watched Sutherland's mobile face as the frustration touched his features. "They both turned left, toward town? The Caprice and Tory?"

"Ah, yes."

"Did you watch the highway after that? After you saw the cars leave?"

"No, ma'am. I was concerned because I had lost sight of Olveda. I mean, his truck was lit up, and the doors were open, but it had been a little bit since I actually saw *him*."

"So the Caprice *could* have turned around and headed south on fifty-six."

"Yes, ma'am," Sutherland said uncomfortably. "It could have. I was focused on Olveda's truck."

"Before all this with the cars leaving the parking lot, you could actually see Olveda near his truck? You could see what he was doing?"

Sutherland shook his head. "No, ma'am. I could see the *top* of his head sometimes. That's all."

"But he didn't close the doors," Estelle said.

"No, ma'am."

The *timing*, Estelle thought. *So very like our Señor Mazón.* More talking to herself than to the flustered deputy, she said aloud, "He escapes from the ambulance, into heavy dusk when light is so tricky. How does he manage the Chevy Caprice, if that was him? If he did, is that just opportunity? Say he does. He drives down to this motel. He might know that Olveda is staying here, he might know what vehicle Olveda is driving. But he *could not* know Olveda was having a fashionably late dinner with local *politicos.*"

"They do that down south, don't they?" Sutherland asked. "Eatin' late and stuff?"

"They do. So very cosmopolitan and *Mexican.*" She turned and regarded the motel, its design flat and angular, trimmed with neon. "And by chance, Mazón slips into the motel, just as you did, Brent, and sees Olveda. He waits for him out by the truck…expecting to see either Olveda or his dinner companions leave, or both. If Leona and the commissioner left by themselves, Mazón would know with reasonable certainty that Olveda is either inside at the bar, or back in his room. But while he waits, there's nothing to tip off the cops…the Caprice has to be local."

"We don't know if he took the Caprice," Sutherland added. "I mean, we don't *know* that."

"Nope. But he's a master opportunist. If he didn't, he could be on foot." She pointed off to the southwest. "Either up to the interstate and hook a ride, or cross-country somehow down to the border." She shook her head. "I bet on the Caprice. From the hospital, he's on foot. It's so easy to find a useful car in the village. Somewhere between the hospital and here."

"And if that's true, he's at the border by now."

Estelle gazed back toward the motel. *Yes, he's at the border,* she thought. Naranjo smiled at something Leona said. *Mazón is on that side of the border, and you're marooned over here, Colonel.* She turned back to Sutherland. "Ask the lieutenant what he wants you to do, Brent. And don't waste another second beating yourself up over this."

"I just let him walk out and get killed, right under my nose."

"You're not the first who's been outfoxed by this man, Brent." The thought crossed her mind that in all likelihood it was a *fortunate* thing that the young deputy and Mazón had not been forced into a confrontation. With a chill, she realized that had fate operated a little differently, she could have lost *two* deputies and a jailer this evening—and an ambulance crew at risk as well.

She reached out and took his elbow. "Talk to L.T. now. See what he wants you to do."

"Yes, ma'am."

Estelle watched him jog off and then she turned her attention to Naranjo. As she approached, she saw Leona's face brighten, but Estelle held up a hand to halt the gush. Leona understood perfectly, but it appeared that she was literally biting her tongue.

"You can cross at the border gate after hours?" she asked Naranjo.

"Of course." The Regál border crossing had not yet achieved twenty-four-hour a day status. But the two gates, one American, one Mexican, would pose no problem with the right phone calls.

"Are you going to come with me?" Despite the gravity of the situation, Estelle knew it was a silly question. The Mexican officer didn't hesitate for an instant. "Of course. What better way to spend a pleasant night."

Chapter Thirty

Sheriff Robert Torrez had left the circle of lights, noise and confusion and driven north on Grande. He saw nothing at the crime scene that demanded his attention—the photos would be taken, the scene measured, the grounds meticulously searched for any trace of evidence. He had a specific destination in mind, and deep in thought, he settled back in the Expedition's seat, two fingers on the bottom of the steering wheel.

The moment Deputy Brent Sutherland mentioned the older model Caprice, Torrez knew the owner. Back when Jerry Steward had decided that the Sheriff's Auxiliary was the way to go, he'd bought the car at a county auction after the vehicle had spent altogether too long patrolling the streets of Posadas. He'd driven it in parades, and attended 4-H shows, athletic events—anything at all where, in his judgment, an "official" car might serve a purpose.

Bob Torrez dismissed Jerry Steward as a wanna-be pest. He didn't consider for a nano-second that Steward might actually *win* the election for sheriff. The odds were about the same as a burro winning the Kentucky Derby.

But nothing about the violent attack on Dominic Olveda at the Posadas Inn matched Jerry Steward's laid-back, almost dim-witted approach to life either, and that made Torrez edgy. The sheriff had had ample opportunity to observe Mazón's behavior during the interviews, to watch the deep, dark eyes calculate without emotion. To strike, or not to strike…like the calm of a Mohave green. What he saw was a human being of a different species from Jerry Steward.

As the big SUV idled up Grande, Torrez fished out his cell phone and pressed one of the tiny buttons. Four rings and the undersheriff picked up.

"Guzman."

"Hey, I'm headed up to pay Jerry a little visit."

Estelle paused. "All right. Brent is sure it's Steward's car that he saw down here."

"Yep. Now we'll find out why. If this is Mazón's doing, are you headed south?"

"Yes. The colonel is with me."

"Be careful." He switched off in time to turn the car onto Piñon, and then in a few yards right onto Sylvester. The Mesa View apartment complex dominated the block, a rundown heap of a building arranged in a shallow horseshoe with communal parking spaces in the middle. Built originally as an ambitious motel, the first owners had discovered that tourists fresh off the interstate and looking for one night's lodging rarely found the place. What did attract were the cheap by-the-week/month/season rates—long term accommodations that the Posadas Inn down at the interchange didn't offer.

An effort had once been made by new owners to make the Mesa View appear southwesterny by sticking on fake vigas, but that brainstorm faded after the landlord had run out of ambition. The eight vigas he'd managed to install provided an interesting architectural study. If the visible end of a viga was just the exterior end of a ceiling beam as that beam carries through the wall, then these eight beams would have been a haphazard delight on the inside.

Torrez surveyed the building, leaning forward against the steering wheel as he keyed the radio. When Mike Sands responded, he said only, "Three oh eight is 10-6 at Mesa View." From his spot at the end of the parking lot, he counted seventeen resident vehicles. None of them was an aging Caprice.

With his phone switched to vibrate and flashlight in hand, he got out of the Expedition and took the long way around the parking area, eventually ending up at the metal stairway leading to the center section's second floor.

Jerry Steward's apartment, 201, was at the far end, and Torrez trod carefully near the porch railing to lessen the resonant ring of his hard-soled boots on the steel and concrete.

Six feet from the door he stopped, listening. A television set somewhere blared through an open window. Reaching out with the flashlight as if it were a baton, the sheriff rapped four times on the door. Nothing. He rapped again, at the same time palming his phone. This time, Dispatcher Mike Sands sounded eager to have something to do.

"Have Alfonso Torrez bring the master key to room 201 up to his favorite cousin. I'm at the room right now," the sheriff said.

"Room 201. That's at the Mesa View, right?"

"Yep." He frowned at the deputy's nervous redundancy.

In thirty seconds, Torrez heard the thump of a door, and then saw the bulky figure of his cousin trudging up the steep metal stairs, knees bowed inward by his weight.

"He left earlier," Alfonso said by way of greeting. "I saw his car pull out a while ago."

"Okay."

"And don't you go kicking in the door, Bobby." He held up the key ring. "I got enough to do around here."

The first two keys didn't fit, but the third attempt rewarded them. "Whatcha after?" He stepped back, not the least bit eager to enter.

Torres nodded his thanks but ignored the question, and gently pushed the door with the butt of the flashlight. The apartment had originally been one of the finer suites when the Mesa View had been designed. Bathroom, kitchenette, living room—the sheriff surveyed it all without changing his position at the door.

"*Ay, chingada,*" Alfonso muttered and backed to the porch railing, holding on with both hands.

"You got that right," Torrez replied. Jerry Steward sat in his favorite armchair—his only armchair, two steps from the television. One hand rested on each arm of the chair, his head fallen back as if he'd taken a nap. His posture mimicked the dead hitman, snoozing into eternity. A sea of blood drenched both Steward and the chair.

The killer had made no attempt at hiding the murder weapon. The aluminum baseball bat lay on the floor against the wall, gore adhered to the metal. The sheriff didn't enter the room, but remained by the door as he dialed.

"Guzman."

"Hey," he said. "See who you can shake loose over there. Somebody did a line drive through the front of Jerry Steward's skull with a baseball bat. Room 201 at the Mesa View."

"Dead?"

"Yep. And somebody took off with his Caprice."

"Signs of a struggle?"

"Don't know yet, but my first guess is not."

"I can spring L.T., Linda, and Tommy. If the State mobile gets here, I'll have them swing that way, too. Forced entry?"

"Don't look like it. Make it ASAP with the team. You headed south yet?"

"About to. Naranjo and I were going to head for the border crossing at Regál, but we can hold off on that if you want me over there. I can come over if you need me."

Torrez was silent for a moment, then replied. "Ain't nothing any of us can do for Jerry. I got this one all right. The way the body is, I'm thinking one hit with a baseball bat. We'll see. You be careful down there if you're thinkin' of crossing the border with Naranjo."

"Oh, *sí.*"

Chapter Thirty-one

The tiny village of Regál nestled on the south side of the San Cristóbal Mountains, facing the open sweep of the Mexican prairie—that prairie broken now and then by jagged volcanic plugs and ash-capped mesas. From the part-time border crossing, the road swept south through that battered landscape toward Janos. Because of the San Cristóbal barrier to the north of the village, it had always seemed to Estelle that Regál belonged to Mexico rather than the United States.

The undersheriff lowered the windows as she drove down toward the village. Cresting a last slight rise a stone's throw from the church, she stopped the car on the pavement and switched off the engine. To the right, the village lay in the darkness. She counted three porch lights, and even as she watched, one of them was switched off.

"Charming little town, I've always thought," Tomás Naranjo whispered.

From far to the south, the yip of a coyote floated across the still air, and that prompted half a dozen village dogs to add their two cents. For a few moments, the chorus filled the night, then lost interest.

"If you drive through the village," he added, "every dog and his cousin will announce you."

"That's okay," Estelle said. "If Mazón came this way, he isn't sitting on someone's front porch, waiting. He would have headed up." She leaned down so she could see to the west, where an arm of the rugged foothills broke and then curved south, slicing the border. The new fence was a black shadow heading east and west from the border crossing behind the church. But a mile west, as the barrier of foothills rose, the towering abomination of steel posts and paneling had been abandoned in favor of the traditional four strand barbed wire demarcation, snaking up and over the rugged natural barrier.

"We'll never find him," she said. "Not under cover of darkness. But we'll find the car."

Certainly much of the modern economy had passed the village by. Regál was the sort of place destined never to know the bright lights of a Dollar store, or an all-night pharmacy—or any pharmacy at all, for that matter. The village was not gridded and surveyed and street-lit. The very darkness of the village worked in Mazón's favor, as did the hodgepodge layout of the community. The fifteen houses had been built as each owner saw fit, with lot lines sometimes marked by rustic fences, sometimes not. Outbuildings in various states of repair were scattered through the village as if a giant hand had swept overhead, sifting them down. Once over the pass and the smooth macadam of State 56, visitors found every lane in the village hard-packed dirt with occasional soft sand pockets or deep ruts in the caliche.

In spots, the narrow lanes wound within a foot or so of a front porch or juniper fence behind which elderly mules dozed.

Estelle started the car and pulled it into gear, idling down the last hundred yards of pavement before swinging off onto the dirt of the first lane into the village. Now after ten, the blue ghosts still lit many of the windows, and she could imagine the folks sitting deep in their old wing-back chairs—the Sanchez clan, the Abuelos, old Marvin Acosta, the widow Fermina Torrez, who was a distant relative of the sheriff, and ten or fifteen others who had shut out the night—now captivated by the modern life of the tube-people.

Letting the car idle, tires crunching on patches of gravel, they wound through the village. Ralph Martinez was standing in the doorway of his adobe home, and he raised a hand in greeting. Estelle slowed as she saw him step carefully out of the house and mosey toward the road, smoke trailing from his cigarette. They met at his mailbox, itself now obsolete and replaced by an ugly cluster box out by the highway.

"Who you lookin' for?" Martinez asked with a lopsided grin. He bent down, and Estelle caught the fragrant aroma from the smoke. He offered his hand, the brown skin now tissue-paper thin. "And who you got there?" He leaned a bit more, knuckles of one hand against the car for support, and squinted at Estelle's passenger.

"Ralph, this is Colonel Tomás Naranjo of the *Judiciales.*"

"Ohhhhhhhhh." It was impossible to tell if the comment was derisive or if Martinez was genuinely impressed. She turned to Naranjo. "Mr. Martinez was postmaster for years and years up in Newton."

"Until they took away my post office," Martinez added. "You know, I've been here now for eighteen years. How about that." He straightened a bit. "Some of my neighbors still consider me an outsider." He puffed another plume of smoke. "So, Sheriff, you know, I got to go into town and talk to your husband."

"He'll be happy to see you."

Martinez coughed a little chuckle. "I don't know about *that.* But I don't piss so good, and I guess I better do something about it. Keeps me awake all night."

"You should go see him."

Martinez looked off to the west. "You after that other car?"

"That depends," Estelle said.

"Brown Chevy? He drove through here just a few minutes ago. Maybe half an hour. Maybe less."

"Did you see him come back out this way?"

Martinez shook his head. "Nope. Now he could have circled around past Trujillo's, but I don't think so. That little bridge over the arroyo has loose boards, and the tires, you know? Make all kinds of noise. I would have heard."

Estelle reached out and patted the back of Martinez's hand. "Thanks, Ralph." She looked squarely at him. "Don't be putting off that appointment, now."

"No, I got to do that." He stepped back as she eased her foot off the brake, turning the car sharply to follow the lane around the west side of Martinez's lot.

"How much do you know about this man?" Naranjo asked.

"Martinez? Or Mazón?"

"The man who calls himself your uncle."

"Only what he's told me. If he's the one responsible for killing Quesada, Olveda, and now Steward, then there are links to all these people that I don't yet understand."

"There are ties," Naranjo said. "What is the expression? 'A falling out of thieves?' Something moved Benedicte Mazón to act against the Ortega brothers in Mazatlán." He shifted in the seat. "I would not be surprised if it is because of your son, my friend. That's what the display of a decade's worth of photographs and articles has to say." When Estelle didn't reply, he added gently, "That explains it all to me, even what has happened here in the States. What is the common factor?"

"Me."

"That's right." He nodded vigorously. "You and your family. I could go so far as to say that this man is protecting you and yours…in his own way. We have suspicions, you know. We *suspect,*" and he drew out the word for emphasis, "that Olveda and his *compadres* are doing nothing so much as establishing a…" He paused, searching for the right word. "A *beachhead* in Posadas. And we are surprised it has not happened before. What a marvelous place—close to the border, a good airport, near the interstate, yet isolated. And now this project of your Mr. Waddell. Imagine the sorts of things something like that can conceal." He sighed. "In this case, however, it is…it *appears* to be, an ambitious and creative group of Costa Ricans who are the entrepreneurs. And it further *appears* that we have some Mexican businessmen," and he said it with heavy sarcasm, "who object to what they see as their turf being invaded."

Estelle carefully guided the car around a trim little barn and the corner of an orchard. Just beyond, the double-wide trailer of Modesto Armijo loomed, and beyond that, the collection of antique farm machinery Modesto had collected over the decades—without a tillable field in sight.

"Do you think Mazón is working on their behalf? His killing of Steward, Olveda, even Quezada has nothing to do with me."

"Except protecting you and yours from being caught in the middle of something ugly. Surely you do not think that these people are simply going to say, 'Ah, well…it looks like we'll have to go elsewhere for our development plans. This Posadas County is too much of a risk.'"

"You're expecting more of this, then."

"Of course. We must not be naive. Mr. Waddell is going to have to be *constantly* on guard. That is what the attempt on your sheriff's life makes clear to me. Working with a non-entity such as Jerry Steward guarding the gates to the county is so much easier than trying to deal with our Robert Torrez…a man who cannot be bribed or intimidated, a man with complete and honest loyalties."

She braked so suddenly that the tires slid in the dirt. Cranking the spotlight around, she snapped it on and played the beam down the row of scrap that constituted Modesto Armijo's outdoor museum.

Three International Scouts all listed badly, tires removed, windshields long gone. A grain harvester, miles from the nearest grain field, loomed beside two aging tractors whose guts were no doubt gummed and rusted into a congealed, useless mess. For whatever reason, Modesto had left a space or two, and then parked a useless, worn-out Suburban with all six doors yawning, a Hilton for the packrats and the investigative towhees. Estelle held the light still. In the space between the Suburban and the nearest tractor, a dusty brown Chevy sedan rested, hood up, doors ajar, all four tires flat. As the light flooded past the hood, it reflected off the chrome spotlight by the driver's front door.

"So," she breathed. Naranjo sucked in a gentle breath but said nothing. Switching off the spot, Estelle found her hand light and got out of the county car. Mindful of the fanged denizens of the dry New Mexican back-country, she approached the row of junk carefully, watching where she put her feet. Naranjo followed, his own light playing patterns on the machinery.

The tire tracks in the stunted grass and crushed, gray weed stalks were fresh. Touching the driver's door to push it open further, she smelled not the dull, musky odor of years in the sun and weather, but the urban aroma of mixed aftershave, cigarette smoke, and sweat.

"The tires were knifed," Naranjo muttered. "But he left the license plate."

"Thoughtful of him," Estelle said. "Maybe he thought we'd never walk around behind it. The flat tires give it the derelict look."

Naranjo stood quietly, two paces away from the Caprice. "You know," he said finally, "if he took the time to wipe the car clean of prints, we lose an important connection."

"It was Mazón," Estelle said flatly. "I can smell him."

"That will be interesting to hear in court," the colonel chuckled.

"I think we can guarantee that Benedicte Mazón will never see a day in court."

"This charade gives him a few more minutes." Naranjo turned and looked west. "It is my understanding that the new fence goes just up into these foothills, not over the crest."

Estelle swept the flashlight beam toward the shadows west of the village. "Over the rise, down a little draw, and then it deadheads into some spectacular, rough country."

"And that's where he went."

"I would think so. Out of view of the cameras, out of view of the blimp, if it's flying. Under cover of darkness, he'll be over the barbed wire and into Mexico in just a couple of hours."

"Then he's our problem," Naranjo said grimly. "You know, we could fly the desert with helicopters and spend a million dollars and never find him. But a man like Mazón will surface eventually. It is only a matter of time." He clapped his hands once without much enthusiasm. "You know, some people would say that he has accomplished what he sought to do. He has protected your son, and now he has neutralized any threat to your village from Olveda and his cronies. He has satisfied whomever he answers to in my country. We may never hear from him again."

"One helicopter on each side of the border fence," Estelle said. "We have to try that. We might get lucky."

"You might. We might." He stretched his head back and look at the panoply of stars. "Come dawn? How far can he be?

"Miles from here, Tomás. And of course, so easy to hide in that country. On top of that, it's impossible to sneak up on someone with a helicopter." Estelle gazed back through the village, just a thin sprinkling of lights. "Or he might be sitting in the dark, behind someone's woodpile, watching us run around in circles. He has all the cards now."

Chapter Thirty-two

The deep hush of five-thirty in the morning blanketed the morgue. The small room with its twin tables, dual sinks, frosted white cabinets and three computers marching side by side seemed all the more cavelike in the quiet. The flow of technicians and staff had not yet started the day.

The assistant state medical examiner, Dr. Alan Perrone, stood with his arms crossed over his chest, waiting for an audience. Sheriff Bobby Torrez relaxed with one hip cocked against the edge of the nearest stainless steel table. Both tables were occupied, the white sheets pulled up to cover the grotesque damage.

Perrone and Torrez looked up as the door opened. Estelle held it for Miles Waddell and Colonel Tomás Naranjo.

"I'm sorry to make you wait," Estelle said. "The colonel had a short staff meeting via phone that he had to attend to."

"You gotta keep this morning interesting, I guess." The physician reached out a hand to the Mexican officer. "Welcome back."

"Thank you, Doctor. We could wish for more convivial circumstances."

"Indeed we could. Miles, I'm sure you have places you'd rather be."

"You got that right." Clearly, Miles Waddell did not relish his visit. Estelle guided him toward the tables with a hand on his right elbow.

Perrone extended his hand like a tour guide. "So," he turned to the sheriff, "Mr. Olveda is on the left, Mr. Steward is right here." He did not reach out to disturb the sheets. "Both violent, sudden attacks, neither with any sign of scuffle or any attempt at self-defense. That in itself is interesting, given that the victims are two adult males capable of *something* by way of self-defense. You have the times locked in place, so *that's* not a problem or issue. In fact, as far as I'm concerned, this is pretty cut and dried."

He stepped around the tables and reached out with both hands to pull down the sheet with the same care someone might use to reveal a painting on an easel. Dominic Olveda's pale face was frozen in surprise. With rubber-gloved thumb and forefinger, Dr. Perrone spread the lips of the single knife wound below the sternum.

"This wound is deep and incapacitating," the physician said. "The autopsy this morning will tell us for sure, but I'd guess the full length of a blade, a single thrust upward slightly, so hard that the handle caused some bruising. Can't tell you about precise angles yet, but we're talking about a violent stab wound to the major epicenter of the body. My theory is that the first wound, this one, gave the killer time to execute the second wound, the deep slash to the throat. The victim most likely wouldn't have been able to struggle. No resistance. Straight-in plunge, then whack. A vicious rake across the throat."

Waddell made an odd little noise, and Perrone looked up sharply. "You're all right?"

"Yeah." Waddell's face was pale. "Humans are always a little different from livestock." He forced a thin smile.

"I sympathize," Perrone said. "My guess is that Mr. Olveda lived just seconds after the attack. Besides probable damage to the heart itself, both jugular and carotid were completely severed."

Estelle thumbed pages in her notebook. "It would have been less than two minutes before the deputy reached the scene of the attack, and another minute or so before the body was found a few yards away. No signs of life."

"Oh, way before that," Perrone nodded. "From a medical point of view, this attack was meant to kill quickly and efficiently...with a knife, which isn't always as easy as Hollywood would have us believe. Whoever did this knew exactly what he was doing." He left the sheet down and turned to the second table.

"In a sense, Mr. Steward's case is the same." He pulled the sheet down far enough to reveal the gate attendant's shattered head. "What we have here is *one* blow. Just one. No defensive evidence, no follow-up attack. The force of the blow was so great that the aluminum bat itself was dented, and that by itself is incredible. I'm visualizing a full, round-house swing. A line drive, so to speak."

He bent town and turned the victim's head slightly. "Right on the bridge of the nose, so hard that the force continued inward, destroying the left orbit. We're looking at bone fragments exploded into the brain. Instantaneous unconsciousness, but with no damage to the heart, it would have continued pumping erratically for a minute or so…maybe even several. That explains the copious blood from the face—eyes, ears, mouth."

He looked at his visitors. "Once again, this isn't the result of a family spat. This isn't a brawl. A single blow, with a weapon of opportunity." He shrugged. "That in itself is interesting. If the same killer accounted for both victims, then you have someone who strikes hard and fast, with no hesitation."

Waddell let out a long sigh. "Christ, why Jerry? It couldn't have been just because the killer needed a car, for God's sakes. He wouldn't have come to the apartment just for that. Of all the places the killer *could* go to steal a damn car."

"Exactly right," Estelle said. "We'll want to talk with Rick Bueler again today, Miles. He had occasion to see Mr. Steward on a daily basis. If there's some connection between Olveda and Steward's death, that's a place to start."

"But what's to gain?" Waddell looked at each of the three officers in turn, hands spread out in frustration. "I mean, *Jerry?* What's he ever done to deserve this? I mean, this is *assassination,* for Christ's sakes. I mean, if you just want his car, take it. Why bash the man's brains out over a damn useless rattletrap?"

"He didn't just want the car, sir."

"You're shitting me. You know who did this, then? And *why* he did it?" He turned to Naranjo. "That's why you're up here?"

"This may be related to events in Mexico," Naranjo said quietly.

Waddell shook his head in frustration. "I'll have Bueler come in right away." He started to fish his cell phone out of his pocket. "Although, you know, he's never said anything about any of this to me."

"Actually, sir, I'd like to meet with him out at the facility. If you would make sure he's available, I'd appreciate it."

"You got it."

"Any surprises, let us know," the sheriff said to Perrone. They were the first words he'd spoken since his arrival at the morgue, and, bemused, Perrone looked at Torrez for a long moment until the sheriff turned to Naranjo. "You'll ride along with the Mexican air unit?"

"Absolutely. They're planning to be in the air at six-thirty from your airport."

"And you'll be at Waddell's," Torrez said to Estelle. "Let's do this. Doc, thanks for meetin' with us." In an uncharacteristic gesture of warmth, the sheriff stuck out his hand to the rancher. "I'm sorry about all this, Miles. We got something going on and we don't have a clue. I'll let you know when we do."

"You're doing an air search of some sort?"

"Yep. State Police on our side of the border, *Federales* on their side. And I don't bet on the results. Good way to waste some of the taxpayers' jet fuel."

"Should I go along?" Waddell asked.

"Nope. The undersheriff is workin' your place. We need you there."

Waddell looked at Estelle. "When?"

"I'm headed that way right now."

Once outside, Miles Waddell took the opportunity as the sheriff and Colonel Naranjo broke off and headed for Torrez's SUV.

"Did Torrez mean what he said?" Waddell asked. "You guys are in the dark about all this?"

"Not quite," Estelle replied. "Close, but not quite."

"Who are we after, then?"

"I'll let you know when I'm sure."

"But he's Mexican, right? That's gotta be."

"Safe guess, sir."

Chapter Thirty-three

"What's your impression of him so far?" Miles Waddell and Estelle watched Rick Beuler's tan Jeep making its dusty way across the mesa-top toward them. The rising sun turned the dust cloud golden. For their rendezvous, Estelle had chosen a mesa promontory, a spit of land like the bow of an enormous ship, on the north rim. They had an unobstructed view of the activity both below and on top of the mesa itself, with little likelihood of interruptions.

"Rick? He's eager. I call him Spook. I never know where the hell he's going to show up," the developer said. "He doesn't talk much, but that's okay with me."

"How much time did he spend with Jerry Steward?"

Waddell thumped his elbow on the fender, a small gesture of frustration. "I didn't pay much attention." His eyebrows wrinkled under the brim of his Stetson. "Should have, I suppose. I'm kinda naive that way. Hire a man, and then trust 'em. That's the way I do business, until circumstances show me otherwise."

"You told us the other day that Dominic Olveda visited here several times."

"Oh, yeah. Well, maybe not several, but at least twice. And that's as far as *I* know. Jesus, this is bad. You know, I kind of liked that little guy." Nodding off across the mesa, Waddell added, "Sometimes I think Olveda was almost as excited about all of this as I am. He even talked about the possibility of what he called a sister site down in Costa Rica. *Big* tourist draw. And you know," and he turned to look at Estelle, "his ideas involving the airport are not half bad. Doesn't get in *my* way, but provides some expansion of services for the area." He grunted in disgust. "Or *did.*"

Other people were just as enthusiastic about moving operations into Posadas County, Estelle thought. And they weren't as enthusiastic as Miles Waddell about sharing the bounty.

Beuler had parked behind Waddell's truck, and he now approached with quiet deference, as if loath to interrupt the conversation. He wore trainers, jeans, and a white western-style shirt. His dark blue baseball cap sported the United Security Resources logo, but otherwise he looked like someone's assistant track coach, lithe and confident as he approached.

"Rick, this is Posadas Undersheriff Estelle Reyes-Guzman," Waddell said. "I think you two have met."

"Briefly, a couple of times," Beuler agreed. "Good to see you up here again." His handshake was a quick pump, and he regarded Estelle expectantly as he slid his dark glasses up on top of his cap. From handshake distance, Estelle saw that Beuler was older than he first appeared when he dismounted from the truck. Sun crinkles touched the corners of his direct, surfer-blue eyes.

Estelle slipped from her clipboard a photo of Benedicte Mazón that Colonel Naranjo had provided and handed both it and the morgue photo of Miguel Quezada, the murdered hit man, to Beuler. "I'd be particularly interested to know if you've encountered either of these two men here at the facility."

Beuler took his time examining the images, and he took an extra minute with Quezada's grim portrait. The crow's feet at the corners of his eyes deepened a fraction. "We won't be expecting return visits from him, I assume."

"No." *And you can hope not from the other,* she thought.

"Not this one," Beuler said, handing back Mazón's official Mexican prison portrait. "But this second…he was up here at least once with the developer from Arizona. Mr. Olveda?"

"Other than with Mr. Waddell, did you see them talk to anyone else?"

Beuler hesitated, and Miles Waddell instantly jumped in. "Anything she needs to know, Rick. Anything at all."

"Mr. Olveda spoke with Jerry Steward, down at the gate. I was across the lot, where the crews were off-loading one of the cable spools for the tram. I saw Mr. Olveda drive in, with this one," and he nodded at the photo, "riding shotgun. They talked with Jerry for quite a while." He looked up at Estelle. "I mentioned that to Sheriff Torrez earlier."

"You didn't hear the conversation between Olveda and Steward?"

"No, ma'am. Every once in a while, Steward would point off toward the northeast. Who knows why."

"Show me how he did that." When Beuler hesitated, Estelle added, "I mean how he was standing, how he gestured. Every detail you can remember."

Beuler frowned, and turned in place. "Like Olveda stood with his hands on his hips, and Steward was like this." He turned some more and reached out toward the distant bulk of Cat Mesa with his left hand. "Then Steward drew a line, sort of, down south, like he was indicating the prairie over across the road."

"Do you remember when this was?"

"No, but it's in my log. Hang on just a moment."

As Beuler jogged back toward his truck, Waddell said, "He's an observant young man."

"I have to wonder how he linked up with USR in the first place." She knew that United Security Resources, a Colorado firm run by a former college classmate and close friend of hers, hired its staff only after exhaustive interviews and background checks. To be handed a security job as complex, and daily growing, as Waddell's *NightZone,* meant that Rick Beuler was far more than just a pretty face.

"All I know," Waddell said, "is that he spent a few years in the Merchant Marines." He shrugged. "Go figure."

"In the Merchants as what?"

"In logistics and planning, I think."

Beuler read as he walked the few yards back from his truck. "The last time I saw them here—and it would be that incident

I was talking about—was this past Tuesday." He followed the line of print across with one index finger. "Zero eleven twenty. They left the premises at zero eleven fifty-one."

"Did you speak with them that day as well?" she asked Waddell.

"Just this past Tuesday morning? Hell, I don't recall the exact time, but maybe." He looked at Beuler. "Did I?"

"You met with Mr. Olveda up by the tram site from zero ten-thirty to zero eleven-fifteen."

Waddell smiled broadly. "When did I have my last cup of coffee?" Before Beuler could answer, Waddell reached out and shook him by the shoulder. "Just kidding, my man. Just kidding."

"When Mr. Olveda spoke with you that day, what did he want to know?" Estelle asked.

"From me?" Waddell's forehead crinkled in concentration. "That visit, let's see." His face brightened. "We were talking about the tram car's capacity. Two tram cars, actually. One goes up, the other comes down. I told him that the Swiss engineers called for a max load of twenty-eight souls." He grinned. "Souls. Just like the airlines. Always makes me edgy. Sounds like they're preparing for something."

"Just that?"

"Pretty much." Waddell regarded the ground. "He was interested in load details about the train—we talked about that some, too. Basically," and he linked his hands together, "it sounded like he was thinking about the flow of customers. You know about that resort deal he's planning at the airport. Hell of a link to us, I'm hoping."

"And all this time Quesada remained in the vehicle?" She took the morgue photo from Beuler. "He didn't talk to you?"

"Nope. In fact, Olveda didn't even introduce him," Waddell said. "I thought maybe he would, but the guy never got out of the truck. That white rig Olveda was driving."

"The tram and the train, then. That was the extent of it?"

"Yep. And some about hunting. What the possibilities along those lines were. I told him absolutely not. Not with bikers, birdwatchers, and what have you. The whole shebang will be posted when the time comes." He smiled broadly. "'Hunt now, Bobby,' I told the sheriff the other day. He didn't seem to mind, but I'm sure there'll be some pissed hunters when it's all closed off. I said there was the possibility of some special hunts, maybe. Then Olveda wanted to know what the flow of visitors was at this point…preliminary interest, that sort of thing. I told him that Jerry had the official log at the gate, and that he should talk to him about that."

"And sure enough, he did."

"Yep. That's what Rick's log says."

"If you want to talk with Steward, we can call him in. He's late anyway," Beuler said.

"And going to be later," Estelle said. "Both Mr. Olveda and Mr. Steward were murdered last night, Mr. Beuler." She held out Mazón's photo again. "We think this man is linked to the killings."

"Jerry was killed last night?"

"That's right."

Beuler's jaw muscles danced as he clenched his teeth. "How?"

"One hit in the face with a baseball bat. While he sat in his living room. Just a few minutes before or after Mr. Olveda was stabbed to death at the Posadas Inn."

Beuler frowned hard, shaking his head slowly. "Can't imagine that." He looked up at Estelle. "Steward not being able to defend himself, I mean. Hell, the man owns an arsenal. I know he had at least one weapon in his car. I know he had his concealed carry card, but we had agreed he *wouldn't* carry at the gate when he was meeting the public. And he was always talking about hunting prairie dogs with his AR."

"I don't think he had time to lift a hand to defend himself," Estelle said. "He wasn't given that chance."

"The choppers are part of the search for the killer?" Beuler glanced skyward. "I saw two just a little bit ago, headin' toward the airport."

"Yes. We think the killer would have headed for the border. But we're not sure. So keep that photo, Mr. Beuler. The man's name is Mazón. If you see him, presume him to be armed and extremely dangerous."

"He killed this man as well?" He reached for the photo of Quesada.

"We think so. With the man's own gun. So…if you see anything unusual, Mr. Beuler. Anyone you don't know or can't verify. Redouble your security efforts. We don't know what this man is after now, and that makes it doubly difficult. You're working alone?"

"At the moment."

"Then there will be an officer or two out shortly to assist you. They will have been briefed. More eyes can't hurt."

"I don't think we need any extra help, ma'am. USR is going to send down another officer or two on Monday."

"Unfortunately, in this case, next week won't do anyone any good," Estelle said. "Trust me on that."

Chapter Thirty-four

A nighttime air search was hopeless, and Torrez had chaffed at the wait for first light. He would have preferred to be by himself, on foot, with a good pair of binoculars. But urgency demanded a quick search.

Despite air support come dawn and, on the Mexican side of the border, more than fifty troops disturbing the desert dust, no sign of Benedicte Mazón was found—not a single track or discarded water bottle. New Mexico Route 56 reached Regál, and where the highway crossed the border and turned into the well-pounded dirt road leading to Tres Santos, soldiers and police sifted through the occasional small groups of people who had reason to be in that section of bleak desert, most heading either northeast toward Palomas, or south to Janos. Mazón was not among them.

On the American side of the border, Sheriff Robert Torrez kept the helicopter pilot, State Police Sergeant Paul Platt, busy avoiding crags and boulders that projected from the mountainous jumble as they flew westward, away from Regál. The "awful thing," as Torrez had heard Estelle's mother refer to the monumental border fence on rare occasions, made the world safe until it arrived westbound in Regál. Westward, through the steep jumble of the San Cristóbals, the fence had not been completed. Locals figured that the towering rock palisades, sheer canyons, and nothing much better on the other side was deterrent enough.

On many occasions, Torrez had hunted the forbidding country, exploring the deeply shaded canyons and occasional wet spots where ancient water still seeped. Years before, he had caught a glimpse of a jaguar, but the big cat had seen him first, and allowed him no closer than a quarter mile…for just a few seconds.

Despite the impossible terrain, the remains of several mine operations still littered the wilderness, dried fragments of support beams like bleached bones among the rocks. In a few accessible places, the faintest scars of wagon tracks marked where iron and beams had been freighted in to staging stations. Higher up on the slopes, the slag piles were modest, testimony that in country where every pick or shovel or stick of dynamite had to be packed in by human mule, even the most ardent prospector gave up the dream after a while.

Even crusty old Reuben Fuentes, Teresa Reyes's uncle and Estelle Reyes' guardian when the teenaged girl had first come to the United States to continue her schooling, had talked about the vast reaches of the San Cristóbals and the riches that probably could be found there with enough effort and risk.

Those seeking an unguarded trail into the United States left behind occasional traces of their efforts—abandoned clothing, empty water jugs, useless personal items. As he hunted, Bob Torrez had often gazed at the forbidding Cristóbals above him, wondering if the bones of immigrants littered the upper crevices, crags, and canyons of their new, permanent home.

Torrez knew that the search for Benedicte Mazón was hopeless, barring a fantastic stroke of luck. There would be no easy capture of this man. Mazón would not panic and run, to be chased down like a weary coyote trying to hide in the stunted desert scrub. The mountains provided perfect cover, giving the fugitive time to think through his strategy for escaping across the prairie country below him.

The chopper announced itself from miles away. Mazón could make himself comfortable on any rock sofa and watch the search efforts, slipping back into shelter if the machine came too close—lessons learned from the jaguar himself. Although Torrez would never have admitted it—if he thought about it at all—the search was probably good politics. That three corpses had been found within the village limits within two days—and Frank Dayan's *Posadas Register* would remind readers lest they should forget—was cause enough for the county sheriff to take to the air in a massive manhunt. That the cooperation was now international was news in itself.

As the morning progressed, the breeze freshened, and with the air movement came first the rough chop as air currents bounced among the mountain's rocks. In the distance, Torrez could see the scud of dust lifting from the Mexican desert, and once in a while the wink of Mexican air support as they criss-crossed the rugged country.

The State Police chopper bucked and kicked against updrafts, and Torrez felt his stomach mixing the acid coffee and what little breakfast he'd grabbed on the way to the airport.

"About another five minutes, and we're out of here," Platt said, his voice unnaturally loud through the headset. Even as he spoke, he rode the chopper up slope toward the ridge summit, reaching for smoother altitude. "If he's anywhere around here, he's laughin' at us."

Torrez pointed at the deep cleft in the south slope. "Fly right down that, out where it fans into the desert."

"We don't own the air out there," the pilot said.

"Don't care," Torrez replied. He remembered the country now below them from a decade before, when he'd bagged a sheep with a long shot and had the mortally wounded animal struggle through the border fence. At that moment, there hadn't been a Mexican cop within a hundred miles, and Torrez hadn't even considered the dim risks of hopping the fence to secure his trophy.

The game of border politics was different now. All Homeland Security really accomplished, Torrez firmly believed, was money wasted on paperwork and ugly fences.

The pilot compromised, heading south over American soil until they could see the barbed-wire border fence below. In a few places, a rough two-track tried to parallel the fence on both sides, enough room for a really ambitious, fearless Jeep driver to coax his vehicle. At that point, Platt reared the chopper to a hover, and spun slowly in place, giving them a 360-degree panorama.

The dirt road to Tres Santos was twelve miles east. Mexican police were swarming. Mazón's only chances were to beat them through the border barrier or relax and wait for them to lose interest.

Torrez looked at his watch for a moment. The evening before, Steward murdered first, then the auto ride to the Posadas Inn. Olveda had been stabbed and slashed to death shortly after nine p.m. And then, including the little diversion of turning north out of the motel's parking lot, the drive to Regál in Steward's car would take forty minutes at a deliberate speed, one that wouldn't run the risk of alerting a patrolling cop. Ten o'clock, maybe, as Mazón parked the Chevy in the village meadow. Estelle and Naranjo had found it shortly afterward, and by that time, Mazón could easily have breached the border. Not a wasted move. And now, he'd had all night.

"He's south now," Torrez said with finality. Mazón could have spent the eight hours of darkness climbing up into the mountains, gaining secure cover. Or he could have crossed through the barbed-wire border fence and headed south. A steady pace, part fast walk and part jog, would net him three miles each hour—with the roll of desert and the plunge of arroyos, he could be ten or fifteen miles deep into Mexico at this moment.

Torrez assumed that Colonel Tomás Naranjo must be thinking the same thing. The dust from his ground search had moved farther and farther south, including the tiny village of Tres Santos, and onward toward Janos. One scruffy little man consumed by the desert—Mazón would take some confidence from that.

Torrez slid his headphones to one side and screwed the tiny ear bug from his cell phone into place. The speed select took him to his undersheriff's number, and he waited patiently while the towers bounced signals around.

"Guzman." The undersheriff's voice sound as if she was crouched inside a fifty-five-gallon drum.

"We're wastin' a lot of jet fuel up here," Torrez said. "He's either taken up residence somewhere up in the mountains, or he's skipped the circle. Naranjo's ground forces might have better luck."

"Don't bet on it, Bobby." The sheriff heard Naranjo's voice in the background, garbled by the static of aircraft radio traffic. Estelle added, "He just said that no one has seen a thing."

"Didn't think so. Look, we'll be back at the airport in half an hour or so. Did Mears finish with Seward's car?"

"He did. Lots of prints, but I know what we'll find when we process them, and it won't be Mazón's. Also two guns, one Sig-Sauer .45 automatic in the glove box and an AR in the trunk, full magazine, ready to go. Both belonged to Steward. Mazón certainly had the opportunity."

"There might have been others. He don't need a damn arsenal, after all. And guns don't seem his choice."

"That's how it looks. And we just finished with Beuler, by the way. There was nothing much he could add, except he had some reservations about Steward's performance."

"No shit."

"It's looking like most of the principal players are out of the show."

"Except Mazón."

"Except him."

"Meet us at the airport?"

"Yes, but you'll get there before I do. I'm just heading south on 14 now."

"You planning to go to Mazatlán later today?"

"*Por dios,* I'd like to, Bobby. But I can't. *Padrino's* son would take me if I asked, and the good colonel has offered. He'd jump at the favor in a heartbeat. But I can't ask that. I'd like to keep pestering *hijo* every fifteen minutes on the phone, but I'm tough. It's actually been half an hour since I last called. He's fine."

Torrez actually laughed. "So tough."

"I have this nightmare of someone walking out on stage when Francisco is halfway through Beethoven, and handing him a cell phone. 'It's your mother, Maestro.'"

"Audience would enjoy that."

"I bet. See you in a bit, Bobby. I think you're right. It's all in the colonel's hands now. At least for the time being."

"The time being? Means what? We ain't goin' down into Mexico."

Estelle hesitated. "It's just that I can't imagine Benedicte Mazón going to all this trouble—following Francisco's career over the years, then finding me, then eliminating five from the other side and making a dangerous sidetrip to the states—*meeting* with me in a public place, risking arrest, then escaping jail. I can't imagine him doing all that and then just disappearing forever like a whiff of smoke."

"So what's he going to do?"

"I wish I knew. But he has to know that we're looking for him. And we're not alone. Remember Quesada, Bobby. Someone gave him his orders, and he took a shot at you. And then Mazón killed *him*. And then he took out Quesada's associate, Olveda. Whoever those two were working for won't forget that. They're not going to let Mazón walk off scot-free. Somebody's plans got jinxed, and he'll be the target."

"Huh. Okay then. You don't need to walk into the middle of a turf war."

Sergeant Platt turned the chopper away from the border, away from the mountains, and headed in a beeline for Posadas Municipal Airport. At one point, Bobby relaxed with his head against the plexi-glass, watching the landscape slide by. As State 56 stretched away toward the village of Posadas, he looked for the white dash that would be his undersheriff's car. The road was empty.

By the time they touched down, the wind was kicking dust in savage little bursts. Sheriff Torrez slid out of the machine, ducking instinctively under the rotors even though they were two feet over his head. Sergeant Jackie Taber walked out on the hot tarmac to meet him.

"Nothing," Torrez grumbled, and the young woman nodded at his one word flight and search report.

"Estelle received a phone call from the Román Diaz family," she said. "Actually, a Mr. Juan Guerrero? She didn't explain. She was having a hard time copying your transmissions from the chopper, so she relayed to me."

Torrez stopped in his tracks, frowning at his sergeant.

"Sir?" Taber prompted.

"You're sure it was *Román* Diaz?" he asked.

"Yes, sir. She said you'd know."

"Yeah, I know." Torrez had already started walking toward his truck, but stopped and turned, looking at Taber but clearly thinking about something else. "She headed that way?"

"*That way,* sir?"

"Román Diaz lives next door to where Teresa Reyes lived in Tres Santos. He's the one with a phone. Probably the only one in town. Did Estelle say she was headed down there?"

"She didn't say, sir."

Torrez spun on his heal and strode back to his truck, dialing his own phone as he did so. Again, he stopped before he reached his destination.

"Sarge, how much head start does she have?"

Taber glanced at her watch. "She called me when she was just outside of Regál, sir. About fifteen minutes ago. Maybe twenty." The sheriff didn't acknowledge the information, and the county Expedition was already in motion before he bothered to slam the driver's door shut.

Chapter Thirty-five

The phone call had come as Estelle Reyes-Guzman idled the car down County Road 14, away from *NightZone*, leaving behind the noise of the development with its own symphony of diesel machinery working in a dozen places at once. Her pulse leaped, assuming even as she flipped open her phone that the caller was her elder son, reporting that all was well in Mazatlán. Instead, an international call code was displayed—Colonel Tomás Naranjo, no doubt.

"Guzman." Her greeting was answered by first silence, and then voices in the background. She distinctly heard the Spanish, someone being urged to *"take it. Talk with her."*

More silence, then a strong voice broke in. "Estelle? This is Román. Román Diaz."

Estelle switched mental gears to Spanish. "What a wonderful surprise, Román! I hope you and yours are well?"

"We are. We are. You know, it's been too long since you've been down to see us. How is Teresa?"

"Actually, she's fine, Román. She's enjoying the experience of being ninety-nine, we hope. How about that."

"This woman will live forever." Román's voice softened. "In our hearts, at the very least. And the family?"

"Fine as can be. Francisco is in Mazatlán this weekend, with concerts."

"I heard about that. *Magnifico.* What a son this young man must be to you."

How did you hear about the concert? Estelle wondered. Román Díaz, father to a now-scattered brood of eight, founder of a successful wood-carving venture in Tres Santos, and for a lifetime a neighbor a stone's throw away from Teresa Reyes' home near the Río Plegado and its ever changing personality. Many connections.

"But listen," and Román spoke now in his heavily accented English. "I have a neighbor who wishes to speak with you." He laughed. "I think this is his first time in a decade with the telephone, so be patient. You remember Juan Guerrero?"

"Of course I do." Did she? The name, yes. But she hadn't seen Juan Guerrero in thirty years, perhaps more. Benedicte Mazón had forced the memory.

Guerrero's voice was soft and husky, and she heard Román say, "No, hold this part close to your mouth."

"Estelita? Is that you?"

"Juan, it is so good to hear your voice! And Esperanza…is she well?" That was always a tricky question when she hadn't heard from a family for decades, especially in rural Mexico, where the most routine health care was a difficult proposition at best.

"Such a woman," Juan Guerrero said. "I am to tell you that you must visit with us."

"I will do that."

"No…I mean soon."

She hesitated. "Are you well, *Señor* Guerrero?" Perhaps the formality would open a door.

"Oh, yes," and he sounded impatient. "I think the police are now looking for your uncle."

She hesitated. "Benedicte Mazón?"

"Ah, then you know."

"Are the police there now?"

"No. We saw a helicopter a few moments ago, but it left. There were two trucks with troops in town, too. But they did not come here. It is very strange."

Her stomach clenched uneasily. "You've seen him? This man who claims to be an uncle of mine?"

"Yes. And you know, it's been a long, long time. He is who he says he is. That night…" His voice trailed off as if the memory was too elusive.

Estelle realized with a start that her car had rolled to a stop. One of the gigantic black and red prairie wasps, what ranchers called a "cow killer," was inspecting the tray that surrounded the windshield wipers.

"You will come down?"

"Did someone ask you to call me, Juan?"

"Yes."

Of course he had, she thought. "Mazón asked this of you?"

"You know, I haven't seen this one since that day. That day when he stood beside the Plegado with me, and we watched it destroy so much. Just a little boy then. And I was there, too." *He cannot bring himself to talk about the family,* Estelle thought. *This one.* "Where is Mazón now, don Guerrero?"

"He is at my house, Estelita. I think he is safe there." *He is safe?* There was a lengthy list of people for whom she cared more about than Benedicte Mazón. If he was in Tres Santos, then every one of them was at risk.

"And he told you to call me?"

"Yes. He said, 'I want her to know why I did what I did.'" That in itself was some relief. When Guerrero had mentioned that the troops had arrived, then pulled back, her first thought was that Colonel Naranjo was playing games. But, if he knew the fugitive was holed up at Guerrero's, then he was providing a portal for Estelle. There was no reason for Mazón to talk with police—even on the remote chance that they would *give* him such an opportunity.

"You'll wait with Román for me, Juan. Don't go back to your home."

"I cannot do that, Estelita. Esperanza is there, you know. I do not see any danger."

"Your wife is keeping *Señor* Mazón company?"

"Yes. There is much to talk about. The old days, you know."

"All right. Then go join them. Keep him talking. I'm on my way. Perhaps twenty minutes."

"All right. My neighbor wants to talk with you."

Román Diaz came back on the line, and Estelle had already kicked the Charger into motion down County Road 14, dust rising high.

"Estelle, are the police really looking for this man? There's an army of them around."

"Yes." A natural enough assumption, given the now departed police chopper and trucks laden with troops. But the government interest had vanished as quickly as it had arrived. Reaching the pavement, she turned right, south-bound, and the Charger quickly shed a layer of dust as it worked its way up to triple digits.

"Juan will be safe with him?" Román asked. "Perhaps I should accompany him back to the house."

"No need," Estelle said. "Please don't do that. The police will do nothing until Colonel Naranjo orders it, and he will talk with me first." *I hope.*

"Ah. Juan did not mention him. But that's good. He is a man we can trust, no?" Before Estelle could verbalize a reply, Román Diaz added, "You know, I knew this Mazón when he was a small boy. Before his family moved to Janos. I have heard stories…"

"Then you know he can be dangerous."

The highway to Regál was empty, the road snaking down from the pass into the village in a series of switchbacks that had rewarded more than one incautious driver with a somersault down into the boulders and trees. The parking lot of the church was empty as well, and just beyond it, she turned into the tiny parking lot bordered by a dozen United States flags, alternating with the bright yellow and red of New Mexico's Zia banner.

The unimposing, non-threatening character of the Regál crossing would be changed within the year as Homeland Security poured millions into a new, high tech, 24/7 facility. Agent Sam Werthiem, a rookie enjoying perhaps the dullest crossing anywhere on the border, sauntered out and looked at Estelle quizzically as she got out of the car, leaving the engine running.

Shotgun in hand, she rounded the back of the Charger and pushed open the trunk lid. In a moment she reappeared with the AR-15 rifle in the other hand.

"I need to leave these with you, Sam," she said. "You have room in your vault?"

"Sure. What's up?"

"I need to visit relatives." She offered an engaging smile, and as the officer took the two long guns, she slipped the holster containing the Beretta off her belt. "This too."

"I guess I can do that. But let me fix you up with the receipt," Werthiem said. Estelle shook her head, already heading back to her car, leaving the agent's arms loaded down with artillery.

"Keep them for me. I won't be long."

She didn't recognize the Mexican officer who now waited on his side of the fence, standing in the shade of the white office building. He eyed the official car with curiosity as Estelle pulled to a stop. Handing him her license, registration, and commission, she read *E.L. Contreras* on his name tag. "I'm meeting some of your officers in Tres Santos, just for a few minutes. Call Colonel Naranjo if you need to."

No doubt, he'd seen her off-loading the weapons, but he looked through the Charger's cage toward the backseat. "You must surrender any firearms or ammunition," he said, hefting his clipboard as if all of his authority rested there.

"I have done so." He would clearly have seen the transfer a moment ago.

He examined her commission documents again. "How long have you worked for the Sheriff's Department?"

"Twenty-four years."

"Ah. Then you know Sheriff Torrez."

"Of course."

"Will he be arriving soon?"

"Perhaps."

He nodded sagely and handed back the paperwork. "We always look forward to seeing him. And you have a pleasant stay, *Señora* Guzman." He nodded toward the dusty two-lane road that was Estelle's only choice, a route that wandered south to disappear over a small rise.

"Thank you." The road was unchanged since she had walked it thirty years before, or when she had raised little contrails of dust while riding her bike. Over the years, she had driven it dozens, maybe hundreds of times. Only six miles now separated her from the village of Tres Santos, and she knew every rock, cactus, and lizard. Still, it was no longer home, and no longer reached out to her heart.

Chapter Thirty-six

A low range of hills obscured the approach to Tres Santos, and once past them, tourists would feel that they were deep in Old Mexico—no border fence in view, no wash of signs blossoming along the route, no dwellings, no cattle, no nothing. The road forced attention—not quite wide enough for two cars, with blind corners and undulations, and no prior warning about what other pathways might merge from out of the desert.

The country south of the hills was surprisingly green, or at least a narrow strip of it was where the Rio Plegado wound down toward the village, its *galleria* of brush, small cottonwoods, even desert willows and walnuts flourished. Fed by springs, the Plegado puddled in the few spots where it surfaced, a true Jekyll and Hyde personality. The focal point of a huge watershed, it had been the Plegado that had swollen and surged half a lifetime ago, triggering a flood wall so powerful that it had swept away the Mazón family pickup at the river crossing south of the village. That was the story, anyway, told by Benedicte Mazón. But she would trust Juan Guerrero's version of the events that had left her an orphan.

As Estelle followed the road that bordered the Plegado, she saw that save for the occasional puddle under the protective shade, most of the riverbed was stone dry. The river—a tiny creek, actually—had become her friend during the years when she had been blissfully ignorant of the disaster. Then, she had been Estelle Florencia Reyes…and had been content to *be* Estelle

Reyes. The name *Mazón* meant nothing to her beyond the man who now made such extraordinary claims.

The Iglesia de los Tres Santos greeted visitors to the little valley, and oversaw the day-to-day life there, but no longer garnered the affectionate glances it once did. Burning to the ground in 1980, the community had made the incomprehensible decision to build a modern frame replacement. A short steeple jutted out of the metal roofing, and although the church was painted brown, it bore no resemblance, neither in appearance nor character, to the original adobe structure that it replaced.

Still, it had lasted now more than three decades without sagging or cracking, and residents had grown used to it. *Utilitario* was the most common compliment.

Estelle swung the car into the church parking lot and paused in the sparse shade of an ancient, black-limbed walnut. With the car windows down, she switched off the low rumble of the engine and let the sounds of the village seep in. Sun pounded on the packed dirt of the lot, and off the white paint of the Charger. Far in the distance, she heard the whine of a power saw—perhaps don Román himself, or one of his sons, at work on more whimsical creations.

Off to the southwest, somewhere below the gray concrete block elementary school, two goats made conversation. The faint thup-thup of helicopter blades carried in from far to the east, too far away to be really intrusive. With a rush of wings, two drab sparrows lit on the stone walkway to the church and regarded her with heads cocked.

Slipping her cell phone out of her pocket, she selected the sheriff's number and waited while it rang, and rang some more. The repeater on top of San Cristóbal peak should have made reception crystal clear. Finally, on the eighth ring, Torrez answered in his usual mid-conversation habit.

"So what are you doing down there?" He didn't sound pleased.

"I'm parked at the Iglesia in Tres Santos, Bobby. Everything is quiet. Juan Guerrero said that Mazón is waiting for me. At the Guerreros'. The police are nearby, but they're pulled back now. Maybe that's Naranjo's doing. I don't know. He's been cagey with me."

"Huh." Whether he was disinterested, disapproving, or just plain Bobby was hard to tell. "What does he want?"

"To talk with me."

"I meant Naranjo. If he knows where Mazón is, why doesn't he just go get him?"

"I think…actually, Bobby, I don't know what I think. Maybe it's a favor to me."

"Hell of a favor. You talked to Naranjo?"

"No. I haven't seen him. I don't know. He may not even be here. There's a presence, though. A chopper is in the neighborhood. I haven't seen any troops yet."

"So you're just walking into that one."

"I suppose so."

"You left your hardware at the crossing?"

"Yes."

"Not the smartest thing."

"It's their law, Bobby." The sheriff knew that as well as anyone, and he would obey that policy at times when it suited him.

"Look, I'm headed toward Regál right now. If you need anything…"

"I don't think so. If Mazón is here, I have nothing to fear from him."

"Yeah, but Naranjo? Don't be gettin' between the two of them. This guy ain't *his* uncle."

"I'll try my best."

"What's your plan, then?"

Estelle paused. "I wish I had one, Bobby. I truly do."

"Listen to Naranjo, then. Talk with him first. It's *his* turf. Don't be tryin' to work this without him."

"I should be back on the other side of the fence," Estelle said, but she said it to herself as she hung up the phone.

It would have been easy to think that she didn't understand Tomás Naranjo. If Benedicte Mazón had taken refuge in Juan Guerrero's home, what stayed the colonel's hand? Mexican law enforcement was not known for its patience, especially with a killer who had struck twice on one side of the border and three times on the other. Simple enough. A truckload of solders to surround the simple little adobe, and Mazón would come out, one way or another. Cheaper to bury than to feed.

She started the car and eased it out of the church parking lot. From this rise, she could count half a dozen new trailer homes and the small general store that had been built since her last visit. The tiny Tienda de Tres Santos would cater to the modest flow of tourists—there were too few residents to support any such undertaking. As she passed, she saw an SUV with Iowa plates at the single gas pump. The hundred liters of fuel might be the store's only sale of the day.

Beyond the store was the first of four river crossings, and the Plegado barely dampened the concrete "upside down bridge," a simple and safe smooth passage across when the water wasn't high. A depth gauge, a striped pole with meter marks, had been installed at each side, and it promised that the Plegado could rage with at least three meters' depth of water charging down the canyon. From trickle to killer.

Her car tires whispered across the concrete of the inverted crossing and she looked up-channel. The story of her family's tragic demise might be entirely apocryphal, of course. Teresa Reyes had never told her anything beyond the basic story of her life that began a year *after* the flood. The one-year-old who she'd taken in had spent the first year of her life nurtured by the church. Mexico was no stranger to orphans, and the church welcomed having the tiny child so comfortably adopted by the widowed school teacher Teresa Reyes. Juan Guerrero had kept the tragedy to himself—as the years passed, there was less and less reason for him to seek out the little girl and speak of the flood. And of course, every other year or so, there were other angry surges of floodwaters, all of them blending into the accepted character of the river. Other residents of the valley had suffered similar fates when they became careless or fatally daring.

The incident that had claimed her family, if Mazón and Guerrero were to be believed, would be legend. Everyone in town would know the story. They might *not* know what had become of the newborn orphan child. A very thin possibility.

True enough, the Mazón family, if that was their name, simply ceased to be. And now, Benedicte Mazón, claiming to be her uncle, had crawled out from under a rock.

The dirt road crossed the Plegado three more times. The road followed the river channel around an ox-bow, and for a few hundred yards the Plegado coursed due west. On the south side of the river, she once more stopped and shut off the engine. This was no sylvan streamlet with shade-dappled waters that enchanted photographers. The deeply scarred banks were supported here and there with the rip-rap manufactured from the crumpled remains of automobiles and trucks too lame to continue their road service. Estelle wondered if, buried somewhere in the sands downstream, the crumpled Mazón family's pickup truck enjoyed the same fate.

Far to the west, she heard just the faintest engine sound, and looked up toward the ridge, a cactus and rock-strewn vantage point that she had climbed dozens of times as a child, often in company with Mateo or Abbie Diaz. A brown SUV had taken one of the rough burro trails to the top, and now parked with a panoramic view of the village. One man got out and rested something on the hood of the truck. Even from 500 yards away, she could guess what it was—and where it would be looking.

"Ay," she breathed. A curious towhee hopped noisily through the brush and emerge to examine her car, pausing for a moment just below the driver's window. The bird's head cocked, and large eyes regarded Estelle. "What do you know about all this?" she whispered. With a brief *nuck,* the bird flew off, disinterested.

She started the car and eased it forward, away from the river. An imposing adobe wall, decorated here and there with bursts of Talavera tile, grew out of the hillside, and where the road skirted close, a sign announced *Casa Diaz.* In another ten yards, an ornate iron gate yawned open. The vegetation hinted that the gate had not been swung closed in years.

The circular gravel driveway brought her to Casa Diaz, a squat fortress of thick adobe walls that horseshoed around a courtyard shaded with pampered cottonwoods and two burly walnut trees. A three-tiered fountain splashed water noisily, the spray almost reaching the two wrought-iron benches. Colonel Tomás Naranjo sat on one of them, leaning forward with his elbows on his knees, chin resting on his hand. As Estelle's county car nosed through the gate, he rose, stepped to the fountain and reached down to turn a brass valve. The fountain water died to a gentle and quiet trickle.

Estelle pulled in only far enough to avoid blocking the gate. She had worked with this man dozens of times over the years, always gently deflecting his personal interest in her. He had never made any secret of his admiration for her and her family.

"I apologize in advance for making all of this needlessly complicated," he said, his elegant English cadence marking each syllable. "Still, it is good to see you here again." He reached out his hands and took Estelle's in both of his, a courtly grip that lingered. His eyes never left hers. "I never tire of visiting this place. It is indeed fortunate that my wife is one of their best customers."

Estelle stopped, turning slightly so that Naranjo had to drop his right hand from the comfortable spot it had found at the small of her back as he escorted her toward one of the benches. She had first met Naranjo when she was but twenty-two. In all of those years, his courtly manner—even deference toward her— had remained unchanged. He had never pressed close enough, either in words or physically, to make her uncomfortable. But there was no need to encourage him. His admiration-from-afar could stay that way.

"I am told that Mazón is here?"

The colonel nodded slowly. "Not exactly *here*, but," and he pointed south with his chin. "At don Guerrero's. I wanted to give you some time with him." A natural enough presumption, she supposed, but not one she eagerly embraced.

"If you have him in custody, we could have met in one of the district offices."

"In a manner of speaking, he is in custody...in that there is nowhere now for him to go." He turned and looked off into the distance, taking in the truck on the ridge. "We do not need to rush into tragedy."

"Means what?" It was one of Bobby Torrez's favorite expressions, a cryptic demand for clarification, and Estelle found it perfectly suited to the way she felt at the moment.

Naranjo almost smiled. "*Señor* Mazón is currently accepting the hospitality of don Juan Guerrero, who is also anxious to speak with you. He tells me that he hasn't seen you for many years."

"We move on."

Naranjo laughed, his handsome face capturing the moment of pure pleasure. "Oh, we do. We do." His head dropped as he removed his dark glasses, two fingers smoothing the mussed hair over his ears. "At this moment, how would *you* like this to...to work? What are your wishes?"

Estelle took a deep breath, wishing the answers were cop-easy. "We have a triple homicide in my jurisdiction, Colonel. You have at least two in yours. If Benedicte Mazón is guilty of any or all of those, then he needs to be in custody." *He won't go quietly,* she thought. *Not this time.*

And as if hearing her thoughts, Naranjo said, "I don't believe the actual apprehension," and he lingered over each of the four syllables in turn, "is going to be so straight-forward. This is a man with everything to lose. It appears to me that he wishes to take a final moment to justify himself to you. That is important to him, it seems."

"I don't care what's important to him, Colonel."

Naranjo shrugged. "No, but it helps to explain his motivation."

"Of course he knows you're here?"

"I am sure of it."

"And he's just sitting in that little cottage and waiting to be arrested? Or shot?"

"He is not waiting for me," Naranjo said patiently. "It is you with whom he wishes to meet."

"Why have you granted the courtesy? He's there—arrest him. Or is it not so simple?"

"Indeed not. I have no desire to visit this *confrontation* on such a gentle and innocent family." He drew himself up, taking a deep breath that savored the dry, clean air. "This place," he said, and then he looked at Estelle with raised eyebrows. "You feel the peace here, no?"

"Colonel, I talked with this man at the hospital in Las Cruces, and I arrested him there. He had his chance to say whatever he wished to me at that time. And then he escaped from the Posadas lockup and killed two more people. That's what interests me."

"And yet you came here today. You could have just let us take him…" Naranjo shrugged as if the outcome of that was a foregone conclusion.

Estelle fell silent. *And why should I care about this man?* she thought. *What do I want to know?*

"Would you speak with *Señor* Guerrero? He is an old man, and none of this is easy for him."

"He's had thirty years to tell his story. I was in Tres Santos at least half a hundred times during those years. What I want is Benedicte Mazón safely in custody, and me back across the border where I belong." Estelle's words rang more harshly than she might have liked. "I want my son out of Mazatlán, out of harm's way." She knew perfectly well the Mexican notion of *familia*. The world could stop until this issue was resolved. Naranjo lifted a hand, begging for patience.

"I would take it as a personal favor if you would at least speak with don Guerrero." A smile touched his generous lips, and Estelle admitted his undeniable attraction.

"I *have* spoken with him on the telephone. But you puzzle me, Tomás." She saw an eyebrow lift slightly at her use of his given name. "You have a fugitive cornered, and I assume you've surrounded him with adequate resources to force the surrender of a modest army." She looked pointedly at the ridge behind them where the truck was still parked. "Yet here we sit."

"Why did you come to Mexico?" Naranjo asked gently.

"I came because *Señor* Dias asked me to—as did don Guerrero. There is a possible link between Mazón and three deaths in our county, but that is a matter for the bureaucrats who arrange extradition papers. And there is a link somehow between all of that and the incident outside the theater in Mazatlán. I am curious, of course."

"You could have simply waited for me to forward the police report—the apprehension report—to you, and then waited for the extradition process to take its course." Naranjo eyed her, eyes appraising.

"If ever."

Naranjo nodded. "There is always that."

"I admit to a deep curiosity, Tomás. If this man is who he claims to be, then he is the last surviving member of my parents' generation. I never knew what happened to my mother and father. I have never known their names. I didn't even know I was *adopted* until I was sixteen, and even then, it was enough to know that the church had had custody of me until Teresa took me in." She shrugged. "So…on that score, there isn't going to be some sudden epiphany here that is going to change my life."

"And your son?"

"My sons," Estelle corrected. "One is as remarkable as the other. If Mazón did something to protect Francisco while the young man was in Mazatlán, I'm grateful." She held up an index finger. "But no more so than if a young city patrolman happened on the two thugs in the alley outside the theater and managed to subdue them before they had the chance to act. I am grateful. Period. *Punto.*"

"Of course. But your son occupies the world's stage at the moment. So to speak. His fame crosses borders."

"Yes, it does. And now it seems highly likely that there is some link between the plan to kidnap the boys and whatever the objective was in Posadas—Mazón apparently chose to terminate both operations in one sweep. That's the way it looks right now. I need to find the answers to that. I'd be interested to find out who he works for."

She regarded Naranjo with interest, wondering how much he was holding back. "You know, the assassin who took a foolish shot at our sheriff? I really don't care if he—whoever he turns out to be—stepped in front of a truck, or had his brains blown out by Benedicte Mazón. He took a rifle shot at our sheriff, and fortunately missed. I could be cynical and say that by dying, Quesada saved us a lot of work and expense and makes the world a better place. Ditto the two brothers in the Mazatlán alley. They have been neatly *removed.* But I *don't* know about *Señor* Dominic Olveda. When he was murdered, he was deep in a meeting with a handful of our county's best and brightest. If Mazón killed him, I want to know the reasons. And Jerry Steward was a harmless guy who I'd guess got caught up in something a whole lot bigger than he was. I want to know what…before it grows."

She stopped, almost embarrassed by her gushing. "So tell me what you know, Colonel."

"We know that three men were in prison together. This man who calls himself your uncle. The two Ortega brothers. A fourth, this Miguel Quesada, was released from a facility in Chihuahua after he made something of a deal with officials, one that included his deportation to Costa Rica. My suspicion that he could not be trusted proved correct. Instead of meeting with the people who had originally employed him, within days he had made contact with Olveda in Chihuahua. Your uncle and the Ortegas were released within a week of each other from a prison…in Chihuahua. Interesting coincidence, no?" Naranjo took a deep breath and settled on the end of a wrought-iron bench near the fountain. "It is not difficult to imagine what might have passed between Mazón and the two young men—the Ortega brothers, even Quesada, while in prison. Stories about your son's performances, Mazón's prideful boasting. But the other two?" He shrugged. "We are as interested in establishing that as you are."

"What do you know about Dominic Olveda? He had presented himself to the Posadas folks as a developer from Arizona, interested in linking with the astronomy project, or at least benefiting from it."

Naranjo leaned forward and clasped his hands, staring at the stonework of the fountain. "Señor Olveda—an interesting man. He has no criminal record. Not a word, not even the slightest insinuation. Yet we know that he is linked with some very interesting names…very powerful people who seek ways to invest a considerable flow of money." He turned and regarded Estelle. "But not Mexican money, we have come to learn. He has made no secret that he is based in Costa Rica. Quesada as well."

"And the Ortega brothers as well."

"Most likely. They are small fish, most difficult to track their movements. And now this man who calls himself your uncle. He is Mexican, of course, and that is curious, is it not? That he should develop ties to Costa Rican interests. Or feeling the need to disrupt them."

"He's accomplished that, certainly."

"It appears that with all his efforts, and not an inconsiderable investment, your rancher Mr. Waddell has made something of a tempting target on that mesa of his."

"Olveda was after that, you think?"

"No, not Waddell's development itself. But," and Naranjo drew a large circle in the air, "the periphery. For some of these people with whom Olveda was associated—Posadas is a most tempting *beachhead* for them, so to speak. What could be more convenient, just at the border. A luxury hotel and conference center, an improved airport away from the urban hustle and bustle." He smiled without much humor. "You must realize that there are these people who wish to establish a firm foothold in your country for their businesses. Sometimes the normal channels are laborious."

"But why the attempt on Torrez?"

Naranjo hesitated at the abrupt change of subject. "I can only tell you what I think."

"And that is?"

Naranjo's brow furrowed. "You see, this Robert Torrez is something of an enigma. So intensely private in some inconvenient ways." He held up both hands. "Yet here he is, related to half the indigenous population of your county. What can transpire without him knowing all the details?" Naranjo shrugged. "In Mexico, he would be a rich man. But," and he shrugged again, "it appears that he is *impervious* to influence." He said the word as if it had a bitter taste. "You see, I know for a fact that there are people on both sides who wish that he was on their payroll. But…" he held up both hands in surrender "…do not think that Olveda's group does not do its homework. In this case, I think it might be the old story. If he is not with them, then he is against them."

Naranjo clapped his hands gently. "He could be a very rich man. And you know, the same applies to you, *agente.*" He rested a hand over his heart. "*Fortunately,* for those of us trying to keep our little corner of the world on an even keel where the law really means something…fortunately we can depend on you. If you say, '*this is so,*' then we *know* it is so. The same is true of this Robert Torrez."

Estelle made an impatient face. "So the upshot of all this is that if Bobby can't be bought, then it would benefit someone to have him removed. Is that what you're saying?"

Naranjo's nod was slow and thoughtful. "Someone more conveniently pliant."

"If he doesn't win the election?"

"He will win," Naranjo said with finality. "And as much as I respect him, I firmly believe that the lieutenant is not a factor. He owns a rental house in Posadas, but he does not live in your county. People know that, and resent it." He shrugged. "I would be surprised to see him win a tenth of the vote. Maybe not that much."

"Lieutenant Adams would be surprised to hear that," Estelle said.

"I'm sure. I do not think that the lieutenant, as good a man as he might be, could have even beaten Jerry Steward. A man, incidentally, who was *not* adverse to various opportunities that might have come his way. You say that he and Olveda had the opportunity to meet at least once—it was not just to discuss the weather, let me assure you."

Estelle looked off to the south where, just beyond yet another twist in the Plegado, Juan Guerrero's little farm nestled.

"Mazón knew all this. Is that what you're telling me?"

Naranjo held up both hands. "What he knows? I would say, how could he *not* know? Thieves around a campfire, plotting and planning…we know how that goes. And then, the notion that there is some instant money to be made by ransoming your son—and *that* only comes about when the first scam seeking money from your mother goes awry? I think that Mazón's affection for your son—his enormous *pride* in him—forced his hand. He refused to see Francisco put at risk, and did what he had to do." The colonel shrugged expressively. "And you know, just between you and me, for that I say, 'bless him.' There needs to be no other reason to give you the opportunity to speak with this man."

"But he didn't stop with those two," Estelle said. "He decided to go after Olveda and the others as well."

"It would appear so. We think he was ordered to do so by Mexican acquaintances that saw a most convenient opportunity to remove the competition. Mazón perceived a threat to you and your family, perhaps, as Olveda and his interests gained a foothold in Posadas County. This Mazón—if not your guardian angel, at least he takes the direct approach. A clean sweep. The brothers in Mazatlán, the assassin sent to remove your sheriff, and then the man who has come to Posadas to build a power base. And for good measure, the American who is more than willing to work with him." Naranjo made a scything motion with his hand. "A workman-like job of it." He smiled, and Estelle thought she saw some satisfaction in the expression.

"You know," he continued, "we might debate for years who is to benefit from the work of *Señor* Mazón. If I were among the group that had contracted with Dominic Olveda to make connections with Posadas County, I would certainly hesitate now with my investment."

He watched the range of emotions on Estelle's dark face, then reached out and touched her shoulder as if brushing away an insect. "Your uncle, if that's who he is, has done what he can to protect you and yours. He does not want you caught in the middle."

"If that's the case."

Naranjo tipped his head in surprise. "You've seen the photograph of Mazón's cell."

"Yes."

"It would be hard to examine that and *not* be assured as to his motives."

"You sound sympathetic."

The colonel shrugged. "How can we not be? I think you underestimate the number of people—no doubt on both sides of the border and around the world—who cherish the young Maestro and his family. The Maestro *and* his family." He hesitated when it appeared that Estelle was about to speak, and when she did not, added, "And now Mr. Waddell has elected to bring the world to Posadas in yet another way, and the *bait*, as it were, is most difficult to pass up. The predators are circling, and I'm afraid will always be doing so." He looked down at the ground and chuckled. "You know, the thought has occurred to me more than once in the past few days that Mr. Waddell must surely miss the wise counsel of your *padrino*. I know they were close."

"We all miss his counsel," Estelle said. "But he will heal and be better than new."

Naranjo ducked his head in agreement. "We all hope so. Now…" and he squared his shoulders abruptly. "Your uncle… you will speak with him?"

"Yes."

He nodded sharply at her instant response. "Let me make a bargain with you. I do not wish to put *Señor* Guerrero or you or anyone else from this place of serenity, in harm's way. I do not wish for you to sit down with Benedicte Mazón while the entire area is surrounded by troops pointing machine guns at you. The bargain is this…whatever *you* decide is the right path, then," and he hunched his shoulders, "then that is what will happen." He rested his hand on Estelle's shoulder once more, a gesture of such warmth that she did not shake it off.

"I have no jurisdiction down here," she said. "No authority of any kind. Those are not decisions that I can make." Regardless of who decided what, she knew what lay in store for Benedicte Mazón as far as Mexican authorities were concerned. Naranjo had no reason to protect the man—except as a personal favor to her.

"I *give* you that authority, *agente,*" he said. "Even though I am in no position myself to do so." He smiled ruefully, then his face grew serious. "Even if Benedicte Mazón should walk away today, do not think that the people who supported the efforts of the late *Señor* Olveda will be content to let this man walk free. Sad to say, if he slips through *our* fingers, he will *not* slip through theirs. They do not take such interference lightly." Estelle remained silent.

"In my world," Naranjo continued, "this man is guilty of assuming the role of judge, jury, and *executioner.* That is against the law on both sides of the border. He could have gone to the authorities with what he knew, but he choose another route." Again the expressive shrug. "That ties our hands."

Naranjo brushed aside his light jacket and drew a large handgun from the small of his back. "Because the world is unpredictable," he said, and extended the Beretta to Estelle butt first.

"I don't need that. Mazón is no threat to me. Neither is Guerrero."

"Just to humor me," Naranjo said. "For the unexpected snake lying across the path." He raised an eyebrow. "Oh, yes. And I would surely hate to have our mutual and determined friend Robert Torrez hunting *me,* should something happen to *you.* The border does not exist for this sheriff of yours, as you well know." He reached to another spot on his belt and removed the small handheld radio. "And this, please. The proper channel is already selected. Just push to talk, and there I will be."

"With troops and their machine guns," Estelle said wryly.

"Just so. I'm afraid *Señor* Mazón's time is limited."

She heaved a heavy sigh, feeling as if she were rooted in place.

"He cannot be allowed to go free," Naranjo said quietly. "In addition to what he has done, there is information surely available. The people he knows, the contacts made. He has managed to manipulate powerful interests in two countries. That information will be valuable to us." He reached out to Estelle's shoulder again. "And to you, as well. *Señor* Olveda surely did not operate in a vacuum. There will be others, I have no doubt, who will pursue his efforts."

For a long moment, Estelle didn't answer. "I understand that," she said finally. "Otherwise, I wouldn't be here in the first place."

A smile traced Naranjo's lips as he hefted his own radio. He partially turned his back to Estelle and spoke rapidly. The truck remained parked on the ridge, and as she surveyed the valley, she saw nothing to indicate a police presence—although they were surely there.

"Whenever you wish." Naranjo lowered the radio. He nodded at the white Charger. "Most distinctive. We will have no trouble keeping you in sight."

"It's a good day for a walk," Estelle said.

"Even easier. Take your time." He drew a circle in the air. "Take your time and close this."

Chapter Thirty-seven

After leaving the colonel standing beside the Diaz fountain, she did not visit the woodcarver's home—even though a noisy, affectionate reunion would be welcome. Instead, she followed the narrow trail toward her mother's cottage on a river bench high enough above the Plegado that flooding had never threatened it. Despite lingering periods of drought, the *galleria* was still thick, almost rank, the heavy-limbed cottonwoods and walnuts noisy with the swarms of insects and the birds that chased them.

She hesitated at the cottage's front door, and turned to gaze down through the thickets to the riverbed. Had her mother been home that day to watch the rampaging river? *What day?* Mazón had not offered a date, nor had she asked. Of course Teresa Reyes would have heard the terrible details of the family swept away, of the child's birth on the river bank, of the sole survivor on her first day in the world being given to the convent orphanage in Janos. She would have known.

Estelle Reyes-Guzman had always understood her birthday anniversary to be July first. Now, perhaps Juan Guerrero could be trusted to provide the correct date.

The small adobe, tiny by American standards, smelled faintly musty. A cheap padlock secured the door. After Teresa had moved to Posadas to live with her adopted daughter, one of the Diaz boys had lived here for a year or so with his bride before moving on. Since then, the small adobe had remained empty.

Skirting the house, she walked down to the grove nearest the riverbed. Nothing remained of the extensive, miniature pueblo towns that she and Robert Diaz had constructed so meticulously in the mud banks near the river, little model Tara Humaran towns that often became the victims of siege by Robert's two brothers.

She slid down the last sheer bank to the dry riverbed and stood, listening intently. Two hundred yards ahead was the river crossing that, legend had it, was the site of tragedy and birth. Not a drop of water stirred now, but when she toed over a polished pebble, its belly was damp. She bent and picked it up, her fingers tracing the smooth shape. She carried it for a dozen yards before letting it go.

To her left, the dirt road snaked through the trees, closing on the riverbed. Reaching the hard-packed gravel crossing with its ribbon of concrete roadway, she stopped again. Up ahead, just visible through the thick brush that tried to grow away from the river, was the clutter of Juan Guerrero's homestead.

So this is how it was, Estelle thought. How desperate they must have been—the wife near to labor, the distraught husband, the two children—to risk such a thing. With the pouring rain pounding upstream, the river would have been chocolate brown, crashing with rapids, swirling around hummocks of gravel and deadwood. She inspected the road, probably little changed since that day forty-five years before, except for the single lane of concrete. How long had…her father? She wasn't even sure of his first name. She tried to picture him, anxious, hunched at the steering wheel of the truck, hand poised at the gear lever, trying to both gauge the river's power and his wife's perilous condition on the seat beside him. Had he driven north, he would have faced three more such river crossings, then the risk of the border crossing, then twenty-eight miles into Posadas. Now, headed south toward Janos and medical help, just this one barrier. He took the gamble, and lost.

"Immediately below the Guerrero *casa,*" the quiet voice said, and she spun around. Benedicte Mazón sat in the deep shade, knees drawn up like a child. "The water carried the truck many yards down the river, into the rocks on the outside of the bend. The force was incredible. There it turned over, only the wheels exposed."

You are under arrest. That's all you need to say.

"And where were you?"

"If you look just to the left of Guerrero's, you can see a portion of the road just visible through the trees. I was standing there with Amelia Guerrero. Juan's oldest. She died on her twentieth birthday, you know. But back then, I was merely visiting, you see. I had been up the stream, visiting with my brother's family. The roaring of the flood had attracted us, and by standing on the verge, we could see clearly. And then we saw the truck. Of course, I immediately knew who it was. My brother had sent one of the Diaz children to tell me they were going to Janos, that Dulce was early, and in some distress. I was to go with them. They had but to cross this one spot."

"Dulce."

"Yes. Dulce and my brother, Hector. And my little cousins, Teodoro and Bernice. My brother's children." Mazón leaned back against the bulging roots of a cottonwood. "Teodoro would have been just old enough to stand on the seat between their *mamá* and *papá*. Perhaps three years old. Bernice was two." Mazón's voice sank to a whisper. "I would visit from time to time, and I remember Teodoro trying to keep up with me...little, stumpy legs, so determined. A beautiful child." He heaved a sigh. "His body was found three days after the crash, more than a mile downstream. Bernice was never found."

A flock of jays swooped low over the riverbed, then dispersed into noisy conversation in the cottonwoods. "Where was the house?"

"My brother's, you mean?"

"Yes."

"Ah. From here, you cannot see it." He pushed himself upright and smoothed his simple cotton shirt. Estelle wondered how many crosshairs were focused on him that moment, how many trigger fingers rested on trigger guards, nervous and twitchy. "All that is left is one corner that faces the church across the road. The bus from Janos uses the property for a turn-around now. Do you wish to see?"

"My mother…Teresa Reyes…she would have known the family."

"Of course."

"And she would have known what happened."

"Certainly."

"She would have known what happened…to me."

"Beyond any doubt. In such a tiny village as this, you know, there are no secrets."

"But then?"

"But then? I was but ten, so I don't recall everything," Mazón said. "A newborn, I suppose, ripped from its mother by the violence of the flood, saved by a brave man who probably didn't even realize what he was doing."

"*Señor* Guerrero."

"Exactly. He slid down the bank, all the while shouting for Amelia and me to 'get back, get back.' I could see that the woman's injuries were ghastly. She had been forced from the crushed truck, and now was battered against the rocks. Guerrero was able to reach her, but what could be done? Enough spark of life remained to give the world this remarkable child." He looked at Estelle, appraising. He sighed. "And the child was bundled up, and went to the hospital in Janos, and in due time from there to the nuns' orphanage. A remarkable child has become a remarkable woman."

"Your parents…your brother Hector's parents…they didn't take her? Or Dulce's family?" *Take her. Why can I not say, 'Take me…?'*

"No. My mother was sickly. Our father died the year before, and she had never recovered from that. Dulce's family lived in Guymas, you know. Hector had met her while he was briefly in the *Federales,* before he was hurt." He shrugged in sympathy. "And the Guerreros did not take the child. There are always many reasons."

"But a year later, Teresa Reyes did."

He nodded. "And is she…?"

"Still well."

"Maybe she will want to discuss that day, maybe not." Estelle didn't reply, and Mazón stood quietly, waiting.

"And now, you," she said finally.

He took his time finding a seat again in the dappled shade of the stream bank. "In all respects but one, mine is a wasted life, *sobrina*." He smiled suddenly, revealing that the years in prison hadn't contributed to an attractive smile. "Despite what you might think, the last few years have been a treasure for me, even though I have been a guest of the Mexican government the whole time. You saw the photograph of my last abode. Do you know how proud I am of what your Francisco has accomplished?"

"You've made that clear."

He regarded her as if he had expected something other than the chill in her tone.

"I did not mean…" he started, then hesitated, looking first toward the north where the tile roof of the Diaz *hacienda* was just visible above the river's galleria, then to the ridge to the west. "I *do* not mean to put you in a difficult position, *sobrina.*"

"Then turn yourself in," she said. "Do that and I will help you. If you resist here and now, they will kill you. It's that simple. If you need an attorney here in Mexico, I will make sure you have one. When Mexican authorities are finished with you, I'm sure you will be extradited to the United States for three homicides there. Regardless of how grateful to you I might be for protecting my son, there is nothing else I can do. There is nothing else I *will* do."

Mazón's expression was kindly, almost paternal. "The years I have spent in prison are enough," he said. "I will not go back." He shrugged. "It is not so hard to live as a fugitive, you know. If I am allowed to do so." He nodded toward the north. "On either side of the border."

"I will not allow you back into my life, *Señor* Mazón. I do not know what you expect, but that isn't going to happen."

"You know, someday…" and he stared long toward the horizon, "it is my fondest wish to hear your son, *mi gran sobrino,* in concert. To sit there in the audience and allow the music to embrace me, to experience the bittersweet rush of emotion that comes when we know the concert must end, that the stage will be empty again."

"You can dream about that," Estelle said.

He grinned at her. "You are a hard woman," he said. "The life you have chosen has made you this way, I think. Working always with the *policia.* You know, my brother—your father—had a stubborn streak, as well. He would have enjoyed an enviable career with the *Federales* had not fate intervened. I look at you now, and am reminded of him." He turned to look upstream. "Where is your car?"

"You don't need it."

He laughed, truly delighted. "Now you are a mind reader."

In the distance, Estelle heard the rumble of a truck, a distinctive sound that carried down the valley, surging now and then as it rounded bends along the river, idling down at the crossings and then powering up and out of the Plegado. The sound abruptly died, and Estelle guessed that the driver had turned into the Diaz *hacienda.* She had heard the old Chevy enough times that there was no doubt about who had arrived in Tres Santos.

"You should speak with Juan Guerrero," Mazón said. "He is waiting up at the house." He rose abruptly, as if eager to accompany her.

"I think I know all I need to know," Estelle replied. "Perhaps some other time, when there are fewer…distractions. Then I will visit him."

This time, the distraction was not Bobby Torrez, whom she expected, but the tan uniform of Colonel Tomás Naranjo. His clothing blended with the dappled earth as he descended quietly from the road to the streambed just north of the crossing where Estelle and Mazón stood. His boots crunched on a patch of gravel, and Mazón turned at the noise. For a moment he stood with his hands on his hips, then relaxed. His right hand drifted to his waistband at his back, slipping under his linen shirt.

Mazón took two or three quick breaths and shook his head. "You must understand, *sobrina,* that if I had not acted, there is no telling what would have happened to your son. You understand that?"

"I do."

"And if I had not taken matters into my own hands, there is no telling what would have happened in Posadas, beginning with the life of your esteemed sheriff. And what might have happened if the wrong people had won a foothold in your community."

"I'm now aware of that."

"And yet still..." he broke off, frowning at the approaching policeman. Naranjo walked with care, placing his steps on the loose cobbles without taking his eyes off Mazón. His right hand rested on the butt of his holstered automatic.

"I am told that your sheriff has arrived at the Diaz hacienda," Naranjo said to Estelle by way of greeting. "I do not know what he has in mind."

"He should be glad simply to be alive," Mazón said.

"I'm sure he is." Naranjo's voice was easy, almost amused, as if he was one of three old friends who had chosen this meeting. Estelle watched as he eased to a stop several paces from Mazón. The colonel could not see the object that Mazón commanded now in his right hand, but Estelle could—a small chrome revolver, the sort of thing that Jerry Steward might have worn strapped to his ankle.

"You know that there is no escaping this tranquil valley," Naranjo added. "I have but to utter a single word," and he held up his radio in his left hand. Estelle could see his finger held the transmit button firmly depressed. Someone—perhaps several someones—was listening to their conversation, and the crosshairs would be steady on their target.

"Perhaps not," Mazón said. "But I wish to talk with the two of you in private, without the eavesdroppers. There may be some sort of accommodation that can be reached."

"The time for accommodation is far behind us."

Mazón turned his head to look at Estelle. "I am the last of your family, you know." His gaze drifted down, and he nodded, assuming correctly that her hand was tucked under the tail of her own jacket for good reason. "That should mean something to you. My life is in your hands, surely."

"Then I will save your life, *Señor* Mazón. Put your hands on your head and drop to your knees."

"*Mi tío grande,*" he whispered. "I would have liked to have heard the *maestro* say those words."

Estelle saw the muscles tense, and Mazón turned just a quarter step, giving his right arm leverage. Naranjo remained inexplicably calm, his right hand on the butt of his automatic, but making no effort to draw it. She had checked the Beretta when Naranjo had given it to her, seen that it was fully loaded, and now let the grip settle comfortably in her hand.

The turn of his body gave Mazón the leverage he needed. Naranjo remained relaxed, radio in hand, even as Mazón made his decision.

"No!" Estelle shouted, and the Beretta came out in one fluid motion even as Mazón's arm tensed and started its arc. More than 400 yards away, a young man's finger eased back on a trigger. With a loud *whack* of impact, the bullet exploded through Mazón's left temple. As if someone had kicked him in the back of the knees, he folded onto the river sand. At the instant his knees touched the sand, the single report of the high-powered rifle reached them.

Estelle decocked the Beretta, and Naranjo stepped close, the radio to his ear as he gave instructions.

"I am sorry this is the route he chose," the colonel said as he tucked the radio away. "Let me." He reached out for the Beretta and Estelle handed it to him without comment. He withdrew a perfectly folded white handkerchief from his hip pocket, snapped it open, and meticulously polished the automatc. He made no effort to avoid his own fingerprints as he did so. Through the efficient process, his gaze never left Mazón's corpse.

"Are you going to be all right?" His question was gently asked, and as he tucked the handgun carefully in his belt, there was no doubt what fiction he had already embraced. The Beretta had never been in her hands. The fact that she now stood in the bottom of a dry Mexican arroyo bottom, her uncle dead at her feet—if she chose, she could embrace that Mazón had brought all this upon himself. Perhaps her uncle had good reason. Had she simply refused to come to Tres Santos, Mazón might have survived for a few hours, maybe a few days. But so many questions had been left unanswered.

"I don't know." She turned at the sound of footsteps crunching down the riverbed. Sheriff Robert Torrez carried one of the department's suppressed AR's relaxed over his shoulder as if he were on the way to a prairie dog town. At the same time, the rhythmic chop of a helicopter approached, still far in the distance.

"I wish we had time to enjoy a casual discussion." Naranjo extended his hand to Torrez in greeting, his face sober. "But it would be best if the two of you bundled yourselves back across the border. I will, of course, send you a full report." He glanced at the rifle, and then at the pistol holstered at Torrez's waist. "Such well-prepared backup is always appreciated, but no doubt there would be some who wouldn't understand. I will provide adequate escort."

The sheriff stepped across to Mazón's corpse and knelt carefully, peering at the stub-nosed revolved that lay partially buried under the man's right leg. "I heard just the one shot a ways off." He looked up at Estelle.

"It all happened so fast," Naranjo said. "But you are probably correct."

"I guess the one was good enough."

Estelle turned away without comment, not wishing to engage in a shooting gallery recap. But then she paused, reaching out a hand to Naranjo's elbow. "Thank you for allowing him this chance," she said. He hesitated, then bowed ever so slightly from the waist. "I'm sorry it didn't work out."

"My truck's just up on the road." Torrez nodded upstream toward the first bend of the riverbed.

"I'd like to walk back to the car." Estelle offered Torrez a tight smile. "Thanks for driving down." His armed response into Mexico had been at considerable risk. She knew that it was something Torrez would just *do,* and that he would never mention it again. Nor would Colonel Tomás Naranjo, who in many ways shared Bobby Torrez's view of border complications. Both lived with the notion that the border fence, and the politics that went with it, demanded no particular imperative. The idea was a holdover from simpler days—if you're chasing a felon, you don't stop the chase at a fence to do paperwork.

She hadn't stopped, either. Now she was left to wonder. At that final moment, even as she drew the heavy automatic from her belt, would training and instinct have taken over? If the Mexican sniper hadn't been so prompt in following Naranjo's orders, would she have pulled the Beretta's trigger? Naranjo had seen the hurt in her eyes as she looked down at the man who claimed to be her uncle, whose last name should have been her own. All that would take some sorting out, and she silently thanked the Mexican colonel for understanding that Monday morning quarterbacking, or even commiseration, was the last thing she needed or wanted just then. The boy who had watched the drama of her own birth now lay dead in the bottom of the streambed. If she never saw the Plegado again, the healing could start.

Chapter Thirty-eight

The belly-dump took up most of the county road, and Estelle pulled far onto the shoulder as it approached. She could hear the rig downshifting, and then the driver rode the Jake as he slowed the hauler first to a crawl, then to a full stop. As he swung down from the truck, she recognized him as one of the crew from McInerney Sand and Gravel.

"Morning, Sheriff." Indeed it was, the sun brilliant, the sky dotted by puffy clouds that an art critic would say were too stereotypical to be real. Arnie Sisson bent down, an elbow planting on the county car's window sill, stained and frayed Isotopes ball cap well back on his round, close-cropped skull. He smelled of the laborer's cologne—cigarettes, diesel, and sweat. "You had a chance to talk with Bill Gastner lately?"

"Good morning. Yes, I have. Just yesterday, in fact."

"Well," and Sisson straightened up, looking back toward the south. "There are sure safer places for him to be than walkin' in the middle of the road. Somebody's gonna hit him, sure as hell if he don't watch out."

"He's on down the road here?" She tried to imagine the logistics of Bill Gastner, still hobbled with the walker, fetching himself out here. She had helped him, in the weeks past, re-educate himself about how to board the SUV, pulling the folding walker in behind him. But Sisson was right…there were safer places to exercise.

"He's just past the cattle guard."

"Ah. Well, thank you. Other than that, how's your day going?"

"It's gonna be hotter'n hell. That's why we start haulin' at four now."

"Wise move." She pulled the car into gear. "Thanks for the tip."

"He might listen to you. I stopped and asked him if I could help, but he just grinned and waved me off."

Estelle nodded. "He *might* listen, but that's doubtful. "

In the seven additional miles to Miles Waddell's development, she passed six more trucks, three white SUVs with government plates, and assorted other contractors and visitors. Despite the salt solution tried first on the road surface, and then the oil film, dust was a constant companion of heavy construction.

She slowed for the cattle guard, and saw that Gastner had parked his flame-red SUV well off the roadway, swinging it around to face north. *Always ready for a fast getaway,* she thought. And sure enough, there he was, a hundred yards down the road, the front wheels of his walker leaving narrow snail trails in the dirt of the shoulder facing northbound traffic.

Despite three weeks of diligent therapy, he still moved as if made of glass. He leaned very little on the walker now, just skating it along in front of him.

She let the car drift along until she was a few yards behind him, then pulled off into what little prairie grass remained. Gastner stopped and then walked himself around in a half circle until he was facing her as she parked and got out of the car.

"Morning, sweetheart. I just got to thinking," he said as she approached.

"Uh, oh." She sidestepped the walker and gave him a long, hard hug.

"Yeah, well. Back and forth across the living room, or up and down the halls in the hospital, just doesn't cut it. And then I thought, well hell…why not get some sunshine and fresh air? I mean diesel and dust is supposed to be some sort of magic home remedy, eh?"

"Does Camille know you're out here, sir?"

"Thank God, no. Are you kidding?" He waved back toward the SUV. "Getting in that crate is the hardest part."

"Life's little challenges," Estelle laughed.

"Yeah, well. One step at a time. If Camille has a fit, she can always call me." He patted his belt where the tiny phone nestled. "We're still on for dinner tonight?"

"Indeed we are."

"The kid arrived safe and sound?"

Estelle laughed. Francisco *had* arrived in high spirits for a brief four-day holiday break from the academy. After submitting to one crushing hug after another, he had spent an hour touching up the tuning of the family's piano—with his younger brother's help. Teresa had commented that the session was unlike any piano tuning *she* had ever heard.

"He and Carlos are planning something for this evening." She turned her head as another truck passed, grimacing against the wash of particulate. "And by the way—unbelievable news, sir." He raised a shaggy eyebrow. "Carlos asked if it was all right to invite Bobby and Gayle? I told him to go ahead but not to hold his breath. Guess what. He biked over to the county building and cornered Bobby in the sheriff's office. They're coming."

Gastner beamed. "Well, all right. I'll believe it when I see them, of course. The menu is what you said?"

"Of course, sir."

He took a deep breath and waved as a tan Jeep passed northbound, then braked hard and turned an abrupt U-turn to park behind Estelle's unit. Rick Bueler, the security chief for *NightZone,* dismounted.

"You arrested him for speeding, Sheriff?" He shook hands first with Gastner, then with Estelle. "Is everything going all right?"

"I think so. I have a meeting this afternoon with the county manager and Mr. Waddell. I had a few things I wanted to run by him beforehand."

"He's up on top this morning. They're pouring the roots for the big dish today. Exciting stuff."

"Hell of a long walk," Gastner groused.

"I'll be happy to give you a tour, sir," Bueler offered.

"No thanks. I'd need a pile of pillows a yard thick in that buggy of yours. In fact," and he shifted a little uncomfortably, "I've had about all the fun I can stand for one day." He set the walker squarely on top of its own tracks, pointed back toward his SUV. "Five o'clock still?"

"Five it is, sir," Estelle replied.

He took a couple of steps and stopped, regarding her with interest. "Talk to Teresa yet?"

Estelle reached out a hand and rested it on his. For a moment, she said nothing, then shook her head. "She has always seemed content with her memories the way they are, *Padrino*. If she brings it up, I'll listen." She smiled. "Otherwise, I'm planning to make liberal use of my mental *delete* key. After the boys, that is. They deserve to know."

"You talked to Carlos about it all already?"

"Just a little. I'll find a quiet time with the two of them. They deserve to know where the bloodline comes from, I suppose."

A red Prius churned its own mini-dust cloud, and Estelle recognized Frank Dayan, the *Posadas Register*'s publisher and most eager cub reporter.

"He doesn't know, does he?"

"No," Estelle said quickly. "And he's not going to. What happened in Mexico will *stay* in Mexico." The Prius swung off the road and stopped, and when Dayan got out, he clutched a small camera.

"Hey, there!" he greeted ebulliently. "All the law there is, west of the Pecos. It's great to see you up and around, Bill."

"Thanks."

"Are you all headed topside?"

"We'll be right behind you," Gastner said gruffly, and Dayan stopped abruptly as if he had stepped into a meeting where he wasn't welcome.

"Right then," he said, and turned back toward the Prius. "See you up there."

As the little car pulled away, Estelle gave Gastner a hug hard enough to make him grimace. "You haven't lost your touch, sir."

To receive a free catalog of Poisoned Pen Press titles, please provide your name and address through one of the following ways:

Phone: 1-800-421-3976
Facsimile: 1-480-949-1707
Email: info@poisonedpenpress.com
Website: www.poisonedpenpress.com

Poisoned Pen Press
6962 E. First Ave. Ste 103
Scottsdale, AZ 85251